Great Short Works
of
HENRY DAVID THOREAU

Great Short Works
of
HENRY DAVID THOREAU

Edited, with an Introduction, by

WENDELL GLICK

PERENNIAL LIBRARY

Harper & Row, Publishers
New York, Cambridge, Philadelphia, San Francisco
London, Mexico City, São Paulo, Singapore, Sydney

Grateful acknowledgment is made for permission to reprint:

The text of *Walden*, "Friendship," "Ktaadn," "Reform and the Reformers," "Resistance to Civil Government," "Slavery in Massachusetts," "A Plea for Captain John Brown," "Life without Principle" from *The Writings of Henry D. Thoreau*. Copyright © 1971, 1972, 1973, 1975, 1980 by the Princeton University Press.

Letter to Henry Williams from *The Correspondence of Henry David Thoreau* edited by Carl Bode and Walter Harding. Copyright © 1958 by New York University. By permission of Houghton Library at Harvard University, and the New York University Press.

First PERENNIAL CLASSIC edition published 1982.

Designer: Jane Weinberger

Library of Congress Cataloging in Publication Data

Thoreau, Henry David, 1817–1862.
    Great short works of Henry David Thoreau.

    (Perennial classic)
    Bibliography: p. 383
    1. Glick, Wendell, 1916–   II. Title.
PS3042.G64   1982   818'.309   82-47560
    ISBN 0-06-080598-6 (pbk.)   AACR2

87 88 89 90 OPM 8 7 6 5 4 3 2

CONTENTS

INTRODUCTION

TEN YEARS AFTER the graduation of the Harvard Class of 1837, the class secretary, Henry Williams, Jr., sent a questionnaire to all surviving members querying them on their personal lives and post-graduation activities. Williams's letter arrived at the time that Henry Thoreau, an undistinguished member of the class, was living in a cabin he had constructed himself on the shore of Walden Pond, where he was engaged, as he later recorded, in transacting some important "private business." He was wholly disinclined to spend his time responding to intrusive requests of this character. Not until he had left the pond, therefore, more than six months later, did he get around to replying grudgingly to Williams's request. In answer to the questions: Where and when were you born? Where were you fitted for college? Are you married? What is your profession or trade? What is your present employment? and What fact of general importance can you mention? Thoreau provided Williams this dry, laconic response:

Concord Sept 30th 1847

Dear Sir,

I confess that I have very little class spirit, and have almost forgotten that I ever spent four years at Cambridge. That must have been in a former state of existence. It is difficult to realize that the old routine is still kept up. However, I will undertake at last to answer your questions as well as I can in spite of a poor memory and a defect of information.

1st then, I was born, they say, on the 12th of July 1817, on what is called the Virginia Road, in the east part of Concord.

2nd I was fitted, or rather made unfit, for College, at Concord Academy & elsewhere, mainly by myself, with the countenance of Phineas Allen, Preceptor.

3d I am not married.

4th I dont know whether mine is a profession, or a trade, or what not. It is not yet learned, and in every instance has been practised before being studied. The mercantile part of it was begun *here* by myself alone.

—It is not one but legion. I will give you some of the monster's heads. I am a Schoolmaster—a Private Tutor, a Surveyor— a Gardener, a Farmer—a Painter, I mean a House Painter, a Carpenter, a Mason, a Day-Laborer, a Pencil-Maker, a Glass-paper Maker, a Writer, and sometimes a Poetaster. If you will act the part of Iolas, and apply a hot iron to any of these heads, I shall be greatly obliged to you.

5th My present employment is to answer such orders as may be expected from so general an advertisement as the above— that is, if I see fit, which is not always the case, for I have found out a way to live without what is commonly called employment or industry attractive or otherwise. Indeed my steadiest employ-ment, if such it can be called, is to keep myself at the top of my condition, and ready for whatever may turn up in heaven or on earth. For the last two or three years I have lived in Concord woods alone, something more than a mile from any neighbor, in a house built entirely by myself.

6th I cannot think of a single general fact of any importance before or since graduating

Yrs &c
HENRY D THOREAU

P S. I beg that the Class will not consider me an object of chari-ty, and if any of them are in want of pecuniary assistance, and will make known their case to me, I will engage to give them some advice of more worth than money.

Scarcely fifteen years later, in May of 1862, one of the most eminent men of the century rose in the First Parish Church in Concord to deliver a final tribute and eulogy to Thoreau, his young friend and neighbor, dead of tu-berculosis. Emerson's personal sadness pervaded his long address to the assembled mourners. But above all, he la-mented that Thoreau's genius had had but 44 years to engage in its "comprehensive calling, the art of living well." It seemed to him, said Emerson, that Thoreau had devoted his life to the search for that rare and inaccessible plant, the *"Edelweisse,* which signifies *Noble Purity."* Then Emerson went on to make a judgment of Thoreau's career that must have seemed, even to Thoreau's friends gathered this spring morning in the First Parish Church, an extravagant one:

The country knows not yet, or in the least part, how great a son it has lost. It seems an injury that he should leave in the midst of his broken task which none else can finish, a kind of indignity to so noble a soul that he should depart out of Nature before yet he has been really shown to his peers for what he is. . . . His soul was made for the noblest society; he had in a short life exhausted the capabilities of this world; wherever there is knowledge, wherever there is virtue, wherever there is beauty, he will find a home.

Time has proved Emerson's perspicuity. That Thoreau has now found a home in the pantheon of those who have most cogently articulated the American ideal of spiritualizing the self is no longer at issue. Emerson's eulogy identified one by one the qualities of Thoreau that augured to Emerson his young friend's immortality. "Noble Purity" was the first, comprised of a scrupulous and unremitting integrity in all that Thoreau had done and said. He had been a man, said Emerson, of "perfect probity," a "truth-speaker," a man of "sincerity itself," who "never had a vice in his life." So severe was the ideal that he had set for himself and others, Emerson observed, that it deprived him "of a healthy sufficiency of human society." His virtues "ran to extremes." The reader of Thoreau's essay on "Friendship," included in this volume, is confronted by an ideal so rarefied, that nearly all personal relationships seem to be precluded.

But to his catalog of Thoreau's personal qualities, Emerson did the unusual thing (in a funeral eulogy) of appending a commentary upon Thoreau's "literary excellence," complete with twenty-two samples of Thoreau's sentences. Recognizing at once what for almost one hundred years interpreters and critics of Thoreau failed to see, Emerson identified Thoreau's calling as that of writer. Writing and "truth-telling" for him, moreover, had been one and the same thing; indeed, he had felt his personal purity to be despoiled by impurity of expression. In the "Conclusion" of *Walden* (here included), in prose as subtle as any American has ever written, Thoreau disclosed his fear that his "expression" might fall short of revealing "the truth of which I have been convinced." Emerson suggested to his auditors one of the clues of Thoreau's genius as a writer that Francis Matthiessen would explicitly identify in *American Renaissance* a century later—that Thoreau's power emanated from his gift of "thinking in images." "He knew the worth of the imagination for the uplifting and consolation of human life [Emerson astutely observed], and liked to throw every thought into a symbol. The fact you tell is of no value, but only the impression. For this reason his presence was poetic." This gift, in "a person of a rare, tender and absolute religion, a person incapable of any profanation, by act or thought," spelled genius. That the genius would seem eccentric to the people of his town, Emerson made no attempt to conceal. But he was convinced that genius would outlive eccentricity.

Though the purpose of this book is to reflect the range of Thoreau's genius, there is no whitewashing of his eccentricities, if such they are. With a young friend on an outing, he inadvertently set his neighbors' woods on fire. Upon failing in his attempts to extinguish the blaze, he coolly contemplated the beauty of the holocaust, later recording the experience in his journal. He preferred spending money on libraries rather than on roads. His exhortations were persistent and at times abrasive. He probed the philosophical and moral underpinnings of American society and found them deficient: "Our sills are rotten," he warned his fellow citizens. "Wash your windows, I say," was his posthumous counsel to his neighbors in "Life without Principle." Thoreau's rhetoric is often fueled by the anger he felt in watching his neighbors waste their lives and settle as a consequence into ennui and "quiet desperation." The homiletic tradition of the New England clergy everywhere penetrates the "sermons" of this crusty descendant of French Huguenot emigrants from France to the Isle of Jersey. "Slavery in Mas-

sachusetts" and "A Plea for Captain John Brown" put to
secular uses the rhetoric of Jonathan Edwards's "Sinners
in the Hands of an Angry God." Thoreau was castigated
by such critics as Lowell and Stevenson for being a
"skulker" who withdrew to Walden Pond rather than
take an active part in the social and political movements
of his age. But the modern reader should recognize in the
imperatives of Thoreau's prose, ranging from whimsical
cajolery to hortatory denunciation, its writer's deep concern for the discontent of his contemporaries, their en-
slavement to custom, and their mistaken values. "I do not
propose to write an ode to dejection," Thoreau an-
nounced on the title page of *Walden*, pointedly separating himself from the theme of Coleridge's "Dejection: An
Ode." Instead, he proposed "to brag as lustily as Chanticleer in the morning, standing on his roost, if only to
wake my neighbors up." During the months when Thoreau was making his final revisions of *Walden*, he might
have read in *Harper's Magazine* Herman Melville's account in "Cock-a-Doodle-Doo!" of an indomitable Shanghai rooster who imparted to the poor, malnourished Mer-
rymusk family of which he was a member "stuff against
despair." In any event, Thoreau's occasional abrasive po-
lemics against values that he deemed enslaving and unworthy should not deflect the reader from the perception
that beneath all of Thoreau's writings is the conviction of
the power of the individual to change, to "live deep and
suck out all the marrow of life," as Thoreau contends in
"Where I Lived and What I Lived For." If we "live
meanly, like ants," he argued, it is because, unlike Melville's rooster, we have lost faith and abdicated our self-
hood. The series of remarkable letters written by Thoreau
to H. G. O. Blake and here anthologized for the first time
apply the premises of *Walden* to the personal problems
of a young stranger who turned to Thoreau for guidance.
In almost thirty letters, Thoreau counsels Blake on how to
live deep and suck out all the marrow of life. "Did ever a
man try heroism, magnanimity, truth, sincerity, and find
that there was no advantage in them? that it was a vain
endeavor?" Thoreau asked in his initial response to
Blake's queries. Throughout nature Thoreau saw ana-

logues of metamorphosis. He concluded *Walden* with the story of "the beautiful bug which came out of the dry leaf of an old table of apple-tree wood" after years of inertia—a story which Melville also used—and argued persistently that renewal, not paralysis, is the norm of all life.

Of Thoreau's affinity for the natural world every reader of Thoreau is at once aware. The depth, the subtlety, and the philosophical complexity of that affinity, however, are still being revealed. Emerson in his eulogy noted Thoreau's "entire love to the fields, hills and waters of his native town," and his acuteness of observation, as if he had had "additional senses." But Emerson knew also that Thoreau was more than a naturalist, and that it was not the fact that was important to him, but the impression or effect of that fact upon his mind. The nature of that impression Emerson could delineate only in a general way: what nature divulged to Thoreau was to Emerson a "secret." "So much knowledge of Nature's secret and genius few others possessed," Emerson observed, "none in a more large and religious synthesis." That "religious synthesis" scholars are now at work exploring. "Walking," "Autumnal Tints," and "Ktaadn," reproduced in this volume, reflect Thoreau's imagination, reshaping, synthesizing, and transforming his observations into art. Facts become transparent as he records them. He sees through them, making them symbolic vehicles for the creation of new forms of intellect and feeling and will, and for the reader, new and intense experiences to be lived through and aesthetically enjoyed. Few American writers match Thoreau in his awareness of the imaginative suggestiveness of sensory facts, or in his gift for transforming them for others into instruments of delight and self-knowledge. "Time is but the stream I go afishing in," he explained in "Where I Lived and What I Lived For." What he fished for, like another Fisher of Men, was Truth. "This alone," he observed, "wears well."

WENDELL GLICK
The University of Minnesota, Duluth

A NOTE ON THE TEXTS

The Writings of Henry D. Thoreau, a complete and definitive edition of Thoreau's works, is currently being produced at Princeton University in accordance with the scrupulous standards of accuracy established by the Center for Editions of American Authors of the Modern Language Association of America. Whenever texts from the Princeton Edition are in print, as in the volumes listed below, *The Great Short Works of Henry David Thoreau* reproduces them, with the permission of the Princeton University Press, Princeton, N.J., 08540, holder of the copyright. "Ktaadn" is from *The Maine Woods,* ed. Joseph J. Moldenhauer (1972); "Friendship" is from *A Week on the Concord and Merrimack Rivers,* ed. Carl F. Hovde et al. (1980). The four chapters from *Walden*— "Where I Lived and What I Lived For," "Reading," "Higher Laws," and "Conclusion"—are from *Walden,* ed. J. Lyndon Shanley (1971). "Reform and the Reformers," "Resistance to Civil Government," "Slavery in Massachusetts," "A Plea for Captain John Brown," and "Life without Principle" are from *Reform Papers,* ed. Wendell Glick (1973).

For the remaining selections, definitive texts have not yet been established, and the source chosen in each case therefore is the first printing, the best text presently available. "A Winter Walk" is from *The Dial* of October 1843. The letters to H. G. O. Blake are from *The Familiar Letters of Thoreau* (Boston and New York, 1894), ed.

F. B. Sanborn. The dated selections from Thoreau's *Journal* are from the *Walden Edition* of *The Writings of Thoreau* (Boston, 1906). "The Shipwreck" is from *Putnam's Monthly Magazine* for June 1855. "Walking" and "Autumnal Tints" are from *The Atlantic Monthly* of June 1862 and October 1862 respectively. Thoreau's letter to Henry Williams, Jr., in the "Introduction" is reprinted from *The Correspondence of Henry David Thoreau*, ed. Walter Harding and Carl Bode by permission of New York University Press, and the Houghton Library, Harvard University.

A WINTER WALK

Published by Emerson in The Dial *for October 1843, this early apprenticeship essay that Thoreau fused from* Journal *extracts invites comparison with the posthumously published "Walking." Thoreau has not yet mastered his craft; his style is mannered, yet here is the beginning of the circular form that would later lend structure to* Walden. *What the essay lacks in the subtlety we have come to expect in Thoreau's prose is partially compensated for by the acuteness of his observation of natural phenomena. The text reproduced here is from the first printing in* The Dial, *the only version of the essay over which Thoreau probably exercised a measure of control.*

THE WIND HAS GENTLY MURMURED through the blinds, or puffed with feathery softness against the windows, and occasionally sighed like a summer zephyr lifting the leaves along the livelong night. The meadow mouse has slept in his snug gallery in the sod, the owl has sat in a hollow tree in the depth of the swamp, the rabbit, the squirrel, and the fox have all been housed. The watchdog has lain quiet on the hearth, and the cattle have stood silent in their stalls. The earth itself has slept, as it were its first, not its last sleep, save when some street-sign or wood-house door, has faintly creaked upon its hinge,

cheering forlorn nature at her midnight work.—The only
sound awake twixt Venus and Mars,—advertising us of a
remote inward warmth, a divine cheer and fellowship,
where gods are met together, but where it is very bleak
for men to stand. But while the earth has slumbered, all
the air has been alive with feathery flakes, descending, as
if some northern Ceres reigned, showering her silvery
grain over all the fields.

We sleep and at length awake to the still reality of a
winter morning. The snow lies warm as cotton or down
upon the window-sill; the broadened sash and frosted
panes admit a dim and private light, which enhances the
snug cheer within. The stillness of the morning is impressive. The floor creaks under our feet as we move toward
the window to look abroad through some clear space over
the fields. We see the roofs stand under their snow burden. From the eaves and fences hang stalactites of snow,
and in the yard stand stalagmites covering some concealed core. The trees and shrubs rear white arms to the
sky on every side, and where were walls and fences, we
see fantastic forms stretching in frolic gambols across the
dusky landscape, as if nature had strewn her fresh designs
over the fields by night as models for man's art.

Silently we unlatch the door, letting the drift fall in,
and step abroad to face the cutting air. Already the stars
have lost some of their sparkle, and a dull leaden mist
skirts the horizon. A lurid brazen light in the east pro-
claims the approach of day, while the western landscape
is dim and spectral still, and clothed in a sombre Tartar-
ean light, like the shadowy realms. They are Infernal
sounds only that you hear,—the crowing of cocks, the
barking of dogs, the chopping of wood, the lowing of
kine, all seem to come from Pluto's barn-yard and beyond the Styx;—not for any melancholy they suggest, but
their twilight bustle is too solemn and mysterious for
earth. The recent tracks of the fox or otter, in the yard,
remind us that each hour of the night is crowded with
events, and the primeval nature is still working and making tracks in the snow. Opening the gate, we tread briskly
along the lone country road, crunching the dry and crisp
snow under our feet, or aroused by the sharp clear creak

of the wood-sled, just starting for the distant market,
from the early farmer's door, where it has lain the summer long, dreaming amid the chips and stubble. For
through the drifts and powdered windows we see the
farmer's early candle, like a paled star, emitting a lonely
beam, as if some severe virtue at its matins there.
And one by one the smokes begin to ascend from the
chimneys amidst the trees and snows.

> The sluggish smoke curls up from some deep dell,
> The stiffened air exploring in the dawn,
> And making slow acquaintance with the day;
> Delaying now upon its heavenward course,
> In wreathed loiterings dallying with itself,
> With as uncertain purpose and slow deed,
> As its half-wakened master by the hearth,
> Whose mind still slumbering and sluggish thoughts
> Have not yet swept into the onward current
> Of the new day;—and now it streams afar,
> The while the chopper goes with step direct,
> And mind intent to swing the early axe.
> First in the dusky dawn he sends abroad
> His early scout, his emissary, smoke,
> The earliest, latest pilgrim from the roof,
> To feel the frosty air, inform the day;
> And while he crouches still beside the hearth,
> Nor musters courage to unbar the door,
> It has gone down the glen with the light wind,
> And o'er the plain unfurled its venturous wreath,
> Draped the tree tops, loitered upon the hill,
> And warmed the pinions of the early bird;
> And now, perchance, high in the crispy air,
> Has caught sight of the day o'er the earth's edge,
> And greets its master's eye at his low door,
> As some refulgent cloud in the upper sky.

We heard the sound of wood-chopping at the farmers'
doors, far over the frozen earth, the baying of the house
dog, and the distant clarion of the cock. The thin and
frosty air conveys only the finer particles of sound to our
ears, with short and sweet vibrations, as the waves subside
soonest on the purest and lightest liquids, in which gross
substances sink to the bottom. They come clear and bell-
like, and from a greater distance in the horizon, as if

there were fewer impediments than in summer to make
them faint and ragged. The ground is sonorous, like seasoned wood, and even the ordinary rural sounds are melodious, and the jingling of the ice on the trees is sweet
and liquid. There is the least possible moisture in the atmosphere, all being dried up, or congealed, and it is of
such extreme tenuity and elasticity, that it becomes a
source of delight. The withdrawn and tense sky seems
groined like the aisles of a cathedral, and the polished air
sparkles as if there were crystals of ice floating in it.
Those who have resided in Greenland, tell us, that, when
it freezes, "the sea smokes like burning turf land, and a
fog or mist arises, called frost smoke," which "cutting
smoke frequently raises blisters on the face and hands,
and is very pernicious to the health." But this pure stinging cold is an elixir to the lungs, and not so much a frozen
mist, as a crystallized mid-summer haze, refined and purified by cold.

The sun at length rises through the distant woods, as if
with the faint clashing swinging sound of cymbals, melting the air with his beams, and with such rapid steps the
morning travels, that already his rays are gilding the distant western mountains. We step hastily along through
the powdery snow, warmed by an inward heat, enjoying
an Indian summer still, in the increased glow of thought
and feeling. Probably if our lives were more conformed
to nature, we should not need to defend ourselves against
her heats and colds, but find her our constant nurse and
friend, as do plants and quadrupeds. If our bodies were
fed with pure and simple elements, and not with a stimulating and heating diet, they would afford no more pasture for cold than a leafless twig, but thrive like the trees,
which find even winter genial to their expansion.

The wonderful purity of nature at this season is a most
pleasing fact. Every decayed stump and moss-grown
stone and rail, and the dead leaves of autumn, are concealed by a clean napkin of snow. In the bare fields and
tinkling woods, see what virtue survives. In the coldest
and bleakest places, the warmest charities still maintain a
foot-hold. A cold and searching wind drives away all contagion, and nothing can withstand it but what has a vir-

tue in it; and accordingly, whatever we meet with in cold
and bleak places, as the tops of mountains, we respect for
a sort of sturdy innocence, a Puritan toughness. All things
beside seem to be called in for shelter, and what stays out
must be part of the original frame of the universe, and of
such valor as God himself. It is invigorating to breathe
the cleansed air. Its greater fineness and purity are visible
to the eye, and we would fain stay out long and late, that
the gales may sigh through us too, as through the leafless
trees, and fit us for the winter:—as if we hoped so to
borrow some pure and steadfast virtue, which will stead
us in all seasons.

At length we have reached the edge of the woods, and
shut out the gadding town. We enter within their covert
as we go under the roof of a cottage, and cross its thresh-
old, all ceiled and banked up with snow. They are glad
and warm still, and as genial and cheery in winter as in
summer. As we stand in the midst of the pines, in the
flickering and checkered light which straggles but little
way into their maze, we wonder if the towns have ever
heard their simple story. It seems to us that no traveller
has ever explored them, and notwithstanding the wonders
which science is elsewhere revealing every day, who
would not like to hear their annals? Our humble villages
in the plain, are their contribution. We borrow from the
forest the boards which shelter, and the sticks which
warm us. How important is their evergreen to the winter,
that portion of the summer which does not fade, the permanent year, the unwithered grass. Thus simply, and
with little expense of altitude, is the surface of the earth
diversified. What would human life be without forests,
those natural cities? From the tops of mountains they appear like smooth shaven lanes, yet whither shall we walk
but in this taller grass?

There is a slumbering subterranean fire in nature
which never goes out, and which no cold can chill. It
finally melts the great snow, and in January or July is
only buried under a thicker or thinner covering. In the
coldest day it flows somewhere, and the snow melts
around every tree. This field of winter rye, which sprouted late last fall, and now speedily dissolves the snow, is

where the fire is very thinly covered. We feel warmed by it. In the winter, warmth stands for all virtue, and we resort in thought to a trickling rill, with its bare stones shining in the sun, and to warm springs in the woods, with as much eagerness as rabbits and robins. The steam which rises from swamps and pools is as dear and domestic as that of our own kettle. What fire could ever equal the sunshine of a winter's-day, when the meadow mice come out by the wallsides, and the chickadee lisps in the defiles of the wood? The warmth comes directly from the sun, and is not radiated from the earth, as in summer; and when we feel his beams on our back as we are treading some snowy dell, we are grateful as for a special kindness, and bless the sun which has followed us into that by-place.

This subterranean fire has its altar in each man's breast, for in the coldest day, and on the bleakest hill, the traveler cherishes a warmer fire within the folds of his cloak than is kindled on any hearth. A healthy man, indeed, is the complement of the seasons, and in winter, summer is in his heart. There is the south. Thither have all birds and insects migrated, and around the warm springs in his breast are gathered the robin and the lark.

In this glade covered with bushes of a year's growth see how the silvery dust lies on every seared leaf and twig, deposited in such infinite and luxurious forms as by their very variety atone for the absence of color. Observe the tiny tracks of mice around every stem, and the triangular tracks of the rabbit. A pure elastic heaven hangs over all, as if the impurities of the summer sky refined and shrunk by the chaste winter's cold, had been winnowed from the heavens upon the earth.

Nature confounds her summer distinction at this season. The heavens seem to be nearer the earth. The elements are less reserved and distinct. Water turns to ice, rain to snow. The day is but a Scandinavian night. The winter is an arctic summer.

How much more living is the life that is in nature, the furred life which still survives the stinging nights, and, from amidst fields and woods covered with frost and snow, sees the sun rise.

> "The foodless wilds
> Pour forth their brown inhabitants."

The grey-squirrel and rabbit are brisk and playful in the remote glens, even on the morning of the cold Friday. Here is our Lapland and Labrador, and for our Esquimaux and Knistenaux, Dog-ribbed Indians, Novazemblaites, and Spitzbergeners, are there not the ice-cutter and wood-chopper, the fox, muskrat, and mink?

Still, in the midst of the arctic day, we may trace the summer to its retreats, and sympathize with some contemporary life. Stretched over the brooks, in the midst of the frost-bound meadows, we may observe the submarine cottages of the caddice worms, the larvae of the Plicipennes. Their small cylindrical caves built around themselves, composed of flags, sticks, grass, and withered leaves, shells and pebbles, in form and color like the wrecks which strew the bottom—now drifting along over the pebbly bottom, now whirling in tiny eddies and dashing down steep falls, or sweeping rapidly along with the current, or else swaying to and fro at the end of some grass blade or root. Anon they will leave their sunken habitations, and crawling up the stems of plants, or floating on the surface like gnats, or perfect insects, henceforth flutter over the surface of the water, or sacrifice their short lives in the flame of our candles at evening. Down yonder little glen the shrubs are drooping under their burden, and the red alder-berries contrast with the white ground. Here are the marks of a myriad feet which have already been abroad. The sun rises as proudly over such a glen, as over the valley of the Seine or the Tiber, and it seems the residence of a pure and self-subsistent valor, such as they never witnessed; which never knew defeat nor fear. Here reign the simplicity and purity of a primitive age, and a health and hope far remote from towns and cities. Standing quite alone, far in the forest, while the wind is shaking down snow from the trees, and leaving the only human tracks behind us, we find our reflections of a richer variety than the life of cities. The chickadee and nut-hatch are more inspiring society than the statesmen and philosophers, and we shall return to these last, as to more vulgar companions. In this lonely glen, with its brook draining the slopes, its creased ice and crystals of all hues, where the spruces and hemlocks stand up on either side, and the rush and sere wild oats in the rivulet itself, our lives are more serene and worthy to contemplate.

As the day advances, the heat of the sun is reflected by the hillsides, and we hear a faint but sweet music, where flows the rill released from its fetters, and the icicles are melting on the trees; and the nut-hatch and partridge are heard and seen. The south wind melts the snow at noon, and the bare ground appears with its withered grass and leaves, and we are invigorated by the perfume which expands from it, as by the scent of strong meats.

Let us go into this deserted woodman's hut, and see how he has passed the long winter nights and the short and stormy days. For here man has lived under this south hill-side, and it seems a civilized and public spot. We have such associations as when the traveller stands by the ruins of Palmyra or Hecatompolis. Singing birds and flowers perchance have begun to appear here, for flowers as well as weeds follow in the footsteps of man. These hemlocks whispered over his head, these hickory logs were his fuel, and these pitch-pine roots kindled his fire; yonder foaming rill in the hollow, whose thin and airy vapor still ascends as busily as ever, though he is far off now, was his well. These hemlock boughs, and the straw upon this raised platform, were his bed, and this broken dish held his drink. But he has not been here this season, for the phæbes built their nest upon this shelf last summer. I find some embers left, as if he had but just gone out, where he baked his pot of beans, and while at evening he smoked his pipe, whose stemless bowl lies in the ashes, chatted with his only companion, if perchance he had any, about the depth of the snow on the morrow, already falling fast and thick without, or disputed whether the last sound was the screech of an owl, or the creak of a bough, or imagination only; and through this broad chimney-throat, in the late winter evening, ere he stretched himself upon the straw, he looked up to learn the progress of the storm, and seeing the bright stars of

Cassiopeia's chair shining brightly down upon him, fell contentedly asleep.

See how many traces from which we may learn the chopper's history. From this stump we may guess the sharpness of his axe, and from the slope of the stroke, on which side he stood, and whether he cut down the tree without going round it or changing hands; and from the flexure of the splinters we may know which way it fell. This one chip contains inscribed on it the whole history of the wood-chopper and of the world. On this scrap of paper, which held his sugar or salt, perchance, or was the wadding of his gun, sitting on a log in the forest, with what interest we read the tattle of cities, of those larger huts, empty and to let, like this, in High-streets, and Broad-ways. The eaves are dripping on the south side of this simple roof, while the titmouse lisps in the pine, and the genial warmth of the sun around the door is somewhat kind and human.

After two seasons, this rude dwelling does not deform the scene. Already the birds resort to it, to build their nests, and you may track to its door the feet of many quadrupeds. Thus, for a long time, nature overlooks the encroachment and profanity of man. The wood still cheerfully and unsuspiciously echoes the strokes of the axe that fells it, and while they are few and seldom, they enhance its wildness, and all the elements strive to naturalize the sound.

Now our path begins to ascend gradually to the top of this high hill, from whose precipitous south side, we can look over the broad country, of forest, and field, and river, to the distant snowy mountains. See yonder thin column of smoke curling up through the woods from some invisible farm-house; the standard raised over some rural homestead. There must be a warmer and more genial spot there below, as where we detect the vapor from a spring forming a cloud above the trees. What fine relations are established between the traveller who discovers this airy column from some eminence in the forest, and him who sits below. Up goes the smoke as silently and naturally as the vapor exhales from the leaves, and as busy disposing itself in wreathes as the housewife on the hearth below. It is a hieroglyphic of man's life, and suggests more intimate and important things than the boiling of a pot. Where its fine column rises above the forest, like an ensign, some human life has planted itself,—and such is the beginning of Rome, the establishment of the arts, and the foundation of empires, whether on the prairies of America, or the steppes of Asia.

And now we descend again to the brink of this woodland lake, which lies in a hollow of the hills, as if it were their expressed juice, and that of the leaves, which are annually steeped in it. Without outlet or inlet to the eye, it has still its history, in the lapse of its waves, in the rounded pebbles on its shore, and on the pines which grow down to its brink. It has not been idle, though sedentary, but, like Abu Musa, teaches that "sitting still at home is the heavenly way; the going out is the way of the world." Yet in its evaporation it travels as far as any. In summer it is the earth's liquid eye; a mirror in the breast of nature. The sins of the wood are washed out in it. See how the woods form an amphitheatre about it, and it is an arena for all the genialness of nature. All trees direct the traveller to its brink, all paths seek it out, birds fly to it, quadrupeds flee to it, and the very ground inclines toward it. It is nature's saloon, where she has sat down to her toilet. Consider her silent economy and tidiness; how the sun comes with his evaporation to sweep the dust from its surface each morning, and a fresh surface is constantly welling up; and annually, after whatever impurities have accumulated herein, its liquid transparency appears again in the spring. In summer a hushed music seems to sweep across its surface. But now a plain sheet of snow conceals it from our eyes, except when the wind has swept the ice bare, and the sere leaves are gliding from side to side, tacking and veering on their tiny voyages. Here is one just keeled up against a pebble on shore, a dry beach leaf, rocking still, as if it would soon start again. A skillful engineer, methinks, might project its course since it fell from the parent stem. Here are all the elements for such a calculation. Its present position, the direction of the wind, the level of the pond, and how much more is given. In its scarred edges and veins is its log rolled up.

We fancy ourselves in the interior of a larger house. The surface of the pond is our deal table or sanded floor, and the woods rise abruptly from its edge, like the walls of a cottage. The lines set to catch pickerel through the ice look like a larger culinary preparation, and the men stand about on the white ground like pieces of forest furniture. The actions of these men, at the distance of half a mile over the ice and snow, impress us as when we read the exploits of Alexander in history. They seem not unworthy of the scenery, and as momentous as the conquest of kingdoms.

Again we have wandered through the arches of the wood, until from its skirts we hear the distant booming of ice from yonder bay of the river, as if it were moved by some other and subtler tide than oceans know. To me it has a strange sound of home, thrilling as the voice of one's distant and noble kindred. A mild summer sun shines over forest and lake, and though there is but one green leaf for many rods, yet nature enjoys a serene health. Every sound is fraught with the same mysterious assurance of health, as well now the creaking of the boughs in January, as the soft sough of the wind in July.

> When Winter fringes every bough
>   With his fantastic wreath,
> And puts the seal of silence now
>   Upon the leaves beneath;
>
> When every stream in its pent-house
>   Goes gurgling on its way,
> And in his gallery the mouse
>   Nibbleth the meadow hay;
>
> Methinks the summer still is nigh,
>   And lurketh underneath,
> As that same meadow mouse doth lie
>   Snug in the last year's heath.
>
> And if perchance the Chickadee
>   List a faint note anon,
> The snow in summer's canopy,
>   Which she herself put on.

Fair blossoms deck the cheerful trees,
  And dazzling fruits depend,
The north wind sighs a summer breeze,
  The nipping frosts to fend,

Bringing glad tidings unto me,
  The while I stand all ear,
Of a serene eternity,
  Which need not winter fear.

Out on the silent pond straightway
  The restless ice doth crack,
And pond sprites merry gambols play
  Amid the deafening rack.

Eager I hasten to the vale,
  As if I heard brave news,
How nature held high festival,
  Which it were hard to lose.

I gambol with my neighbor ice,
  And sympathizing quake,
As each new crack darts in a trice
  Across the gladsome lake.

One with the cricket in the ground,
  And faggot on the hearth,
Resounds the rare domestic sound
  Along the forest path.

Before night we will take a journey on skates along the
course of this meandering river, as full of novelty to one
who sits by the cottage fire all the winter's day, as if it
were over the polar ice, with captain Parry or Franklin;
following the winding of the stream, now flowing amid
hills, now spreading out into far meadows, and forming a
myriad coves and bays where the pine and hemlock over-
arch. The river flows in the rear of the towns, and we see
all things from a new and wilder side. The fields and
gardens come down to it with a frankness, and freedom
from pretension, which they do not wear on the highway.
It is the outside and edge of the earth. Our eyes are not
offended by violent contrasts. The last rail of the farmer's
fence is some swaying willow bough, which still preserves
its freshness, and here at length all fences stop, and we no
longer cross any road. We may go far up within the

country now by the most retired and level road, never climbing a hill, but by broad levels ascending to the upland meadows. It is a beautiful illustration of the law of obedience, the flow of a river; the path for a sick man, a highway down which an acorn cup may float secure with its freight. Its slight occasional falls, whose precipices would not diversify the landscape, are celebrated by mist and spray, and attract the traveller from far and near. From the remote interior, its current conducts him by broad and easy steps, or by one gentle inclined plain, to the sea. Thus by an early and constant yielding to the inequalities of the ground, it secures itself the easiest passage.

No dominion of nature is quite closed to man at all times, and now we draw near to the empire of the fishes. Our feet glide swiftly over unfathomed depths, where in summer our line tempted the pout and perch, and where the stately pickerel lurked in the long corridors, formed by the bulrushes. The deep, impenetrable marsh, where the heron waded, and bittern squatted, is made pervious to our swift shoes, as if a thousand railroads had been made into it. With one impulse we are carried to the cabin of the muskrat, that earliest settler, and see him dart away under the transparent ice, like a furred fish, to his hole in the bank; and we glide rapidly over meadows where lately "the mower whet his scythe," through beds of frozen cranberries mixed with meadow grass. We skate near to where the blackbird, the pewee, and the kingbird hung their nests over the water, and the hornets builded from the maple on the swamp. How many gay warblers now following the sun, have radiated from this nest of silver birch and thistle down. On the swamp's outer edge was hung the supermarine village, where no foot penetrated. In this hollow tree the wood-duck reared her brood, and slid away each day to forage in yonder fen.

In winter, nature is a cabinet of curiosities, full of dried specimens, in their natural order and position. The meadows and forests are a *hortus siccus*. The leaves and grasses stand perfectly pressed by the air without screw or gum, and the bird's nests are not hung on an artificial twig, but where they builded them. We go about dry

shod to inspect the summer's work in the rank swamp,
and see what a growth have got the alders, the willows,
and the maples; testifying to how many warm suns, and
fertilizing dews and showers. See what strides their
boughs took in the luxuriant summer,—and anon these
dormant buds will carry them onward and upward another span into the heavens.

Occasionally we wade through fields of snow, under
whose depths the river is lost for many rods, to appear
again to the right or left, where we least expected; still
holding on its way underneath, with a faint, stertorous,
rumbling sound, as if, like the bear and marmot, it too
had hibernated, and we had followed its faint summer
trail to where it earthed itself in snow and ice. At first we
should have thought that rivers would be empty and dry
in mid winter, or else frozen solid till the spring thawed
them; but their volume is not diminished even, for only a
superficial cold bridges their surface. The thousand
springs which feed the lakes and streams are flowing still.
The issues of a few surface springs only are closed, and
they go to swell the deep reservoirs. Nature's wells are
below the frost. The summer brooks are not filled with
snow-water, nor does the mower quench his thirst with
that alone. The streams are swollen when the snow melts
in the spring, because nature's work has been delayed,
the water being turned into ice and snow, whose particles
are less smooth and round, and do not find their level so
soon.

Far over the ice, between the hemlock woods and
snow-clad hills, stands the pickerel fisher, his lines set in
some retired cove, like a Finlander, with his arms thrust
into the pouches of his dreadnought; with dull, snowy,
fishy thoughts, himself a finless fish, separated a few
inches from his race; dumb, erect, and made to be enveloped in clouds and snows, like the pines on shore. In
these wild scenes, men stand about in the scenery, or
move deliberately and heavily, having sacrificed the
sprightliness and vivacity of towns to the dumb sobriety
of nature. He does not make the scenery less wild, more
than the jays and muskrats, but stands there as a part of
it, as the natives are represented in the voyages of early

navigators, at Nootka sound, and on the North-west coast, with their furs about them, before they were tempted to loquacity by a scrap of iron. He belongs to the natural family of man, and is planted deeper in nature and has more root than the inhabitants of towns. Go to him, ask what luck, and you will learn that he too is a worshipper of the unseen. Hear with what sincere deference and waving gesture in his tone, he speaks of the lake pickerel, which he has never seen, his primitive and ideal race of pickerel. He is connected with the shore still, as by a fish-line, and yet remembers the season when he took fish through the ice on the pond, while the peas were up in his garden at home.

But now, while we have loitered, the clouds have gathered again, and a few straggling snow-flakes are beginning to descend. Faster and faster they fall, shutting out the distant objects from sight. The snow falls on every wood and field, and no crevice is forgotten; by the river and the pond, on the hill and in the valley. Quadrupeds are confined to their coverts, and the birds sit upon their perches this peaceful hour. There is not so much sound as in fair weather, but silently and gradually every slope, and the grey walls and fences, and the polished ice, and the sere leaves, which were not buried before, are concealed, and the tracks of men and beasts are lost. With so little effort does nature reassert her rule, and blot out the traces of men. Hear how Homer has described the same. "The snow flakes fall thick and fast on a winter's day. The winds are lulled, and the snow falls incessant, covering the top of the mountains, and the hills, and the plains where the lotus tree grows, and the cultivated fields, and they are falling by the inlets and shores of the foaming sea, but are silently dissolved by the waves." The snow levels all things, and infolds them deeper on the bosom of nature, as, in the slow summer, vegetation creeps up to the entablature of the temple, and the turrets of the castle, and helps her to prevail over art.

The surly night-wind rustles through the wood, and warns us to retrace our steps, while the sun goes down behind the thickening storm, and birds seek their roosts, and cattle their stalls.

> "Drooping the lab'rer ox
> Stands covered o'er with snow, and *now* demands
> The fruit of all his toil."

Though winter is represented in the almanac as an old
man, facing the wind and sleet, and drawing his cloak
about him, we rather think of him as a merry wood-
chopper, and warm-blooded youth, as blithe as summer.
The unexplored grandeur of the storm keeps up the spirits of the traveller. It does not trifle with us, but has a
sweet earnestness. In winter we lead a more inward life.
Our hearts are warm and merry, like cottages under
drifts, whose windows and doors are half concealed, but
from whose chimneys the smoke cheerfully ascends. The
imprisoning drifts increase the sense of comfort which
the house affords, and in the coldest days we are content
to sit over the hearth and see the sky through the chimney top, enjoying the quiet and serene life that may be
had in a warm corner by the chimney side, or feeling our
pulse by listening to the low of cattle in the street, or the
sound of the flail in distant barns all the long afternoon.
No doubt a skilful physician could determine our health
by observing how these simple and natural sounds affected us. We enjoy now, not an oriental, but a boreal leisure,
around warm stoves and fire-places, and watch the shadow of motes in the sunbeams.

Sometimes our fate grows too homely and familiarly
serious ever to be cured. Consider how for three months
the human destiny is wrapped in furs. The good Hebrew
revelation takes no cognizance of all this cheerful snow. Is
there no religion for the temperate and frigid zones? We
know of no scripture which records the pure benignity of
the gods on a New England winter night. Their praises
have never been sung, only their wrath deprecated. The
best scripture, after all, records but a meagre faith. Its
saints live reserved and austere. Let a brave devout man
spend the year in the woods of Maine or Labrador, and
see if the Hebrew scriptures speak adequately of his condition and experience, from the setting in of winter to the
breaking up of the ice.

Now commences the long winter evening around the
farmer's hearth, when the thoughts of the indwellers

travel far abroad, and men are by nature and necessity charitable and liberal to all creatures. Now is the happy resistance to cold, when the farmer reaps his reward, and thinks of his preparedness for winter, and through the glittering panes, sees with equanimity "the mansion of the northern bear," for now the storm is over,

> "The full ethereal round,
> Infinite worlds disclosing to the view,
> Shines out intensely keen; and all one cope
> Of starry glitter glows from pole to pole."

KTAADN

Thoreau's keeping an imaginary mountain anchored east of Concord for his private climbing, as he confided in his Journal *and to his friend, Blake, did not preclude his climbing real mountains. His ascent of wild Ktaadn (Katadin) in September of 1846, "made of Chaos and Old Night," confronted him with the sobering possibility that man and nature may be alien and irreconcilable, and that civilized life in America may be an aberration. Though "Ktaadn and the Maine Woods" was first published in the* Union Magazine, *July through November, 1848, the text reproduced here is from* The Maine Woods *in the definitive Princeton Edition, edited by Joseph J. Moldenhauer (1972).*

BY SIX O'CLOCK, having mounted our packs and a good blanket full of trout, ready dressed, and swung up such baggage and provision as we wished to leave behind upon the tops of saplings, to be out of the reach of bears, we started for the summit of the mountain, distant, as Uncle George said the boatmen called it, about four miles, but as I judged, and as it proved, nearer fourteen. He had never been any nearer the mountain than this, and there was not the slightest trace of man to guide us further in this direction. At first, pushing a few rods up the Aboljacknagesic, or "open-land stream," we fastened our bat-

teau to a tree, and travelled up the north side, through
burnt lands, now partially overgrown with young aspens,
and other shrubbery; but soon, recrossing this stream,
where it was about fifty or sixty feet wide, upon a jam of
logs and rocks, and you could cross it by this means almost anywhere, we struck at once for the highest peak,
over a mile or more of comparatively open land still, very
gradually ascending the while. Here it fell to my lot, as
the oldest mountain-climber, to take the lead: so scanning
the woody side of the mountain, which lay still at an indefinite distance, stretched out some seven or eight miles
in length before us, we determined to steer directly for
the base of the highest peak, leaving a large slide, by
which, as I have since learned, some of our predecessors
ascended, on our left. This course would lead us parallel
to a dark seam in the forest, which marked the bed of a
torrent, and over a slight spur, which extended southward
from the main mountain, from whose bare summit we
could get an outlook over the country, and climb directly
up the peak, which would then be close at hand. Seen
from this point, a bare ridge at the extremity of the open
land, Ktaadn presented a different aspect from any
mountain I have seen, there being a greater proportion of
naked rock, rising abruptly from the forest; and we
looked up at this blue barrier as if it were some fragment
of a wall which anciently bounded the earth in that direction. Setting the compass for a north-east course,
which was the bearing of the southern base of the highest
peak, we were soon buried in the woods.

We soon began to meet with traces of bears and moose,
and those of rabbits were everywhere visible. The tracks
of moose, more or less recent, to speak literally covered
every square rod on the sides of the mountain; and these
animals are probably more numerous there now than
ever before, being driven into this wilderness from all
sides by the settlements. The track of a full-grown moose
is like that of a cow, or larger, and of the young, like that
of a calf. Sometimes we found ourselves travelling in
faint paths, which they had made, like cow-paths in the
woods, only far more indistinct, being rather openings,
affording imperfect vistas through the dense underwood,

than trodden paths; and everywhere twigs had been browsed by them, clipt as smoothly as if by a knife. The bark of trees was stript up by them to the height of eight or nine feet, in long narrow strips, an inch wide, still showing the distinct marks of their teeth. We expected nothing less than to meet a herd of them every moment, and our Nimrod held his shooting-iron in readiness; but we did not go out of our way to look for them, and, though numerous, they are so wary, that the unskilful hunter might range the forest a long time before he could get sight of one. They are sometimes dangerous to encounter, and will not turn out for the hunter, but furiously rush upon him, and trample him to death, unless he is lucky enough to avoid them by dodging round a tree. The largest are nearly as large as a horse, and weigh sometimes one thousand pounds; and it is said that they can step over a five-foot gate in their ordinary walk. They are described as exceedingly awkward-looking animals, with their long legs and short bodies, making a ludicrous figure when in full run, but making great headway nevertheless. It seemed a mystery to us how they could thread these woods, which it required all our suppleness to accomplish, climbing, stooping, and winding, alternately. They are said to drop their long and branching horns, which usually spread five or six feet, on their backs, and make their way easily by the weight of their bodies. Our boatmen said, but I know not with how much truth, that their horns are apt to be gnawed away by vermin while they sleep. Their flesh, which is more like beef than venison, is common in Bangor market.

We had proceeded on thus seven or eight miles, till about noon, with frequent pauses to refresh the weary ones, crossing a considerable mountain stream, which we conjectured to be Murch Brook, at whose mouth we had camped, all the time in woods, without having once seen the summit, and rising very gradually, when the boatmen, beginning to despair a little, and fearing that we were leaving the mountain on one side of us, for they had not entire faith in the compass, McCauslin climbed a tree, from the top of which he could see the peak, when it appeared that we had not swerved from a right line, the compass down below still ranging with his arm, which pointed to the summit. By the side of a cool mountain rill, amid the woods, where the water began to partake of the purity and transparency of the air, we stopped to cook some of our fishes, which we had brought thus far in order to save our hard bread and pork, in the use of which we had put ourselves on short allowance. We soon had a fire blazing, and stood around it, under the damp and sombre forest of firs and birches, each with a sharpened stick, three or four feet in length, upon which he had spitted his trout, or roach, previously well gashed and salted, our sticks radiating like the spokes of a wheel from one centre, and each crowding his particular fish into the most desirable exposure, not with the truest regard always to his neighbor's rights. Thus we regaled ourselves, drinking meanwhile at the spring, till one man's pack, at least, was considerably lightened, when we again took up our line of march.

At length we reached an elevation sufficiently bare to afford a view of the summit, still distant and blue, almost as if retreating from us. A torrent, which proved to be the same we had crossed, was seen tumbling down in front, literally from out of the clouds. But this glimpse at our whereabouts was soon lost, and we were buried in the woods again. The wood was chiefly yellow birch, spruce, fir, mountain-ash, or round-wood, as the Maine people call it, and moose-wood. It was the worst kind of travelling; sometimes like the densest scrub-oak patches with us. The cornel, or bunch-berries, were very abundant, as well as Solomon's seal and moose-berries. Blue-berries were distributed along our whole route; and in one place the bushes were drooping with the weight of the fruit, still as fresh as ever. It was the seventh of September. Such patches afforded a grateful repast, and served to bait the tired party forward. When any lagged behind, the cry of "blue-berries" was most effectual to bring them up. Even at this elevation we passed through a moose-yard, formed by a large flat rock, four or five rods square, where they tread down the snow in winter. At length, fearing that if we held the direct course to the summit, we should not find any water near our camping-ground, we gradually swerved to the west, till, at four o'clock, we struck again the torrent which I have mentioned, and here, in view of the summit, the weary party decided to camp that night.

While my companions were seeking a suitable spot for this purpose, I improved the little daylight that was left in climbing the mountain alone. We were in a deep and narrow ravine, sloping up to the clouds, at an angle of nearly forty-five degrees, and hemmed in by walls of rock, which were at first covered with low trees, then with impenetrable thickets of scraggy birches and spruce-trees, and with moss, but at last bare of all vegetation but lichens, and almost continually draped in clouds. Following up the course of the torrent which occupied this—and I mean to lay some emphasis on this word up—pulling myself up by the side of perpendicular falls of twenty or thirty feet, by the roots of firs and birches, and then, perhaps, walking a level rod or two in the thin stream, for it took up the whole road, ascending by huge steps, as it were, a giant's stairway, down which a river flowed, I had soon cleared the trees, and paused on the successive shelves, to look back over the country. The torrent was from fifteen to thirty feet wide, without a tributary, and seemingly not diminishing in breadth as I advanced; but still it came rushing and roaring down, with a copious tide, over and amidst masses of bare rock, from the very clouds, as though a water-spout had just burst over the mountain. Leaving this at last, I began to work my way, scarcely less arduous than Satan's anciently through Chaos, up the nearest, though not the highest peak. At first scrambling on all fours over the tops of ancient black spruce-trees, (Abies nigra,) old as the flood, from two to ten or twelve feet in height, their tops flat and spreading, and their foliage blue and nipt with cold, as if for centuries they had ceased growing upward against the bleak sky, the solid cold. I walked some good rods erect upon the tops of these trees, which were overgrown with moss and mountain-cranberries. It seemed that in the course of time they had filled up the intervals between the huge rocks, and the cold wind had uniformly levelled all over. Here the principle of vegetation was hard put to it. There was apparently a belt of this kind running quite round the mountain, though, perhaps, nowhere so remarkable as here. Once, slumping through, I looked down ten feet, into a dark and cavernous region, and saw the stem of a spruce, on whose top I stood, as on a mass of coarse basketwork, fully nine inches in diameter at the ground. These holes were bears' dens, and the bears were even then at home. This was the sort of garden I made my way *over,* for an eighth of a mile, at the risk, it is true, of treading on some of the plants, not seeing any path *through* it— certainly the most treacherous and porous country I ever travelled.

> "———nigh founder'd, on he fares,
> Treading the crude consistence, half on foot,
> Half flying."

But nothing could exceed the toughness of the twigs, —not one snapped under my weight, for they had slowly grown. Having slumped, scrambled, rolled, bounced, and walked, by turns, over this scraggy country, I arrived upon a side-hill, or rather side-mountain, where rocks, gray, silent rocks, were the flocks and herds that pastured, chewing a rocky cud at sunset. They looked at me with hard gray eyes, without a bleat or a low. This brought me to the skirt of a cloud, and bounded my walk that night. But I had already seen that Maine country when I turned about, waving, flowing, rippling, down below.

When I returned to my companions, they had selected a camping-ground on the torrent's edge, and were resting on the ground; one was on the sick list, rolled in a blanket, on a damp shelf of rock. It was a savage and dreary scenery enough; so wildly rough, that they looked long to find a level and open space for the tent. We could not well camp higher, for want of fuel; and the trees here seemed so evergreen and sappy, that we almost doubted if they would acknowledge the influence of fire; but fire prevailed at last, and blazed here, too, like a good citizen of the world. Even at this height we met with frequent traces of moose, as well as of bears. As here was no cedar, we made our bed of coarser feathered spruce; but at any rate the feathers were plucked from the live tree. It was,

perhaps, even a more grand and desolate place for a
night's lodging than the summit would have been, being
in the neighborhood of those wild trees, and of the torrent. Some more aerial and finer-spirited winds rushed
and roared through the ravine all night, from time to
time arousing our fire, and dispersing the embers about.
It was as if we lay in the very nest of a young whirlwind.
At midnight, one of my bedfellows, being startled in his
dreams by the sudden blazing up to its top of a fir-tree,
whose green boughs were dried by the heat, sprang up,
with a cry, from his bed, thinking the world on fire, and
drew the whole camp after him.

In the morning, after whetting our appetite on some
raw pork, a wafer of hard bread, and a dipper of con-
densed cloud or water-spout, we all together began to
make our way up the falls, which I have described; this
time choosing the right hand, or highest peak, which was
not the one I had approached before. But soon my companions were lost to my sight behind the mountain ridge
in my rear, which still seemed ever retreating before me,
and I climbed alone over huge rocks, loosely poised, a
mile or more, still edging toward the clouds—for though
the day was clear elsewhere, the summit was concealed
by mist. The mountain seemed a vast aggregation of loose
rocks, as if sometime it had rained rocks, and they lay as
they fell on the mountain sides, nowhere fairly at rest,
but leaning on each other, all rocking-stones, with cavities
between, but scarcely any soil or smoother shelf. They
were the raw materials of a planet dropped from an unseen quarry, which the vast chemistry of nature would
anon work up, or work down, into the smiling and verdant plains and valleys of earth. This was an undone extremity of the globe; as in lignite we see coal in the process of formation.

At length I entered within the skirts of the cloud which
seemed forever drifting over the summit, and yet would
never be gone, but was generated out of that pure air as
fast as it flowed away; and when, a quarter of a mile
further, I reached the summit of the ridge, which those
who have seen in clearer weather say is about five miles
long, and contains a thousand acres of table-land, I was
deep within the hostile ranks of clouds, and all objects

were obscured by them. Now the wind would blow me
out a yard of clear sunlight, wherein I stood; then a gray,
dawning light was all it could accomplish, the cloud-line
ever rising and falling with the wind's intensity. Sometimes it seemed as if the summit would be cleared in a
few moments and smile in sunshine: but what was gained
on one side was lost on another. It was like sitting in a
chimney and waiting for the smoke to blow away. It was,
in fact, a cloud-factory,—these were the cloud-works,
and the wind turned them off done from the cool, bare
rocks. Occasionally, when the windy columns broke in to
me, I caught sight of a dark, damp crag to the right or
left; the mist driving ceaselessly between it and me. It
reminded me of the creations of the old epic and dramat-
ic poets, of Atlas, Vulcan, the Cyclops, and Prometheus.
Such was Caucasus and the rock where Prometheus was
bound. Æschylus had no doubt visited such scenery as
this. It was vast, Titanic, and such as man never inhabits.
Some part of the beholder, even some vital part, seems to
escape through the loose grating of his ribs as he ascends.
He is more lone than you can imagine. There is less of
substantial thought and fair understanding in him, than
in the plains where men inhabit. His reason is dispersed
and shadowy, more thin and subtile like the air. Vast,
Titanic, inhuman Nature has got him at disadvantage,
caught him alone, and pilfers him of some of his divine
faculty. She does not smile on him as in the plains. She
seems to say sternly, why came ye here before your time?
This ground is not prepared for you. Is it not enough that
I smile in the valleys? I have never made this soil for thy
feet, this air for thy breathing, these rocks for thy neighbors. I cannot pity nor fondle thee here, but forever relentlessly drive thee hence to where I *am* kind. Why seek
me where I have not called thee, and then complain because you find me but a stepmother? Shouldst thou
freeze or starve, or shudder thy life away, here is no
shrine, nor altar, nor any access to my ear.

> "Chaos and ancient Night, I come no spy
> With purpose to explore or to disturb
> The secrets of your realm, but * * *
> * * * * * * * * as my way
> Lies through your spacious empire up to light."

The tops of mountains are among the unfinished parts of the globe, whither it is a slight insult to the gods to climb and pry into their secrets, and try their effect on our humanity. Only daring and insolent men, perchance, go there. Simple races, as savages, do not climb mountains—their tops are sacred and mysterious tracts never visited by them. Pomola is always angry with those who climb to the summit of Ktaadn.

According to Jackson, who in his capacity of geological surveyor of the state, has accurately measured it—the altitude of Ktaadn is 5,300 feet, or a little more than one mile above the level of the sea—and he adds: "It is then evidently the highest point in the State of Maine, and is the most abrupt granite mountain in New England." The peculiarities of that spacious table-land on which I was standing, as well as the remarkable semicircular precipice or basin on the eastern side, were all concealed by the mist. I had brought my whole pack to the top, not knowing but I should have to make my descent to the river, and possibly to the settled portion of the state alone and by some other route, and wishing to have a complete outfit with me. But at length, fearing that my companions would be anxious to reach the river before night, and knowing that the clouds might rest on the mountain for days, I was compelled to descend. Occasionally, as I came down, the wind would blow me a vista open through which I could see the country eastward, boundless forests, and lakes, and streams, gleaming in the sun, some of them emptying into the East Branch. There were also new mountains in sight in that direction. Now and then some small bird of the sparrow family would flit away before me, unable to command its course, like a fragment of the gray rock blown off by the wind.

I found my companions where I had left them, on the side of the peak, gathering the mountain cranberries, which filled every crevice between the rocks, together with blue berries, which had a spicier flavor the higher up they grew, but were not the less agreeable to our palates. When the country is settled and roads are made, these cranberries will perhaps become an article of commerce. From this elevation, just on the skirts of the clouds, we could overlook the country west and south for a hundred miles. There it was, the State of Maine, which we had seen on the map, but not much like that. Immeasurable forest for the sun to shine on, that eastern *stuff* we hear of in Massachusetts. No clearing, no house. It did not look as if a solitary traveller had cut so much as a walking-stick there. Countless lakes,—Moosehead in the southwest, forty miles long by ten wide, like a gleaming silver platter at the end of the table; Chesuncook eighteen long by three wide, without an island; Millinocket, on the south, with its hundred islands; and a hundred others without a name; and mountains also, whose names, for the most part, are known only to the Indians. The forest looked like a firm grass sward, and the effect of these lakes in its midst has been well compared by one who has since visited this same spot, to that of a "mirror broken into a thousand fragments, and wildly scattered over the grass, reflecting the full blaze of the sun." It was a large farm for somebody, when cleared. According to the Gazetteer, which was printed before the boundary question was settled, this single Penobscot county in which we were, was larger than the whole State of Vermont, with its fourteen counties; and this was only a part of the wild lands of Maine. We are concerned now, however, about natural, not political limits. We were about eighty miles as the bird flies from Bangor, or one hundred and fifteen as we had ridden, and walked, and paddled. We had to console ourselves with the reflection that this view was probably as good as that from the peak, as far as it went, and what were a mountain without its attendant clouds and mists? Like ourselves, neither Bailey nor Jackson had obtained a clear view from the summit.

Setting out on our return to the river, still at an early hour in the day, we decided to follow the course of the torrent, which we supposed to be Murch Brook, as long as it would not lead us too far out of our way. We thus travelled about four miles in the very torrent itself, continually crossing and recrossing it, leaping from rock to rock, and jumping with the stream down falls of seven or eight feet, or sometimes sliding down on our backs in a thin sheet of water. This ravine had been the scene of an extraordinary freshet in the spring, apparently accompanied by a slide from the mountain. It must have been filled with a stream of stones and water, at least twenty feet above the present level of the torrent. For a rod or two on either side of its channel, the trees were barked and splintered up to their tops, the birches bent over, twisted, and sometimes finely split like a stable-broom; some a foot in diameter snapped off, and whole clumps of trees bent over with the weight of rocks piled on them. In one place we noticed a rock two or three feet in diameter, lodged nearly twenty feet high in the crotch of a tree. For the whole four miles, we saw but one rill emptying in, and the volume of water did not seem to be increased from the first. We travelled thus very rapidly with a downward impetus, and grew remarkably expert at leaping from rock to rock, for leap we must, and leap we did, whether there was any rock at the right distance or not. It was a pleasant picture when the foremost turned about and looked up the winding ravine, walled in with rocks and the green forest, to see at intervals of a rod or two, a red-shirted or green-jacketed mountaineer against the white torrent, leaping down the channel with his pack on his back, or pausing upon a convenient rock in the midst of the torrent to mend a rent in his clothes, or unstrap the dipper at his belt to take a draught of the water. At one place we were startled by seeing, on a little sandy shelf by the side of the stream, the fresh print of a man's foot, and for a moment realized how Robinson Crusoe felt in a similar case; but at last we remembered that we had struck this stream on our way up, though we could not have told where, and one had descended into the ravine for a drink. The cool air above, and the continual bathing of our bodies in mountain water, alternate foot, sitz, douche, and plunge baths, made this walk exceedingly refreshing, and we had travelled only a mile or two after leaving the torrent, before every thread of our clothes was as dry as usual, owing perhaps to a peculiar quality in the atmosphere.]

After leaving the torrent, being in doubt about our course, Tom threw down his pack at the foot of the loftiest spruce tree at hand, and shinned up the bare trunk

some twenty feet, and then climbed through the green
tower, lost to our sight, until he held the topmost spray in
his hand.* McCauslin, in his younger days, had marched
through the wilderness with a body of troops, under General Somebody, and with one other man did all the scout-
ing and spying service. The General's word was: "Throw
down the top of that tree," and there was no tree in the
Maine woods so high that it did not lose its top in such a
case. I have heard a story of two men being lost once in
these woods, nearer to the settlements than this, who
climbed the loftiest pine they could find, some six feet in
diameter at the ground, from whose top they discovered
a solitary clearing and its smoke. When at this height,
some two hundred feet from the ground, one of them
became dizzy, and fainted in his companion's arms, and
the latter had to accomplish the descent with him, alternately fainting and reviving, as best he could. To Tom we
cried, where away does the summit bear? where the
burnt lands? The last he could only conjecture; he de-
scried, however, a little meadow and pond, lying probably in our course, which we concluded to steer for. On
reaching this secluded meadow, we found fresh tracks of
moose on the shore of the pond, and the water was still
unsettled as if they had fled before us. A little further, in
a dense thicket, we seemed to be still on their trail. It was
a small meadow, of a few acres, on the mountain side,
concealed by the forest, and perhaps never seen by a
white man before, where one would think that the moose
might browse and bathe, and rest in peace. Pursuing this
course, we soon reached the open land, which went slop-

---

* "The spruce-tree," says Springer in '51, "is generally selected, principally for the superior facilities which its numerous
limbs afford the climber. To gain the first limbs of this tree,
which are from twenty to forty feet from the ground, a smaller
tree is undercut and lodged against it, clambering up which the
top of the spruce is reached. In some cases, when a very elevated position is desired, the spruce-tree is lodged against the trunk
of some lofty pine, up which we ascend to a height twice that of
the surrounding forest."

To indicate the direction of pines, he throws down a branch,
and a man at the ground takes the bearing.

ing down some miles toward the Penobscot.

Perhaps I most fully realized that this was primeval, untamed, and forever untameable *Nature*, or whatever else men call it, while coming down this part of the mountain. We were passing over "Burnt Lands," burnt by lightning, perchance, though they showed no recent marks of fire hardly so much as a charred stump, but looked rather like a natural pasture for the moose and deer, exceedingly wild and desolate, with occasional strips of timber crossing them, and low poplars springing up, and patches of blueberries here and there. I found myself traversing them familiarly, like some pasture run to waste, or partially reclaimed by man; but when I reflected what man, what brother or sister or kinsman of our race made it and claimed it, I expected the proprietor to rise up and dispute my passage. It is difficult to conceive of a region uninhabited by man. We habitually presume his presence and influence everywhere. And yet we have not seen pure Nature, unless we have seen her thus vast, and drear, and inhuman, though in the midst of cities. Nature was here something savage and awful, though beautiful. I looked with awe at the ground I trod on, to see what the Powers had made there, the form and fashion and material of their work. This was that Earth of which we have heard, made out of Chaos and old Night. Here was no man's garden, but the unhandselled globe. It was not lawn, nor pasture, nor mead, nor woodland, nor lea, nor arable, nor waste-land. It was the fresh and natural surface of the planet Earth, as it was made forever and ever,—to be the dwelling of man, we say,—so Nature made it, and man may use it if he can. Man was not to be associated with it. It was Matter, vast, terrific,—not his Mother Earth that we have heard of, not for him to tread on, or be buried in,—no, it were being too familiar even to let his bones lie there—the home this of Necessity and Fate. There was there felt the presence of a force not bound to be kind to man. It was a place for heathenism and superstitious rites,—to be inhabited by men nearer of kin to the rocks and to wild animals than we. We walked over it with a certain awe, stopping from time to time to pick the blueberries which grew there, and had a smart and spicy taste. Perchance where *our* wild pines stand, and leaves lie on their forest floor in Concord, there were once reapers, and husbandmen planted grain; but here not even the surface had been scarred by man, but it was a specimen of what God saw fit to make this world. What is it to be admitted to a museum, to see a myriad of particular things, compared with being shown some star's surface, some hard matter in its home! I stand in awe of my body, this matter to which I am bound has become so strange to me. I fear not spirits, ghosts, of which I am one,—*that* my body might,—but I fear bodies, I tremble to meet them. What is this Titan that has possession of me? Talk of mysteries!—think of our life in nature,—daily to be shown matter, to come in contact with it,—rocks, trees, wind on our cheeks! the *solid* earth! the *actual* world! the *common sense!* *Contact! Contact!* *Who* are we? *where* are we?

Ere long we recognized some rocks and other features in the landscape which we had purposely impressed on our memories, and quickening our pace, by two o'clock we reached the batteau.* Here we had expected to dine on trout, but in this glaring sunlight they were slow to take the bait, so we were compelled to make the most of the crumbs of our hard bread and our pork, which were both nearly exhausted. Meanwhile we deliberated whether we should go up the river a mile farther to Gibson's clearing on the Sowadnehunk, where there was a deserted log hut, in order to get a half-inch auger, to mend one of our spike-poles with. There were young spruce trees enough around us, and we had a spare spike, but nothing to make a hole with. But as it was uncertain whether we should find any tools left there, we patched up the broken pole as well as we could for the downward voyage, in which there would be but little use for it. Moreover, we were unwilling to lose any time in this expedition, lest the wind should rise before we reached the larger lakes, and detain us, for a moderate wind produces quite a sea on

---

*The bears had not touched things on our possessions. They sometimes tear a batteau to pieces for the sake of the tar with which it is besmeared.

these waters, in which a batteau will not live for a moment; and on one occasion McCauslin had been delayed a week at the head of the North Twin, which is only four miles across. We were nearly out of provisions, and ill prepared in this respect for what might possibly prove a week's journey round by the shore, fording innumerable streams, and threading a trackless forest, should any accident happen to our boat.

It was with regret that we turned our backs on Chesuncook, which McCauslin had formerly logged on, and the Allagash lakes. There were still longer rapids and portages above; among the last the Rippogenus Portage, which he described as the most difficult on the river, and three miles long. The whole length of the Penobscot is two hundred and seventy-five miles, and we are still nearly one hundred miles from its source. Hodge, the assistant State Geologist, passed up this river in 1837, and by a portage of only one mile and three-quarters, crossed over into the Allagash, and so went down that into the St. John, and up the Madawaska to the Grand Portage across to the St. Lawrence. His is the only account that I know, of an expedition through to Canada in this direction. He thus describes his first sight of the latter river, which, to compare small things with great, is like Balboa's first sight of the Pacific from the mountains of the Isthmus of Darien. "When we first came in sight of the St. Lawrence," he says, "from the top of a high hill, the view was most striking, and much more interesting to me from having been shut up in the woods for the two previous months. Directly before us lay the broad river, extending across nine or ten miles, its surface broken by a few islands and reefs; and two ships riding at anchor near the shore. Beyond, extended ranges of uncultivated hills, parallel with the river. The sun was just going down behind them, and gilding the whole scene with its parting rays."

About four o'clock the same afternoon, we commenced our return voyage, which would require but little if any poling. In shooting rapids, the boatmen use large and broad paddles, instead of poles, to guide the boat with. Though we glided so swiftly and often smoothly down, where it had cost us no slight effort to get up, our present voyage was attended with far more danger: for if we once fairly struck one of the thousand rocks by which we were surrounded, the boat would be swamped in an instant. When a boat is swamped under these circumstances, the boatmen commonly find no difficulty in keeping afloat at first, for the current keeps both them and their cargo up for a long way down the stream; and if they can swim, they have only to work their way gradually to the shore. The greatest danger is of being caught in an eddy behind some larger rock, where the water rushes up stream faster than elsewhere it does down, and being carried round and round under the surface till they are drowned. McCauslin pointed out some rocks which had been the scene of a fatal accident of this kind. Sometimes the body is not thrown out for several hours. He himself had performed such a circuit once, only his legs being visible to his companions; but he was fortunately thrown out in season to recover his breath.* In shooting the rapids, the boatman has this problem to solve: to choose a circuitous and safe course amid a thousand sunken rocks, scattered over a quarter or half a mile, at the same time that he is moving steadily on at the rate of fifteen miles an hour. Stop he cannot; the only question is, where will he go? The bow-man chooses the course with all his eyes about him, striking broad off with his paddle, and drawing the boat by main force into her course. The stern-man faithfully follows the bow.

We were soon at the Aboljacarmegus Falls. Anxious to avoid the delay as well as the labor of the portage here, our boatmen went forward first to reconnoitre, and concluded to let the batteau down the falls, carrying the baggage only over the portage. Jumping from rock to rock until nearly in the middle of the stream, we were ready to receive the boat and let her down over the first fall, some six or seven feet perpendicular. The boatmen stand

---

*I cut this from a newspaper. "On the 11th (instant?) [May, '49], on Rappogenes Falls, Mr. John Delantee, of Orono, Me., was drowned while running logs. He was a citizen of Orono, and was twenty-six years of age. His companions found his body, enclosed it in bark, and buried it in the solemn woods."

upon the edge of a shelf of rock where the fall is perhaps
nine or ten feet perpendicular, in from one to two feet of
rapid water, one on each side of the boat, and let it slide
gently over, till the bow is run out ten or twelve feet in
the air; then letting it drop squarely, while one holds the
painter, the other leaps in, and his companion following,
they are whirled down the rapids to a new fall, or to
smooth water. In a very few minutes they had accomplished a passage in safety, which would be as fool-hardy
for the unskilful to attempt as the descent of Niagara itself. It seemed as if it needed only a little familiarity, and
a little more skill to navigate down such falls as Niagara
itself with safety. At any rate, I should not despair of such
men in the rapids above Table-Rock, until I saw them
actually go over the falls, so cool, so collected, so fertile in
resources are they. One might have thought that these
were falls, and that falls were not to be waded through
with impunity like a mud-puddle. There was really danger of their losing their sublimity in losing their power to
harm us. Familiarity breeds contempt. The boatman
pauses, perchance, on some shelf beneath a table-rock under the fall, standing in some cove of back-water two feet
deep, and you hear his rough voice come up through the
spray, coolly giving directions how to launch the boat this
time.

Having carried round Pockwockomus Falls, our oars
soon brought us to the Katepskonegan, or Oak Hall carry,
where we decided to camp half way over, leaving our
batteau to be carried over in the morning on fresh shoulders. One shoulder of each of the boatmen showed a red
spot as large as one's hand, worn by the batteau on this
expedition; and this shoulder, as it did all the work, was
perceptibly lower than its fellow, from long service. Such
toil soon wears out the strongest constitution. The drivers
are accustomed to work in the cold water in the spring,
rarely ever dry; and if one falls in all over, he rarely
changes his clothes till night, if then, even. One who takes
this precaution is called by a particular nickname, or is
turned off. None can lead this life who are not almost
amphibious. McCauslin said soberly, what is at any rate a
good story to tell, that he had seen where six men were

wholly under water at once, at a jam, with their shoulders
to handspikes. If the log did not start, then they had to
put out their heads to breathe. The driver works as long
as he can see, from dark to dark, and at night has not
time to eat his supper and dry his clothes fairly, before he
is asleep on his cedar bed. We lay that night on the very
bed made by such a party, stretching our tent over the
poles which were still standing, but reshingling the damp
and faded bed with fresh leaves.

In the morning, we carried our boat over and launched
it, making haste lest the wind should rise. The boatmen
ran down Passamagamet, and, soon after, Ambejijis Falls,
while we walked round with the baggage. We made a
hasty breakfast at the head of Ambejijis lake, on the re-
mainder of our pork, and were soon rowing across its
smooth surface again, under a pleasant sky, the mountain
being now clear of clouds in the northeast. Taking turns
at the oars, we shot rapidly across Deep Cove, the Foot of
Pamadumcook, and the North Twin, at the rate of six
miles an hour, the wind not being high enough to disturb
us, and reached the Dam at noon. The boatmen went
through one of the log sluices in the batteau, where the
fall was ten feet at the bottom, and took us in below.
Here was the longest rapid in our voyage, and perhaps
the running this was as dangerous and arduous a task as
any. Shooting down sometimes at the rate, as we judged,
of fifteen miles an hour, if we struck a rock, we were
split from end to end in an instant. Now like a bait bobbing for some river monster amid the eddies, now darting
to this side of the stream, now to that, gliding swift and
smooth near to our destruction, or striking broad off with
the paddle and drawing the boat to right or left with all
our might, in order to avoid a rock. I suppose that it was
like running the rapids of the Sault de Ste. Marie, at the
outlet of Lake Superior, and our boatmen probably dis-
played no less dexterity than the Indians there do. We
soon ran through this mile, and floated in Quakish lake.

After such a voyage, the troubled and angry waters,
which once had seemed terrible and not to be trifled
with, appeared tamed and subdued; they had been
bearded and worried in their channels, pricked and

whipped into submission with the spike-pole and paddle, gone through and through with impunity, and all their spirit and their danger taken out of them, and the most swollen and impetuous rivers seemed but playthings henceforth. I began, at length, to understand the boatman's familiarity with and contempt for the rapids. "Those Fowler boys," said Mrs. McCauslin, "are perfect ducks for the water." They had run down to Lincoln, according to her, thirty or forty miles, in a batteau, in the night, for a doctor, when it was so dark that they could not see a rod before them, and the river was swollen so as to be almost a continuous rapid, so that the doctor *cried*, when they brought him up by daylight, "Why, Tom, how did you see to steer?" "We didn't steer much,—only kept her straight." And yet they met with no accident. It is true, the more difficult rapids are higher up than this.

When we reached the Millinocket opposite to Tom's house, and were waiting for his folks to set us over, for we had left our batteau above the Grand Falls, we discovered two canoes with two men in each, turning up this stream from Shad Pond, one keeping the opposite side of a small island before us, while the other approached the side where we were standing, examining the banks carefully for muskrats as they came along. The last proved to be Louis Neptune and his companion, now at last on their way up to Chesuncook after moose; but they were so disguised that we hardly knew them. At a little distance, they might have been taken for Quakers, with their broad-brimmed hats, and overcoats with broad capes, the spoils of Bangor, seeking a settlement in this Sylvania,—or, nearer at hand, for fashionable gentlemen, the morning after a spree. Met face to face, these Indians in their native woods looked like the sinister and slouching fellows whom you meet picking up strings and paper in the streets of a city. There is, in fact, a remarkable and unexpected resemblance between the degraded savage and the lowest classes of the great city. The one is no more a child of nature than the other. In the progress of degradation, the distinction of races is soon lost. Neptune at first was only anxious to know what we "kill," seeing some partridges in the hands of one of the party, but we had assumed too much anger to permit of a reply. We thought Indians had some honor before. But—"Me been sick. O, me unwell now. You make bargain, then me go." They had in fact been delayed so long by a drunken frolic at the Five Islands, and they had not yet recovered from its effects. They had some young musquash in their canoes, which they dug out of the banks with a hoe for food, not for their skins, for musquash are their principal food on these expeditions. So they went on up the Millinocket, and we kept down the bank of the Penobscot, after recruiting ourselves with a draught of Tom's beer, leaving Tom at his home.

Thus a man shall lead his life away here on the edge of the wilderness, on Indian Millinocket stream, in a new world, far in the dark of a continent, and have a flute to play at evening here, while his strains echo to the stars, amid the howling of wolves; shall live, as it were, in the primitive age of the world, a primitive man. Yet he shall spend a sunny day, and in this century be my contemporary; perchance shall read some scattered leaves of literature, and sometimes talk with me. Why read history then if the ages and the generations are now? He lives three thousand years deep into time, an age not yet described by poets. Can you well go further back in history than this? Ay! ay!—for there turns up but now into the mouth of Millinocket stream a still more ancient and primitive man, whose history is not brought down even to the former. In a bark vessel sewn with the roots of the spruce, with horn-beam paddles he dips his way along. He is but dim and misty to me, obscured by the æons that lie between the bark canoe and the batteau. He builds no house of logs, but a wigwam of skins. He eats no hot-bread and sweet-cake, but musquash and moose-meat and the fat of bears. He glides up the Millinocket and is lost to my sight, as a more distant and misty cloud is seen flitting by behind a nearer, and is lost in space. So he goes about his destiny, the red face of man.

After having passed the night and buttered our boots for the last time at Uncle George's, whose dogs almost devoured him for joy at his return, we kept on down the river the next day about eight miles on foot, and then

took a batteau with a man to pole it to Mattawamkeag,
ten more. At the middle of that very night, to make a
swift conclusion to a long story, we dropped our buggy
over the half-finished bridge at Oldtown, where we
heard the confused din and clink of a hundred saws
which never rust, and at six o'clock the next morning one
of the party was steaming his way to Massachusetts.

What is most striking in the Maine wilderness is, the
continuousness of the forest, with fewer open intervals or
glades than you had imagined. Except the few burnt
lands, the narrow intervals on the rivers, the bare tops of
the high mountains, and the lakes and streams, the forest
is uninterrupted. It is even more grim and wild than you
had anticipated, a damp and intricate wilderness, in the
spring everywhere wet and miry. The aspect of the country indeed is universally stern and savage, excepting the
distant views of the forest from hills, and the lake prospects, which are mild and civilizing in a degree. The
lakes are something which you are unprepared for: they
lie up so high exposed to the light, and the forest is diminished to a fine fringe on their edges, with here and
there a blue mountain, like amethyst jewels set around
some jewel of the first water,—so anterior, so superior to
all the changes that are to take place on their shores, even
now civil and refined, and fair, as they can ever be.
These are not the artificial forests of an English king—a
royal preserve merely. Here prevail no forest laws, but
those of nature. The aborigines have never been dispos-
sessed, nor nature disforested.

It is a country full of evergreen trees, of mossy silver
birches and watery maples, the ground dotted with insip-
id, small red berries, and strewn with damp and moss-
grown rocks—a country diversified with innumerable
lakes and rapid streams, peopled with trout and various
species of *leucisci*, with salmon, shad and pickerel, and
other fishes; the forest resounding at rare intervals with
the note of the chicadee, the blue-jay, and the woodpeck-
er, the scream of the fish-hawk and the eagle, the laugh
of the loon, and the whistle of ducks along the solitary
streams; and at night, with the hooting of owls and howling of wolves; in summer, swarming with myriads of

black flies and mosquitoes, more formidable than wolves
to the white man. Such is the home of the moose, the
bear, the caribou, the wolf, the beaver, and the Indian.
Who shall describe the inexpressible tenderness and immortal life of the grim forest, where Nature, though it be
mid-winter, is ever in her spring, where the moss-grown
and decaying trees are not old, but seem to enjoy a perpetual youth; and blissful, innocent Nature, like a serene
infant, is too happy to make a noise, except by a few
tinkling, lisping birds and trickling rills?

What a place to live, what a place to die and be buried
in! There certainly men would live forever, and laugh at
death and the grave. There they could have no such
thoughts as are associated with the village graveyard,—
that make a grave out of one of those moist evergreen
hummocks!

> Die and be buried who will,
> I mean to live here still;
> My nature grows ever more young
> The primitive pines among.

I am reminded by my journey how exceedingly new
this country still is. You have only to travel for a few days
into the interior and back parts even of many of the old
states, to come to that very America which the North-
men, and Cabot, and Gosnold, and Smith and Raleigh
visited. If Columbus was the first to discover the islands,
Americus Vespucius, and Cabot, and the Puritans, and
we their descendants, have discovered only the shores of
America. While the republic has already acquired a history world-wide, America is still unsettled and unexplored. Like the English in New Holland, we live only on
the shores of a continent even yet, and hardly know
where the rivers come from which float our navy. The
very timber and boards, and shingles, of which our
houses are made, grew but yesterday in a wilderness
where the Indian still hunts and the moose runs wild.
New-York has her wilderness within her own borders;
and though the sailors of Europe are familiar with the
soundings of her Hudson, and Fulton long since invented
the steamboat on its waters, an Indian is still necessary to

guide her scientific men to its head-waters in the Adirondac country.

Have we even so much as discovered and settled the shores? Let a man travel on foot along the coast, from the Passamaquoddy to the Sabine, or to the Rio Bravo, or to wherever the end is now, if he is swift enough to overtake it, faithfully following the windings of every inlet and of every cape, and stepping to the music of the surf—with a desolate fishing-town once a week, and a city's port once a month to cheer him, and putting up at the light-houses, when there are any, and tell me if it looks like a discovered and settled country, and not rather, for the most part, like a desolate island, and No-man's Land.

We have advanced by leaps to the Pacific, and left many a lesser Oregon and California unexplored behind us. Though the railroad and the telegraph have been established on the shores of Maine, the Indian still looks out from her interior mountains over all these to the sea. There stands the city of Bangor, fifty miles up the Penobscot, at the head of navigation for vessels of the largest class, the principal lumber depot on this continent, with a population of twelve thousand, like a star on the edge of night, still hewing at the forests of which it is built, already overflowing with the luxuries and refinement of Europe, and sending its vessels to Spain, to England, and to the West Indies for its groceries,—and yet only a few axe-men have gone "up river" into the howling wilderness which feeds it. The bear and deer are still found within its limits; and the moose, as he swims the Penobscot, is entangled amid its shipping and taken by foreign sailors in its harbor. Twelve miles in the rear, twelve miles of railroad, are Orono and the Indian Island, the home of the Penobscot tribe, and then commence the batteau and the canoe, and the military road; and, sixty miles above, the country is virtually unmapped and unexplored, and there still waves the virgin forest of the New World.

LETTERS TO H. G. O. BLAKE

The remarkable series of letters written by Thoreau to Harrison Gray Otis Blake of Worcester has been generally ignored by critics and readers of Thoreau. Numbering twenty-seven in all, and spanning most of Thoreau's productive lifetime, from March 1848 to November 1860, the letters reveal Thoreau's Weltanschauung *in its successive stages with unusual clarity. Blake's honest inquisitiveness about matters of importance to both men elicited from Thoreau responses that were candid, direct, and unselfconscious. The selection made here is of the most philosophical, least anecdotal of the series. The texts are from* The Familiar Letters of Thoreau *(Boston and New York, 1894) edited by F. B. Sanborn, and are the best presently available. "You will perceive," Thoreau wrote to Blake, "that I am as often talking to myself, perhaps, as speaking to you."*

Concord, March 27, 1848.

I AM GLAD TO HEAR that any words of mine, though spoken so long ago that I can hardly claim identity with their author, have reached you. It gives me pleasure, because I have therefore reason to suppose that I have uttered what concerns men, and that it is not in vain that

man speaks to man. This is the value of literature. Yet
those days are so distant, in every sense, that I have had
to look at that page again, to learn what was the tenor of
my thoughts then. I should value that article, however, if
only because it was the occasion of your letter.

I do believe that the outward and the inward life correspond; that if any should succeed to live a higher life,
others would not know of it; that difference and distance
are one. To set about living a true life is to go a journey
to a distant country, gradually to find ourselves surrounded by new scenes and men; and as long as the old are
around me, I know that I am not in any true sense living
a new or a better life. The outward is only the outside of
that which is within. Men are not concealed under habits,
but are revealed by them; they are their true clothes. I
care not how curious a reason they may give for their
abiding by them. Circumstances are not rigid and un-
yielding, but our habits are rigid. We are apt to speak
vaguely sometimes, as if a divine life were to be grafted
on to or built over this present as a suitable foundation.
This might do if we could so build over our old life as to
exclude from it all the warmth of our affection, and ad-
dle it, as the thrush builds over the cuckoo's egg, and lays
her own atop, and hatches that only; but the fact is, we—
so thin is the partition—hatch them both, and the cuckoo's always by a day first, and that young bird crowds the
young thrushes out of the nest. No. Destroy the cuckoo's
egg, or build a new nest.

Change is change. No new life occupies the old bodies;—they decay. *It* is born, and grows, and flourishes.
Men very pathetically inform the old, accept and wear it.
Why put up with the almshouse when you may go to
heaven? It is embalming,—no more. Let alone your oint-
ments and your linen swathes, and go into an infant's
body. You see in the catacombs of Egypt the result of
that experiment,—that is the end of it.

I do believe in simplicity. It is astonishing as well as
sad, how many trivial affairs even the wisest man thinks
he must attend to in a day; how singular an affair he
thinks he must omit. When the mathematician would

solve a difficult problem, he first frees the equation of all incumbrances, and reduces it to its simplest terms. So simplify the problem of life, distinguish the necessary and the real. Probe the earth to see where your main roots run. I would stand upon facts. Why not see,—use our eyes? Do men know nothing? I know many men who, in common things, are not to be deceived; who trust no moonshine; who count their money correctly, and know how to invest it; who are said to be prudent and knowing, who yet will stand at a desk the greater part of their lives, as cashiers in banks, and glimmer and rust and finally go out there. If they *know* anything, what under the sun do they do that for? Do they know what *bread* is? or what it is for? Do they know what life is? If they *knew* something, the places which know them now would know them no more forever.

This, our respectable daily life, on which the man of common sense, the Englishman of the world, stands so squarely, and on which our institutions are founded, is in fact the veriest illusion, and will vanish like the baseless fabric of a vision; but that faint glimmer of reality which sometimes illuminates the darkness of daylight for all men, reveals something more solid and enduring than adamant, which is in fact the corner-stone of the world.

Men cannot conceive of a state of things so fair that it cannot be realized. Can any man honestly consult his experience and say that it is so? Have we any facts to appeal to when we say that our dreams are premature? Did you ever hear of a man who had striven all his life faithfully and singly toward an object and in no measure obtained it? If a man constantly aspires, is he not elevated? Did ever a man try heroism, magnanimity, truth, sincerity, and find that there was no advantage in them? that it was a vain endeavor? Of course we do not expect that our paradise will be a garden. We know not what we ask. To look at literature;—how many fine thoughts has every man had! how few fine thoughts are expressed! Yet we never have a fantasy so subtle and ethereal, but that *talent merely*, with more resolution and faithful persistency, after a thousand failures, might fix and engrave it in distinct and enduring words, and we should see that our dreams are the solidest facts that we know. But I speak not of dreams.

What can be expressed in words can be expressed in life.

My actual life is a fact, in view of which I have no occasion to congratulate myself; but for my faith and aspiration I have respect. It is from these that I speak. Every man's position is in fact too simple to be described. I have sworn no oath. I have no designs on society, or nature, or God. I am simply what I am, or I begin to be that. I *live* in the *present*. I only remember the past, and anticipate the future. I love to live. I love reform better than its modes. There is no history of how bad became better. I believe something, and there is nothing else but that. I know that I am. I know that another is who knows more than I, who takes interest in me, whose creature, and yet whose kindred, in one sense, am I. I know that the enterprise is worthy. I know that things work well. I have heard no bad news.

As for positions, combinations, and details,—what are they? In clear weather, when we look into the heavens, what do we see but the sky and the sun?

If you would convince a man that he does wrong, do right. But do not care to convince him. Men will believe what they see. Let them see.

Pursue, keep up with, circle round and round your life, as a dog does his master's chaise. Do what you love. Know your own bone; gnaw at it, bury it, unearth it, and gnaw it still. Do not be too moral. You may cheat yourself out of much life so. Aim above morality. Be not simply good; be good for something. All fables, indeed, have their morals; but the innocent enjoy the story. Let nothing come between you and the light. Respect men and brothers only. When you travel to the Celestial City, carry no letter of introduction. When you knock, ask to see God,—none of the servants. In what concerns you much, do not think that you have companions: know that you are alone in the world.

Thus I write at random. I need to see you, and I trust I

shall, to correct my mistakes. Perhaps you have some oracles for me.

HENRY THOREAU.

Concord, May 2, 1848.

"WE MUST HAVE our bread." But what is our bread? Is it baker's bread? Methinks it should be very *home-made* bread. What is our meat? Is it butcher's meat? What is that which we *must* have? Is that bread which we are now earning sweet? Is it not bread which has been suffered to sour, and then been sweetened with an alkali, which has undergone the vinous, the acetous, and sometimes the putrid fermentation, and then been whitened with vitriol? Is this the bread which we must have? Man must earn his bread by the sweat of his brow, truly, but also by the sweat of his brain within his brow. The body can feel the body only. I have tasted but little bread in my life. It has been mere grub and provender for the most part. Of bread that nourished the brain and the heart, scarcely any. There is absolutely none even on the table of the rich.

There is not one kind of food for all men. You must and you will feed those faculties which you exercise. The laborer whose body is weary does not require the same food with the scholar whose brain is weary. Men should not labor foolishly like brutes, but the brain and the body should always, or as much as possible, work and rest together, and then the work will be of such a kind that when the body is hungry the brain will be hungry also, and the same food will suffice for both; otherwise the food which repairs the waste energy of the over-wrought body will oppress the sedentary brain, and the degenerate scholar will come to esteem all food vulgar, and all getting a living drudgery.

How shall we earn our bread is a grave question; yet it is a sweet and inviting question. Let us not shirk it, as is usually done. It is the most important and practical question which is put to man. Let us not answer it hastily. Let us not be content to get our bread in some gross, careless, and hasty manner. Some men go a-hunting, some a-fishing, some a-gaming, some to war; but none have so pleasant a time as they who in earnest seek to earn their bread. It is true actually as it is true really; it is true materially as it is true spiritually, that they who seek honestly and sincerely, with all their hearts and lives and strength, to earn their bread, do earn it, and it is sure to be very sweet to them. A very little bread,—a very few crumbs are enough, if it be of the right quality, for it is infinitely nutritious. Let each man, then, earn at least a crumb of bread for his body before he dies, and know the taste of it,—that it is identical with the bread of life, and that they both go down at one swallow.

Our bread need not ever be sour or hard to digest. What Nature is to the mind she is also to the body. As she feeds my imagination, she will feed my body; for what she says she means, and is ready to do. She is not simply beautiful to the poet's eye. Not only the rainbow and sunset are beautiful, but to be fed and clothed, sheltered and warmed aright, are equally beautiful and inspiring. There is not necessarily any gross and ugly fact which may not be eradicated from the life of man. We should endeavor practically in our lives to correct all the defects which our imagination detects. The heavens are as deep as our aspirations are high. So high as a tree aspires to grow, so high it will find an atmosphere suited to it. Every man should stand for a force which is perfectly irresistible. How can any man be weak who dares *to be* at all? Even the tenderest plants force their way up through the hardest earth, and the crevices of rocks; but a man no material power can resist. What a wedge, what a beetle, what a catapult, is an *earnest* man! What can resist him?

It is a momentous fact that a man may be *good,* or he may be *bad;* his life may be *true,* or it may be *false;* it may be either a shame or a glory to him. The good man builds himself up; the bad man destroys himself.

But whatever we do we must do confidently (if we are timid, let us, then, act timidly), not expecting more light, but having light enough. If we confidently expect more, then let us wait for it. But what is this which we have? Have we not already waited? Is this the beginning of time? Is there a man who does not see clearly beyond, though only a hair's breadth beyond where he at any time stands?

If one hesitates in his path, let him not proceed. Let him respect his doubts, for doubts, too, may have some divinity in them. That we have but little faith is not sad, but that we have but little faithfulness. By faithfulness faith is earned. When, in the progress of a life, a man swerves, though only by an angle infinitely small, from his proper and allotted path (and this is never done quite unconsciously even at first; in fact, that was his broad and scarlet sin,—ah, he knew of it more than he can tell), then the drama of his life turns to tragedy, and makes haste to its fifth act. When once we thus fall behind ourselves, there is no accounting for the obstacles which rise up in our path, and no one is so wise as to advise, and no one so powerful as to aid us while we abide on that ground. Such are cursed with *duties*, and the *neglect of their duties*. For such the decalogue was made, and other far more voluminous and terrible codes.

These departures,—who have not made them?—for they are as faint as the parallax of a fixed star, and at the commencement we say they are nothing,—that is, they originate in a kind of sleep and forgetfulness of the soul when it is taught. A man cannot be too circumspect in order to keep in the straight road, and be sure that he sees all that he may at any time see, that so he may distinguish his true path.

You ask if there is no doctrine of sorrow in my philosophy. Of acute sorrow I suppose that I know comparatively little. My saddest and most genuine sorrows are apt to be but transient regrets. The place of sorrow is supplied, perchance, by a certain hard and proportionably barren indifference. I am of kin to the sod, and partake largely of its dull patience,—in winter expecting the sun of spring. In my cheapest moments I am apt to think that it is not my business to be "seeking the spirit," but as much its business to be seeking me. I know very well what Goethe meant when he said that he never had a chagrin but he made a poem out of it. I have altogether too much patience of this kind. I am too easily contented with a

slight and almost animal happiness. My happiness is a
good deal like that of the woodchucks.

Methinks I am never quite committed, never wholly
the creature of my moods, but always to some extent
their critic. My only integral experience is in my vision. I
see, perchance, with more integrity than I feel.

But I need not tell you what manner of man I am,—
my virtues or my vices. You can guess if it is worth the
while; and I do not discriminate them well.

I do not write this at my hut in the woods. I am at
present living with Mrs. Emerson, whose house is an old
home of mine, for company during Mr. Emerson's absence.

You will perceive that I am as often talking to myself,
perhaps, as speaking to you.

Concord, August 10, 1849.

MR. BLAKE,—I write now chiefly to say, before it is too
late, that I shall be glad to see you in Concord, and will
give you a chamber, etc., in my father's house, and as
much of my poor company as you can bear.

I am in too great haste this time to speak to your, or
out of my, condition. I might say,—you might say,—
comparatively speaking, be not anxious to avoid poverty.
In this way the wealth of the universe may be securely
invested. What a pity if we do not live this short time
according to the laws of the long time,—the eternal laws!
Let us see that we stand erect here, and do not lie along
by our *whole length* in the dirt. Let our meanness be our
footstool, not our cushion. In the midst of this labyrinth
let us live a *thread* of life. We must act with so rapid and
resistless a purpose in *one* direction, that our vices will
necessarily trail behind. The nucleus of a comet is almost
a star. Was there ever a genuine dilemma? The laws of
earth are for the feet, or inferior man; the laws of heaven
are for the head, or superior man; the latter are the former sublimed and expanded, even as radii from the
earth's centre go on diverging into space. Happy the man
who observes the heavenly and the terrestrial law in just
proportion; whose every faculty, from the soles of his feet

to the crown of his head, obeys the law of its level; who neither stoops nor goes on tiptoe, but lives a balanced life, acceptable to nature and to God.

These things I say; other things I do.

I am sorry to hear that you did not receive my book earlier. I directed it and left it in Munroe's shop to be sent to you immediately, on the twenty-sixth of May, before a copy had been sold.

Will you remember me to Mr. Brown, when you see him next: he is well remembered by

HENRY THOREAU.

I still owe you a worthy answer.

Concord, November 20, 1849.

MR. BLAKE,—I have not forgotten that I am your debtor. When I read over your letters, as I have just done, I feel that I am unworthy to have received or to answer them, though they are addressed, as I would have them, to the ideal of me. It behoves me, if I would reply, to speak out of the rarest part of myself.

At present I am subsisting on certain wild flavors which nature wafts to me, which unaccountably sustain me, and make my apparently poor life rich. Within a year my walks have extended themselves, and almost every afternoon (I read, or write, or make pencils in the forenoon, and by the last means get a living for my body) I visit some new hill, or pond, or wood, many miles distant. I am astonished at the wonderful retirement through which I move, rarely meeting a man in these excursions, never seeing one similarly engaged, unless it be my companion, when I have one. I cannot help feeling that of all the human inhabitants of nature hereabouts, only we two have leisure to admire and enjoy our inheritance.

"Free in this world as the birds in the air, disengaged from every kind of chains, those who have practiced the *yoga* gather in Brahma the certain fruit of their works."

Depend upon it, that, rude and careless as I am, I would fain practice the *yoga* faithfully.

"The yogi, absorbed in contemplation, contributes in his degree to creation: he breathes a divine perfume, he hears wonderful things. Divine forms traverse him without tearing him, and, united to the nature which is proper to him, he goes, he acts as animating original matter."

To some extent, and at rare intervals, even I am a yogi.

I know little about the affairs of Turkey, but I am sure that I know something about barberries and chestnuts, of which I have collected a store this fall. When I go to see my neighbor, he will formally communicate to me the latest news from Turkey, which he read in yesterday's mail,—"Now Turkey by this time looks determined, and Lord Palmerston"—Why, I would rather talk of the bran, which, unfortunately, was sifted out of my bread this morning, and thrown away. It is a fact which lies nearer to me. The newspaper gossip with which our hosts abuse our ears is as far from a true hospitality as the viands which they set before us. We did not need them to feed our bodies, and the news can be bought for a penny. We want the inevitable news, be it sad or cheering, wherefore and by what means they are extant this *new* day. If they are well, let them whistle and dance; if they are dyspeptic, it is their duty to complain, that so they may in any case be *entertaining*. If words were invented to conceal thought, I think that newspapers are a great improvement on a bad invention. Do not suffer your life to be taken by newspapers.

I thank you for your hearty appreciation of my book. I am glad to have had such a long talk with you, and that you had patience to listen to me to the end. I think that I had the advantage of you, for I chose my own mood, and in one sense your mood too,—that is, a quiet and attentive reading mood. Such advantage has the writer over the talker. I am sorry that you did not come to Concord in your vacation. Is it not time for another vacation? I am here yet, and Concord is here.

You will have found out by this time who it is that writes this, and will be glad to have you write to him, without his subscribing himself

HENRY D. THOREAU.

P.S.—It is so long since I have seen you, that, as you will perceive, I have to speak, as it were, *in vacuo,* as if I were sounding hollowly for an echo, and it did not make much odds what kind of a sound I made. But the gods do not hear any rude or discordant sound, as we learn from the echo; and I know that the nature toward which I launch these sounds is so rich that it will modulate anew and wonderfully improve my rudest strain.

Concord, April 3, 1850.

MR. BLAKE,—I thank you for your letter, and I will endeavor to record some of the thoughts which it suggests, whether pertinent or not. You speak of poverty and dependence. Who are poor and dependent? Who are rich and independent? When was it that men agreed to respect the appearance and not the reality? Why should the appearance *appear?* Are we well acquainted, then, with the reality? There is none who does not lie hourly in the respect he pays to false appearance. How sweet it would be to treat men and things, for an hour, for just what they are! We wonder that the sinner does not confess his sin. When we are weary with travel, we lay down our load and rest by the wayside. So, when we are weary with the burden of life, why do we not lay down this load of falsehoods which we have volunteered to sustain, and be refreshed as never mortal was? Let the beautiful laws prevail. Let us not weary ourselves by resisting them. When we would rest our bodies we cease to support them; we recline on the lap of earth. So, when we would rest our spirits, we must recline on the Great Spirit. Let things alone; let them weigh what they will; let them soar or fall. To succeed in letting only one thing alone in a winter morning, if it be only one poor frozen-thawed apple that hangs on a tree, what a glorious achievement! Methinks it lightens through the dusky universe. What an infinite wealth we have discovered! God reigns, *i.e.,* when we take a liberal view,—when a liberal view is presented us.

Let God alone if need be. Methinks, if I loved him more, I should keep him,—I should keep myself rather,—at a more respectful distance. It is not when I am going to meet him, but when I am just turning away and leaving him alone, that I discover that God is. I say, God. I am not sure that that is the name. You will know whom I mean.

If for a moment we make way with our petty selves, wish no ill to anything, apprehend no ill, cease to be but as the crystal which reflects a ray,—what shall we not reflect! What a universe will appear crystallized and radiant around us!

I should say, let the Muse lead the Muse,—let the understanding lead the understanding, though in any case it is the farthest forward which leads them both. If the muse accompany, she is no muse, but an amusement. The Muse should lead like a star which is very far off; but that does not imply that we are to follow foolishly, falling into sloughs and over precipices, for it is not foolishness, but understanding, which is to follow, which the Muse is appointed to lead, as a fit guide of a fit follower.

Will you live? or will you be embalmed? Will you live, though it be astride of a sunbeam; or will you repose safely in the catacombs for a thousand years? In the former case, the worst accident that can happen is that you may break your neck. Will you break your heart, your soul, to save your neck? Necks and pipe-stems are fated to be broken. Men make a great ado about the folly of demanding too much of life (or of eternity?), and of endeavoring to live according to that demand. It is much ado about nothing. No harm ever came from that quarter. I am not afraid that I shall exaggerate the value and significance of life, but that I shall not be up to the occasion which it is. I shall be sorry to remember that I was there, but noticed nothing remarkable,—not so much as a prince in disguise; lived in the golden age a hired man; visited Olympus even, but fell asleep after dinner, and did not hear the conversation of the gods. I lived in Judæa eighteen hundred years ago, but I never knew that there was such a one as Christ among my contemporaries! If there is anything more glorious than a congress of men a-framing or amending of a constitution going on, which I suspect there is, I desire to see the morning papers. I am greedy of the faintest rumor, though it were got by listening at the key-hole. I will dissipate myself in that direction.

I am glad to know that you find what I have said on Friendship worthy of attention. I wish I could have the benefit of your criticism; it would be a rare help to me. Will you not communicate it?

Concord, May 28, 1850.

Mr. Blake,—"I never found any contentment in the life which the newspapers record,"—anything of more value than the cent which they cost. Contentment in being covered with dust an inch deep! We who walk the streets, and hold time together, are but the refuse of ourselves, and that life is for the shells of us,—of our body and our mind,—for our scurf,—a thoroughly *scurvy* life. It is coffee made of coffee-grounds the twentieth time, which was only coffee the first time,—while the living water leaps and sparkles by our doors. I know some who, in their charity, give their coffee-grounds to the poor! We, demanding news, and putting up with *such* news! Is it a new convenience, or a new accident, or, rather, a new perception of the truth that we want!

You say that "the serene hours in which friendship, books, nature, thought, seem alone primary considerations, visit you but faintly." Is not the attitude of expectation somewhat divine?—a sort of home-made divineness? Does it not compel a kind of sphere-music to attend on it? And do not its satisfactions merge at length, by insensible degrees, in the enjoyment of the thing expected?

What if I should forget to write about my not writing? It is not worth the while to make that a theme. It is as if I had written every day. It is as if I had never written before. I wonder that you think so much about it, for not writing is the most like writing, in my case, of anything I know.

Why will you not relate to me your dream? That would be to realize it somewhat. You tell me that you dream, but not what you dream. I can *guess* what comes to pass. So do the frogs dream. Would that I knew what. I have never found out whether they are awake or asleep,—whether it is day or night with them.

I am preaching, mind you, to bare walls, that is to myself; and if you have chanced to come in and occupy a pew, do not think that my remarks are directed at you particularly, and so slam the seat in disgust. This discourse was written long before these exciting times.

Some absorbing employment on your higher ground,— your upland farm,—whither no cart-path leads, but where the life everlasting grows; there you raise a crop which needs not to be brought down into the valley to a market; which you barter for heavenly products.

Do you separate distinctly enough the support of your body, from that of your essence? By how distinct a course commonly are these two ends attained! Not that they should not be attained by one and the same means,— that, indeed, is the rarest success,—but there is no half and half about it.

I shall be glad to read my lecture to a small audience in Worcester such as you describe, and will only require that my expenses be paid. If only the parlor be large enough for an echo, and the audience will embarrass themselves with hearing as much as the lecturer would otherwise embarrass himself with reading. But I warn you that this is no better calculated for a promiscuous audience than the last two which I read to you. It requires, in every sense, a concordant audience.

I will come on next Saturday and spend Sunday with you if you wish it. Say so if you do.

"Drink deep, or taste not the Pierian spring."

Be not deterred by melancholy on the path which leads to immortal health and joy. When they tasted of the water of the river over which they were to go, they thought it tasted a little bitterish to the palate, but it proved sweeter when it was down.

H.D.T.

Concord, August 9, 1850.

MR. BLAKE,—I received your letter just as I was rushing to Fire Island beach to recover what remained of Margaret Fuller, and read it on the way. That event and its train, as much as anything, have prevented my answering it before. It is wisest to speak when you are spoken to. I will now endeavor to reply, at the risk of having nothing to say.

I find that actual events, notwithstanding the singular prominence which we all allow them, are far less real than the creations of my imagination. They are truly visionary and insignificant,—all that we commonly call life and death,—and affect me less than my dreams. This petty stream which from time to time swells and carries away the mills and bridges of our habitual life, and that mightier stream or ocean on which we securely float,— what makes the difference between them? I have in my pocket a button which I ripped off the coat of the Marquis of Ossoli, on the seashore, the other day. Held up, it intercepts the light,—an actual button,—and yet all the life it is connected with is less substantial to me, and interests me less, than my faintest dream. Our thoughts are the epochs in our lives: all else is but as a journal of the winds that blew while we were here.

I say to myself, Do a little more of that work which you have confessed to be good. You are neither satisfied nor dissatisfied with yourself, without reason. Have you not a thinking faculty of inestimable value? If there is an experiment which you would like to try, try it. Do not entertain doubts if they are not agreeable to you. Remember that you need not eat unless you are hungry. Do not read the newspapers. Improve every opportunity to be melancholy. As for health, consider yourself well. Do not engage to find things as you think they are. Do what nobody else can do for you. Omit to do anything else. It is not easy to make our lives respectable by any course of activity. We must repeatedly withdraw into our shells of thought, like the tortoise, somewhat helplessly; yet there is more than philosophy in that.

Do not waste any reverence on my attitude. I merely manage to sit up where I have dropped. I am sure that my acquaintances mistake me. They ask my advice on high matters, but they do not know even how poorly on't I am for hats and shoes. I have hardly a shift. Just as shabby as I am in my outward apparel, ay, and more lamentably shabby, am I in my inward substance. If I should turn myself inside out, my rags and meanness would indeed appear. I am something to him that made me, undoubtedly, but not much to any other that he has made.

Would it not be worth while to discover nature in Milton? be native to the universe? I, too, love Concord best, but I am glad when I discover, in oceans and wildernesses far away, the material of a million Concords: indeed, I am lost, unless I discover them. I see less difference between a city and a swamp than formerly. It is a swamp, however, too dismal and dreary even for me, and I should be glad if there were fewer owls, and frogs, and mosquitoes in it. I prefer ever a more cultivated place, free from miasma and crocodiles. I am so sophisticated, and I will take my choice.

As for missing friends,—what if we do miss one another? Have we not agreed on a rendezvous? While each wanders his own way through the wood, without anxiety, ay, with serene joy, though it be on his hands and knees, over rocks and fallen trees, he cannot but be in the right way. There is no wrong way to him. How can he be said to miss his friend, whom the fruits still nourish and the elements sustain? A man who missed his friend at a turn, went on buoyantly, dividing the friendly air, and humming a tune to himself, ever and anon kneeling with delight to study each little lichen in his path, and scarcely made three miles a day for friendship. As for conforming outwardly, and living your own life inwardly, I do not think much of that. Let not your right hand know what your left hand does in that line of business. It will prove a failure. Just as successfully can you walk against a sharp steel edge which divides you cleanly right and left. Do you wish to try your ability to resist distension? It is a greater strain than any soul can long endure. When you get God to pulling one way, and the devil the other, each having his feet well braced,—to say nothing of the conscience sawing transversely,—almost any timber will give away.

I do not dare invite you earnestly to come to Concord, because I know too well that the berries are not thick in my fields, and we should have to take it out in viewing the landscape. But come, on every account, and we will see—one another.

Concord, July 21, 1852.

MR. BLAKE,—I am too stupidly well these days to write to you. My life is almost altogether outward,—all shell and no tender kernel; so that I fear the report of it would be only a nut for you to crack, with no meat in it for you to eat. Moreover, you have not cornered me up, and I enjoy such large liberty in writing to you, that I feel as vague as the air. However, I rejoice to hear that you have attended so patiently to anything which I have said heretofore, and have detected any truth in it. It encourages me to say more,—not in this letter, I fear, but in some book which I may write one day. I am glad to know that I am as much to any mortal as a persistent and consistent scarecrow is to a farmer,—such a bundle of straw in a man's clothing as I am, with a few bits of tin to sparkle in the sun dangling about me, as if I were hard at work there in the field. However, if this kind of life saves any man's corn,—why, he is the gainer. I am not afraid that you will flatter me as long as you know what I am, as well as what I think, or aim to be, and distinguish between these two, for then it will commonly happen that if you praise the last you will condemn the first.

I remember that walk to Asnebumskit very well,—a fit place to go to on a Sunday; one of the true temples of the earth. A temple, you know, was anciently "an open place without a roof," whose walls served merely to shut out the world and direct the mind toward heaven; but a modern *meeting-house* shuts out the heavens, while it crowds the world into still closer quarters. Best of all is it when, as on a mountaintop, you have for all walls your own elevation and deeps of surrounding ether. The partridge-berries, watered with mountain dews which are

gathered there, are more memorable to me than the
words which I last heard from the pulpit at least; and for
my part, I would rather look toward Rutland than Jerusa-
lem. Rutland,—modern town,—land of ruts,—trivial and
worn,—not too sacred,—with no holy sepulchre, but profane green fields and dusty roads, and opportunity to live
as holy a life as you can,—where the sacredness, if there
is any, is all in yourself and not in the place.

I fear that your Worcester people do not often enough
go to the hilltops, though, as I am told, the springs lie
nearer to the surface on your hills than in your valleys.
They have the reputation of being Free-Soilers. Do they
insist on a free atmosphere, too, that is, on freedom for
the head or brain as well as the feet? If I were consciously
to join any party, it would be that which is the most free
to entertain thought.

All the world complain nowadays of a press of trivial
duties and engagements, which prevents their employing
themselves on some higher ground they know of; but, undoubtedly, if they were made of the right stuff to work
on that higher ground, provided they were released from
all those engagements, they would now at once fulfill the
superior engagement, and neglect all the rest, as naturally
as they breathe. They would never be caught saying that
they had no time for this, when the dullest man knows
that this is all that he has time for. No man who acts from
a sense of duty ever puts the lesser duty above the greater. No man has the desire and the ability to work on high
things, but he has also the ability to build himself a high
staging.

As for passing *through* any great and glorious experience, and rising *above* it, as an eagle might fly athwart
the evening sky to rise into still brighter and fairer regions of the heavens, I cannot say that I ever sailed so
creditably; but my bark ever seemed thwarted by some
side wind, and went off over the edge, and now only
occasionally tacks back toward the centre of that sea
again. I have outgrown nothing good, but, I do not fear to
say, fallen behind by whole continents of virtue, which
should have been passed as islands in my course; but I
trust—what else can I trust? that, with a stiff wind, some

Friday, when I have thrown some of my cargo over-board, I may make up for all that distance lost.

Perchance the time will come when we shall not be content to go back and forth upon a raft to some huge Homeric or Shakespearean Indiaman that lies upon the reef, but build a bark out of that wreck and others that are buried in the sands of this desolate island, and such new timber as may be required, in which to sail away to whole new worlds of light and life, where our friends are.

Write again. There is one respect in which you did not finish your letter: you did not write it with ink, and it is not so good, therefore, against or for you in the eye of the law, nor in the eye of

H.D.T.

September, 1852.

MR. BLAKE,—Here come the sentences which I prom-ised you. You may keep them, if you will regard and use them as the disconnected fragments of what I may find to be a completer essay, on looking over my journal, at last, and may claim again.

I send you the thoughts on Chastity and Sensuality with diffidence and shame, not knowing how far I speak to the condition of men generally, or how far I betray my peculiar defects. Pray enlighten me on this point if you can.

Love.

What the essential difference between man and wom-an is, that they should be thus attracted to one another, no one has satisfactorily answered. Perhaps we must ac-knowledge the justness of the distinction which assigns to man the sphere of wisdom, and to woman that of love, though neither belongs exclusively to either. Man is con-tinually saying to woman, Why will you not be more wise? Woman is continually saying to man, Why will you not be more loving? It is not in their wills to be wise or to be loving; but, unless each is both wise and loving, there can be neither wisdom nor love.

All transcendent goodness is one, though appreciated in
different ways, or by different senses. In beauty we see it,
in music we hear it, in fragrance we scent it, in the palat-
able the pure palate tastes it, and in rare health the whole
body feels it. The variety is in the surface or manifesta-
tion; but the radical identity we fail to express. The lover
sees in the glance of his beloved the same beauty that in
the sunset paints the western skies. It is the same daimon,
here lurking under a human eyelid, and there under the
closing eyelids of the day. Here, in small compass, is the
ancient and natural beauty of evening and morning.
What loving astronomer has ever fathomed the ethereal
depths of the eye?

The maiden conceals a fairer flower and sweeter fruit
than any calyx in the field; and, if she goes with averted
face, confiding in her purity and high resolves, she will
make the heavens retrospective, and all nature humbly
confess its queen.

Under the influence of this sentiment, man is a string
of an Æolian harp, which vibrates with the zephyrs of
the eternal morning.

There is at first thought something trivial in the com-
monness of love. So many Indian youths and maidens
along these banks have in ages past yielded to the influence of this great civilizer. Nevertheless, this generation is
not disgusted nor discouraged, for love is no individual's
experience; and though we are imperfect mediums, it
does not partake of our imperfection; though we are finite, it is infinite and eternal; and the same divine influence broods over these banks, whatever race may inhabit
them, and perchance still would, even if the human race
did not dwell here.

Perhaps an instinct survives through the intensest actual love, which prevents entire abandonment and devotion, and makes the most ardent lover a little reserved. It
is the anticipation of change. For the most ardent lover is
not the less practically wise and seeks a love which will
last forever.

Considering how few poetical friendships there are, it
is remarkable that so many are married. It would seem as
if men yielded too easy an obedience to nature without

consulting their genius. One may be drunk with love without being any nearer to finding his mate. There is more of good nature than of good sense at the bottom of most marriages. But the good nature must have the counsel of the good spirit or Intelligence. If common sense had been consulted, how many marriages would never have taken place; if uncommon or divine sense, how few marriages such as we witness would ever have taken place!

Our love may be ascending or descending. What is its character, if it may be said of it—

> "We must *respect* the souls above
> But only *those below* we *love*."

Love is a severe critic. Hate can pardon more than love. They who aspire to love worthily, subject themselves to an ordeal more rigid than any other.

Is your friend such a one that an increase of worth on your part will surely make her more your friend? Is she retained—is she attracted by more nobleness in you,—by more of that virtue which is peculiarly yours; or is she indifferent and blind to that? Is she to be flattered and won by your meeting her on any other than the ascending path? Then duty requires that you separate from her.

Love must be as much a light as a flame.

Where there is not discernment, the behavior even of the purest soul may in effect amount to coarseness.

A man of fine perceptions is more truly feminine than a merely sentimental woman. The heart is blind; but love is not blind. None of the gods is so discriminating.

In love and friendship the imagination is as much exercised as the heart; and if either is outraged the other will be estranged. It is commonly the imagination which is wounded first, rather than the heart,—it is so much the more sensitive.

Comparatively, we can excuse any offense against the heart, but not against the imagination. The imagination knows—nothing escapes its glance from out its eyry—and it controls the breast. My heart may still yearn toward the valley, but my imagination will not permit me to jump off the precipice that debars me from it, for it is wounded, its wings are clipt, and it cannot fly, even descendingly. Our "blundering hearts!" some poet says. The imagination never forgets; it is a re-membering. It is not foundationless, but most reasonable, and it alone uses all the knowledge of the intellect.

Love is the profoundest of secrets. Divulged, even to the beloved, it is no longer Love. As if it were merely I that loved you. When love ceases, then it is divulged.

In our intercourse with one we love, we wish to have answered those questions at the end of which we do not raise our voice; against which we put no interrogation-mark,—answered with the same unfailing, universal aim toward every point of the compass.

I require that thou knowest everything without being told anything. I parted from my beloved because there was one thing which I had to tell her. She *questioned* me. She should have known all by sympathy. That I had to tell it her was the difference between us,—the misunderstanding.

A lover never hears anything that he is *told*, for that is commonly either false or stale; but he hears things taking place, as the sentinels heard Trenck mining in the ground, and thought it was moles.

The relation may be profaned in many ways. The parties may not regard it with equal sacredness. What if the lover should learn that his beloved dealt in incantations and philters! What if he should hear that she consulted a clairvoyant! The spell would be instantly broken.

If to chaffer and higgle are bad in trade, they are much worse in Love. It demands directness as of an arrow.

There is danger that we lose sight of what our friend is absolutely, while considering what she is to us alone.

The lover wants no partiality. He says, Be so kind as to be just.

> Canst thou love with thy mind,
>   And reason with thy heart?
> Canst thou be kind,
>   And from thy darling part?
>
> Canst thou range earth, sea, and air,
> And so meet me everywhere?
> Through all events I will pursue thee,
> Through all persons I will woo thee.

I need thy hate as much as thy love. Thou wilt not repel me entirely when thou repellest what is evil in me.

> Indeed, indeed, I cannot tell,
> Though I ponder on it well,
> Which were easier to state,
> All my love or all my hate.
> Surely, surely, thou wilt trust me
> When I say thou doth disgust me.
> O, I hate thee with a hate
> That would fain annihilate;
> Yet, sometimes, against my will,
> My dear Friend, I love thee still.
> It were treason to our love,
> And a sin to God above,
> One iota to abate
> Of a pure, impartial hate.

It is not enough that we are truthful; we must cherish and carry out high purposes to be truthful about.

It must be rare, indeed, that we meet with one to whom we are prepared to be quite ideally related, as she to us. We should have no reserve; we should give the whole of ourselves to that society; we should have no duty aside from that. One who could bear to be so wonderfully and beautifully exaggerated every day. I would take my friend out of her low self and set her higher, infinitely higher, and *there* know her. But, commonly, men are as much afraid of love as of hate. They have lower engagements. They have near ends to serve. They have not imagination enough to be thus employed about a human being, but must be coopering a barrel, forsooth.

What a difference, whether, in all your walks, you meet only strangers, or in one house is one who knows you, and whom you know. To have a brother or a sister! To have a gold mine on your farm! To find diamonds in the gravel heaps before your door! How rare these things are! To share the day with you,—to people the earth. Whether to have a god or a goddess for companion in your walks, or to walk alone with hinds and villains and carles. Would not a friend enhance the beauty of the landscape as much as a deer or hare? Everything would acknowledge and serve such a relation; the corn in the field, and the cranberries in the meadow. The flowers would bloom, and the birds sing, with a new impulse. There would be more fair days in the year.

The object of love expands and grows before us to eternity, until it includes all that is lovely, and we become all that can love.

Chastity and Sensuality.

The subject of sex is a remarkable one, since, though its phenomena concern us so much, both directly and indirectly, and, sooner or later, it occupies the thoughts of all, yet all mankind, as it were, agree to be silent about it, at least the sexes commonly one to another. One of the most interesting of all human facts is veiled more completely than any mystery. It is treated with such secrecy and awe as surely do not go to any religion. I believe that it is unusual even for the most intimate friends to communicate the pleasures and anxieties connected with this fact,—much as the external affair of love, its comings and goings, are bruited. The Shakers do not exaggerate it so much by their manner of speaking of it, as all mankind by their manner of keeping silence about it. Not that men should speak on this or any subject without having anything worthy to say; but it is plain that the education of man has hardly commenced,—there is so little genuine intercommunication.

In a pure society, the subject of marriage would not be so often avoided,—from shame and not from reverence, winked out of sight, and hinted at only; but treated naturally and simply,—perhaps simply avoided, like the kindred mysteries. If it cannot be spoken of for shame, how can it be acted of? But, doubtless, there is far more purity, as well as more impurity, than is apparent.

Men commonly couple with their idea of marriage a slight degree at least of sensuality; but every lover, the world over, believes in its inconceivable purity.

If it is the result of a pure love, there can be nothing sensual in marriage. Chastity is something positive, not negative. It is the virtue of the married especially. All lusts or base pleasures must give place to loftier delights.

They who meet as superior beings cannot perform the deeds of inferior ones. The deeds of love are less questionable than any action of an individual can be, for, it being founded on the rarest mutual respect, the parties incessantly stimulate each other to a loftier and purer life, and the act in which they are associated must be pure and noble indeed, for innocence and purity can have no equal. In this relation we deal with one whom we respect more religiously even than we respect our better selves, and we shall necessarily conduct as in the presence of God. What presence can be more awful to the lover than the presence of his beloved?

If you seek the warmth even of affection from a similar motive to that from which cats and dogs and slothful persons hug the fire,—because your temperature is low through sloth,—you are on the downward road, and it is but to plunge yet deeper into sloth. Better the cold affection of the sun, reflected from fields of ice and snow, or his warmth in some still, wintry dell. The warmth of celestial love does not relax, but nerves and braces its enjoyer. Warm your body by healthful exercise, not by cowering over a stove. Warm your spirit by performing independently noble deeds, not by ignobly seeking the sympathy of your fellows who are no better than yourself. A man's social and spiritual discipline must answer to his corporeal. He must lean on a friend who has a hard breast, as he would lie on a hard bed. He must drink cold water for his only beverage. So he must not hear sweetened and colored words, but pure and refreshing truths. He must daily bathe in truth cold as spring water, not warmed by the sympathy of friends.

Can love be in aught allied to dissipation? Let us love by refusing, not accepting one another. Love and lust are far asunder. The one is good, the other bad. When the affectionate sympathize by their higher natures, there is love; but there is danger that they will sympathize by their lower natures, and then there is lust. It is not necessary that this be deliberate, hardly even conscious; but, in the close contact of affection, there is danger that we may stain and pollute one another; for we cannot embrace but with an entire embrace.

We must love our friend so much that she shall be associated with our purest and holiest thoughts alone. When
there is impurity, we have "descended to meet," though.
we knew it not.

The *luxury* of affection,—there's the danger. There
must be some nerve and heroism in our love, as of a winter morning. In the religion of all nations a purity is hinted at, which, I fear, men never attain to. We may love
and not elevate one another. The love that takes us as it
finds us degrades us. What watch we must keep over the
fairest and purest of our affections, lest there be some
taint about them! May we so love as never to have occasion to repent of our love!

There is to be attributed to sensuality the loss to language of how many pregnant symbols! Flowers, which,
by their infinite hues and fragrance, celebrate the marriage of the plants, are intended for a symbol of the open
and unsuspected beauty of all true marriage, when man's
flowering season arrives.

Virginity, too, is a budding flower, and by an impure
marriage the virgin is deflowered. Whoever loves flowers, loves virgins and chastity. Love and lust are as far
asunder as a flower-garden is from a brothel.

J. Biberg, in the "Amœnitates Botanicæ," edited by
Linnæus, observes (I translate from the Latin): "The organs of generation, which, in the animal kingdom, are for
the most part concealed by nature, as if they were to be
ashamed of, in the vegetable kingdom are exposed to the
eyes of all; and, when the nuptials of plants are celebrated, it is wonderful what delight they afford to the beholder, refreshing the senses with the most agreeable col-
or and the sweetest odor; and, at the same time, bees and
other insects, not to mention the humming-bird, extract
honey from their nectaries, and gather wax from their
effete pollen." Linnæus himself calls the calyx the *thala-
mus*, or bridal chamber; and the corolla the *aulaeum*, or
tapestry of it, and proceeds to explain thus every part of
the flower.

Who knows but evil spirits might corrupt the flowers
themselves, rob them of their fragrance and their fair
hues, and turn their marriage into a secret shame and

defilement? Already they are of various qualities, and there is one whose nuptials fill the lowlands in June with the odor of carrion.

The intercourse of the sexes, I have dreamed, is incredibly beautiful, too fair to be remembered. I have had thoughts about it, but they are among the most fleeting and irrecoverable in my experience. It is strange that men will talk of miracles, revelation, inspiration, and the like, as things past, while love remains.

A true marriage will differ in no wise from illumination. In all perception of the truth there is a divine ecstasy, an inexpressible delirium of joy, as when a youth embraces his betrothed virgin. The ultimate delights of a true marriage are one with this.

No wonder that, out of such a union, not as end, but as accompaniment, comes the undying race of man. The womb is a most fertile soil.

Some have asked if the stock of men could not be improved,—if they could not be bred as cattle. Let Love be purified, and all the rest will follow. A pure love is thus, indeed, the panacea for all the ills of the world.

The only excuse for reproduction is improvement. Nature abhors repetition. Beasts merely propagate their kind; but the offspring of noble men and women will be superior to themselves, as their aspirations are. By their fruits ye shall know them.

Concord, February 27, 1853.

Mr. Blake,—I have not answered your letter before, because I have been almost constantly in the fields surveying of late. It is long since I have spent many days so profitably in a pecuniary sense; so unprofitably, it seems to me, in a more important sense. I have earned just a dollar a day for seventy-six days past; for, though I charge at a higher rate for the days which are seen to be spent, yet so many more are spent than appears. This is instead of lecturing, which has not offered, to pay for that book which I printed. I have not only cheap hours, but cheap weeks and months; that is, weeks which are

bought at the rate I have named. Not that they are quite
lost to me, or make me very melancholy, alas! for I too
often take a cheap satisfaction in so spending them,
—weeks of pasturing and browsing, like beeves and
deer,—which give me animal health, it may be, but create a tough skin over the soul and intellectual part. Yet, if
men should offer my body a maintenance for the work of
my head alone, I feel that it would be a dangerous temp-
tation.

As to whether what you speak of as the "world's way"
(which for the most part is my way), or that which is
shown me, is the better, the former is imposture, the latter is truth. I have the coldest confidence in the last.
There is only such hesitation as the appetites feel in following the aspirations. The clod hesitates because it is inert, wants *animation*. The one is the way of death, the
other of life everlasting. My hours are not "cheap in such
a way that *I* doubt whether the world's way would not
have been better," but cheap in such a way that I doubt
whether the world's way, which I have adopted for the
time, could be worse. The whole enterprise of this nation,
which is not an upward, but a westward one, toward Oregon, California, Japan, etc., is totally devoid of interest to
me; whether performed on foot, or by a Pacific railroad.
It is not illustrated by a thought; it is not warmed by a
sentiment; there is nothing in it which one should lay
down his life for, nor even his gloves,—hardly which one
should take up a newspaper for. It is perfectly heathenish,—a filibustering *toward* heaven by the great western
route. No; they may go their way to their manifest destiny, which I trust is not mine. May my seventy-six dollars,
whenever I get them, help to carry me in the other direction! I see them on their winding way, but no music is
wafted from their host,—only the rattling of change in
their pockets. I would rather be a captive knight, and let
them all pass by, than be free only to go whither they are
bound. What end do they propose to themselves beyond
Japan? What aims more lofty have they than the prairie
dogs?

As it respects these things, I have not changed an opinion one iota from the first. As the stars looked to me

when I was a shepherd in Assyria, they look to me now, a New-Englander. The higher the mountain on which you stand, the less change in the prospect from year to year, from age to age. Above a certain height there is no change. I am a Switzer on the edge of the glacier, with his advantages and disadvantages, goitre, or what not. (You may suspect it to be some kind of swelling at any rate.) I have had but one *spiritual* birth (excuse the word), and now whether it rains or snows, whether I laugh or cry, fall farther below or approach nearer to my standard; whether Pierce or Scott is elected,—not a new scintillation of light flashes on me, but ever and anon, though with longer intervals, the same surprising and everlastingly new light dawns to me, with only such variations as in the coming of the natural day, with which, indeed, it is often coincident.

As to how to preserve potatoes from rotting, your opinion may change from year to year; but as to how to preserve your soul from rotting, I have nothing to learn, but something to practice.

Thus I declaim against them; but I in my folly am the world I condemn.

I very rarely, indeed, if ever, "feel any itching to be what is called useful to my fellow-men." Sometimes—it may be when my thoughts for want of employment fall into a beaten path or humdrum—I have dreamed idly of stopping a man's horse that was running away; but, perchance, I wished that he might run, in order that I might stop him;—or of putting out a fire; but then, of course, it must have got well a-going. Now, to tell the truth, I do not dream much of acting upon horses before they run, or of preventing fires which are not yet kindled. What a foul subject is this of doing good! instead of minding one's life, which should be his business; doing good as a dead carcass, which is only fit for manure, instead of as a living man,—instead of taking care to flourish, and smell and taste sweet, and refresh all mankind to the extent of our capacity and quality. People will sometimes try to persuade you that you have done something from that motive, as if you did not already know enough about it. If I ever *did* a man any good, in their sense, of course it was something exceptional and insignificant compared with the good or evil which I am constantly doing by being what I am. As if you were to preach to ice to shape itself into burning-glasses, which are sometimes useful, and so the peculiar properties of ice be lost. Ice that merely performs the office of a burning-glass does not do its duty.

The problem of life becomes, one cannot say by how many degrees, more complicated as our material wealth is increased,—whether that needle they tell of was a gateway or not,—since the problem is not merely nor mainly to get life for our bodies, but by this or a similar discipline to get life for our souls; by cultivating the lowland farm on right principles, that is, with this view, to turn it into an upland farm. You have so many more talents to account for. If I accomplish as much more in spiritual work as I am richer in worldly goods, then I am just as worthy, or worth just as much, as I was before, and no more. I see that, in my own case, money *might* be of great service to me, but probably it would not be; for the difficulty now is, that I do not improve my opportunities, and therefore I am not prepared to have my opportunities increased. Now, I warn you, if it be as you say, you have got to put on the pack of an upland farmer in good earnest the coming spring, the lowland farm being cared for; ay, you must be selecting your seeds forthwith, and doing what winter work you can; and, while others are raising potatoes and Baldwin apples for you, you must be raising apples of the Hesperides for them. (Only hear how he preaches!) No man can suspect that he is the proprietor of an upland farm,—upland in the sense that it will produce nobler crops, and better repay cultivation in the long run,—but he will be perfectly sure that he ought to cultivate it.

Though we are desirous to earn our bread, we need not be anxious to *satisfy* men for it,—though we shall take care to pay them,—but God, who alone gave it to us. Men may in effect put us in the debtors' jail for that matter, simply for paying our whole debt to God, which includes our debt to them, and though we have His receipt for it,—for His paper is dishonored. The cashier will tell you that He has no stock in his bank.

How prompt we are to satisfy the hunger and thirst of our bodies; how slow to satisfy the hunger and thirst of our *souls!* Indeed, we would-be-practical folks cannot use this word without blushing because of our infidelity, having starved this substance almost to a shadow. We feel it to be as absurd as if a man were to break forth into a eulogy on *his dog*, who hasn't any. An ordinary man will work every day for a year at shoveling dirt to support his body, or a family of bodies; but he is an extraordinary man who will work a whole day in a year for the support of his soul. Even the priests, the men of God, so called, for the most part confess that they work for the support of the body. But he alone is the truly enterprising and practical man who succeeds in *maintaining* his soul here. Have not we our everlasting life to get? and is not that the only excuse at last for eating, drinking, sleeping, or even carrying an umbrella when it rains? A man might as well devote himself to raising pork, as to fattening the bodies, or temporal part merely, of the whole human family. If we made the true distinction we should almost all of us be seen to be in the almshouse for souls.

I am much indebted to you because you look so steadily at the better side, or rather the true centre of me (for our true centre may, and perhaps oftenest does, lie entirely aside from us, and we are in fact eccentric), and, as I have elsewhere said, "give me an opportunity to live." You speak as if the image or idea which I see were reflected from me to you; and I see it again reflected from you to me, because we stand at the right angle to one another; and so it goes zigzag to what successive reflecting surfaces, before it is all dissipated or absorbed by the more unreflecting, or differently reflecting,—who knows? Or, perhaps, what you see directly, you refer to me. What a little shelf is required, by which we may impinge upon another, and build there our eyry in the clouds, and all the heavens we see above us we refer to the crags around and beneath us. Some piece of mica, as it were, in the face or eyes of one, as on the Delectable Mountains, slanted at the right angle, reflects the heavens to us. But, in the slow geological upheavals and depressions, these mutual angles are disturbed, these suns set, and new ones rise to us. That ideal which I worshiped was a greater stranger to the mica than to me. It was not the hero I admired, but the reflection from his epaulet or helmet. It is nothing (for us) permanently inherent in another, but his attitude or relation to what we prize, that we admire. The meanest man may glitter with micacious particles to his fellow's eye. These are the spangles that adorn a man. The highest union,—the only *un*-ion (don't laugh), or central oneness, is the coincidence of visual rays. Our club-room was an apartment in a constellation where our visual rays met (and there was no debate about the restaurant). The way between us is over the mount.

Your words make me think of a man of my acquaintance whom I occasionally meet, whom you, too, appear to have met, one Myself, as he is called. Yet, why not call him *Your*self? If you have met with him and know him, it is all I have done; and surely, where there is a mutual acquaintance, the *my* and *thy* make a distinction without a difference.

I do not wonder that you do not like my Canada story. It concerns me but little, and probably is not worth the time it took to tell it. Yet I had absolutely no design whatever in my mind, but simply to report what I saw. I have inserted all of myself that was implicated, or made the excursion. It has come to an end, at any rate; they will print no more, but return me my MS, when it is but little more than half done, as well as another I had sent them, because the editor requires the liberty to omit the heresies without consulting me,—a privilege California is not rich enough to bid for.

I thank you again and again for attending to me; that is to say, I am glad that you hear me and that you also are glad. Hold fast to your most indefinite, waking dream. The very green dust on the walls is an organized vegetable; the atmosphere has its fauna and flora floating in it; and shall we think that dreams are but dust and ashes, are always disintegrated and crumbling thoughts, and not dust-like thoughts trooping to their standard with music,—systems beginning to be organized? These expectations,—these are roots, these are nuts, which even the poorest man has in his bin, and roasts or cracks them occasionally in winter evenings,—which even the poor debtor retains with his bed and his pig, *i.e.*, his idleness and sensuality. Men go to the opera because they hear there a faint expression in sound of this news which is never quite distinctly proclaimed. Suppose a man were to sell the hue, the least amount of coloring matter in the superficies of his thought, for a farm,—were to exchange an absolute and infinite value for a relative and finite one,—to gain the whole world and lose his own soul!

Do not wait as long as I have before you write. If you will look at another star, I will try to supply my side of the triangle.

Tell Mr. Brown that I remember him, and trust that he remembers me.

P.S.—Excuse this rather flippant preaching, which does not cost me enough; and do not think that I mean you *always*, though your letter *requested* the subjects.

Concord, April 10, 1853.

Mr. Blake,—Another singular kind of spiritual football,—really nameless, handle-less, homeless, like myself,—a mere arena for thoughts and feelings; definite enough outwardly, indefinite more than enough inwardly. But I do not know why we should be styled "misters" or "masters:" we come so near to being anything or nothing, and seeing that we are mastered, and not wholly sorry to be mastered, by the least phenomenon. It seems to me that we are the mere creatures of thought,—one of the lowest forms of intellectual life, we men,—as the sunfish is of animal life. As yet our thoughts have acquired no definiteness nor solidity; they are purely molluscous, not vertebrate; and the height of our existence is to float upward in an ocean where the sun shines,—appearing only like a vast soup or chowder to the eyes of the immortal navigators. It is wonderful that I can be here, and you there, and that we can correspond, and do many other things, when, in fact, there is so little of us, either or both, anywhere. In a few minutes, I expect, this slight

film or dash of vapor that I am will be what is called
asleep,—resting! forsooth from what? Hard work? and
thought? The hard work of the dandelion down, which
floats over the meadow all day; the hard work of a pis-
mire that labors to raise a hillock all day, and even by
moonlight. Suddenly I can come forward into the utmost
apparent distinctness, and speak with a sort of emphasis
to you; and the next moment I am so faint an entity, and
make so slight an impression, that nobody can find the
traces of me. I try to hunt myself up, and find the little of
me that is discoverable is falling asleep, and then I assist
and tuck it up. It is getting late. How can *I* starve or
feed? Can *I* be said to sleep? There is not enough of me
even for that. If you hear a noise,—'taint I,—'taint I,—as
the dog says with a tin-kettle tied to his tail. I read of
something happening to another the other day: how happens it that nothing ever happens to me? A dandelion
down that never alights,—settles,—blown off by a boy to
see if his mother wanted him,—some divine boy in the
upper pastures.

Well, if there really is another such a meteor sojourn-
ing in these spaces, I would like to ask you if you know
whose estate this is that we are on? For my part I enjoy it
well enough, what with the wild apples and the scenery;
but I shouldn't wonder if the owner set his dog on me
next. I could remember something not much to the purpose, probably; but if I stick to what I do know, then—

It is worth the while to live respectably unto ourselves.
We can possibly *get along* with a neighbor, even with a
bedfellow, whom we respect but very little; but as soon as
it comes to this, that we do not respect ourselves, then we
do not get along at all, no matter how much money we
are paid for halting. There are old heads in the world
who cannot help me by their example or advice to live
worthily and satisfactorily to myself; but I believe that it
is in my power to elevate myself this very hour above the
common level of my life. It is better to have your head in
the clouds, and know where you are, if indeed you cannot get it above them, than to breathe the clearer atmosphere below them, and think that you are in paradise.

Once you were in Milton doubting what to do. To live

a better life,—this surely can be done. Dot and carry one. Wait not for a clear sight, for that you are to get. What you see clearly you may omit to do. Milton and Worcester? It is all Blake, Blake. Never mind the rats in the wall; the cat will take care of them. All that men have said or are is a very faint rumor, and it is not worth the while to remember or refer to that. If you are to meet God, will you refer to anybody out of that court? How shall men know how I succeed, unless they are in at the life? I did not see the "Times" reporter there.

Is it not delightful to provide one's self with the necessaries of life,—to collect dry wood for the fire when the weather grows cool, or fruits when we grow hungry?—not till then. And then we have all the time left for thought!

Of what use were it, pray, to get a little wood to burn, to warm your body this cold weather, if there were not a divine fire kindled at the same time to warm your spirit?

> "Unless above himself he can
> Erect himself, how poor a thing is man!"

I cuddle up by my stove, and there I get up another fire which warms fire itself. Life is so short that it is not wise to take roundabout ways, nor can we spend much time in waiting. Is it absolutely necessary, then, that we should do as we are doing? Are we chiefly under obligations to the devil, like Tom Walker? Though it is late to leave off this wrong way, it will seem early the moment we begin in the right way; instead of mid-afternoon, it will be early morning with us. We have not got half way to dawn yet.

As for the lectures, I feel that I have something to say, especially on Traveling, Vagueness, and Poverty; but I cannot come now. I will wait till I am fuller, and have fewer engagements. Your suggestions will help me much to write them when I am ready. I am going to Haverhill to-morrow, surveying, for a week or more. You met me on my last errand thither.

I trust that you realize what an exaggerater I am,—that I lay myself out to exaggerate whenever I have an opportunity,—pile Pelion upon Ossa, to reach heaven so. Expect no trivial truth from me, unless I am on the witness-stand. I will come as near to lying as you can drive a coach-and-four. If it isn't thus and so with me, it is with something. I am not particular whether I get the shells or meat, in view of the latter's worth.

I see that I have not at all answered your letter, but there is time enough for that.

Concord, December 19, 1853.

MR. BLAKE,—My debt has accumulated so that I should have answered your last letter at once, if I had not been the subject of what is called a press of engagements, having a lecture to write for last Wednesday, and survey-ing more than usual besides. It has been a kind of run-ning fight with me,—the enemy not always behind me, I trust.

True, a man cannot lift himself by his own waistbands, because he cannot get out of himself; but he can expand himself (which is better, there being no up nor down in nature), and so split his waistbands, being already within himself.

You speak of doing and being, and the vanity, real or apparent, of much doing. The suckers—I think it is they—make nests in our river in the spring of more than a cart-load of small stones, amid which to deposit their ova. The other day I opened a muskrat's house. It was made of weeds, five feet broad at base, and three feet high, and far and low within it was a little cavity, only a foot in diameter, where the rat dwelt. It may seem triv-ial, this piling up of weeds, but so the race of muskrats is preserved. We must heap up a great pile of doing for a small diameter of being. Is it not imperative on us that we *do* something, if we only work in a treadmill? And, indeed, some sort of revolving is necessary to produce a centre and nucleus of being. What exercise is to the body, employment is to the mind and morals. Consider what an amount of drudgery must be performed,—how much humdrum and prosaic labor goes to any work of the least value. There are so many layers of mere white lime in every shell to that thin inner one so beautifully tinted.

Let not the shell-fish think to build his house of that
alone; and pray, what are its tints to him? Is it not his
smooth, close-fitting shirt merely, whose tints *are not* to
him, being in the dark, but only when he is gone or dead,
and his shell is heaved up to light, a wreck upon the
beach, do they appear. With him, too, it is a Song of the
Shirt, "Work,—work,—work!" And the work is not merely a police in the gross sense, but in the higher sense a
discipline. If it is surely the means to the highest end we
know, can any work be humble or disgusting? Will it not
rather be elevating as a ladder, the means by which we
are translated?

How admirably the artist is made to accomplish his
self-culture by devotion to his art! The wood-sawyer,
through his effort to do his work well, becomes not merely a better wood-sawyer, but measurably a better *man*.
Few are the men that can work on their navels,—only
some Brahmins that I have heard of. To the painter is
given some paint and canvas instead; to the Irishman a
hog, typical of himself. In a thousand apparently humble
ways men busy themselves to make some right take the
place of some wrong,—if it is only to make a better
paste-blacking,—and they are themselves *so much* the
better morally for it.

You say that you do not succeed much. Does it concern
you enough that you do not? Do you work hard enough
at it? Do you get the benefit of discipline out of it? If so,
persevere. Is it a more serious thing than to walk a thousand miles in a thousand successive hours? Do you get
any corns by it? Do you ever think of hanging yourself on
account of failure?

If you are going into that line,—going to besiege the
city of God,—you must not only be strong in engines, but
prepared with provisions to starve out the garrison. An
Irishman came to see me to-day, who is endeavoring to
get his family out to this New World. He rises at half past
four, milks twenty-eight cows (which has swollen the
joints of his fingers), and eats his breakfast, without any
milk in his tea or coffee, before six; and so on, day after
day, for six and a half dollars a month; and thus he keeps
his virtue in him, if he does not add to it; and he regards

me as a gentleman able to assist him; but if I ever get to
be a gentleman, it will be by working after my fashion
harder than he does. If my joints are not swollen, it must
be because I deal with the teats of celestial cows before
breakfast (and the milker in this case is always allowed
some of the milk for his breakfast), to say nothing of the
flocks and herds of Admetus afterward.

It is the art of mankind to polish the world, and every
one who works is scrubbing in some part.

If the work is high and far,

> You must not only aim aright,
> But draw the bow with all your might.

You must qualify yourself to use a bow which no humbler archer can bend.

> "Work,—work,—work!"

Who shall know it for a bow? It is not of yew-tree. It is
straighter than a ray of light; flexibility is not known for
one of its qualities.

December 22.

So far I had got when I was called off to survey. Pray
read the life of Haydon the painter, if you have not. It is
a small revelation for these latter days; a great satisfaction
to know that he has lived, though he is now dead. Have
you met with the letter of a Turkish cadi at the end of
Layard's "Ancient Babylon"? that also is refreshing, and
a capital comment on the whole book which precedes
it,—the Oriental genius speaking through him.

Those Brahmins "put it through." They come off, or
rather stand still, conquerors, with some withered arms or
legs at least to show; and they are said to have cultivated
the faculty of abstraction to a degree unknown to Europeans. If we cannot sing of faith and triumph, we will
sing our despair. We will be that kind of bird. There are
day owls, and there are night owls, and each is beautiful
and even musical while about its business.

Might you not find some positive work to do with your
back to Church and State, letting your back do all the

rejection of them? Can you not *go* upon your pilgrimage, Peter, along the winding mountain path whither you face? A step more will make those funereal church bells over your shoulder sound far and sweet as a natural sound.

"Work,—work,—work!"

Why not make a *very large* mud-pie and bake it in the sun! Only put no Church nor State into it, nor upset any other pepper-box that way. Dig out a woodchuck,—for that has nothing to do with rotting institutions. Go ahead.

Whether a man spends his day in an ecstasy or despondency, he must do some work to show for it, even as there are flesh and bones to show for him. We are superior to the joy we experience.

Your last two letters, methinks, have more nerve and will in them than usual, as if you had erected yourself more. Why are not they good work, if you only had a hundred correspondents to tax you?

Make your failure tragical by the earnestness and steadfastness of your endeavor, and then it will not differ from success. Prove it to be the inevitable fate of mortals,—of one mortal,—if you can.

You said that you were writing on Immortality. I wish you would communicate to me what you know about that. You are sure to live while that is your theme.

Thus I write on some text which a sentence of your letters may have furnished.

I think of coming to see you as soon as I get a new coat, if I have money enough left. I will write to you again about it.

Concord, January 21, 1854.

MR. BLAKE,—My coat is at last done, and my mother and sister allow that I am *so far* in a condition to go abroad. I feel as if I had gone abroad the moment I put it on. It is, as usual, a production strange to me, the wearer,—invented by some Count D'Orsay; and the maker of it was not acquainted with any of my real depressions or elevations. He only measured a peg to hang it on, and might have made the loop big enough to go over my head. It requires a not quite innocent indifference, not to say insolence, to wear it. Ah! the process by which we get our coats is not what it should be. Though the Church declares it righteous, and its priest pardons me, my own good genius tells me that it is hasty, and coarse, and false. I expect a time when, or rather an integrity by which, a man will get his coat as honestly and as perfectly fitting as a tree its bark. Now our garments are typical of our conformity to the ways of the world, *i. e.*, of the devil, and to some extent react on us and poison us, like that shirt which Hercules put on.

I think to come and see you next week, on Monday, if nothing hinders. I have just returned from court at Cambridge, whither I was called as a witness, having surveyed a water-privilege, about which there is a dispute, since you were here.

Ah! what foreign countries there are, greater in extent than the United States or Russia, and with no more souls to a square mile, stretching away on every side from every human being with whom you have no sympathy. Their humanity affects me as simply monstrous. Rocks, earth, brute beasts, comparatively are not so strange to me. When I sit in the parlors and kitchens of some with whom my business brings me—I was going to say in contact—(business, like misery, makes strange bedfellows), I feel a sort of awe, and as forlorn as if I were cast away on a desolate shore. I think of Riley's Narrative and his sufferings. You, who soared like a merlin with your mate through the realms of æther, in the presence of the unlike, drop at once to earth, a mere amorphous squab, divested of your air-inflated pinions. (By the way, excuse this writing, for I am using the stub of the last feather I chance to possess.) You travel on, however, through this dark and desert world; you see in the distance an intelligent and sympathizing lineament; stars come forth in the dark, and oases appear in the desert.

But (to return to the subject of coats), we are wellnigh smothered under yet more fatal coats, which do not fit us, our whole lives long. Consider the cloak that our employment or station is; how rarely men treat each other for what in their true and naked characters they are; how we use and tolerate pretension; how the judge is clothed with dignity which does not belong to him, and the trembling witness with humility that does not belong to him, and the criminal, perchance, with shame or impudence which no more belong to him. It does not matter so much, then, what is the fashion of the cloak with which we cloak these cloaks. Change the coat; put the judge in the criminal-box, and the criminal on the bench, and you might think that you had changed the men.

No doubt the thinnest of all cloaks is conscious deception or lies; it is sleazy and frays out; it is not close-woven like cloth; but its meshes are a coarse network. A man can afford to lie only at the intersection of the threads; but truth puts in the filling, and makes a consistent stuff.

I mean merely to suggest how much the station affects the demeanor and self-respectability of the parties, and that the difference between the judge's coat of cloth and the criminal's is insignificant compared with, or only partially significant of, the difference between the coats which their respective stations permit them to wear. What airs the judge may put on over his coat which the criminal may not! The judge's opinion (*sententia*) of the criminal *sentences* him, and is read by the clerk of the court, and published to the world, and executed by the sheriff; but the criminal's opinion of the judge has the weight of a sentence, and is published and executed only in the supreme court of the universe,—a court not of common pleas. How much juster is the one than the other? Men are continually *sentencing* each other; but, whether we be judges or criminals, the sentence is ineffectual unless we continue ourselves.

I am glad to hear that I do not always limit your vision when you look this way; that you sometimes see the light through me; that I am here and there windows, and not all dead wall. Might not the community sometimes petition a man to remove himself as a nuisance, a darkener of the day, a too large mote?

Concord, August 8, 1854.

Mr. Blake,—Methinks I have spent a rather unprofitable summer thus far. I have been too much with the world, as the poet might say. The completest performance of the highest duties it imposes would yield me but little satisfaction. Better the neglect of all such, because your life passed on a level where it was impossible to recognize them. Latterly, I have heard the very flies buzz too distinctly, and have accused myself because I did not still this superficial din. We must not be too easily distracted by the crying of children or of dynasties. The Irishman erects his sty, and gets drunk, and jabbers more and more under my eaves, and I am responsible for all that filth and folly. I find it, as ever, very unprofitable to have much to do with men. It is sowing the wind, but not reaping even the whirlwind; only reaping an unprofitable calm and stagnation. Our conversation is a smooth, and civil, and never-ending speculation merely. I take up the thread of it again in the morning, with very much such courage as the invalid takes his prescribed Seidlitz powders. Shall I help you to some of the mackerel? It would be more respectable if men, as has been said before, instead of being such pigmy desperates, were Giant Despairs. Emerson says that his life is so unprofitable and shabby for the most part, that he is driven to all sorts of resources, and, among the rest, to men. I tell him that we differ only in our resources. Mine is to get away from men. They very rarely affect me as grand or beautiful; but I know that there is a sunrise and a sunset every day. In the summer, this world is a mere watering-place,—a Saratoga,—drinking so many tumblers of Congress water; and in the winter, is it any better, with its oratorios? I have seen more men than usual, lately; and, well as I was acquainted with one, I am surprised to find what vulgar fellows they are. They do a little business commonly each day, in order to pay their board, and then they congregate in sitting-rooms and feebly fabulate and paddle in the social slush; and when I think that they have sufficiently relaxed, and am prepared to see them steal away to their shrines, they go unashamed to their beds, and take on a new layer of sloth. They may be single, or have families in their *faineancy*. I do not meet men who can have nothing to do with me because they have so much to do with themselves. However, I trust that a very few cherish purposes which they never declare. Only think, for a moment, of a man about his affairs! How we should respect him! How glorious he would appear! Not working for any corporation, its agent, or president, but fulfilling the end of his being! A man about *his business* would be the cynosure of all eyes.

The other evening I was determined that I would silence this shallow din; that I would walk in various directions and see if there was not to be found any depth of silence around. As Bonaparte sent out his horsemen in the Red Sea on all sides to find shallow water, so I sent forth my mounted thoughts to find deep water. I left the village and paddled up the river to Fair Haven Pond. As the sun went down, I saw a solitary boatman disporting on the smooth lake. The falling dews seemed to strain and purify the air, and I was soothed with an infinite stillness. I got the world, as it were, by the nape of the neck, and held it under in the tide of its own events, till it was drowned, and then I let it go down stream like a dead dog. Vast hollow chambers of silence stretched away on every side, and my being expanded in proportion, and filled them. Then first could I appreciate sound, and find it musical.

But now for your news. Tell us of the year. Have you fought the good fight? What is the state of your crops? Will your harvest answer well to the seed-time, and are you cheered by the prospect of stretching cornfields? Is there any blight on your fields, any murrain in your herds? Have you tried the size and quality of your potatoes? It does one good to see their balls dangling in the lowlands. Have you got your meadow hay before the fall rains shall have set in? Is there enough in your barns to keep your cattle over? Are you killing weeds nowadays? or have you earned leisure to go a-fishing? Did you plant any Giant Regrets last spring, such as I saw advertised? It is not a new species, but the result of cultivation and a fertile soil. They are excellent for sauce. How is it with your marrow squashes for winter use? Is there likely to be

a sufficiency of fall feed in your neighborhood? What is
the state of the springs? I read that in your county there
is more water on the hills than in the valleys. Do you find
it easy to get all the help you require? Work early and
late, and let your men and teams rest at noon. Be careful
not to drink too much sweetened water, while at your
hoeing, this hot weather. You can bear the heat much
better for it.

Concord, December 19, 1854.

MR. BLAKE,—I suppose you have heard of my truly
providential meeting with Mr. [T.] Brown; providential
because it saved me from the suspicion that my words
had fallen altogether on stony ground, when it turned out
that there was some Worcester soil there. You will allow
me to consider that I correspond with him through you.

I confess that I am a very bad correspondent, so far as
promptness of reply is concerned; but then I am sure to
answer sooner or later. The longer I have forgotten you,
the more I remember you. For the most part I have not
been idle since I saw you. How does the world go with
you? or rather, how do you get along without it? I have
not yet learned to live, that I can see, and I fear that I
shall not very soon. I find, however, that in the long run
things correspond to my original idea,—that they correspond to nothing else so much; and thus a man may really be a true prophet without any great exertion. The day
is never so dark, not the night even, but that the laws at
least of light still prevail, and so may make it light in our
minds if they are open to the truth. There is considerable
danger that a man will be crazy between dinner and supper; but it will not directly answer any good purpose that
I know of, and it is just as easy to be sane. We have got to
know what both life and death are, before we can begin
to live after our own fashion. Let us be learning our
a-b-c's as soon as possible. I never yet knew the sun to be
knocked down and rolled through a mud-puddle; he
comes out honor-bright from behind every storm. Let us
then take sides with the sun, seeing we have so much
leisure. Let us not put all we prize into a football to be

kicked, when a bladder will do as well.

When an Indian is burned, his body may be broiled, it may be no more than a beefsteak. What of that? They may broil his *heart*, but they do not therefore broil his *courage*,—his principles. Be of good courage! That is the main thing.

If a man were to place himself in an attitude to bear manfully the greatest evil that can be inflicted on him, he would find suddenly that there was no such evil to bear; his brave back would go a-begging. When Atlas got his back made up, that was all that was required. (In this case α *priv.*; not *pleon.*, and $\tau\lambda\tilde{\eta}\mu\iota$.) The world rests on principles. The wise gods will never make underpinning of a man. But as long as he crouches, and skulks, and shirks his work, every creature that has weight will be treading on his toes, and crushing him; he will himself tread with one foot on the other foot.

The monster is never just there where we think he is. What is truly monstrous is our cowardice and sloth.

Have no idle disciplines like the Catholic Church and others; have only positive and fruitful ones. Do what you know you ought to do. Why should we ever go abroad, even across the way, to ask a neighbor's advice? There is a nearer neighbor within us incessantly telling us how we should behave. But we wait for the neighbor without to tell us of some false, easier way.

They have a census-table in which they put down the number of the insane. Do you believe that they put them all down there? Why, in every one of these houses there is at least one man fighting or squabbling a good part of his time with a dozen pet demons of his own breeding and cherishing, which are relentlessly gnawing at his vitals; and if perchance he resolve at length that he will courageously combat them, he says, "Ay! ay! I will attend to you after dinner!" And, when that time comes, he concludes that he is good for another stage, and reads a column or two about the *Eastern War!* Pray, to be in earnest, where is Sevastopol? Who is Menchikoff? and Nicholas behind there? who the Allies? Did not we fight a little (little enough to be sure, but just enough to make it interesting) at Alma, at Balaclava, at Inkermann? We love to fight far from home. Ah! the Minié musket is the king of weapons. Well, let us get one then.

I just put another stick into my stove,—a pretty large mass of white oak. How many men will do enough this cold winter to pay for the fuel that will be required to warm them? I suppose I have burned up a pretty good-sized tree to-night,—and for what? I settled with Mr. Tarbell for it the other day; but that wasn't the final settlement. I got off cheaply from him. At last, one will say, "Let us see, how much wood did you burn, sir?" And I shall shudder to think that the next question will be, "What did you do while you were warm?" Do we think the ashes will pay for it? that God is an ash-man? It is a fact that we have got to render an account for the deeds done in the body.

Who knows but we shall be better the next year than we have been the past? At any rate, I wish you a really *new* year,—commencing from the instant you read this,—and happy or unhappy, according to your deserts.

Concord, September 26, 1855.

MR. BLAKE,—The other day I thought that my health must be better,—that I gave at last a sign of vitality,— because I experienced a slight chagrin. But I do not see how strength is to be got into my legs again. These months of feebleness have yielded few, if any, thoughts, though they have not passed without serenity, such as our sluggish Musketaquid suggests. I hope that the harvest is to come. I trust that you have at least warped up the stream a little daily, holding fast by your anchors at night, since I saw you, and have kept my place for me while I have been absent.

Mr. Ricketson of New Bedford has just made me a visit of a day and a half, and I have had a quite good time with him. He and Channing have got on particularly well together. He is a man of very simple tastes, notwithstanding his wealth; a lover of nature; but, above all, singularly frank and plain-spoken. I think that you might enjoy meeting him.

Sincerity is a great but rare virtue, and we pardon to it much complaining, and the betrayal of many weaknesses. R. says of himself, that he sometimes thinks that he has all the infirmities of genius without the genius; is wretched without a hair-pillow, etc.; expresses a great and awful uncertainty with regard to "God," "Death," his "immortality;" says, "If I only knew," etc. He loves Cowper's "Task" better than anything else; and thereafter, perhaps, Thomson, Gray, and even Howitt. He has evidently suffered for want of sympathizing companions. He says that he sympathizes with much in my books, but much in them is naught to him,—"namby-pamby,"—"stuff,"— "mystical." Why will not I, having common sense, write in plain English always; *teach* men in detail how to live a simpler life, etc.; not go off into _____ ? But I say that I have no scheme about it,—no designs on men at all; and, if I had, my mode would be to tempt them with the fruit, and not with the manure. To what end do I lead a simple life at all, pray? That I may teach others to simplify their lives?—and so all our lives be *simplified* merely, like an algebraic formula? Or not, rather, that I may make use of the ground I have cleared, to live more worthily and profitably? I would fain lay the most stress forever on that which is the most important,—imports the most to me,—though it were only (what it is likely to be) a vibration in the air. As a preacher, I should be prompted to tell men, not so much how to get their wheat-bread cheaper, as of the bread of life compared with which *that* is bran. Let a man only taste these loaves, and he becomes a skillful economist at once. He'll not waste much time in earning those. Don't spend your time in drilling soldiers, who may turn out hirelings after all, but give to undrilled peasantry a *country* to fight for. The schools begin with what they call the elements, and where do they end?

I was glad to hear the other day that Higginson and _____ were gone to Ktaadn; it must be so much better to go to than a Woman's Rights or Abolition Convention; better still, to the delectable primitive mounts within you, which you have dreamed of from your youth up, and seen, perhaps, in the horizon, but never climbed.

But how do *you* do? Is the air sweet to you? Do you

find anything at which you can work, accomplishing
something solid from day to day? Have you put sloth and
doubt behind, considerably?—had one redeeming dream
this summer? I dreamed, last night, that I could vault
over any height it pleased me. That was *something*; and I
contemplated myself with a slight satisfaction in the
morning for it.

Methinks I will write to you. Methinks you will be glad
to hear. We will stand on solid foundations to one another,—I a column planted on this shore, you on that. We
meet the same sun in his rising. We were built slowly,
and have come to our bearing. We will not mutually fall
over that we may meet, but will grandly and eternally
guard the straits. Methinks I see an inscription on you,
which the architect made, the stucco being worn off to it.
The name of that ambitious worldly king is crumbling
away. I see it toward sunset in favorable lights. Each
must read for the other, as might a sailer-by. Be sure you
are star-y-pointing still. How is it on your side? I will not
require an answer until you think I have paid my debts
to you.

I have just got a letter from Ricketson, urging me to
come to New Bedford, which possibly I may do. He says
I can wear my old clothes there.

Let me be remembered in your quiet house.

Concord, December 9, 1855.

Mr. Blake,—Thank you! thank you for going a-wood-
ing with me,—and enjoying it,—for being warmed by
my wood fire. I have indeed enjoyed it much alone. I see
how I might enjoy it yet more with company,—how we
might help each other to live. And to be admitted to Nature's hearth costs nothing. None is excluded, but ex-
cludes himself. You have only to push aside the curtain.

I am glad to hear that you were there too. There are
many more such voyages, and longer ones, to be made on
that river, for it is the water of life. The Ganges is nothing to it. Observe its reflections,—no idea but is familiar
to it. That river, though to dull eyes it seems terrestrial
wholly, flows through Elysium. What powers bathe in it

invisible to villagers! Talk of its shallowness,—that hay-carts can be driven through it at midsummer; its depth passeth my understanding. If, forgetting the allurements of the world, I could drink deeply enough of it; if, cast adrift from the shore, I could with complete integrity float on it, I should never be seen on the Mill-dam again. If there is any depth in me, there is a corresponding depth in it. It is the cold blood of the gods. I paddle and bathe in their artery.

I do not want a stick of wood for so trivial a use as to burn even, but they get it over night, and carve and gild it that it may please my eye. What persevering lovers they are! They will supply us with fagots wrapped in the daintiest packages, and freight paid; sweet-scented woods, and bursting into flower, and resounding as if Orpheus had just left them,—these shall be our fuel, and we still prefer to chaffer with the wood-merchant!

The jug we found still stands draining bottom up on the bank, on the sunny side of the house. That river,—who shall say exactly whence it came, and whither it goes? Does aught that flows come from a higher source? Many things drift downward on its surface which would enrich a man. If you could only be on the alert all day, and every day! And the nights are as long as the days.

Do you not think you could contrive thus to get woody fibre enough to bake your wheaten bread with? Would you not perchance have tasted the sweet crust of another kind of bread in the mean while, which ever hangs ready baked on the bread-fruit trees of the world?

Talk of burning your smoke after the wood has been consumed! There is a far more important and warming heat, commonly lost, which precedes the burning of the wood. It is the smoke of industry, which is incense. I had been so thoroughly warmed in body and spirit, that when at length my fuel was housed, I came near selling it to the ash-man, as if I had extracted all its heat.

You should have been here to help me get in my boat. The last time I used it, November 27th, paddling up the Assabet, I saw a great round pine log sunk deep in the water, and with labor got it aboard. When I was floating this home so gently, it occurred to me why I had found

it. It was to make wheels with to roll my boat into winter
quarters upon. So I sawed off two thick rollers from one
end, pierced them for wheels, and then of a joist which I
had found drifting on the river in the summer I made an
axletree, and on this I rolled my boat out.

Miss Mary Emerson is here,—the youngest person in
Concord, though about eighty,—and the most apprehen-
sive of a genuine thought; earnest to know of your inner
life; most stimulating society; and exceedingly witty withal. She says they called her old when she was young, and
she has never grown any older. I wish you could see her.

My books did not arrive till November 30th, the cargo
of the Asia having been complete when they reached
Liverpool. I have arranged them in a case which I made
in the mean while, partly of river boards. I have not
dipped far into the new ones yet. One is splendidly
bound and illuminated. They are in English, French, Latin, Greek, and Sanscrit. I have not made out the signfi-
cance of this godsend yet.

Farewell, and bright dreams to you!

                              Concord, March 13, 1856.

Mr. Blake,—It is high time I sent you a word. I have
not heard from Harrisburg since offering to go there, and
have not been invited to lecture anywhere else the past
winter. So you see I am fast growing rich. This is quite
right, for such is my relation to the lecture-goers, I should
be surprised and alarmed if there were any great call for
me. I confess that I am considerably alarmed even when
I hear that an individual wishes to meet me, for my experience teaches me that we shall thus only be made certain
of a mutual strangeness, which otherwise we might never
have been aware of.

I have not yet recovered strength enough for such a
walk as you propose, though pretty well again for cir-
cumscribed rambles and chamber work. Even now, I am
probably the greatest walker in Concord,—to its disgrace
be it said. I remember our walks and talks and sailing in
the past with great satisfaction, and trust that we shall
have more of them erelong,—have more woodings-up,—

for even in the spring we must still seek "fuel to maintain
our fires."

As you suggest, we would fain value one another for
what we are absolutely, rather than relatively. How will
this do for a symbol of sympathy?

As for compliments, even the stars praise me, and I
praise them. They and I sometimes belong to a mutual
admiration society. Is it not so with you? I know you of
old. Are you not tough and earnest to be talked at,
praised, or blamed? Must *you* go out of the room because
you are the subject of conversation? Where will you go
to, pray? Shall we look into the "Letter Writer" to see
what compliments are admissible? I am not afraid of
praise, for I have practiced it on myself. As for my deserts, I never took an account of that stock, and in this
connection care not whether I am deserving or not.
When I hear praise coming, do I not elevate and arch
myself to hear it like the sky, and as impersonally? Think
I appropriate any of it to my weak legs? No. Praise away
till all is blue.

I see by the newspapers that the season for making sugar is at hand. Now is the time, whether you be rock, or
white-maple, or hickory. I trust that you have prepared a
store of sap-tubs and sumach-spouts, and invested largely
in kettles. Early the first frosty morning, tap your maples,—the sap will not run in summer, you know. It matters not how little juice you get, if you get all you can,
and boil it down. I made just one crystal of sugar once,
one twentieth of an inch cube, out of a pumpkin, and it
sufficed. Though the yield be no greater than that, this is
not less the season for it, and it will be not the less sweet,
nay, it will be infinitely the sweeter.

Shall, then, the maple yield sugar, and not man? Shall
the farmer be thus active, and surely have so much sugar
to show for it, before this very March is gone,—while I

read the newspaper? While he works in his sugar-camp let me work in mine,—for sweetness is in me, and to sugar it shall come,—it shall not all go to leaves and wood. Am I not a *sugar-maple* man, then? Boil down the sweet sap which the spring causes to flow within you. Stop not at syrup,—go on to sugar, though you present the world with but a single crystal,—a crystal not made from trees in your yard, but from the new life that stirs in your pores. Cheerfully skim your kettle, and watch it set and crystallize, making a holiday of it if you will. Heaven will be propitious to you as to him.

Say to the farmer, There is your crop; here is mine. Mine is a sugar to sweeten sugar with. If you will listen to me, I will sweeten your whole load,—your whole life.

Then will the callers ask, Where is Blake? He is in his sugar-camp on the mountain-side. Let the world await him. Then will the little boys bless you, and the great boys too, for such sugar is the origin of many condiments,—Blakians in the shops of Worcester, of new form, with their mottoes wrapped up in them. Shall men taste only the sweetness of the maple and the cane the coming year?

A walk over the crust to Asnybumskit, standing there in its inviting simplicity, is tempting to think of,—making a fire on the snow under some rock! The very poverty of outward nature implies an inward wealth in the walker. What a Golconda is he conversant with, thawing his fingers over such a blaze! But—but—

Have you read the new poem, "The Angel in the House"? Perhaps you will find it good for you.

Concord, May 21, 1856.

MR. BLAKE,—I have not for a long time been *putting such thoughts together* as I should like to read to the company you speak of. I have enough of that sort to say, or even read, but not time now to arrange it. Something I have prepared might prove for their entertainment or refreshment perchance; but I would not like to have a hat carried round for it. I have just been reading some papers to see if they would do for your company; but though I thought pretty well of them as long as I read them to myself, when I got an auditor to try them on, I felt that they would not answer. How could I let you drum up a company to hear them? In fine, what I have is either too scattered or loosely arranged, or too light, or else is too scientific and matter of fact (I run a good deal into that of late) for so hungry a company.

I am still a learner, not a teacher, feeding somewhat omnivorously, browsing both stalk and leaves; but I shall perhaps be enabled to speak with the more precision and authority by and by,—if philosophy and sentiment are not buried under a multitude of details.

I do not refuse, but accept your invitation, only changing the time. I consider myself invited to Worcester once for all, and many thanks to the inviter. As for the Harvard excursion, will you let me suggest another? Do you and Brown come to Concord on Saturday, if the weather promises well, and spend the Sunday here on the river or hills, or both. So we shall save some of our money (which is of next importance to our souls), and lose—I do not know what. You say you *talked* of coming here before; now *do* it. I do not propose this because I think that I am worth your spending time with, but because I hope that we may prove flint and steel to one another. It is at most only an hour's ride farther, and you can at any rate do what you please when you get here.

Then we will see if we have any apology to offer for our existence. So come to Concord,—come to Concord,—come to Concord! or—your suit shall be defaulted.

As for the dispute about solitude and society, any comparison is impertinent. It is an idling down on the plain at the base of a mountain, instead of climbing steadily to its top. Of course you will be glad of all the society you can get to go up with. Will you go to glory with me? is the burden of the song. I love society so much that I swallowed it all at a gulp,—that is, all that came in my way. It is not that we love to be alone, but that we love to soar, and when we do soar, the company grows thinner and thinner till there is none at all. It is either the Tribune on the plain, a sermon on the mount, or a very private ecstasy still higher up. We are not the less to aim at the sum-

mits, though the multitude does not ascend them. Use all
the society that will abet you. But perhaps I do not enter
into the spirit of your talk.

Eagleswood, N.J., November 19, 1856.

MR. BLAKE,—I have been here much longer than I expected, but have deferred answering you, because I could
not foresee when I should return. I do not know yet within three or four days. This uncertainty makes it impossible for me to appoint a day to meet you, until it shall be
too late to hear from you again. I think, therefore, that I
must go straight home. I feel some objection to reading
that "What shall it profit" lecture *again* in Worcester;
but if you are quite sure that it will be worth the while (it
is a grave consideration), I will even make an independent journey from Concord for that purpose. I have read
three of my old lectures (that included) to the Eagleswood people, and, unexpectedly, with rare success,—*i. e.*,
I was aware that what I was saying was silently taken in
by their ears.

You must excuse me if I write mainly a business letter
now, for I am sold for the time,—am merely Thoreau the
surveyor here,—and solitude is scarcely obtainable in
these parts.

Alcott has been here three times, and, Saturday before
last, I went with him and Greeley, by invitation of the
last, to G.'s farm, thirty-six miles north of New York. The
next day A. and I heard Beecher preach; and what was
more, we visited Whitman the next morning (A. had already seen him), and were much interested and provoked. He is apparently the greatest democrat the world
has seen. Kings and aristocracy go by the board at once,
as they have long deserved to. A remarkably strong
though coarse nature, of a sweet disposition, and much
prized by his friends. Though peculiar and rough in his
exterior, his skin (all over (?)) red, he is essentially a gentleman. I am still somewhat in a quandary about him,—
feel that he is essentially strange to me, at any rate; but I
am surprised by the sight of him. He is very broad, but,
as I have said, not fine. He said that I misapprehended

him. I am not quite sure that I do. He told us that he loved to ride up and down Broadway all day on an omnibus, sitting beside the driver, listening to the roar of the carts, and sometimes gesticulating and declaiming Homer at the top of his voice. He has long been an editor and writer for the newspapers,—was editor of the "New Orleans Crescent" once; but now has no employment but to read and write in the forenoon, and walk in the afternoon, like all the rest of the scribbling gentry.

I shall probably be in Concord next week; so you can direct to me there.

Concord, December 6, 1856.

Mr. Blake,—I trust that you got a note from me at Eagleswood, about a fortnight ago. I passed through Worcester on the morning of the 25th of November, and spent several hours (from 3:30 to 6:20) in the travelers' room at the depot, as in a dream, it now seems. As the first Harlem train unexpectedly connected with the first from Fitchburg, I did not spend the forenoon with you as I had anticipated, on account of baggage, etc. If it had been a seasonable hour, I should have seen you,—*i. e.*, if you had not gone to a horse-race. But think of making a call at half past three in the morning! (would it not have implied a three o'clock in the morning courage in both you and me?) as it were, ignoring the fact that mankind are really not at home,—are not out, but so deeply in that they cannot be seen,—nearly half their hours at this season of the year.

I walked up and down the main street, at half past five, in the dark, and paused long in front of Brown's store, trying to distinguish its features; considering whether I might safely leave his "Putnam" in the door-handle, but concluded not to risk it. Meanwhile a watchman (?) seemed to be watching me, and I moved off. Took another turn round there, and had the very earliest offer of the Transcript from an urchin behind, whom I actually could not see, it was so dark. So I withdrew, wondering if you and B. would know if I had been there. You little dream who is occupying Worcester when you

are all asleep. Several things occurred there that night
which I will venture to say were not put into the Transcript. A cat caught a mouse at the depot, and gave it to
her kitten to play with. So that world-famous tragedy
goes on by night as well as by day, and nature is *emphat-
ically* wrong. Also I saw a young Irishman kneel before
his mother, as if in prayer, while she wiped a cinder out
of his eye with her tongue; and I found that it was never
too late (or early?) to learn something. These things tran-
spired while you and B. were, to all practical purposes,
nowhere, and good for nothing,—not even for society,—
not for horse-races,—nor the taking back of a "Putnam's
Magazine." It is true, I might have recalled you to life,
but it would have been a cruel act, considering the kind
of life you would have come back to.

However, I would fain write to you now by broad daylight, and report to you some of my life, such as it is, and
recall you to your life, which is not always lived by you,
even by daylight. Blake! Brown! are you awake? are you
aware what an ever-glorious morning this is,—what long-
expected, never-to-be-repeated opportunity is now offered to get life and knowledge?

For my part, I am trying to wake up,—to wring slum-
ber out of my pores; for, generally, I take events as un-
concernedly as a fence post,—absorb wet and cold like it,
and am pleasantly tickled with lichens slowly spreading
over me. Could I not be content, then, to be a cedar post,
which lasts twenty-five years? Would I not rather be that
than the farmer that set it? or he that preaches to the
farmer? and go to the heaven of posts at last? I think I
should like that as well as any would like it. But I should
not care if I sprouted into a living tree, put forth leaves
and flowers, and bore fruit.

I am grateful for what I am and have. My thanksgiving
is perpetual. It is surprising how contented one can be
with nothing definite,—only a sense of existence. Well,
anything for variety. I am ready to try this for the next
ten thousand years, and exhaust it. How sweet to think of!
my extremities well charred, and my intellectual part too,
so that there is no danger of worm or rot for a long while.
My breath is sweet to me. O how I laugh when I think of

my vague, indefinite riches. No run on my bank can drain it, for my wealth is not possession but enjoyment.

What are all these years made for? and now another winter comes, so much like the last? Can't we satisfy the beggars once for all?

Have you got in your wood for this winter? What else have you got in? Of what use a great fire on the hearth, and a confounded little fire in the heart? Are you prepared to make a decisive campaign,—to pay for your costly tuition,—to pay for the suns of past summers,—for happiness and unhappiness lavished upon you?

Does not Time go by swifter than the swiftest equine trotter or racker?

Stir up Brown. Remind him of his duties, which outrun the date and span of Worcester's years past and to come. Tell him to be sure that he is on the main street, however narrow it may be, and to have a lit sign, visible by night as well as by day.

Are they not patient waiters,—they who wait for us? But even they shall not be losers.

December 7.

That Walt Whitman, of whom I wrote to you, is the most interesting fact to me at present. I have just read his second edition (which he gave me), and it has done me more good than any reading for a long time. Perhaps I remember best the poem of Walt Whitman, an American, and the Sun-Down Poem. There are two or three pieces in the book which are disagreeable, to say the least; simply sensual. He does not celebrate love at all. It is as if the beasts spoke. I think that men have not been ashamed of themselves without reason. No doubt there have always been dens where such deeds were unblushingly recited, and it is no merit to compete with their inhabitants. But even on this side he has spoken more truth than any American or modern that I know. I have found his poem exhilarating, encouraging. As for its sensuality,—and it may turn out to be less sensual than it appears,—I do not so much wish that those parts were not written, as that men and women were so pure that they could read them without harm, that is, without understanding them. One woman told me that no woman could read it,—as if a man could read what a woman could not. Of course Walt Whitman can communicate to us no experience, and if we are shocked, whose experience is it that we are reminded of?

On the whole, it sounds to me very brave and American, after whatever deductions. I do not believe that all the sermons, so called, that have been preached in this land put together are equal to it for preaching.

We ought to rejoice greatly in him. He occasionally suggests something a little more than human. You can't confound him with the other inhabitants of Brooklyn or New York. How they must shudder when they read him! He is awfully good.

To be sure I sometimes feel a little imposed on. By his heartiness and broad generalities he puts me into a liberal frame of mind prepared to see wonders,—as it were, sets me upon a hill or in the midst of a plain,—stirs me well up, and then—throws in a thousand of brick. Though rude, and sometimes ineffectual, it is a great primitive poem,—an alarum or trumpet-note ringing through the American camp. Wonderfully like the Orientals, too, considering that when I asked him if he had read them, he answered, "No: tell me about them."

I did not get far in conversation with him,—two more being present,—and among the few things which I chanced to say, I remember that one was, in answer to him as representing America, that I did not think much of America or of politics, and so on, which may have been somewhat of a damper to him.

Since I have seen him, I find that I am not disturbed by any brag or egoism in his book. He may turn out the least of a braggart of all, having a better right to be confident.

He is a great fellow.

Concord, August 18, 1857.

MR. BLAKE,—Fifteenthly. It seems to me that you need some absorbing pursuit. It does not matter much what it is, so it be honest. Such employment will be favorable to your development in more characteristic and important directions. You know there must be impulse enough for steerage way, though it be not toward your port, to prevent your drifting helplessly on to rocks or shoals. Some sails are set for this purpose only. There is the large fleet of scholars and men of science, for instance, always to be seen standing off and on every coast, and saved thus from running on to reefs, who will at last run into their proper haven, we trust.

It is a pity you were not here with Brown and Wiley. I think that in this case, *for a rarity*, the more the merrier.

You perceived that I did not entertain the idea of our going together to Maine on such an excursion as I had planned. The more I thought of it, the more imprudent it appeared to me. I did think to have written to you before going, though not to propose your going also; but I went at last very suddenly, and could only have written a business letter, if I had tried, when there was no business to be accomplished. I have now returned, and think I have had a quite profitable journey, chiefly from associating with an intelligent Indian. My companion, Edward Hoar, also found his account in it, though he suffered considerably from being obliged to carry unusual loads over wet and rough "carries,"—in one instance five miles through a swamp, where the water was frequently up to our knees, and the fallen timber higher than our heads. He went over the ground three times, not being able to carry all his load at once. This prevented his ascending Ktaadn. Our best nights were those when it rained the hardest, on account of the mosquitoes. I speak of these things, which were not unexpected, merely to account for my not inviting you.

Having returned, I flatter myself that the world appears in some respects a little larger, and not, as usual, smaller and shallower, for having extended my range. I have made a short excursion into the new world which the Indian dwells in, or is. He begins where we leave off. It is worth the while to detect new faculties in man,—he is so much the more divine.

Concord, November 16, 1857.

MR. BLAKE,—You have got the start again. It was I
that owed you a letter or two, if I mistake not.

They make a great ado nowadays about hard times;
but I think that the community generally, ministers and
all, take a wrong view of the matter, though some of the
ministers preaching according to a formula may pretend
to take a right one. This general failure, both private and
public, is rather occasion for rejoicing, as reminding us
whom we have at the helm,—that justice is always done.
If our merchants did not most of them fail, and the banks
too, my faith in the old laws of the world would be stag-
gered. The statement that ninety-six in a hundred doing
such business surely break down is perhaps the sweetest
fact that statistics have revealed,—exhilarating as the fragrance of sallows in spring. Does it not say somewhere,
"The Lord reigneth, let the earth rejoice"? If thousands
are thrown out of employment, it suggests that they were
not well employed. Why don't they take the hint? It is
not enough to be industrious; so are the ants. What are
you industrious about?

The merchants and company have long laughed at
transcendentalism, higher laws, etc., crying, "None of
your moonshine," as if they were anchored to something
not only definite, but sure and permanent. If there was
any institution which was presumed to rest on a solid and
secure basis, and more than any other represented this
boasted common sense, prudence, and practical talent, it
was the bank; and now those very banks are found to be
mere reeds shaken by the wind. Scarcely one in the land
has kept its promise. It would seem as if you only need
live forty years in any age of this world, to see its most
promising government become the government of Kansas, and banks nowhere. Not merely the Brook Farm and
Fourierite communities, but now the community generally has failed. But there is the moonshine still, serene, beneficent, and unchanged. Hard times, I say, have this value, among others, that they show us what such promises
are worth,—where the *sure* banks are. I heard some Mr.
Eliot praised the other day because he had paid some of
his debts, though it took nearly all he had (why, I've done

as much as that myself many times, and a little more), and then gone to board. What if he has? I hope he's got a good boarding-place, and can pay for it. It's not everybody that can. However, in my opinion, it is cheaper to keep house,—*i.e.*, if you don't keep too big a one.

Men will tell you sometimes that "money's hard." That shows it was not made to eat, I say. Only think of a man in this new world, in his log cabin, in the midst of a corn and potato patch, with a sheepfold on one side, talking about money being hard! So are flints hard; there is no alloy in them. What has that to do with his raising his food, cutting his wood (or breaking it), keeping in-doors when it rains, and, if need be, spinning and weaving his clothes? Some of those who sank with the steamer the other day found out that money was *heavy* too. Think of a man's priding himself on this kind of wealth, as if it greatly enriched him. As if one struggling in mid-ocean with a bag of gold on his back should gasp out, "I am worth a hundred thousand dollars." I see them struggling just as ineffectually on dry land, nay, even more hopelessly, for, in the former case, rather than sink, they will finally let the bag go; but in the latter they are pretty sure to hold and go down with it. I see them swimming about in their great-coats, collecting their rents, really *getting their dues*, drinking bitter draughts which only increase their thirst, becoming more and more water-logged, till finally they sink plumb down to the bottom. But enough of this.

Have you ever read Ruskin's books? If not, I would recommend you to try the second and third volumes (not parts) of his "Modern Painters." I am now reading the fourth, and have read most of his other books lately. They are singularly good and encouraging, though not without crudeness and bigotry. The themes in the volumes referred to are Infinity, Beauty, Imagination, Love of Nature, etc.,—all treated in a very living manner. I am rather surprised by them. It is remarkable that these things should be said with reference to painting chiefly, rather than literature. The "Seven Lamps of Architecture," too, is made of good stuff; but, as I remember, there is too much about art in it for me and the Hottentots. We want to know about matters and things in general. Our house is as yet a hut.

You must have been enriched by your solitary walk over the mountains. I suppose that I feel the same awe when on their summits that many do on entering a church. To see what kind of earth that is on which you have a house and garden somewhere, perchance! It is equal to the lapse of many years. You must ascend a mountain to learn your relation to matter, and so to your own body, for *it* is at home there, though *you* are not. It might have been composed there, and will have no farther to go to return to dust there, than in your garden; but your spirit inevitably comes away, and brings your body with it, if it lives. Just as awful really, and as glorious, is your garden. See how I can play with my fingers! They are the funniest companions I have ever found. Where did they come from? What strange control I have over them! *Who* am I? What are they?—those little peaks—call them Madison, Jefferson, Lafayette. What is *the matter? My* fingers do I say? Why, erelong, they may form the top-most crystal of Mount Washington. I go up there to see my body's cousins. There are some fingers, toes, bowels, etc., that I take an interest in, and therefore I am interested in all their relations.

Let me suggest a theme for you: to state to yourself precisely and completely what that walk over the mountains amounted to for you,—returning to this essay again and again, until you are satisfied that all that was important in your experience is in it. Give this good reason to yourself for having gone over the mountains, for mankind is ever going over a mountain. Don't suppose that you can tell it precisely the first dozen times you try, but at 'em again, especially when, after a sufficient pause, you suspect that you are touching the heart or summit of the matter, reiterate your blows there, and account for the mountain to yourself. Not that the story need be long, but it will take a long while to make it short. It did not take very long to get over the mountain, you thought; but have you got over it indeed? If you have been to the top of Mount Washington, let me ask, what did you find there? That is the way they prove witnesses, you know.

Going up there and being blown on is nothing. We never do much climbing while we are there, but we eat our luncheon, etc., very much as at home. It is after we get home that we really go over the mountain, if ever. What did the mountain say? What did the mountain do?

I keep a mountain anchored off eastward a little way, which I ascend in my dreams both awake and asleep. Its broad base spreads over a village or two, which do not know it; neither does it know them, nor do I when I ascend it. I can see its general outline as plainly now in my mind as that of Wachusett. I do not invent in the least, but state exactly what I see. I find that I go up it when I am light-footed and earnest. It ever smokes like an altar with its sacrifice. I am not aware that a single villager frequents it or knows of it. I keep this mountain to ride instead of a horse.

Do you not mistake about seeing Moosehead Lake from Mount Washington? That must be about one hundred and twenty miles distant, or nearly twice as far as the Atlantic, which last some doubt if they can see thence. Was it not Umbagog?

Dr. Solger has been lecturing in the vestry in this town on Geography, to Sanborn's scholars, for several months past, at five P.M. Emerson and Alcott have been to hear him. I was surprised when the former asked me, the other day, if I was not going to hear Dr. Solger. What, to be sitting in a meeting-house cellar at that time of day, when you might possibly be out-doors! I never thought of such a thing. What was the sun made for? If he does not prize daylight, I do. Let him lecture to owls and dormice. He must be a wonderful lecturer indeed who can keep me indoors at such an hour, when the night is coming in which no man can walk.

Are you in want of amusement nowadays? Then play a little at the game of getting a living. There never was anything equal to it. Do it temperately, though, and don't sweat. Don't let this secret out, for I have a design against the Opera. OPERA ! ! Pass along the exclamations, devil.

Now is the time to become conversant with your wood-pile (this comes under Work for the Month), and be sure you put some warmth into it by your mode of getting it.

Do not consent to be passively warmed. An intense degree of that is the hotness that is threatened. But a positive warmth within can withstand the fiery furnace, as the vital heat of a living man can withstand the heat that cooks meat.

Concord, January 1, 1859.

Mr. Blake,—It may interest you to hear that Cholmondeley has been this way again, *via* Montreal and Lake Huron, going to the West Indies, or rather to Weiss-nicht-wo, whither he urges me to accompany him. He is rather more demonstrative than before, and, on the whole, what would be called "a good fellow,"—is a man of principle, and quite reliable, but very peculiar. I have been to New Bedford with him, to show him a whaling town and Ricketson. I was glad to hear that you had called on R. How did you like him? I suspect that you did not see one another fairly.

I have lately got back to that glorious society called Solitude, where we meet our friends continually, and can imagine the outside world also to be peopled. Yet some of my acquaintance would fain hustle me into the almshouse for *the sake of society*, as if I were pining for that diet, when I seem to myself a most befriended man, and find constant employment. However, they do not believe a word I say. They have got a club, the handle of which is in the Parker House at Boston, and with this they beat me from time to time, expecting to make me tender or minced meat, so fit for a club to dine off.

> "Hercules with his club
> The Dragon did drub;
> But More of More Hall,
> With nothing at all,
> He slew the Dragon of Wantley."

Ah! that More of More Hall knew what fair play was. Channing, who wrote to me about it once, brandishing the club vigorously (being set on by another, probably), says *now*, seriously, that he is sorry to find by my letters that I am "absorbed in politics," and adds, begging my

pardon for his plainness, "Beware of an extraneous life!"
and so he does his duty, and washes his hands of me. I tell
him that it is as if he should say to the sloth, that fellow
that creeps so slowly along a tree, and cries *ai* from time
to time, "Beware of dancing!"

The doctors are all agreed that I am suffering for want
of society. Was never a case like it. First, I did not know
that I was suffering at all. Secondly, as an Irishman might
say, I had thought it was indigestion of the society I got.

As for the Parker House, I went there once, when the
Club was away, but I found it hard to see through the
cigar smoke, and men were deposited about in chairs
over the marble floor, as thick as legs of bacon in a
smoke-house. It was all smoke, and no salt, Attic or other.
The only room in Boston which I visit with alacrity is the
Gentlemen's Room at the Fitchburg Depot, where I wait
for the cars, sometimes for two hours, in order to get out
of town. It is a paradise to the Parker House, for no
smoking is allowed, and there is far more retirement. A
large and respectable club of us hire it (Town and Country Club), and I am pretty sure to find some one there
whose face is set the same way as my own.

My last essay, on which I am still engaged, is called
Autumnal Tints. I do not know how readable (*i. e.*, by me
to others) it will be.

I met Mr. James the other night at Emerson's, at an
Alcottian conversation, at which, however, Alcott did not
talk much, being disturbed by James's opposition. The
latter is a hearty man enough, with whom you can differ
very satisfactorily, on account of both his doctrines and
his good temper. He utters *quasi* philanthropic dogmas in
a metaphysic dress; but they are for all practical purposes
very crude. He charges society with all the crime committed, and praises the criminal for committing it. But I
think that all the remedies he suggests out of his head—
for he goes no farther, hearty as he is—would leave us
about where we are now. For, of course, it is not by a gift
of turkeys on Thanksgiving Day that he proposes to convert the criminal, but by a true sympathy with each
one,—with him, among the rest, who lyingly tells the
world from the gallows that he has never been treated

kindly by a single mortal since he was born. But it is not
so easy a thing to sympathize with another, though you
may have the best disposition to do it. There is Dobson
over the hill. Have not you and I and all the world been
trying, ever since he was born, to sympathize with him?
(as doubtless he with us), and yet we have got no farther
than to send him to the House of Correction once at least;
and he, on the other hand, as I hear, has sent us to another place several times. This is the real state of things, as I
understand it, as least so far as James's remedies go. We
are now, alas! exercising what charity we actually have,
and new laws would not give us any more. But, perchance, we might make some improvements in the House
of Correction. You and I are Dobson; what will James do
for us?

Have you found at last in your wanderings a place
where the solitude is sweet?

What mountain are you camping on nowadays?
Though I had a good time at the mountains, I confess
that the journey did not bear any fruit that I know of. I
did not expect it would. The mode of it was not simple
and adventurous enough. You must first have made an
infinite demand, and not unreasonably, but after a corresponding outlay, have an all-absorbing purpose, and at
the same time that your feet bear you hither and thither,
travel much more in imagination.

To let the mountains slide,—live at home like a traveler. It should not be in vain that these things are shown us
from day to day. Is not each withered leaf that I see in
my walks something which I have traveled to find?—
traveled, who can tell how far? What a fool he must be
who thinks that his El Dorado is anywhere but where he
lives!

We are always, methinks, in some kind of ravine,
though our bodies may walk the smooth streets of
Worcester. Our souls (I use this word for want of a better)
are ever perched on its rocky sides, overlooking that lowland. (What a more than Tuckerman's Ravine is the body
itself, in which the "soul" is encamped, when you come
to look into it! However, eagles always have chosen such
places for their eyries.)

Thus is it ever with your fair cities of the plain. Their streets may be paved with silver and gold, and six carriages roll abreast in them, but the real *homes* of the citizens are in the Tuckerman's ravines which ray out from that centre into the mountains round about, one for each man, woman, and child. The masters of life have so ordered it. That is their *beau-ideal* of a country seat. There is no danger of being *tuckered* out before you get to it.

So we live in Worcester and in Concord, each man taking his exercise regularly in his ravine, like a lion in his cage, and sometimes spraining his ankle there. We have very few clear days, and a great many small plagues which keep us busy. Sometimes, I suppose, you hear a neighbor halloo (Brown, may be) and think it is a bear. Nevertheless, on the whole, we think it very grand and exhilarating, this ravine life. It is a capital advantage withal, living so high, the excellent drainage of that city of God. Routine is but a shallow and insignificant sort of ravine, such as the ruts are, the conduits of puddles. But these ravines are the source of mighty streams, precipitous, icy, savage, as they are, haunted by bears and loup-cerviers; there are born not only Sacos and Amazons, but prophets who will redeem the world. The at last smooth and fertilizing water at which nations drink and navies supply themselves begins with melted glaciers, and burst thunder-spouts. Let us pray that, if we are not flowing through some Mississippi valley which we fertilize,—and it is not likely we are,—we may know ourselves shut in between grim and mighty mountain walls amid the clouds, falling a thousand feet in a mile, through dwarfed fir and spruce, over the rocky insteps of slides, being exercised in our minds, and so developed.

Concord, September 26, 1859.

Mr. Blake,—I am not sure that I am in a fit mood to write to you, for I feel and think rather too much like a business man, having some very irksome affairs to attend to these months and years on account of my family. This is the way I am serving King Admetus, confound him! If

it were not for my relations, I would let the wolves prey
on his flocks to their bellies' content. Such fellows you
have to deal with! herdsmen of some other king, or of the
same, who tell no tale, but in the sense of counting their
flocks, and then lie drunk under a hedge. How is your
grist ground? Not by some murmuring stream, while you
lie dreaming on the bank; but, it seems, you must take
hold with your hands, and shove the wheel round. You
can't depend on streams, poor feeble things! You can't
depend on worlds, left to themselves; but you've got to oil
them and goad them along. In short, you've got to carry
on two farms at once,—the farm on the earth and the
farm in your mind. Those Crimean and Italian battles
were mere boys' play,—they are the scrapes into which
truants get. But what a battle a man must fight everywhere to maintain his standing army of thoughts, and
march with them in orderly array through the always
hostile country! How many enemies there are to sane
thinking! Every soldier has succumbed to them before he
enlists for those other battles. Men may sit in chambers,
seemingly safe and sound, and yet despair, and turn out
at last only hollowness and dust within, like a Dead Sea
apple. A standing army of numerous, brave, and well-
disciplined thoughts, and you at the head of them,
marching straight to your goal,—how to bring this about
is the problem, and Scott's Tactics will not help you to it.
Think of a poor fellow begirt only with a sword-belt, and
no such staff of athletic thoughts! his brains rattling as he
walks and *talks!* These are your prætorian guard. It is
easy enough to maintain a family, or a state, but it is hard
to maintain these children of your brain (or say, rather,
these guests that trust to enjoy your hospitality), they
make such great demands; and yet, he who does only the
former, and loses the power to *think* originally, or as only
he ever can, fails miserably. Keep up the fires of thought,
and all will go well.

Zouaves?—pish! How you can overrun a country,
climb any rampart, and carry any fortress, with an army
of *alert* thoughts!—thoughts that send their bullets home
to heaven's door,—with which you can *take* the whole
world, without paying for it, or robbing anybody. See,

the conquering hero comes! You *fail* in your thoughts, or you *prevail* in your thoughts only. Provided you *think* well, the heavens falling, or the earth gaping, will be music for you to march by. No foe can ever see you, or you him; you cannot so much as *think* of him. Swords have no edges, bullets no penetration, for such a contest. In your mind must be a liquor which will dissolve the world whenever it is dropt in it. There is no universal solvent but this, and all things together cannot saturate it. It will hold the universe in solution, and yet be as translucent as ever. The vast machine may indeed roll over our toes, and we not know it, but it would rebound and be staved to pieces like an empty barrel, if it should strike fair and square on the smallest and least angular of a man's thoughts.

You seem not to have taken Cape Cod the right way. I think that you should have persevered in walking on the beach and on the bank, even to the land's end, however soft, and so, by long knocking at Ocean's gate, have gained admittance at last,—better, if separately, and in a storm, not knowing where you would sleep by night, or eat by day. Then you should have given a day to the sand behind Provincetown, and ascended the hills there, and been blown on considerably. I hope that you like to remember the journey better than you did to make it.

I have been confined at home all this year, but I am not aware that I have grown any rustier than was to be expected. One while I explored the bottom of the river pretty extensively. I have engaged to read a lecture to Parker's society on the 9th of October next.

I am off—a barberrying.

Concord, October 31, 1859.

MR. BLAKE,—I spoke to my townsmen last evening on "The Character of Captain Brown, now in the clutches of the slaveholder." I should like to speak to any company at Worcester who may wish to hear me; and will come if only my expenses are paid. I think we should express ourselves at once, while Brown is alive. The sooner the better. Perhaps Higginson may like to have a meeting.

Wednesday evening would be a good time. The people here are deeply interested in the matter. Let me have an answer as soon as may be.

P.S.—I may be engaged toward the end of the week.

HENRY D. THOREAU.

Concord, May 20, 1860.

MR. BLAKE,—I must endeavor to pay some of my debts to you. To begin where we left off, then.

The presumption is that *we* are always the same; our opportunities, and Nature herself, fluctuating. Look at mankind. No great difference between two, apparently; perhaps the same height, and breadth, and weight; and yet, to the man who sits most east, this life is a weariness, routine, dust and ashes, and he drowns his imaginary *cares* (!) (a sort of friction among his vital organs) in a bowl. But to the man who sits most west, his *contemporary* (!), it is a field for all noble endeavors, an elysium, the dwelling-place of heroes and demigods. The former complains that he has a thousand affairs to attend to; but he does not realize that his affairs (though they may be a thousand) and he are one.

Men and boys are learning all kinds of trades but how to make *men* of themselves. They learn to make houses; but they are not so well housed, they are not so contented in their houses, as the woodchucks in their holes. What is the use of a house if you have n't got a tolerable planet to put it on?—if you cannot tolerate the planet it is on? Grade the ground first. If a man believes and expects great things of himself, it makes no odds where you put him, or what you show him (of course *you* cannot put him anywhere, nor show him anything), he will be surrounded by grandeur. He is in the condition of a healthy and hungry man, who says to himself,—How sweet this crust is! If he despairs of himself, then Tophet is his dwelling-place, and he is in the condition of a sick man who is disgusted with the fruits of finest flavor.

Whether he sleeps or wakes,—whether he runs or walks,—whether he uses a microscope or a telescope, or his naked eye,—a man never discovers anything, never overtakes anything, or leaves anything behind, but himself. Whatever he says or does, he merely reports himself. If he is in love, he *loves;* if he is in heaven, he *enjoys;* if he is in hell, he *suffers.* It is his condition that determines his locality.

The principal, the only thing a man makes, is his condition of fate. Though commonly he does not know it, nor put up a sign to this effect, "My own destiny made and mended here." [Not *yours.*] He is a master-workman in the business. He works twenty-four hours a day at it, and gets it done. Whatever else he neglects or botches, no man was ever known to neglect this work. A great many pretend to make *shoes* chiefly, and would scout the idea that they make the hard times which they experience.

Each reaching and aspiration is an instinct with which all nature consists and coöperates, and therefore it is not in vain. But alas! each relaxing and desperation is an instinct too. To be active, well, happy, implies rare courage. To be ready to fight in a duel or a battle implies desperation, or that you hold your life cheap.

If you take this life to be simply what old religious folks pretend (I mean the effete, gone to seed in a drought, mere human galls stung by the devil once), then all your joy and serenity is reduced to grinning and bearing it. The fact is, you have got to take the world on your shoulders like Atlas, and "put along" with it. You will do this for an idea's sake, and your success will be in proportion to your devotion to ideas. It may make your back ache occasionally, but you will have the satisfaction of hanging it or twirling it to suit yourself. Cowards suffer, heroes enjoy. After a long day's walk with it, pitch it into a hollow place, sit down and eat your luncheon. Unexpectedly, by some immortal thoughts, you will be compensated. The bank whereon you sit will be a fragrant and flowery one, and your world in the hollow a sleek and light gazelle.

Where is the "unexplored land" but in our own untried enterprises? To an adventurous spirit any place—London, New York, Worcester, or his own yard—is "unexplored land," to seek which Fremont and Kane travel so far. To a sluggish and defeated spirit even the Great Basin and

the Polaris are trivial places. If they can get there (and,
indeed, they are there now), they will want to sleep, and
give it up, just as they always do. These are the regions of
the Known and of the Unknown. What is the use of going
right over the old track again? There is an adder in the
path which your own feet have worn. You must make
tracks into the Unknown. That is what you have your
board and clothes for. Why do you ever mend your
clothes, unless that, wearing them, you may mend your
ways? Let us sing.

Concord, November 4, 1860.

MR. BLAKE,—I am glad to hear any particulars of your
excursion. As for myself, I looked out for you somewhat
on that Monday, when, it appears, you passed Monadnoc;
turned my glass upon several parties that were ascending
the mountain half a mile on one side of us. In short, I
came as near to seeing you as you to seeing me. I have no
doubt that we should have had a good time if you had
come, for I had, all ready, two good spruce houses, in
which you could stand up, complete in all respects, half a
mile apart, and you and B. could have lodged by yourselves in one, if not with us.

We made an excellent beginning of our mountain life.
You may remember that the Saturday previous was a
stormy day. Well, we went up in the rain,—wet through,—
and found ourselves in a cloud there at mid-afternoon, in
no situation to look about for the best place for a camp.
So I proceeded at once, through the cloud, to that memorable stone, "chunk yard," in which we made our humble
camp once, and there, after putting our packs under a
rock, having a good hatchet, I proceeded to build a substantial house, which Channing declared the handsomest
he ever saw. (He never camped out before, and was, no
doubt, prejudiced in its favor.) This was done about dark,
and by that time we were nearly as wet as if we had
stood in a hogshead of water. We then built a fire before
the door, directly on the site of our little camp of two
years ago, and it took a long time to burn through its
remains to the earth beneath. Standing before this, and

turning round slowly, like meat that is roasting, we were as dry, if not drier, than ever, after a few hours, and so at last, we "turned in."

This was a great deal better than going up there in fair weather, and having no adventure (not knowing how to appreciate either fair weather or foul) but dull, commonplace sleep in a useless house, and before a comparatively useless fire,—such as we get every night. Of course we thanked our stars, when we saw them, which was about midnight, that they had seemingly withdrawn for a season. We had the mountain all to ourselves that afternoon and night. There was nobody going up that day to engrave his name on the summit, nor to gather blueberries. The genius of the mountains saw us starting from Concord, and it said, There come two of our folks. Let us get ready for them—Get up a serious storm, that will send a-packing these holiday guests. (They may have their say another time.) Let us receive them with true mountain hospitality,—kill the fatted cloud. Let them know the value of a spruce roof, and of a fire of dead spruce stumps. Every bush dripped tears of joy at our advent. Fire did its best, and received our thanks. What could fire have done in fair weather? Spruce roof got its share of our blessings. And then, such a view of the wet rocks, with the wet lichens on them, as we had the next morning, but did not get again!

We and the mountain had a sound season, as the saying is. How glad we were to be wet, in order that we might be dried! How glad we were of the storm which made our house seem like a new home to us! This day's experience was indeed lucky, for we did not have a thundershower during all our stay. Perhaps our host reserved this attention in order to attempt us to come again.

Our next house was more substantial still. One side was rock, good for durability; the floor the same; and the roof which I made would have upheld a horse. I stood on it to do the shingling.

I noticed, when I was at the White Mountains last, several nuisances which render traveling thereabouts unpleasant. The chief of these was the mountain houses. I might have supposed that the main attraction of that region, even to citizens, lay in its wildness and unlikeness to the city, and yet they make it as much like the city as they can afford to. I heard that the Crawford House was lighted with gas, and had a large saloon, with its band of music, for dancing. But give me a spruce house made in the rain.

An old Concord farmer tells me that he ascended Monadnoc once, and danced on the top. How did that happen? Why, he being up there, a party of young men and women came up, bringing boards and a fiddler; and, having laid down the boards, they made a level floor, on which they danced to the music of the fiddle. I suppose the tune was "Excelsior." This reminds me of the fellow who climbed to the top of a very high spire, stood upright on the ball, and hurrahed for—what? Why, for Harrison and Tyler. That's the kind of sound which most ambitious people emit when they culminate. They are wont to be singularly frivolous in the thin atmosphere; they can't contain themselves, though our comfort and their safety require it; it takes the pressure of many atmospheres to do this; and hence they helplessly evaporate there. It would seem that as they ascend, they breathe shorter and shorter, and, at each *expiration,* some of their wits leave them, till, when they reach the pinnacle, they are so light-headed as to be fit only to show how the wind sits. I suspect that Emerson's criticism called "Monadnoc" was inspired, not by remembering the inhabitants of New Hampshire as they are in the valleys, so much as by meeting some of them on the mountain top.

After several nights' experience, Channing came to the conclusion that he was "lying outdoors," and inquired what was the largest beast that might nibble his legs there. I fear that he did not improve all the night, as he might have done, to sleep. I had asked him to go and spend a week there. We spent five nights, being gone six days, for C. suggested that six working days made a week, and I saw that he was ready to *decamp.* However, he found his account in it as well as I.

We were seen to go up in the rain, grim and silent, like two genii of the storm, by Fassett's men or boys; but we were never identified afterward, though we were the subject of some conversation which we overheard. Five hundred persons at least came on to the mountain while we were there, but not one found our camp. We saw one party of three ladies and two gentlemen spread their blankets and spend the night on the top, and heard them converse; but they did not know that they had neighbors who were comparatively old settlers. We spared them the chagrin which that knowledge would have caused them, and let them print their story in a newspaper accordingly.

Yes, to meet men on an honest and simple footing, meet with rebuffs, suffer from sore feet, as you did,—ay, and from a sore heart, as perhaps you also did,—all that is excellent. What a pity that that young prince could not enjoy a little of the legitimate experience of traveling— be dealt with simply and truly, though rudely. He might have been invited to some hospitable house in the country, had his bowl of bread and milk set before him, with a clean pinafore; been told that there were the punt and the fishing-rod, and he could amuse himself as he chose; might have swung a few birches, dug out a woodchuck, and had a regular good time, and finally been sent to bed with the boys,—and so never have been introduced to Mr. Everett at all. I have no doubt that this would have been a far more memorable and valuable experience than he got.

The snow-clad summit of Mount Washington must have been a very interesting sight from Wachusett. How wholesome winter is, seen far or near; how good, above all mere sentimental, warm-blooded, short-lived, soft-hearted, *moral* goodness, commonly so-called. Give me the goodness which has forgotten its own deeds,—which God has seen to be good, and let be. None of your *just made perfect*,—pickled eels! All that will save them will be their picturesqueness, as with blasted trees. Whatever is, and is not ashamed to be, is good. I value no moral goodness or greatness unless it is good or great, even as that snowy peak is. Pray, how could thirty feet of bowels improve it? Nature is goodness crystallized. You looked into the land of promise. Whatever beauty we behold, the more it is distant, serene, and cold, the purer and more durable it is. It is better to warm ourselves with ice than with fire.

Tell Brown that he sent me more than the price of the book, viz., a word from himself, for which I am greatly his debtor.

Concord, May 3, 1861.

MR. BLAKE,—I am still as much an invalid as when you and Brown were here, if not more of one, and at this rate there is danger that the cold weather may come again, before I get over my bronchitis. The doctor accordingly tells me that I must "clear out" to the West Indies, or elsewhere,—he does not seem to care much where. But I decide against the West Indies, on account of their muggy heat in the summer, and the South of Europe, on account of the expense of time and money, and have at last concluded that it will be most expedient for me to try the air of Minnesota, say somewhere about St. Paul's. I am only waiting to be well enough to start. Hope to get off within a week or ten days.

The inland air may help me at once, or it may not. At any rate, I am so much of an invalid, that I shall have to study my comfort in traveling to a remarkable degree,— stopping to rest, etc., etc., if need be. I think to get a through ticket to Chicago, with liberty to stop frequently on the way, making my first stop of consequence at Niagara Falls, several days or a week, at a private boarding-house; then a night or day at Detroit; and as much at Chicago as my health may require. At Chicago I can decide at what point (Fulton, Dunleith, or another) to strike the Mississippi, and take a boat to St. Paul's.

I trust to find a private boarding-house in one or various agreeable places in that region, and spend my time there. I expect, and shall be prepared, to be gone three months; and I would like to return by a different route,— perhaps Mackinaw and Montreal.

I have thought of finding a companion, of course, yet not seriously, because I had no right to offer myself as a companion to anybody, having such a peculiarly private and all-absorbing but miserable business as *my* health, and not altogether *his*, to attend to, causing me to stop here and go there, etc., etc., unaccountably.

Nevertheless, I have just now decided to let you know of my intention, thinking it barely possible that you might like to make a part or the whole of this journey at the same time, and that perhaps your own health may be such as to be benefited by it.

Pray let me know if such a statement offers any temptations to you. I write in great haste for the mail, and must omit all the moral.

[Thoreau died on May 6, 1862.]

REFORM AND THE REFORMERS

Thoreau did not publish this essay in his lifetime. At his death he left two manuscript drafts of it, however; and at about the time he was writing A Week in 1848, had apparently attempted to develop a finished essay. The manuscripts are now preserved in the Houghton Library of Harvard University, and from them this text was edited. It is not clear whom among the reformers of his time he was thinking of when he argued that persons feeling the urge to reform others should begin with themselves, but the most plausible candidates are William Lloyd Garrison and his followers who occasionally visited Concord and the Thoreau home. The text reproduced here is from Reform Papers *(1973) in the Princeton Edition, edited by Wendell Glick.*

THE REFORMERS ARE NO DOUBT the true ancestors of the next generation; the Conservative belongs to a decaying family, and has not learned that he who seeks to save his 'life' shall lose it. Both are sick, but the one is already convalescent. His disease is not organic but acute, and he looks forward to coming springs with hope. He is not sick of any incurable disorder, of plague or consumption; but of tradition and conformity and infidelity; but the other is still taking his bitters and quack medicines patiently, and will grow worse yet. The heads of conservatives have a puny and deficient look, a certain callowness and concavity, as if they were prematurely exposed on one or both sides, or were made to lie or pack together, as when several nuts are formed under the same burr where only one should have been. We wonder to see such a head wear a whole hat. Such as these naturally herd together for mutual protection. They say *We* and *Our*, as if they had never been assured of an individual existence. *Our* Indian policy; *our* coast defences, *our* national character. They are what are called public men, fashionable men, ambitious men, chaplains of the army or navy; men of property, standing and respectability, for the most part, and in all cases created by society. Sometimes even they are embarked in "Great Causes" which have been stranded on the shores of society in a previous age, carrying them through with a kind of reflected and traditionary nobleness, certainly disinterestedness. The Conservative has many virtues which the Reformer has not—ofttimes a singular and unexpected liberality and courtesy, a decided practicalness and reverence for facts, and with a little less irritability, or more indifference would be the more tolerable companion. He is the steward of society, and in this office at least is faithful and generous. He is a dutiful son but a tyrannical father, and does not foresee that unimaginable epoch when the rising generation will have attained to a level with the risen. Rather he is himself a son all his days, and never arrives at such maturity as to be informed that he and such as he are now mankind and the latest generation, the occupants and proprietors of the globe, but he still feels it to be his chief duty to preserve the law and order and institutions which he finds existing.

It is remarkable how well men train. The teamster rolls out of his cradle into a Tom-and-Jerry—and goes at once to look after his team—to fodder and water his horses, without standing agape at his position. What is the destiny of man, compared with the shipping interests? What does he care for—his creator? doesn't he drive for Squire Make-a-Stir?

The ladies of the land with equal bravery are weavers of toilet cushions and tidies not to betray too green an interest in their fates. Men now take snuff into their noses, but if they had been so advised in season, they would have put it into their ears and eyes. They may gravely deny this, but do not believe them.

In the midst of all this disorder and imperfection in human affairs which he would rather avoid to think of comes the Reformer, the impersonation of disorder and imperfection; to heal and reform them; seeking to discover the divine order and conform to it; and earnestly asking the cooperation of men.

No doubt the evil is great and manifest, and something must certainly be done; and his zeal is in proportion to the urgency of the case—but I know of few radicals as yet who are radical enough, and have not got this name rather by meddling with the exposed roots of innocent institutions than with their own.

The disease and disorder in society are wont to be referred to the false relations in which men live one to another, but strictly speaking there can be no such thing as a false relation; if the condition of the things related is true. False relations grow out of false conditions. The inmate of a poorhouse would be more pauper still on a desolate island, and the convict would find his prison and prison discipline there.

It is not the worst reason why the reform should be a private and individual enterprise, that perchance the evil may be private also. From what southern plains comes up the voice of wailing,—under what latitudes reside the heathen to whom we would send light,—and who is that intemperate and brutal man whom he would redeem?

Now, if anything ail a man so that he does not perform his functions; especially if his digestion is poor, though he may have considerable nervous strength left; if he has failed in all his undertakings hitherto; if he has committed some heinous sin and partially repents, what does he do? He sets about reforming the world. Do ye hear it, ye Woloffs, ye Patagonians, ye Tartars, ye Nez Percés? The world is going to be reformed, formed once for all. Presto—Change! Methinks I hear the glad tidings spreading over the green prairies of the west; over the silent South

American pampas, parched African deserts, and stretching Siberian versts; through the populous Indian and Chinese villages, along the Indus, the Ganges, and Hydaspes.

There is no reformer on the globe, no such philanthropic—benevolent and charitable man—now engaged in any good work anywhere, sorely afflicted by the sight of misery around him, and animated by the desire to relieve it, who would not instantly and unconsciously sign off from these pure labors, and betake himself to purer, if he had but righted some obscure, and perhaps unrecognized private grievance. Let but the spring come to him, let the morning rise over his couch, and he will forsake his generous companions, without apology or explanation!

The Reformer who comes recommending any institution or system to the adoption of men, must not rely solely on logic and argument, or on eloquence and oratory for his success, but see that he represents one pretty perfect institution in himself, the centre and circumference of all others, an erect man.

I ask of all Reformers, of all who are recommending Temperance—Justice—Charity—Peace, the Family, Community or Associative life, not to give us their theory and wisdom only, for these are no proof, but to carry around with them each a small specimen of his own manufactures, and to despair of ever recommending anything of which a small sample at least cannot be exhibited: that the Temperance man let me know the savor of Temperance, if it be good, the Just man permit to enjoy the blessings of liberty while with him, the Community man allow me to taste the sweets of the Community life in his society.

I cannot bear to be told to wait for good results, I pine as much for good beginnings. We never come to final results, and it is too late to start from perennial beginnings.

But alas, when we ask the schemer to show us the material of which his structure is to be built. He exhibits only fair looking words, resolute and solid words for the underpinning, convenient and homely words for the body of the edifice, poems and flights of the imagination for the dome and cupola.

Men know very well how to distinguish barren words

from those which are cousin to a deed, and the promising
or threatening speaker is only rated at his faculty and
resolution to do what he says. The phlegmatic audience
which sits near the doors know that the speaker does not
mean to abolish property or dissolve the family tie, or do
without human governments all over the world tonight,
but that simply, he has agreed to be the speaker and—
they have agreed to be the audience. They may chance
to know that the lecturer against the use of money is paid
for his lecture, and that is the precept which they hear
and believe, and they have a great deal of sympathy with
him.

After all the peace lectures and non resistance meetings
it was never yet learned from them how any of the
speakers would conduct in an emergency, because a very
important disputant, one Mr. Resistance was not present
to offer his arguments.

There are not only books, but lectures and sermons of
fiction, whether written or extemporaneous. The modern
Reformers are a class of *improvvisânti* more wonderful
and amusing than the Italians.

What the prophets even have said is forgotten, and the
oracles are decayed, but what heroes and saints have
done is still remembered, and posterity will tell it again
and again.

We rarely see the Reformer who is fairly launched in
his enterprise, bringing about the right state of things
with hearty and effective tugs, and not rather preparing
and grading the way through the minds of the people.
What if the community were to pull altogether says he!
—Aye, what if two—what if one even were to work harmoniously and with all his energies! say I. No wonder you
plead for my cooperation—I could exert myself considerably. It would be worth the while methinks to have my
traces hitched to some good institution.

There certainly can be no greater folly than for men to
set about to prove a truth at their leisure who have no
other business with it. As if one were to proclaim that he
was going a long journey, and because one of his neighbors was inattentive or did not believe it, should put it
off. To the man of industry and work it is not quite essen-

tial that I should *think* with him. When my neighbor is going to build a house, whether for me or for himself, he does not come to me and reproach or pity me for living in a shed, but he digs the cellar and raises the frame, and makes haste to get the roof done, that he may do the inside-work more comfortably, and he knows very well what assistance he can count upon in these labors.

For the most part by simply agreeing in opinion with the preacher and Reformer I defend myself and get rid of him, for he really asks for no sympathy with deeds,— and this trick it would be well for the irritable Conservative to know and practise.

The great benefactors of their race have been single and singular and not masses of men. Whether in poetry or history it is the same: Minerva—Ceres—Neptune—Prometheus—Socrates—Christ—Luther—Columbus—Arkwright.

There is no objection to action in societies or communities when it is the individual using the society as his instrument, rather than the society using the individual. While one's inspiration is so high and pure as to be necessarily solitary and not to be made a subject of sympathy or congratulation, he may safely use any instrument in his way, whether wood or iron or masses of men. But when the vote of the society rises to a level with his own prayers, and its resolution in the least confirms his own, he may suspect himself, or he may suspect his companions. There have been meetings, religious, political and reformatory, to which men came a hundred miles—though all they had to offer were—some resolutions! What becomes of resolutions that have been offered?

In every society there is or was at least one individual, its founder and leader, who did not belong to it but who imparted to it whatever life and efficiency it had, and sad indeed is the condition of that society, and it is the condition of most, which is deprived of its head—and soul—for the members can still vote,—and as it were by force of galvanism, a spasmodic action be kept up in the body, and men call it life, and expect virtue and character from senseless nerves and muscles. Such societies, as they prize life, will have recourse to dinners and tea-parties that the members may not utterly fail for want of a belly also.

Consider, after all, how very private and silent an affair it is to lead a life—that we do not consider our duties, or the actions of our life, as in a caucus or convention of men, where the subject has been before the meeting a long time, and many resolutions have been proposed and passed, and now one speaker has the floor and then another, and the subject is fairly under discussion; but the convention where our most private and intimate affairs are discussed is very thinly attended, almost we are not there ourselves, that is the go-to-meeting part of us. It is very still, and few resolutions get passed. Few words are spoken, and the hours are not counted!

Next and nearest to that unfortunate man even whom we would stand by in our philanthropy is the mystery of his life. It is nearer than cold or hunger for they are but the outside of it—it is between him and them, and do what we will, we must leave him alone with that.

The information which the gods vouchsafe to give us is never concerning anything which we wished to know. We are not wise enough to put a question to them. Tell me some truth about society and you will annihilate it. What though we are its ailing members and prisoners. We cannot always be detained by your measures for reform. All that is called hindrance without is but occasion within. The prisoner who is free in spirit, on whose innocent life some rays of light and hope still fall, will not delay to be a reformer of prisons, an inventor of superior prison disciplines, but walks forth free on the path by which those rays penetrated to his cell. Has the Green Mountain boy made no better nor more thrilling discovery than that the church is rotten and the state corrupt? Thank heaven, we have not to choose our calling out of those enterprises which society has to offer. Is he then indeed called, who chooses to what he is called? Obey your calling rather, and it will not be whither your neighbors and kind friends and patrons expect or desire, but be true nevertheless, and choose not, nor go whither they call you. "Thy lot or portion of life, is seeking after thee; therefore be at rest from seeking after it."

From the side to which all eyes are turned, and the hue and cry leads, from the effort which the state abets, and the church prays for, the least profitable result comes, the least performance issues.

We would have some pure product of man's hands, some pure labor, some life got in this old trade of getting a living—some work done which shall not be a mending, a cobbling, a reforming. Show me the mountain boy, the city boy, who never heard of an abuse, who has not *chosen* his calling. It is the delight of the ages, the free labor of man, even the creative and beautiful arts.

> Be sure your fate
> Doth keep apart its state;
> Not linked with any band,
> Even the nobles of the land;
> In tented fields with cloth of gold
> No place doth hold,
> But is more chivalrous than they are,
> And sigheth for a nobler war;
> A finer strain its trumpet sings,
> A brighter gleam its armor flings.
> The life that I aspire to live
> No man proposeth me,
> Only the promise of my heart
> Wears its emblazonry.

How long shall vice give a home to virtue? One generation abandons the enterprises of another. Many an institution which was thought to be an essential part of the order of society, has, in the true order of events, been left like a stranded vessel on the sand.

When a zealous Reformer would fain discourse to me, I would have him consider first if he has anything to say to me. All simple and necessary speech between men is sweet; but it takes calamity, it takes death or great good fortune commonly to bring them together. We are sages and proud to speak when we are the bearers of great news, even though it be hard; to tell a man of the welfare of his kindred in foreign parts, or even that his house is on fire, is a great good fortune, and seems to relate us to him by a worthier tie.

It is a great blessing to have to do with men, to be called to them as simply as into the field of your occupation. It refreshes and invigorates us. But this happiness is rare. For the most part we can only treat one another to our wit, our good manners and equanimity, and though we have eagles to give we demand of each other only coppers. We pray that our companion will demand of us truth, sincerity, love and noble behavior, for now these virtues lie impossible to us, and we only know them by their names. Only lovers know the value and magnanimity of truth, while traders prize a cheap honesty, and neighbors and acquaintances a cheap civility.

If you have nothing to say let me have your silence, for that is good and fertile. Silence is the ambrosial night in the intercourse of men in which their sincerity is recruited and takes deeper root.—There are such vices as frivolity, garrulity, and verbosity, not to mention prophanity, growing out of the abuse of speech which does not belong wholly to antiquity, and none have imparted a more cheerless aspect to society.

A man must serve another and a better use than any he can consciously render. Every class and order in the universe is the heaven of certain gifts to men. There is a whole class of musk bearing animals, and each flower has its peculiar odor. And all these together go to make the general wholesome and invigorating atmosphere. So each man should take care to emit his fragrance, and after all perform some such office as hemlock boughs, or dried and healing herbs. Though you are a Reformer we want not your reasons, your good roots and foundations—nor your uprightness and benevolence which are your stem and leaves—but we want the flower and fruit of the man—that some fragrance at least as of fresh spring life can be wafted over from thee to me. This is consolation and that charity that hides a multitude of sins. Our companion must be a sort of appreciable wealth to us or at least make us sensible of our own riches—in his degree an apostle á Mercury, á Ceres, á Minerva, the bearer of diverse gifts to us. He must bring me the morning light untarnished, and the evening red undimmed. There must be the hilarity of spring in his mirth, the summer's serenity in his joy, the autumnal ripeness in his wisdom, and the repose and abundance of winter in his silence. He should impart his courage and not his despair; his health and ease, and not his disease, and take care that this does not spread by contagion.

It is rare that we are able to impart wealth to our fellows, and do not surround them with our own cast off griefs as an atmosphere, and name it sympathy. If we would indeed reform mankind by truly Indian, botanic, magnetic, or *natural* means, let us strive first to be as simple and well as nature ourselves.

I would say therefore to the anxious speculator and philanthropist—Let us dispel the clouds which hang over our own brows—take up a little life into your pores, endeavor to encourage the flow of sap in your veins, find your soil, strike root and grow—Apollo's waters and God will give the increase. Help to clothe the human field with green. Be green and flourishing plants in God's nursery, and not such complaining bleeding trees as Dante saw in the Infernal Regions.

If your branches wither, send out your fibres into every kingdom of nature for its contribution—lift up your boughs into the heavens for etherial and starry influences, let your roots like those of the willow wander wider, deeper, to some moist and fertile spot in the earth, and make firm your trunk against the elements.

Be fast rooted withal in your native soil of originality and independence, your virgin-mould of unexhausted strength and fertility—Nor suffer yourself ever to be transplanted again into the foreign and ungenial regions of tradition and conformity, or the lean and sandy soils of public opinion.

What! to be blown about, a creature of the affections, preaching love and good will and charity, with these tender fibres all bare in a cold world, and not a brother kind enough to throw a spade-full of earth over them! Better try what virtue there is in sand even, and cover your roots with the first exhausted soil you can find.

Who shall tell what blossoms, what fruits, what public and private advantage may push up through this rind we call a man? The traveller may stand by him as a perennial fountain in the desert and slake his thirst forever.

The wind rustling the leaves, the brags of some chil-

dren have thrilled me more than the lives of the greatest
and holiest men. What idle sorrow and stereotyped despair in the saints! What wavering performance in the
heroes! Even the prophets and redeemers have rather
consoled the fears than satisfied the free demands and
hopes of man! We know nowhere recorded a simple and
irrepressible satisfaction with the gift of life, a memorable and unbribed praise of God. So long as the Reformers
are earnest enough and pleased with their own conceptions, they may entertain me, but when the time comes
that their theme is exhausted, and only the sad alternative is left to do the things they have said; and they
would rather that I should do them, then they are intoler-
able companions.

I like the old world and I like the new—winter and
summer, hay and grass,—but the death that presumes to
give laws to life, and persists in affirming essential disease
and disorder to the child who has just begun to bathe his
senses and his understanding in the perception of order
and beauty—that perseveres in maturing its schemes of
life till its last days are come, is not to be compared to
anything in nature. The growing man or youth, is a fact
which commonly we do not enough allow for in our speculations—but to remember which would be fatal to many
a fine theory. Speak for yourself, old man. When we are
oppressed by the heat and turmoil of the noon, we should
remember that the sun which scorches us with his beams,
is gilding the hills of morning and awaking the woodland
quires for other men. So too it must not be forgotten, the
evening exhibits in the still rear of day a beauty to which
the morning and the noon are strangers.

It is hard to make those who have talked much, especially preachers and lecturers, deepen their speech, and
give it fresh sincerity and significance. It will be a long
time before they understand what you mean. They will
wonder if you don't value fluency. But the drains flow.
Turn your back, and wait till you hear their words ring
solid, and they will have cause to thank you! How infinitely trackless yet passable are we. Is not our own interi-
or white on the chart? Inward is a direction which no

traveller has taken. Inward is the bourne which all travellers seek and from which none desire to return. There are the sources of the Nile and Niger.

Every man is the lord of a realm beside which the earthly empire of the Czars is but a petty state—with its ocean borders—its mountain ranges, and its trackless paradises of unfallen nature. And, O ye Reformers! if the good Gods have given ye any high ray of truth to be wrought into life, here in your own realms without let or hindrance is the application to be made.

Those who dwell in Oregon and the far west are not so solitary as the enterprising and independent thinker, applying his discoveries to his own life. This is the way we would see a man striving with his axe and kettle to take up his abode. To this rich soil should the New Englander wend his way. Here is Wisconsin and the farthest west. It is simple, independent, original, natural life.

Most whom I meet in the streets are, so to speak, outward bound, they live out and out, are going and coming, looking before and behind, all out of doors and in the air. I would fain see them inward bound, retiring in and in, farther and farther every day, and when I inquired for them I should not hear, that they had gone abroad anywhere, to Rondont or Sackets Harbor, but that they had withdrawn deeper within the folds of being.

England and France, Spain and Portugal, Gold Coast and Slave Coast, all front upon this private sea, but no bark from them has ventured out of sight of land,—though it is without a doubt the direct way to India.

I would say then to my vagrant countrymen—Go not to any foreign theater for spectacles, but consider first that there is nothing which can delight or astonish the eyes, but you may discover it all in yourselves. One hastens to Southern Africa perchance to chase the giraffe; but that is not the game he would be after. How long, pray, would a man hunt giraffes, if he could?—What was the meaning of that Exploring Expedition with all its parade and expense, but a recognition of the fact that there are continents and seas in the moral world to which every man is an inlet, yet unexplored by him; but that it is easier to sail many thousand miles through cold and

storms and savage cannibals, in a government ship, with
500 men and boys to steer and sail for one, than it is to
explore the private sea, the Atlantic and Pacific ocean of
one's being alone.

> *Erret, et extremos alter scrutetur Iberos.*
> *Plus habet hic vitae, plus habet ille viae.*

> Let the other wander and scrutinize the
>   outlandish Australians.
> This one has more of God, that one has
>   more of the road.

Here is demanded the eye and the nerve. Only the defeated and deserters go to the wars—Cowards that run
away and enlist. O ye Chivalry, ye could not fight a duel
with your lives, and so ye challenged a man!

I met a pilgrim travel-worn, who could speak all
tongues and conform himself to the customs of all nations;—who carried a passport to all countries, and was
naturalized in all climes, who had vanquished all the chi-
meras and caused the Sphinx to go and dash her head
against a stone—who never retraced his steps nor returned to his native land and was reputed to have travelled further than all the travellers. He bore for device on
his shield these words only—"Know Thyself."

> "Direct your eye sight inward, and you'll find
>   A thousand regions in your mind
> Yet undiscovered. Travel them, and be
>   Expert in home-cosmographie."

Most revolutions in society have not power to interest,
still less alarm us, but tell me that our rivers are drying
up, or the genus pine dying out in the country, and I
might attend. Some events in history are more remarkable than important, like eclipses of the sun by which all
are attracted, but whose effects no one takes the trouble
to calculate. Revolutions are never sudden. The most important is commonly some silent and unobtrusive fact in
history. In the year 449 three Saxon cyules arrived on the
British coast. "Three scipen gode comen mid than flode."

To the sick the doctors wisely recommended a change
of air and scenery. Who chains me to this dull town?

There is this moment proposed to me every kind of life

that men lead anywhere or at any time—or that imagination can paint. By another spring I may be a mail carrier in Peru, or a South African planter, or a Siberian exile, or a Greenland whaler, or a settler on the Columbia River—or a Canton merchant, or a soldier in Mexico, or a mackerel fisher off Cape Sable, or a Robinson Crusoe in the Pacific, or a silent navigator of any sea.

How many are now standing on the European coast whom another spring will find located on the Wisconsin or the Sacramento!

I can move away from public opinion, from government, from religion, from education, from society. Shall I be reckoned a rateable poll in the county of Middlesex, or be rated at one spear under the palm trees of Guinea? Shall I raise corn and potatoes in Massachusetts, or figs and olives in Asia Minor? Sit out the day in my office in State street, or ride it out on the steppes of Tartary? For my Brobdingnag I may sail to Patagonia, for my Lilliput to Lapland. In Arabia and Persia my days' adventures may surpass the Arabian Nights entertainments. I may be a logger on the head waters of the Penobscot, to be recorded in fable hereafter as an amphibious river God by as sounding a name as Triton or Proteus.—Carry furs from Nootka to China and so be more renowned than Jason and his Golden Fleece, or join a South Sea exploring expedition to be recounted hereafter along with the Periplus of Hanno.

And how many more things may I do with which there is none to be compared!

Thank Heaven here is not all the world. The buckeye does not grow in New England, and the mocking bird is rarely heard here. Why should I fall behind the summer and the migrations of birds? Shall we not compete with the buffalo who keeps pace with the seasons, cropping the pastures of the Colorado till a greener and sweeter grass awaits him by the Yellowstone? The wild-goose is more a cosmopolite than we,—he breaks his fast in Canada—takes a luncheon in the Susquehanna, and plumes himself for the night in a Louisiana bayou. The pigeon carries an acorn in his crop from the King of Holland's to Mason and Dixon's Line. Yet we think if rail-fences are

pulled down and stone walls set up on our farms, bounds
are henceforth set to our lives and our fates decided. If
you are chosen town-clerk forsooth, you cannot go to
Tierra del Fuego this summer.

But what would all this activity amount to—?

> Goosey goosey gander
> Where shall I wander?
> Up stairs down stairs
> In a lady's chamber?

Shall we not stretch our legs?—Why shall we pause this
side of sundown? We will not then be immigrants still
further into our native country. Let us start now on that
fartherest western way which does not pause at the Mississippi or the Pacific, pushing on by day and night, sun
down—moon down—stars down—and at last earth down
too.

RESISTANCE TO CIVIL GOVERNMENT

[CIVIL DISOBEDIENCE]

"Resistance to Civil Government," Thoreau's most famous essay, is considered by many to rank with John Stuart Mill's "On Liberty" as a classic statement of the relation of the individual to the state. On one level it can be read as Thoreau's personal response to his incarceration for refusing to pay his poll tax to support what he considered to be the immoral war with Mexico; but readers generally have construed it more broadly as a successful definition of the dividing line between the prerogatives of all governments and the basic rights of the governed. Moral principles, to Thoreau, are the private domain of the individual citizen, and governments are oppressive which attempt to legislate them. At the invitation of Elizabeth Peabody, Thoreau contributed this essay to the periodical Aesthetic Papers, *which expired in 1849 after its first issue. The second printing of the essay was in the posthumous* A Yankee in Canada, *with Anti-Slavery and Reform Papers (Boston, 1866), edited by Ellery Channing and Sophia Thoreau, where the title "Civil Disobedience" first appeared. Since no evidence has ever been discovered that Thoreau authorized the new title, and textual scholars do not alter an*

author's text in the absence of evidence that the author so wished, the name that Thoreau gave the essay in 1849 is the one used here. The text is that of Reform Papers (1973) *in the Princeton Edition, edited by Wendell Glick.*

I HEARTILY ACCEPT the motto,—"That government is best which governs least;" and I should like to see it acted up to more rapidly and systematically. Carried out, it finally amounts to this, which also I believe,—"That government is best which governs not at all;" and when men are prepared for it, that will be the kind of government which they will have. Government is at best but an expedient; but most governments are usually, and all governments are sometimes, inexpedient. The objections which have been brought against a standing army, and they are many and weighty, and deserve to prevail, may also at last be brought against a standing government. The standing army is only an arm of the standing government. The government itself, which is only the mode which the people have chosen to execute their will, is equally liable to be abused and perverted before the people can act through it. Witness the present Mexican war, the work of comparatively a few individuals using the standing government as their tool; for, in the outset, the people would not have consented to this measure.

This American government,—what is it but a tradition, though a recent one, endeavoring to transmit itself unimpaired to posterity, but each instant losing some of its integrity? It has not the vitality and force of a single living man; for a single man can bend it to his will. It is a sort of wooden gun to the people themselves; and, if ever they should use it in earnest as a real one against each other, it will surely split. But it is not the less necessary for this; for the people must have some complicated machinery or other, and hear its din, to satisfy that idea of government which they have. Governments show thus how successfully men can be imposed on, even impose on themselves, for their own advantage. It is excellent, we must all allow; yet this government never of itself furthered any enterprise, but by the alacrity with which it got out of its way. *It* does not keep the country free. *It* does not settle the West. *It* does not educate. The character inherent in the American people has done all that has been accomplished; and it would have done somewhat more, if the government had not sometimes got in its way. For government is an expedient by which men would fain succeed in letting one another alone; and, as has been said, when it is most expedient, the governed are most let alone by it. Trade and commerce, if they were not made of India rubber, would never manage to bounce over the obstacles which legislators are continually putting in their way; and, if one were to judge these men wholly by the effects of their actions, and not partly by their intentions, they would deserve to be classed and punished with those mischievous persons who put obstructions on the railroads.

But, to speak practically and as a citizen, unlike those who call themselves no-government men, I ask for, not at once no government, but *at once* a better government. Let every man make known what kind of government would command his respect, and that will be one step toward obtaining it.

After all, the practical reason why, when the power is once in the hands of the people, a majority are permitted, and for a long period continue, to rule, is not because they are most likely to be in the right, nor because this seems fairest to the minority, but because they are physically the strongest. But a government in which the majority rule in all cases cannot be based on justice, even as far as men understand it. Can there not be a government in which majorities do not virtually decide right and wrong, but conscience?—in which majorities decide only those questions to which the rule of expediency is applicable? Must the citizen ever for a moment, or in the least degree, resign his conscience to the legislator? Why has every man a conscience, then? I think that we should be men first, and subjects afterward. It is not desirable to cultivate a respect for the law, so much as for the right. The only obligation which I have a right to assume, is to do at any time what I think right. It is truly enough said, that a corporation has no conscience; but a corporation of conscientious men is a corporation *with* a conscience. Law never made men a whit more just; and, by means of their respect for it, even the well-disposed are daily made the agents of injustice. A common and natural result of an undue respect for law is, that you may see a file of soldiers, colonel, captain, corporal, privates, powder-monkeys and all, marching in admirable order over hill and dale to the wars, against their wills, aye, against their common sense and consciences, which makes it very steep marching indeed, and produces a palpitation of the heart. They have no doubt that it is a damnable business in which they are concerned; they are all peaceably inclined. Now, what are they? Men at all? or small moveable forts and magazines, at the service of some unscrupulous man in power? Visit the Navy Yard, and behold a marine, such a man as an American government can make, or such as it can make a man with its black arts, a mere shadow and reminiscence of humanity, a man laid out alive and standing, and already, as one may say, buried under arms with funeral accompaniments, though it may be

> "Not a drum was heard, not a funeral note,
>   As his corse to the rampart we hurried;
> Not a soldier discharged his farewell shot
>   O'er the grave where our hero we buried."

The mass of men serve the State thus, not as men mainly, but as machines, with their bodies. They are the standing army, and the militia, jailers, constables, *posse comitatus*, &c. In most cases there is no free exercise whatever of the judgment or of the moral sense; but they put themselves on a level with wood and earth and stones, and wooden men can perhaps be manufactured that will serve the purpose as well. Such command no more respect than men of straw, or a lump of dirt. They have the same sort of worth only as horses and dogs. Yet such as these even are commonly esteemed good citizens. Others, as most legislators, politicians, lawyers, ministers, and office-holders, serve the State chiefly with their heads; and, as they rarely make any moral distinctions, they are as likely to serve the devil, without intending it, as God. A very few, as heroes, patriots, martyrs, reformers in the great sense, and *men*, serve the State with their consciences also, and so necessarily resist it for the most part; and they are commonly treated by it as enemies. A wise man will only be useful as a man, and will not submit to be "clay," and "stop a hole to keep the wind away," but leave that office to his dust at least:—

> "I am too high-born to be propertied,
> To be a secondary at control,
> Or useful serving-man and instrument
> To any sovereign state throughout the world."

He who gives himself entirely to his fellow-men appears to them useless and selfish; but he who gives himself partially to them is pronounced a benefactor and philanthropist.

How does it become a man to behave toward this American government to-day? I answer that he cannot without disgrace be associated with it. I cannot for an instant recognize that political organization as *my* government which is the *slave's* government also.

All men recognize the right of revolution; that is, the right to refuse allegiance to and to resist the government, when its tyranny or its inefficiency are great and unendurable. But almost all say that such is not the case now. But such was the case, they think, in the Revolution of '75. If one were to tell me that this was a bad government because it taxed certain foreign commodities brought to its ports, it is most probable that I should not make an ado about it, for I can do without them: all machines have their friction; and possibly this does enough good to counterbalance the evil. At any rate, it is a great evil to make a stir about it. But when the friction comes to have its machine, and oppression and robbery are organized, I say, let us not have such a machine any longer. In other words, when a sixth of the population of a nation which has undertaken to be the refuge of liberty are slaves, and a whole country is unjustly overrun and conquered by a foreign army, and subjected to military law, I think that it is not too soon for honest men to rebel and revolutionize. What makes this duty the more urgent is the fact, that the country so overrun is not our own, but ours is the invading army.

Paley, a common authority with many on moral questions, in his chapter on the "Duty of Submission to Civil Government," resolves all civil obligation into expediency; and he proceeds to say, "that so long as the interest of the whole society requires it, that is, so long as the established government cannot be resisted or changed without public inconveniency, it is the will of God that the established government be obeyed, and no longer." ... "This principle being admitted, the justice of every particular case of resistance is reduced to a computation of the quantity of the danger and grievance on the one side, and of the probability and expense of redressing it on the other." Of this, he says, every man shall judge for himself. But Paley appears never to have contemplated those cases to which the rule of expediency does not apply, in which a people, as well as an individual, must do justice, cost what it may. If I have unjustly wrested a plank from a drowning man, I must restore it to him though I drown myself. This, according to Paley, would be inconvenient. But he that would save his life, in such a case, shall lose it. This people must cease to hold slaves, and to make war on Mexico, though it cost them their existence as a people.

In their practice, nations agree with Paley; but does any one think that Massachusetts does exactly what is right at the present crisis?

> "A drab of state, a cloth-o'-silver slut,
> To have her train borne up, and her soul trail in the dirt."

Practically speaking, the opponents to a reform in Massachusetts are not a hundred thousand politicians at the South, but a hundred thousand merchants and farmers here, who are more interested in commerce and agriculture than they are in humanity, and are not prepared to do justice to the slave and to Mexico, *cost what it may.* I quarrel not with far-off foes, but with those who, near at home, co-operate with, and do the bidding of those far away, and without whom the latter would be harmless. We are accustomed to say, that the mass of men are unprepared; but improvement is slow, because the few are not materially wiser or better than the many. It is not so important that many should be as good as you, as that there be some absolute goodness somewhere; for that will leaven the whole lump. There are thousands who are *in opinion* opposed to slavery and to the war, who yet in effect do nothing to put an end to them; who, esteeming themselves children of Washington and Franklin, sit down with their hands in their pockets, and say that they know not what to do, and do nothing; who even postpone the question of freedom to the question of free-trade, and quietly read the prices-current along with the latest advices from Mexico, after dinner, and, it may be, fall asleep over them both. What is the price-current of an honest man and patriot to-day? They hesitate, and they regret, and sometimes they petition; but they do nothing in earnest and with effect. They will wait, well-disposed, for others to remedy the evil, that they may no longer have it to regret. At most, they give only a cheap vote, and a feeble countenance and God-speed, to the right, as it goes by them. There are nine hundred and ninety-nine patrons of virtue to one virtuous man; but it is easier to deal with the real possessor of a thing than with the temporary guardian of it.

All voting is a sort of gaming, like chequers or backgammon, with a slight moral tinge to it, a playing with right and wrong, with moral questions; and betting naturally accompanies it. The character of the voters is not staked. I cast my vote, perchance, as I think right; but I am not vitally concerned that that right should prevail. I am willing to leave it to the majority. Its obligation, therefore, never exceeds that of expediency. Even voting *for the right* is *doing* nothing for it. It is only expressing to men feebly your desire that it should prevail. A wise man will not leave the right to the mercy of chance, nor wish it to prevail through the power of the majority. There is but little virtue in the action of masses of men. When the majority shall at length vote for the abolition of slavery, it will be because they are indifferent to slavery, or because there is but little slavery left to be abolished by their vote. *They* will then be the only slaves.

Only *his* vote can hasten the abolition of slavery who asserts his own freedom by his vote.

I hear of a convention to be held at Baltimore, or elsewhere, for the selection of a candidate for the Presidency, made up chiefly of editors, and men who are politicians by profession; but I think, what is it to any independent, intelligent, and respectable man what decision they may come to, shall we not have the advantage of his wisdom and honesty, nevertheless? Can we not count upon some independent votes? Are there not many individuals in the country who do not attend conventions? But no: I find that the respectable man, so called, has immediately drifted from his position, and despairs of his country, when his country has more reason to despair of him. He forthwith adopts one of the candidates thus selected as the only *available* one, thus proving that he is himself *available* for any purposes of the demagogue. His vote is of no more worth than that of any unprincipled foreigner or hireling native, who may have been bought. Oh for a man who is a *man*, and, as my neighbor says, has a bone in his back which you cannot pass your hand through! Our statistics are at fault: the population has been returned too large. How many *men* are there to a square thousand miles in this country? Hardly one. Does not America offer any inducement for men to settle here? The American has dwindled into an Odd Fellow,—one who may be known by the development of his organ of gregariousness, and a manifest lack of intellect and cheerful self-reliance; whose first and chief concern, on coming into the world, is to see that the alms-houses are in good repair; and, before yet he has lawfully donned the virile garb, to collect a fund for the support of the widows and orphans that may be; who, in short, ventures to live only by the aid of the mutual insurance company, which has promised to bury him decently.

It is not a man's duty, as a matter of course, to devote himself to the eradication of any, even the most enormous wrong; he may still properly have other concerns to engage him; but it is his duty, at least, to wash his hands of it, and, if he gives it no thought longer, not to give it practically his support. If I devote myself to other pursuits and contemplations, I must first see, at least, that I do not pursue them sitting upon another man's shoulders. I must get off him first, that he may pursue his contemplations too. See what gross inconsistency is tolerated. I have heard some of my townsmen say, "I should like to have them order me out to help put down an insurrection of the slaves, or to march to Mexico,—see if I would go;" and yet these very men have each, directly by their allegiance, and so indirectly, at least, by their money, furnished a substitute. The soldier is applauded who refuses to serve in an unjust war by those who do not refuse to sustain the unjust government which makes the war; is applauded by those whose own act and authority he disregards and sets at nought; as if the State were penitent to that degree that it hired one to scourge it while it sinned, but not to that degree that it left off sinning for a moment. Thus, under the name of order and civil government, we are all made at last to pay homage to and support our own meanness. After the first blush of sin, comes its indifference; and from immoral it becomes, as it were, unmoral, and not quite unnecessary to that life which we have made.

The broadest and most prevalent error requires the most disinterested virtue to sustain it. The slight reproach to which the virtue of patriotism is commonly liable, the noble are most likely to incur. Those who, while they disapprove of the character and measures of a government, yield to it their allegiance and support, are undoubtedly its most conscientious supporters, and so frequently the most serious obstacles to reform. Some are petitioning the State to dissolve the Union, to disregard the requisitions of the President. Why do they not dissolve it themselves,—the union between themselves and the State,—and refuse to pay their quota into its treasury? Do not they stand in the same relation to the State, that the State does to the Union? And have not the same reasons prevented the State from resisting the Union, which have prevented them from resisting the State?

How can a man be satisfied to entertain an opinion merely, and enjoy *it*? Is there any enjoyment in it, if his opinion is that he is aggrieved? If you are cheated out of a single dollar by your neighbor, you do not rest satisfied with knowing that you are cheated, or with saying that you are cheated, or even with petitioning him to pay you your due; but you take effectual steps at once to obtain the full amount, and see that you are never cheated again. Action from principle,—the perception and the performance of right,—changes things and relations; it is essentially revolutionary, and does not consist wholly with any thing which was. It not only divides states and churches, it divides families; aye, it divides the *individual*, separating the diabolical in him from the divine.

Unjust laws exist: shall we be content to obey them, or shall we endeavor to amend them, and obey them until we have succeeded, or shall we transgress them at once? Men generally, under such a government as this, think that they ought to wait until they have persuaded the majority to alter them. They think that, if they should resist, the remedy would be worse than the evil. But it is the fault of the government itself that the remedy *is* worse than the evil. *It* makes it worse. Why is it not more apt to anticipate and provide for reform? Why does it not cherish its wise minority? Why does it cry and resist before it is hurt? Why does it not encourage its citizens to be on the alert to point out its faults, and *do* better than it would have them? Why does it always crucify Christ, and excommunicate Copernicus and Luther, and pronounce Washington and Franklin rebels?

One would think, that a deliberate and practical denial of its authority was the only offence never contemplated by government; else, why has it not assigned its definite, its suitable and proportionate penalty? If a man who has no property refuses but once to earn nine shillings for the State, he is put in prison for a period unlimited by any law that I know, and determined only by the discretion of those who placed him there; but if he should steal ninety times nine shillings from the State, he is soon permitted to go at large again.

If the injustice is part of the necessary friction of the machine of government, let it go, let it go: perchance it will wear smooth,—certainly the machine will wear out. If the injustice has a spring, or a pulley, or a rope, or a

crank, exclusively for itself, then perhaps you may consider whether the remedy will not be worse than the evil;
but if it is of such a nature that it requires you to be the
agent of injustice to another, then, I say, break the law.
Let your life be a counter friction to stop the machine.
What I have to do is to see, at any rate, that I do not lend
myself to the wrong which I condemn.

As for adopting the ways which the State has provided
for remedying the evil, I know not of such ways. They
take too much time, and a man's life will be gone. I have
other affairs to attend to. I came into this world, not
chiefly to make this a good place to live in, but to live in
it, be it good or bad. A man has not every thing to do, but
something; and because he cannot do *every thing*, it is
not necessary that he should do *something* wrong. It is
not my business to be petitioning the governor or the legislature any more than it is theirs to petition me; and, if
they should not hear my petition, what should I do then?
But in this case the State has provided no way: its very
Constitution is the evil. This may seem to be harsh and
stubborn and unconciliatory; but it is to treat with the
utmost kindness and consideration the only spirit that can
appreciate or deserves it. So is all change for the better,
like birth and death which convulse the body.

I do not hesitate to say, that those who call themselves
abolitionists should at once effectually withdraw their
support, both in person and property, from the government of Massachusetts, and not wait till they constitute a
majority of one, before they suffer the right to prevail
through them. I think that it is enough if they have God
on their side, without waiting for that other one. Moreover, any man more right than his neighbors, constitutes
a majority of one already.

I meet this American government, or its representative
the State government, directly, and face to face, once a
year, no more, in the person of its tax-gatherer; this is the
only mode in which a man situated as I am necessarily
meets it; and it then says distinctly, Recognize me; and
the simplest, the most effectual, and, in the present pos-
ture of affairs, the indispensablest mode of treating with
it on this head, of expressing your little satisfaction with

and love for it, is to deny it then. My civil neighbor, the tax-gatherer, is the very man I have to deal with,—for it is, after all, with men and not with parchment that I quarrel,—and he has voluntarily chosen to be an agent of the government. How shall he ever know well what he is and does as an officer of the government, or as a man, until he is obliged to consider whether he shall treat me, his neighbor, for whom he has respect, as a neighbor and well-disposed man, or as a maniac and disturber of the peace, and see if he can get over this obstruction to his neighborliness without a ruder and more impetuous thought or speech corresponding with his action? I know this well, that if one thousand, if one hundred, if ten men whom I could name,—if ten *honest* men only,—aye, if *one* HONEST man, in this State of Massachusetts, *ceasing to hold slaves*, were actually to withdraw from this co-partnership, and be locked up in the county jail therefor, it would be the abolition of slavery in America. For it matters not how small the beginning may seem to be: what is once well done is done for ever. But we love better to talk about it: that we say is our mission. Reform keeps many scores of newspapers in its service, but not one man. If my esteemed neighbor, the State's ambassa-dor, who will devote his days to the settlement of the question of human rights in the Council Chamber, in-stead of being threatened with the prisons of Carolina, were to sit down the prisoner of Massachusetts, that State which is so anxious to foist the sin of slavery upon her sister,—though at present she can discover only an act of inhospitality to be the ground of a quarrel with her,—the Legislature would not wholly waive the subject the fol-lowing winter.

Under a government which imprisons any unjustly, the true place for a just man is also a prison. The proper place to-day, the only place which Massachusetts has pro-vided for her freer and less desponding spirits, is in her prisons, to be put out and locked out of the State by her own act, as they have already put themselves out by their principles. It is there that the fugitive slave, and the Mex-ican prisoner on parole, and the Indian come to plead the wrongs of his race, should find them; on that separate, but more free and honorable ground, where the State places those who are not *with* her but *against* her,—the only house in a slave-state in which a free man can abide with honor. If any think that their influence would be lost there, and their voices no longer afflict the ear of the State, that they would not be as an enemy within its walls, they do not know by how much truth is stronger than error, nor how much more eloquently and effectively he can combat injustice who has experienced a little in his own person. Cast your whole vote, not a strip of paper merely, but your whole influence. A minority is powerless while it conforms to the majority; it is not even a minority then; but it is irresistible when it clogs by its whole weight. If the alternative is to keep all just men in prison, or give up war and slavery, the State will not hesitate which to choose. If a thousand men were not to pay their tax-bills this year, that would not be a violent and bloody measure, as it would be to pay them, and enable the State to commit violence and shed innocent blood. This is, in fact, the definition of a peaceable revolution, if any such is possible. If the tax-gatherer, or any other public officer, asks me, as one has done, "But what shall I do?" my answer is, "If you really wish to do any thing, resign your office." When the subject has refused allegiance, and the officer has resigned his office, then the revolution is accomplished. But even suppose blood should flow. Is there not a sort of blood shed when the conscience is wounded? Through this wound a man's real manhood and immortality flow out, and he bleeds to an everlasting death. I see this blood flowing now.

I have contemplated the imprisonment of the offender, rather than the seizure of his goods,—though both will serve the same purpose,—because they who assert the purest right, and consequently are most dangerous to a corrupt State, commonly have not spent much time in accumulating property. To such the State renders comparatively small service, and a slight tax is wont to appear exorbitant, particularly if they are obliged to earn it by special labor with their hands. If there were one who lived wholly without the use of money, the State itself would hesitate to demand it of him. But the rich man—

not to make any invidious comparison—is always sold to
the institution which makes him rich. Absolutely speaking, the more money, the less virtue; for money comes
between a man and his objects, and obtains them for him;
and it was certainly no great virtue to obtain it. It puts to
rest many questions which he would otherwise be taxed
to answer; while the only new question which it puts is
the hard but superfluous one, how to spend it. Thus his
moral ground is taken from under his feet. The opportunities of living are diminished in proportion as what are
called the "means" are increased. The best thing a man
can do for his culture when he is rich is to endeavour to
carry out those schemes which he entertained when he
was poor. Christ answered the Herodians according to
their condition. "Show me the tribute-money," said he;—
and one took a penny out of his pocket;—if you use money which has the image of Cæsar on it, and which he has
made current and valuable, that is, *if you are men of the
State,* and gladly enjoy the advantages of Cæsar's government, then pay him back some of his own when he demands it; "Render therefore to Cæsar that which is Cæsar's, and to God those things which are God's,"—leaving
them no wiser than before as to which was which; for
they did not wish to know.

When I converse with the freest of my neighbors, I
perceive that, whatever they may say about the magni-
tude and seriousness of the question, and their regard for
the public tranquillity, the long and the short of the matter is, that they cannot spare the protection of the existing
government, and they dread the consequences of disobedience to it to their property and families. For my own
part, I should not like to think that I ever rely on the
protection of the State. But, if I deny the authority of the
State when it presents its tax-bill, it will soon take and
waste all my property, and so harass me and my children
without end. This is hard. This makes it impossible for a
man to live honestly and at the same time comfortably in
outward respects. It will not be worth the while to accu-
mulate property; that would be sure to go again. You
must hire or squat somewhere, and raise but a small crop,
and eat that soon. You must live within yourself, and de-

pend upon yourself, always tucked up and ready for a start, and not have many affairs. A man may grow rich in Turkey even, if he will be in all respects a good subject of the Turkish government. Confucius said,—"If a State is governed by the principles of reason, poverty and misery are subjects of shame; if a State is not governed by the principles of reason, riches and honors are the subjects of shame." No: until I want the protection of Massachusetts to be extended to me in some distant southern port, where my liberty is endangered, or until I am bent solely on building up an estate at home by peaceful enterprise, I can afford to refuse allegiance to Massachusetts, and her right to my property and life. It costs me less in every sense to incur the penalty of disobedience to the State, than it would to obey. I should feel as if I were worth less in that case.

Some years ago, the State met me in behalf of the church, and commanded me to pay a certain sum toward the support of a clergyman whose preaching my father attended, but never I myself. "Pay it," it said, "or be locked up in the jail." I declined to pay. But, unfortunately, another man saw fit to pay it. I did not see why the schoolmaster should be taxed to support the priest, and not the priest the schoolmaster; for I was not the State's schoolmaster, but I supported myself by voluntary subscription. I did not see why the lyceum should not present its tax-bill, and have the State to back its demand, as well as the church. However, at the request of the selectmen, I condescended to make some such statement as this in writing:—"Know all men by these presents, that I, Henry Thoreau, do not wish to be regarded as a member of any incorporated society which I have not joined." This I gave to the town-clerk; and he has it. The State, having thus learned that I did not wish to be regarded as a member of that church, has never made a like demand on me since; though it said that it must adhere to its original presumption that time. If I had known how to name them, I should then have signed off in detail from all the societies which I never signed on to; but I did not know where to find a complete list.

I have paid no poll-tax for six years. I was put into a

jail once on this account, for one night; and, as I stood
considering the walls of solid stone, two or three feet
thick, the door of wood and iron, a foot thick, and the
iron grating which strained the light, I could not help
being struck with the foolishness of that institution which
treated me as if I were mere flesh and blood and bones,
to be locked up. I wondered that it should have concluded at length that this was the best use it could put me to,
and had never thought to avail itself of my services in
some way. I saw that, if there was a wall of stone between me and my townsmen, there was a still more difficult one to climb or break through, before they could get
to be as free as I was. I did not for a moment feel confined, and the walls seemed a great waste of stone and
mortar. I felt as if I alone of all my townsmen had paid
my tax. They plainly did not know how to treat me, but
behaved like persons who are underbred. In every threat
and in every compliment there was a blunder; for they
thought that my chief desire was to stand the other side
of that stone wall. I could not but smile to see how indus-
triously they locked the door on my meditations, which
followed them out again without let or hinderance, and
they were really all that was dangerous. As they could
not reach me, they had resolved to punish my body; just
as boys, if they cannot come at some person against
whom they have a spite, will abuse his dog. I saw that the
State was half-witted, that it was timid as a lone woman
with her silver spoons, and that it did not know its friends
from its foes, and I lost all my remaining respect for it,
and pitied it.

Thus the State never intentionally confronts a man's
sense, intellectual or moral, but only his body, his senses.
It is not armed with superior wit or honesty, but with
superior physical strength. I was not born to be forced. I
will breathe after my own fashion. Let us see who is the
strongest. What force has a multitude? They only can
force me who obey a higher law than I. They force me to
become like themselves. I do not hear of *men* being
forced to live this way or that by masses of men. What
sort of life were that to live? When I meet a government
which says to me, "Your money or your life," why should
I be in haste to give it my money? It may be in a great

strait, and not know what to do: I cannot help that. It must help itself; do as I do. It is not worth the while to snivel about it. I am not responsible for the successful working of the machinery of society. I am not the son of the engineer. I perceive that, when an acorn and a chestnut fall side by side, the one does not remain inert to make way for the other, but both obey their own laws, and spring and grow and flourish as best they can, till one, perchance, overshadows and destroys the other. If a plant cannot live according to its nature, it dies; and so a man.

The night in prison was novel and interesting enough. The prisoners in their shirt-sleeves were enjoying a chat and the evening air in the door-way, when I entered. But the jailer said, "Come, boys, it is time to lock up;" and so they dispersed, and I heard the sound of their steps returning into the hollow apartments. My room-mate was introduced to me by the jailer, as "a first-rate fellow and a clever man." When the door was locked, he showed me where to hang my hat, and how he managed matters there. The rooms were whitewashed once a month; and this one, at least, was the whitest, most simply furnished, and probably the neatest apartment in the town. He naturally wanted to know where I came from, and what brought me there; and, when I had told him, I asked him in my turn how he came there, presuming him to be an honest man, of course; and, as the world goes, I believe he was. "Why," said he, "they accuse me of burning a barn; but I never did it." As near as I could discover, he had probably gone to bed in a barn when drunk, and smoked his pipe there; and so a barn was burnt. He had the reputation of being a clever man, had been there some three months waiting for his trial to come on, and would have to wait as much longer; but he was quite domesticated and contented, since he got his board for nothing, and thought that he was well treated.

He occupied one window, and I the other; and I saw, that, if one stayed there long, his principal business would be to look out the window. I had soon read all the tracts that were left there, and examined where former prisoners had broken out, and where a grate had been sawed off, and heard the history of the various occupants of that room; for I found that even here there was a history and a gossip which never circulated beyond the walls of the jail. Probably this is the only house in the town where verses are composed, which are afterward printed in a circular form, but not published. I was shown quite a long list of verses which were composed by some young men who had been detected in an attempt to escape, who avenged themselves by singing them.

I pumped my fellow-prisoner as dry as I could, for fear I should never see him again; but at length he showed me which was my bed, and left me to blow out the lamp.

It was like travelling into a far country, such as I had never expected to behold, to lie there for one night. It seemed to me that I never had heard the town-clock strike before, nor the evening sounds of the village; for we slept with the windows open, which were inside the grating. It was to see my native village in the light of the middle ages, and our Concord was turned into a Rhine stream, and visions of knights and castles passed before me. They were the voices of old burghers that I heard in the streets. I was an involuntary spectator and auditor of whatever was done and said in the kitchen of the adjacent village-inn,—a wholly new and rare experience to me. It was a closer view of my native town. I was fairly inside of it. I never had seen its institutions before. This is one of its peculiar institutions; for it is a shire town. I began to comprehend what its inhabitants were about.

In the morning, our breakfasts were put through the hole in the door, in small oblong-square tin pans, made to fit, and holding a pint of chocolate, with brown bread, and an iron spoon. When they called for the vessels again, I was green enough to return what bread I had left; but my comrade seized it, and said that I should lay that up for lunch or dinner. Soon after, he was let out to work at haying in a neighboring field, whither he went every day, and would not be back till noon; so he bade me good-day, saying that he doubted if he should see me again.

When I came out of prison,—for some one interfered, and paid the tax,—I did not perceive that great changes had taken place on the common, such as he observed who went in a youth, and emerged a tottering and gray-headed man; and yet a change had to my eyes come over the scene,—the town, and State, and country,—greater than any that mere time could effect. I saw yet more distinctly the State in which I lived. I saw to what extent the people among whom I lived could be trusted as good neighbors and friends; that their friendship was for summer weather only; that they did not greatly purpose to do right; that they were a distinct race from me by their prejudices and superstitions, as the Chinamen and Malays are; that, in their sacrifices to humanity, they ran no risks, not even to their property; that, after all, they were not so noble but they treated the thief as he had treated them, and hoped, by a certain outward observance and a few prayers, and by walking in a particular straight though useless path from time to time, to save their souls. This may be to judge my neighbors harshly; for I believe that most of them are not aware that they have such an institution as the jail in their village.

It was formerly the custom in our village, when a poor debtor came out of jail, for his acquaintances to salute him, looking through their fingers, which were crossed to represent the grating of a jail window, "How do ye do?" My neighbors did not thus salute me, but first looked at me, and then at one another, as if I had returned from a long journey. I was put into jail as I was going to the shoemaker's to get a shoe which was mended. When I was let out the next morning, I proceeded to finish my errand, and, having put on my mended shoe, joined a huckleberry party, who were impatient to put themselves under my conduct; and in half an hour,—for the horse was soon tackled,—was in the midst of a huckleberry field, on one of our highest hills, two miles off; and then the State was nowhere to be seen.

This is the whole history of "My Prisons."

I have never declined paying the highway tax, because I am as desirous of being a good neighbor as I am of being a bad subject; and, as for supporting schools, I am doing my part to educate my fellow-countrymen now. It is for no particular item in the tax-bill that I refuse to pay it. I simply wish to refuse allegiance to the State, to withdraw and stand aloof from it effectually. I do not care to trace the course of my dollar, if I could, till it buys a man, or a musket to shoot one with,—the dollar is innocent,—but I am concerned to trace the effects of my allegiance. In fact, I quietly declare war with the State, after my fashion, though I will still make what use and get what advantage of her I can, as is usual in such cases.

If others pay the tax which is demanded of me, from a sympathy with the State, they do but what they have already done in their own case, or rather they abet injustice to a greater extent than the State requires. If they pay the tax from a mistaken interest in the individual taxed, to save his property or prevent his going to jail, it is because they have not considered wisely how far they let their private feelings interfere with the public good.

This, then, is my position at present. But one cannot be too much on his guard in such a case, lest his action be biassed by obstinacy, or an undue regard for the opinions of men. Let him see that he does only what belongs to himself and to the hour.

I think sometimes, Why, this people mean well; they are only ignorant; they would do better if they knew how: why give your neighbors this pain to treat you as they are not inclined to? But I think, again, this is no reason why I should do as they do, or permit others to suffer much greater pain of a different kind. Again, I sometimes say to myself, When many millions of men, without heat, without ill-will, without personal feeling of any kind, demand of you a few shillings only, without the possibility, such is their constitution, of retracting or altering their present demand, and without the possibility, on your side, of appeal to any other millions, why expose yourself to this overwhelming brute force? You do not resist cold and hunger, the winds and the waves, thus obstinately; you quietly submit to a thousand similar necessities. You do not put your head into the fire. But just in proportion as I regard this as not wholly a brute force, but partly a human force, and consider that I have relations to those millions as to so many millions of men, and not of mere brute or inanimate things, I see that appeal is possible, first and instantaneously, from them to the Maker of them, and, secondly, from them to themselves. But, if I put my head deliberately into the fire, there is no appeal to fire or to the Maker of fire, and I have only myself to blame. If I could convince myself that I have any right to be satisfied with men as they are, and to treat them accordingly, and not according, in some respects, to my requisitions and expectations of what they and I ought to be, then, like a good Mussulman and fatalist, I should endeavor to be satisfied with things as they are, and say it is the will of God. And, above all, there is this difference between resisting this and a purely brute or natural force, that I can resist this with some effect; but I cannot expect, like Orpheus, to change the nature of the rocks and trees and beasts.

I do not wish to quarrel with any man or nation. I do not wish to split hairs, to make fine distinctions, or set myself up as better than my neighbors. I seek rather, I may say, even an excuse for conforming to the laws of the land. I am but too ready to conform to them. Indeed I have reason to suspect myself on this head; and each year, as the tax-gatherer comes round, I find myself disposed to review the acts and position of the general and state governments, and the spirit of the people, to discover a pretext for conformity. I believe that the State will soon be able to take all my work of this sort out of my hands, and then I shall be no better a patriot than my fellow-countrymen. Seen from a lower point of view, the Constitution, with all its faults, is very good; the law and the courts are very respectable; even this State and this American government are, in many respects, very admirable and rare things, to be thankful for, such as a great many have described them; but seen from a point of view a little higher, they are what I have described them; seen from a higher still, and the highest, who shall say what they are, or that they are worth looking at or thinking of at all?

However, the government does not concern me much, and I shall bestow the fewest possible thoughts on it. It is not many moments that I live under a government, even in this world. If a man is thought-free, fancy-free, imagination-free, that which *is not* never for a long time appearing *to be* to him, unwise rulers or reformers cannot fatally interrupt him.

I know that most men think differently from myself; but those whose lives are by profession devoted to the study of these or kindred subjects, content me as little as any. Statesmen and legislators, standing so completely within the institution, never distinctly and nakedly behold it. They speak of moving society, but have no resting-place without it. They may be men of a certain experience and discrimination, and have no doubt invented ingenious and even useful systems, for which we sincerely thank them; but all their wit and usefulness lie within certain not very wide limits. They are wont to forget that the world is not governed by policy and expediency. Webster never goes behind government, and so cannot speak with authority about it. His words are wisdom to those legislators who contemplate no essential reform in the existing government; but for thinkers, and those who legislate for all time, he never once glances at the subject. I know of those whose serene and wise speculations on this theme would soon reveal the limits of his mind's range and hospitality. Yet, compared with the cheap professions of most reformers, and the still cheaper wisdom and eloquence of politicians in general, his are almost the only sensible and valuable words, and we thank Heaven for him. Comparatively, he is always strong, original, and, above all, practical. Still his quality is not wisdom, but prudence. The lawyer's truth is not Truth, but consistency, or a consistent expediency. Truth is always in harmony with herself, and is not concerned chiefly to reveal the justice that may consist with wrong-doing. He well deserves to be called, as he has been called, the Defender of the Constitution. There are really no blows to be given by him but defensive ones. He is not a leader, but a follower. His leaders are the men of '87. "I have never made an effort," he says, "and never propose to make an effort; I have never countenanced an effort, and never mean to countenance an effort, to disturb the arrangement as originally made, by which the various States came into the Union." Still thinking of the sanction which the Constitution gives to slavery, he says, "Because it was a part of the original compact,—let it stand." Notwithstanding his special acuteness and ability, he is unable to take a fact out of its merely political relations, and behold it as it lies absolutely to be disposed of by the intellect,—what, for instance, it behoves a man to do here in America to-day with regard to slavery,—but ventures, or is driven, to make some such desperate answer as the following, while professing to speak absolutely, and as a private man,—from which what new and singular code of social duties might be inferred?—"The manner," says he, "in which the governments of those States where slavery exists are to regulate it, is for their own consideration, under their responsibility to their constituents, to the general laws of propriety, humanity, and justice, and to God. Associations formed elsewhere, springing from a feeling of humanity, or any other cause, have nothing whatever to do with it. They have never received any encouragement from me, and they never will."*

They who know of no purer sources of truth, who have traced up its stream no higher, stand, and wisely stand, by the Bible and the Constitution, and drink at it there with reverence and humility; but they who behold where it comes trickling into this lake or that pool, gird up their loins once more, and continue their pilgrimage toward its fountain-head.

No man with a genius for legislation has appeared in America. They are rare in the history of the world. There are orators, politicians, and eloquent men, by the thousand; but the speaker has not yet opened his mouth to speak, who is capable of settling the much-vexed questions of the day. We love eloquence for its own sake, and not for any truth which it may utter, or any heroism it may inspire. Our legislators have not yet learned the comparative value of free-trade and of freedom, of union, and of rectitude, to a nation. They have no genius or talent for comparatively humble questions of taxation

---

*These extracts have been inserted since the Lecture was read.

and finance, commerce and manufactures and agriculture. If we were left solely to the wordy wit of legislators in Congress for our guidance, uncorrected by the seasonable experience and the effectual complaints of the people, America would not long retain her rank among the nations. For eighteen hundred years, though perchance I have no right to say it, the New Testament has been written; yet where is the legislator who has wisdom and practical talent enough to avail himself of the light which it sheds on the science of legislation?

The authority of government, even such as I am willing to submit to,—for I will cheerfully obey those who know and can do better than I, and in many things even those who neither know nor can do so well,—is still an impure one: to be strictly just, it must have the sanction and consent of the governed. It can have no pure right over my person and property but what I concede to it. The progress from an absolute to a limited monarchy, from a limited monarchy to a democracy, is a progress toward a true respect for the individual. Is a democracy, such as we know it, the last improvement possible in government? Is it not possible to take a step further towards recognizing and organizing the rights of man? There will never be a really free and enlightened State, until the State comes to recognize the individual as a higher and independent power, from which all its own power and authority are derived, and treats him accordingly. I please myself with imagining a State at last which can afford to be just to all men, and to treat the individual with respect as a neighbor; which even would not think it inconsistent with its own repose, if a few were to live aloof from it, not meddling with it, nor embraced by it, who fulfilled all the duties of neighbors and fellow-men. A State which bore this kind of fruit, and suffered it to drop off as fast as it ripened, would prepare the way for a still more perfect and glorious State, which also I have imagined, but not yet anywhere seen.

FRIENDSHIP

Into A Week on the Concord and Merrimack Rivers
(1849) Thoreau incorporated a number of short pieces
that he had written in the preceding decade. "Friendship" *is one such essay; it comprises a good portion of
the* "Wednesday" *chapter of* A Week. *Thoreau's insis-
tence that total trust between persons be a* sine qua non
*of friendship explains, in part, why his close personal
relationships were few, and illuminates Emerson's observation at Thoreau's funeral that his "virtues ran to
extremes." The text of "Friendship" printed here is
from the definitive Princeton Edition of* A Week, *edited
by Carl F. Hovde et al. (1980).*

FRIENDSHIP IS EVANESCENT in every man's experience,
and remembered like heat lightning in past summers.
Fair and flitting like a summer cloud;—there is always
some vapor in the air, no matter how long the drought;
there are even April showers. Surely from time to time,
for its vestiges never depart, it floats through our atmosphere. It takes place, like vegetation in so many materials, because there is such a law, but always without permanent form, though ancient and familiar as the sun and
moon, and as sure to come again. The heart is forever
inexperienced. They silently gather as by magic, these
never failing, never quite deceiving visions, like the

bright and fleecy clouds in the calmest and clearest days.
The Friend is some fair floating isle of palms eluding the
mariner in Pacific seas. Many are the dangers to be en-
countered, equinoctial gales and coral reefs, ere he may
sail before the constant trades. But who would not sail
through mutiny and storm even over Atlantic waves, to
reach the fabulous retreating shores of some continent
man? The imagination still clings to the faintest tradition
of

THE ATLANTIDES.

The smothered streams of love, which flow
More bright than Phlegethon, more low,
Island us ever, like the sea,
In an Atlantic mystery.
Our fabled shores none ever reach,
No mariner has found our beach,
Only our mirage now is seen,
And neighboring waves with floating green,
Yet still the oldest charts contain
Some dotted outline of our main;
In ancient times midsummer days
Unto the western islands' gaze,
To Teneriffe and the Azores,
Have shown our faint and cloud-like shores.

But sink not yet, ye desolate isles,
Anon your coast with commerce smiles,
And richer freights ye'll furnish far
Than Africa or Malabar.
Be fair, be fertile evermore,
Ye rumored but untrodden shore,
Princes and monarchs will contend
Who first unto your land shall send,
And pawn the jewels of the crown
To call your distant soil their own.

Columbus has sailed westward of these isles by the
mariner's compass, but neither he nor his successors have
found them. We are no nearer than Plato was. The earnest seeker and hopeful discoverer of this New World always haunts the outskirts of his time, and walks through
the densest crowd uninterrupted, and as it were in a
straight line.—

Sea and land are but his neighbors,
And companions in his labors,
Who on the ocean's verge and firm land's end
Doth long and truly seek his Friend.
Many men dwell far inland,
But he alone sits on the strand.
Whether he ponders men or books,
Always still he seaward looks,
Marine news he ever reads,
And the slightest glances heeds,
Feels the sea breeze on his cheek
At each word the landsmen speak,
In every companion's eye
A sailing vessel doth descry;
In the ocean's sullen roar
From some distant port he hears,
Of wrecks upon a distant shore,
And the ventures of past years.

Who does not walk on the plain as amid the columns of Tadmore of the desert? There is on the earth no institution which Friendship has established; it is not taught by any religion; no scripture contains its maxims. It has no temple, nor even a solitary column. There goes a rumor that the earth is inhabited, but the shipwrecked mariner has not seen a foot-print on the shore. The hunter has found only fragments of pottery and the monuments of inhabitants.

However, our fates at least are social. Our courses do not diverge; but as the web of destiny is woven it is fulled, and we are cast more and more into the centre. Men naturally, though feebly, seek this alliance, and their actions faintly foretell it. We are inclined to lay the chief stress on likeness and not on difference, and in foreign bodies we admit that there are many degrees of warmth below blood heat, but none of cold above it.

Mencius says: "If one loses a fowl or a dog, he knows well how to seek them again; if one loses the sentiments of his heart, he does not know how to seek them again. . . . The duties of practical philosophy consist only in seeking after those sentiments of the heart which we have lost; that is all."

One or two persons come to my house from time to time, there being proposed to them the faint possibility of intercourse. They are as full as they are silent, and wait for my plectrum to stir the strings of their lyre. If they could ever come to the length of a sentence, or hear one, on that ground which they are dreaming of! They speak faintly, and do not obtrude themselves. They have heard some news, which none, not even they themselves, can impart. It is a wealth they can bear about them which can be expended in various ways. What came they out to seek?

No word is oftener on the lips of men than Friendship, and indeed no thought is more familiar to their aspirations. All men are dreaming of it, and its drama, which is always a tragedy, is enacted daily. It is the secret of the universe. You may thread the town, you may wander the country, and none shall ever speak of it, yet thought is every where busy about it, and the idea of what is possible in this respect affects our behavior toward all new men and women, and a great many old ones. Nevertheless, I can remember only two or three essays on this subject in all literature. No wonder that the Mythology, and Arabian Nights, and Shakspeare, and Scott's novels, entertain us,—we are poets and fablers and dramatists and novelists ourselves. We are continually acting a part in a more interesting drama than any written. We are dreaming that our Friends are our *Friends,* and that we are our Friends' *Friends.* Our actual Friends are but distant relations of those to whom we are pledged. We never exchange more than three words with a Friend in our lives, on that level to which our thoughts and feelings almost habitually rise. One goes forth prepared to say "Sweet Friends!" and the salutation is "Damn your eyes!" But never mind; faint heart never won true Friend. O my Friend, may it come to pass, once, that when you are my Friend I may be yours.

Of what use the friendliest disposition even, if there are no hours given to Friendship, if it is forever postponed to unimportant duties and relations? Friendship is first, Friendship last. But it is equally impossible to forget our Friends, and to make them answer to our ideal.

When they say farewell, then indeed we begin to keep them company. How often we find ourselves turning our backs on our actual Friends, that we may go and meet their ideal cousins. I would that I were worthy to be any man's Friend.

What is commonly honored with the name of Friendship is no very profound or powerful instinct. Men do not, after all, *love* their Friends greatly. I do not often see the farmers made seers and wise to the verge of insanity by their Friendship for one another. They are not often transfigured and translated by love in each other's presence. I do not observe them purified, refined, and elevated by the love of a man. If one abates a little the price of his wood, or gives a neighbor his vote at town-meeting, or a barrel of apples, or lends him his wagon frequently, it is esteemed a rare instance of Friendship. Nor do the farmers' wives lead lives consecrated to Friendship. I do not see the pair of farmer Friends of either sex prepared to stand against the world. There are only two or three couples in history. To say that a man is your Friend, means commonly no more than this, that he is not your enemy. Most contemplate only what would be the accidental and trifling advantages of Friendship, as that the Friend can assist in time of need, by his substance, or his influence, or his counsel; but he who foresees such advantages in this relation proves himself blind to its real advantage, or indeed wholly inexperienced in the relation itself. Such services are particular and menial, compared with the perpetual and all-embracing service which it is. Even the utmost good-will and harmony and practical kindness are not sufficient for Friendship, for Friends do not live in harmony merely, as some say, but in melody. We do not wish for Friends to feed and clothe our bodies,—neighbors are kind enough for that,—but to do the like office to our spirits. For this few are rich enough, however well disposed they may be. For the most part we stupidly confound one man with another. The dull distinguish only races or nations, or at most classes, but the wise man, individuals. To his Friend a man's peculiar character appears in every feature and in every action, and it is thus drawn out and improved by him.

Think of the importance of Friendship in the education of men.

> "He that hath love and judgment too,
> Sees more than any other doe."

It will make a man honest; it will make him a hero; it will make him a saint. It is the state of the just dealing with the just, the magnanimous with the magnanimous, the sincere with the sincere, man with man.—
And it is well said by another poet,

> "Why love among the virtues is not known,
> Is that love is them all contract in one."

All the abuses which are the object of reform with the philanthropist, the statesman, and the housekeeper, are unconsciously amended in the intercourse of Friends. A Friend is one who incessantly pays us the compliment of expecting from us all the virtues, and who can appreciate them in us. It takes two to speak the truth,—one to speak, and another to hear. How can one treat with magnanimity mere wood and stone? If we dealt only with the false and dishonest, we should at last forget how to speak truth. Only lovers know the value and magnanimity of truth, while traders prize a cheap honesty, and neighbors and acquaintance a cheap civility. In our daily intercourse with men, our nobler faculties are dormant and suffered to rust. None will pay us the compliment to expect nobleness from us. Though we have gold to give, they demand only copper. We ask our neighbor to suffer himself to be dealt with truly, sincerely, nobly; but he answers no by his deafness. He does not even hear this prayer. He says practically,—I will be content if you treat me as no better than I should be, as deceitful, mean, dishonest and selfish. For the most part, we are contented so to deal and to be dealt with, and we do not think that for the mass of men there is any truer and nobler relation possible. A man may have *good* neighbors, so called, and acquaintances, and even companions, wife, parents, brothers, sisters, children, who meet himself and one another on this ground only. The State does not demand justice of its members, but thinks that it succeeds very well with the least degree of it, hardly more than rogues practice; and so do the neighborhood and the family. What is commonly called Friendship even is only a little more honor among rogues.

But sometimes we are said to *love* another, that is to stand in a true relation to him, so that we give the best to, and receive the best from, him. Between whom there is hearty truth there is love; and in proportion to our truthfulness and confidence in one another, our lives are divine and miraculous, and answer to our ideal. There are passages of affection in our intercourse with mortal men and women, such as no prophecy had taught us to expect, which transcend our earthly life, and anticipate heaven for us. What is this Love that may come right into the middle of a prosaic Goffstown day, equal to any of the gods? that discovers a new world, fair and fresh and eternal, occupying the place of this old one, when to the common eye a dust has settled on the universe? which world cannot else be reached, and does not exist. What other words, we may almost ask, are memorable and worthy to be repeated than those which love has inspired? It is wonderful that they were ever uttered. They are few and rare, indeed, but, like a strain of music, they are incessantly repeated and modulated by the memory. All other words crumble off with the stucco which overlies the heart. We should not dare to repeat them now aloud. We are not competent to hear them at all times.

The books for young people say a great deal about the *selection* of Friends; it is because they really have nothing to say about *Friends*. They mean associates and confidants merely. "Know that the contrariety of foe and Friend proceeds from God." Friendship takes place between those who have an affinity for one another, and is a perfectly natural and inevitable result. No professions nor advances will avail. Even speech, at first, necessarily has nothing to do with it; but it follows after silence, as the buds in the graft do not put forth into leaves till long after the graft has taken. It is a drama in which the parties have no part to act. We are all Mussulmen and fatalists in this respect. Impatient and uncertain lovers think that they must say or do something kind whenever they meet; they must never be cold. But they who are Friends, do not do what they *think* they must, but what they *must*. Even their Friendship is to some extent but a sublime phenomenon to them.

The true and not despairing Friend will address his Friend in some such terms as these.

"I never asked thy leave to let me love thee,—I have a right. I love thee not as something private and personal, which is *your own*, but as something universal and worthy of love, *which I have found*. O how I think of you! You are purely good,—you are infinitely good. I can trust you forever. I did not think that humanity was so rich. Give me an opportunity to live."

"You are the fact in a fiction,—you are the truth more strange and admirable than fiction. Consent only to be what you are. I alone will never stand in your way."

"This is what I would like,—to be as intimate with you as our spirits are intimate,—respecting you as I respect my ideal. Never to profane one another by word or action, even by a thought. Between us, if necessary, let there be no acquaintance."

"I have discovered you; how can you be concealed from me?"

The Friend asks no return but that his Friend will religiously accept and wear and not disgrace his apotheosis of him. They cherish each other's hopes. They are kind to each other's dreams.

Though the poet says, "'Tis the pre-eminence of Friendship to impute excellence," yet we can never praise our Friend, nor esteem him praiseworthy, nor let him think that he can please us by any *behavior*, or ever *treat* us well enough. That kindness which has so good a reputation elsewhere can least of all consist with this relation, and no such affront can be offered to a Friend, as a conscious good-will, a friendliness which is not a necessity of the Friend's nature.

The sexes are naturally most strongly attracted to one another, by constant constitutional differences, and are most commonly and surely the complements of each other. How natural and easy it is for man to secure the attention of woman to what interests himself. Men and women of equal culture, thrown together, are sure to be of a certain value to one another, more than men to men. There exists already a natural disinterestedness and liberality in such society, and I think that any man will more confidently carry his favorite books to read to some circle of intelligent women, than to one of his own sex. The visit of man to man is wont to be an interruption, but the sexes naturally expect one another. Yet Friendship is no respecter of sex; and perhaps it is more rare between the sexes, than between two of the same sex.

Friendship is, at any rate, a relation of perfect equality. It cannot well spare any outward sign of equal obligation and advantage. The nobleman can never have a Friend among his retainers, nor the king among his subjects. Not that the parties to it are in all respects equal, but they are equal in all that respects or affects their Friendship. The one's love is exactly balanced and represented by the other's. Persons are only the vessels which contain the nectar, and the hydrostatic paradox is the symbol of love's law. It finds its level and rises to its fountain-head in all breasts, and its slenderest column balances the ocean.—

> "And love as well the shepherd can
> As can the mighty nobleman."

The one sex is not, in this respect, more tender than the other. A hero's love is as delicate as a maiden's.

Confucius said, "Never contract Friendship with a man that is not better than thyself." It is the merit and preservation of Friendship, that it takes place on a level higher than the actual characters of the parties would seem to warrant. The rays of light come to us in such a curve that every man whom we meet appears to be taller than he actually is. Such foundation has civility. My Friend is that one whom I can associate with my choicest thought. I always assign to him a nobler employment in my absence than I ever find him engaged in; and I imagine that the hours which he devotes to me were snatched from a higher society. The sorest insult which I ever received from a Friend was, when he behaved with the license which only long and cheap acquaintance allows to one's faults, in my presence, without shame, and still addressed me in friendly accents. Beware, lest thy Friend learn at last to tolerate one frailty of thine, and so an obstacle be raised to the progress of thy love. There are times when we have had enough even of our Friends, when we begin inevitably to profane one another, and must withdraw religiously into solitude and silence, the better to prepare ourselves for a loftier intimacy. Silence is the ambrosial night in the intercourse of Friends, in which their sincerity is recruited and takes deeper root.

Friendship is never established as an understood relation. Do you demand that I be less your Friend that you may know it? Yet what right have I to think that another cherishes so rare a sentiment for me? It is a miracle which requires constant proofs. It is an exercise of the purest imagination and the rarest faith. It says by a silent but eloquent behavior,—"I will be so related to thee as thou canst imagine; even so thou mayest believe. I will spend truth,—all my wealth on thee,"—and the Friend responds silently through his nature and life, and treats his Friend with the same divine courtesy. He knows us literally through thick and thin. He never asks for a sign of love, but can distinguish it by the features which it naturally wears. We never need to stand upon ceremony with him with regard to his visits. Wait not till I invite thee, but observe that I am glad to see thee when thou comest. It would be paying too dear for thy visit to ask for it. Where my Friend lives there are all riches and every attraction, and no slight obstacle can keep me from him. Let me never have to tell thee what I have not to tell. Let our intercourse be wholly above ourselves, and draw us up to it. The language of Friendship is not words but meanings. It is an intelligence above language. One imagines endless conversations with his Friend, in which the tongue shall be loosed, and thoughts be spoken without hesitancy, or end; but the experience is commonly far otherwise. Acquaintances may come and go, and have a word ready for every occasion; but what puny word shall he utter whose very breath is thought and meaning? Suppose you go to bid farewell to your Friend who is setting out on a journey; what other outward sign do you know

of than to shake his hand? Have you any palaver ready
for him then? any box of salve to commit to his pocket?
any particular message to send by him? any statement
which you had forgotten to make?—as if you could forget any thing.—No, it is much that you take his hand and
say Farewell; that you could easily omit; so far custom
has prevailed. It is even painful, if he is to go, that he
should linger so long. If he must go, let him go quickly.
Have you any *last* words? Alas, it is only the word of
words, which you have so long sought and found not; *you*
have not a *first* word yet. There are few even whom I
should venture to call earnestly by their most proper
names. A name pronounced is the recognition of the individual to whom it belongs. He who can pronounce my
name aright, he can call me, and is entitled to my love
and service. Yet reserve is the freedom and abandonment
of lovers. It is the reserve of what is hostile or indifferent
in their natures, to give place to what is kindred and har-
monious.

The violence of love is as much to be dreaded as that of
hate. When it is durable it is serene and equable. Even its
famous pains begin only with the ebb of love, for few are
indeed lovers, though all would fain be. It is one proof of
a man's fitness for Friendship that he is able to do without that which is cheap and passionate. A true Friendship
is as wise as it is tender. The parties to it yield implicitly
to the guidance of their love, and know no other law nor
kindness. It is not extravagant and insane, but what it
says is something established henceforth, and will bear to
be stereotyped. It is a truer truth, it is better and fairer
news, and no time will ever shame it, or prove it false.
This is a plant which thrives best in a temperate zone,
where summer and winter alternate with one another.
The Friend is a *necessarius*, and meets his Friend on
homely ground; not on carpets and cushions, but on the
ground and on rocks they will sit, obeying the natural
and primitive laws. They will meet without any outcry,
and part without loud sorrow. Their relation implies such
qualities as the warrior prizes; for it takes a valor to open
the hearts of men as well as the gates of castles. It is not
an idle sympathy and mutual consolation merely, but a

heroic sympathy of aspiration and endeavor.

> "When manhood shall be matched so
>   That fear can take no place,
> Then weary *works* make warriors
>   Each other to embrace."

The Friendship which Wawatam testified for Henry the fur-trader, as described in the latter's "Adventures," so almost bare and leafless, yet not blossomless nor fruitless, is remembered with satisfaction and security. The stern imperturbable warrior, after fasting, solitude, and mortification of body, comes to the white man's lodge, and affirms that he is the white brother whom he saw in his dream, and adopts him henceforth. He buries the hatchet as it regards his friend, and they hunt and feast and make maple-sugar together. "Metals unite from fluxility; birds and beasts from motives of convenience; fools from fear and stupidity; and just men at sight." If Wawatam would taste the "white man's milk" with his tribe, or take his bowl of human broth made of the trader's fellow-countrymen, he first finds a place of safety for his Friend, whom he has rescued from a similar fate. At length, after a long winter of undisturbed and happy intercourse in the family of the chieftain in the wilderness, hunting and fishing, they return in the spring to Michilimackinac to dispose of their furs; and it becomes necessary for Wawatam to take leave of his Friend at the Isle aux Outardes, when the latter, to avoid his enemies, proceeded to the Sault de Sainte Marie, supposing that they were to be separated for a short time only. "We now exchanged farewells," says Henry, "with an emotion entirely reciprocal. I did not quit the lodge without the most grateful sense of the many acts of goodness which I had experienced in it, nor without the sincerest respect for the virtues which I had witnessed among its members. All the family accompanied me to the beach; and the canoe had no sooner put off than Wawatam commenced an address to the Kichi Manito, beseeching him to take care of me, his brother, till we should next meet.—We had proceeded to too great a distance to allow of our hearing his voice, before Wawatam had ceased to offer up his prayers." We never hear of him again.

Friendship is not so kind as is imagined; it has not much human blood in it, but consists with a certain disregard for men and their erections, the Christian duties and humanities, while it purifies the air like electricity. There may be the sternest tragedy in the relation of two who are more than usually innocent and true to their highest instincts. We may call it an essentially heathenish intercourse, free and irresponsible in its nature, and practising all the virtues gratuitously. It is not the highest sympathy merely, but a pure and lofty society, a fragmentary and godlike intercourse of ancient date, still kept up at intervals, which, remembering itself, does not hesitate to disregard the humbler rights and duties of humanity. It requires immaculate and godlike qualities full-grown, and exists at all only by condescension and anticipation of the remotest future. We love nothing which is merely good and not fair, if such a thing is possible. Nature puts some kind of blossom before every fruit, not simply a calix behind it. When the Friend comes out of his heathenism and superstition, and breaks his idols, being converted by the precepts of a newer testament; when he forgets his mythology, and treats his Friend like a Christian, or as he can afford; then Friendship ceases to be Friendship, and becomes charity; that principle which established the almshouse is now beginning with its charity at home, and establishing an almshouse and pauper relations there.

As for the number which this society admits, it is at any rate to be begun with one, the noblest and greatest that we know, and whether the world will ever carry it further, whether, as Chaucer affirms,

> "There be mo sterres in the skie than a pair,"

remains to be proved;—

> "And certaine he is well begone
> Among a thousand that findeth one."

We shall not surrender ourselves heartily to any while we are conscious that another is more deserving of our love. Yet Friendship does not stand for numbers; the Friend does not count his Friends on his fingers; they are not numerable. The more there are included by this bond, if they are indeed included, the rarer and diviner the quality of the love that binds them. I am ready to believe that as private and intimate a relation may exist by which three are embraced, as between two. Indeed we cannot have too many friends; the virtue which we appreciate we to some extent appropriate, so that thus we are made at last more fit for every relation of life. A base Friendship is of a narrowing and exclusive tendency, but a noble one is not exclusive; its very superfluity and dispersed love is the humanity which sweetens society, and sympathizes with foreign nations; for though its foundations are private, it is in effect, a public affair and a public advantage, and the Friend, more than the father of a family, deserves well of the state.

The only danger in Friendship is that it will end. It is a delicate plant though a native. The least unworthiness, even if it be unknown to one's self, vitiates it. Let the Friend know that those faults which he observes in his Friend his own faults attract. There is no rule more invariable than that we are paid for our suspicions by finding what we suspected. By our narrowness and prejudices we say, I will have so much and such of you, my Friend, no more. Perhaps there are none charitable, none disinterested, none wise, noble, and heroic enough, for a true and lasting Friendship.

I sometimes hear my Friends complain finely that I do not appreciate their fineness. I shall not tell them whether I do or not. As if they expected a vote of thanks for every fine thing which they uttered or did. Who knows but it was finely appreciated. It may be that your silence was the finest thing of the two. There are some things which a man never speaks of, which are much finer kept silent about. To the highest communications we only lend a silent ear. Our finest relations are not simply kept silent about, but buried under a positive depth of silence, never to be revealed. It may be that we are not even yet acquainted. In human intercourse the tragedy begins, not when there is misunderstanding about words, but when silence is not understood. Then there can never be an explanation. What avails it that another loves you, if he does not understand you? Such love is a curse. What sort of companions are they who are presuming always that their silence is more expressive than yours? How foolish, and inconsiderate, and unjust, to conduct as if you were the only party aggrieved! Has not your Friend always equal ground of complaint? No doubt my Friends sometimes speak to me in vain, but they do not know what things I hear which they are not aware that they have spoken. I know that I have frequently disappointed them by not giving them words when they expected them, or such as they expected. Whenever I see my Friend I speak to him, but the expector, the man with the ears, is not he. They will complain too that you are hard. O ye that would have the cocoa-nut wrong side outwards, when next I weep I will let you know. They ask for words and deeds, when a true relation is word and deed. If they know not of these things, how can they be informed? We often forbear to confess our feelings, not from pride, but for fear that we could not continue to love the one who required us to give such proof of our affection.

I know a woman who possesses a restless and intelligent mind, interested in her own culture, and earnest to enjoy the highest possible advantages, and I meet her with pleasure as a natural person who not a little provokes me, and I suppose is stimulated in turn by myself. Yet our acquaintance plainly does not attain to that degree of confidence and sentiment which women, which all, in fact, covet. I am glad to help her, as I am helped by her; I like very well to know her with a sort of stranger's privilege, and hesitate to visit her often, like her other Friends. My nature pauses here, I do not well know why. Perhaps she does not make the highest demand on me, a religious demand. Some, with whose prejudices or peculiar bias I have no sympathy, yet inspire me with confidence, and I trust that they confide in me also as a religious heathen at least,—a good Greek. I too have principles as well founded as their own. If this person could conceive that, without wilfulness, I associate with her as far as our destinies are coincident, as far as our Good Geniuses permit, and still value such intercourse, it would be a grateful assurance to me. I feel as if I appeared careless, indifferent, and without principle to her, not expecting more, and yet not content with less. If she could know that I make an infinite demand on myself, as well as on all others, she would see that this true though incomplete intercourse, is infinitely better than a more unreserved but falsely grounded one, without the principle of growth in it. For a companion, I require one who will make an equal demand on me with my own genius. Such a one will always be rightly tolerant. It is suicide and corrupts good manners to welcome any less than this. I value and trust those who love and praise my aspiration rather than my performance. If you would not stop to look at me, but look whither I am looking and further, then my education could not dispense with your company.

My love must be as free
  As is the eagle's wing,
Hovering o'er land and sea
  And every thing.

I must not dim my eye
  In thy saloon,
I must not leave my sky
  And nightly moon.

Be not the fowler's net
  Which stays my flight,
And craftily is set
  T' allure the sight.

But be the favoring gale
  That bears me on,
And still doth fill my sail
  When thou art gone.

I cannot leave my sky
  For thy caprice,
True love would soar as high
  As heaven is.

The eagle would not brook
  Her mate thus won,
Who trained his eye to look
  Beneath the sun.

Few things are more difficult than to help a Friend in matters which do not require the aid of Friendship, but

only a cheap and trivial service, if your Friendship wants
the basis of a thorough practical acquaintance. I stand in
the friendliest relation, on social and spiritual grounds, to
one who does not perceive what practical skill I have, but
when he seeks my assistance in such matters, is wholly
ignorant of that one with whom he deals; does not use my
skill, which in such matters is much greater than his, but
only my hands. I know another, who, on the contrary, is
remarkable for his discrimination in this respect; who
knows how to make use of the talents of others when he
does not possess the same; knows when not to look after
or oversee, and stops short at his man. It is a rare pleasure
to serve him, which all laborers know. I am not a little
pained by the other kind of treatment. It is as if, after the
friendliest and most ennobling intercourse, your Friend
should use you as a hammer and drive a nail with your
head, all in good faith; notwithstanding that you are a
tolerable carpenter, as well as his good Friend, and would
use a hammer cheerfully in his service. This want of perception is a defect which all the virtues of the heart cannot supply.—

> The Good how can we trust?
> Only the Wise are just.
> The Good we use,
> The Wise we cannot choose.
> These there are none above;
> The Good they know and love,
> But are not known again
> By those of lesser ken.
> They do not charm us with their eyes,
> But they transfix with their advice;
> No partial sympathy they feel
> With private woe or private weal,
> But with the universe joy and sigh,
> Whose knowledge is their sympathy.

Confucius said, "To contract ties of Friendship with
any one, is to contract Friendship with his virtue. There
ought not be any other motive in Friendship." But men
wish us to contract Friendship with their vice also. I have
a Friend who wishes me to see that to be right which I
know to be wrong. But if Friendship is to rob me of my

eyes, if it is to darken the day, I will have none of it. It should be expansive and inconceivably liberalizing in its effects. True Friendship can afford true knowledge. It does not depend on darkness and ignorance. A want of discernment cannot be an ingredient in it. If I can see my Friend's virtues more distinctly than another's, his faults too are made more conspicuous by contrast. We have not so good a right to hate any as our Friend. Faults are not the less faults because they are invariably balanced by corresponding virtues, and for a fault there is no excuse, though it may appear greater than it is in many ways. I have never known one who could bear criticism, who could not be flattered, who would not bribe his judge, or was content that the truth should be loved always better than himself.

If two travellers would go their way harmoniously together, the one must take as true and just a view of things as the other, else their path will not be strewn with roses. Yet you can travel profitably and pleasantly even with a blind man, if he practises common courtesy, and when you converse about the scenery will remember that he is blind but that you can see; and you will not forget that his sense of hearing is probably quickened by his want of sight. Otherwise you will not long keep company. A blind man, and a man in whose eyes there was no defect, were walking together, when they came to the edge of a precipice,—"Take care! my friend," said the latter, "here is a steep precipice; go no further this way."—"I know better," said the other, and stepped off.

It is impossible to say all that we think, even to our truest Friend. We may bid him farewell forever sooner than complain, for our complaint is too well grounded to be uttered. There is not so good an understanding between any two, but the exposure by the one of a serious fault in the other will produce a misunderstanding in proportion to its heinousness. The constitutional differences which always exist, and are obstacles to a perfect Friendship, are forever a forbidden theme to the lips of Friends. They advise by their whole behavior. Nothing can reconcile them but love. They are fatally late when they undertake to explain and treat with one another like foes. Who will take an apology for a Friend? They must apologize like dew and frost, which are off again with the sun, and which all men know in their hearts to be beneficent. The necessity itself for explanation,—what explanation will atone for that? True love does not quarrel for slight reasons, such mistakes as mutual acquaintances can explain away, but alas, however slight the apparent cause, only for adequate and fatal and everlasting reasons, which can never be set aside. Its quarrel, if there is any, is ever recurring, notwithstanding the beams of affection which invariably come to gild its tears; as the rainbow, however beautiful and unerring a sign, does not promise fair weather for ever, but only for a season. I have known two or three persons pretty well, and yet I have never known advice to be of use but in trivial and transient matters. One may know what another does not, but the utmost kindness cannot impart what is requisite to make the advice useful. We must accept or refuse one another as we are. I could tame a hyena more easily than my Friend. He is a material which no tool of mine will work. A naked savage will fell an oak with a firebrand, and wear a hatchet out of the rock by friction, but I cannot hew the smallest chip out of the character of my Friend, either to beautify or deform it.

The lover learns at last that there is no person quite transparent and trustworthy, but every one has a devil in him that is capable of any crime in the long run. Yet, as an oriental philosopher has said, "Although Friendship between good men is interrupted, their principles remain unaltered. The stalk of the lotus may be broken, and the fibres remain connected."

Ignorance and bungling with love are better than wisdom and skill without. There may be courtesy, there may be even temper, and wit, and talent, and sparkling conversation, there may be good-will even,—and yet the humanest and divinest faculties pine for exercise. Our life without love is like coke and ashes. Men may be pure as alabaster and Parian marble, elegant as a Tuscan villa, sublime as Niagara, and yet if there is no milk mingled with the wine at their entertainments, better is the hospitality of Goths and Vandals. My Friend is not of some other race or family of men, but flesh of my flesh, bone of my bone. He is my real brother. I see his nature groping yonder so like mine. We do not live far apart. Have not the fates associated us in many ways? It says, in the Vishnu Purana: "Seven paces together is sufficient for the friendship of the virtuous, but thou and I have dwelt together." Is it of no significance that we have so long partaken of the same loaf, drank at the same fountain, breathed the same air, summer and winter, felt the same heat and cold; that the same fruits have been pleased to refresh us both, and we have never had a thought of different fibre the one from the other!

> Nature doth have her dawn each day,
>   But mine are far between;
> Content, I cry, for sooth to say,
>   Mine brightest are I ween.
>
> For when my sun doth deign to rise,
>   Though it be her noontide,
> Her fairest field in shadow lies,
>   Nor can my light abide.
>
> Sometimes I bask me in her day,
>   Conversing with my mate,
> But if we interchange one ray,
>   Forthwith her heats abate.
>
> Through his discourse I climb and see,
>   As from some eastern hill,
> A brighter morrow rise to me
>   Than lieth in her skill.
>
> As 't were two summer days in one,
>   Two Sundays come together,
> Our rays united make one sun,
>   With fairest summer weather.

As surely as the sunset in my latest November shall translate me to the ethereal world, and remind me of the ruddy morning of youth; as surely as the last strain of music which falls on my decaying ear shall make age to be forgotten, or, in short, the manifold influences of nature survive during the term of our natural life, so surely my Friend shall forever be my Friend, and reflect a ray

of God to me, and time shall foster and adorn and consecrate our Friendship, no less than the ruins of temples. As
I love nature, as I love singing birds, and gleaming stubble, and flowing rivers, and morning and evening, and
summer and winter, I love thee my Friend.

But all that can be said of Friendship, is like botany to
flowers. How can the understanding take account of its
friendliness?

Even the death of Friends will inspire us as much as
their lives. They will leave consolation to the mourners, as
the rich leave money to defray the expenses of their funerals, and their memories will be incrusted over with
sublime and pleasing thoughts, as monuments of other
men are overgrown with moss; for our Friends have no
place in the graveyard.

This to our cis-Alpine and cis-Atlantic Friends.

Also this other word of entreaty and advice to the large
and respectable nation of Acquaintances, beyond the
mountains;—Greeting.

My most serene and irresponsible neighbors, let us see
that we have the whole advantage of each other; we will
be useful, at least, if not admirable, to one another. I
know that the mountains which separate us are high, and
covered with perpetual snow, but despair not. Improve
the serene winter weather to scale them. If need be, soft-
en the rocks with vinegar. For here lie the verdant plains
of Italy ready to receive you. Nor shall I be slow on my
side to penetrate to your Provence. Strike then boldly at
head or heart or any vital part. Depend upon it the timber is well seasoned and tough, and will bear rough usage; and if it should crack, there is plenty more where it
came from. I am no piece of crockery that cannot be
jostled against my neighbor without danger of being broken by the collision, and must needs ring false and jar-
ringly to the end of my days, when once I am cracked;
but rather one of the old fashioned wooden trenchers,
which one while stands at the head of the table, and at
another is a milking-stool, and at another a seat for children, and finally goes down to its grave not unadorned
with honorable scars, and does not die till it is worn out.

Nothing can shock a brave man but dulness. Think how many rebuffs every man has experienced in his day; perhaps has fallen into a horse-pond, eaten fresh-water clams, or worn one shirt for a week without washing. Indeed, you cannot receive a shock unless you have an electric affinity for that which shocks you. Use me, then, for I am useful in my way, and stand as one of many petitioners, from toadstool and henbane up to dahlia and violet, supplicating to be put to my use, if by any means ye may find me serviceable; whether for a medicated drink or bath, as balm and lavender; or for fragrance, as verbena and geranium; or for sight, as cactus; or for thoughts, as pansy.—These humbler, at least, if not those higher uses.

Ah my dear Strangers and Enemies, I would not forget you. I can well afford to welcome you. Let me subscribe myself Yours ever and truly—your much obliged servant. We have nothing to fear from our foes; God keeps a standing army for that service; but we have no ally against our Friends, those ruthless Vandals.

THE JOURNAL

*For the whole of his adult life, from October 1837 when
he was twenty, to November of 1861, six months before
his death in May of 1862, Thoreau recorded his
thoughts in his Journal, which in the aggregate comprises almost three million words. The range of his
moods is broad, from light-hearted whimsy to satire and
irony. A large portion of his published work had its in-
ception in this comprehensive autobiography of his intellect and imagination. Revealed in the Journal is a
man for whom no experience was insignificant in his
personal search for self-knowledge. The reader should
bear in mind that Thoreau never intended to publish
these materials. Texts for the following excerpts are
from the Walden Edition of 1906, under the dates indi-
cated in the table of contents. The Princeton Editors
have not yet established the definitive texts.*

SETTING FIRE TO THE CONCORD WOODS

I once set fire to the woods. Having set out, one April
day, to go to the sources of Concord River in a boat with
a single companion, meaning to camp on the bank at
night or seek a lodging in some neighboring country inn
or farmhouse, we took fishing tackle with us that we

might fitly procure our food from the stream, Indian-like. At the shoemaker's near the river, we obtained a match, which we had forgotten. Though it was thus early in the spring, the river was low, for there had not been much rain, and we succeeded in catching a mess of fish sufficient for our dinner before we had left the town, and by the shores of Fair Haven Pond we proceeded to cook them. The earth was uncommonly dry, and our fire, kindled far from the woods in a sunny recess in the hillside on the east of the pond, suddenly caught the dry grass of the previous year which grew about the stump on which it was kindled. We sprang to extinguish it at first with our hands and feet, and then we fought it with a board obtained from the boat, but in a few minutes it was beyond our reach; being on the side of a hill, it spread rapidly upward, through the long, dry, wiry grass interspersed with bushes.

"Well, where will this end?" asked my companion. I saw that it might be bounded by Well Meadow Brook on one side, but would, perchance, go to the village side of the brook. "It will go to town," I answered. While my companion took the boat back down the river, I set out through the woods to inform the owners and to raise the town. The fire had already spread a dozen rods on every side and went leaping and crackling wildly and irreclaimably toward the wood. That way went the flames with wild delight, and we felt that we had no control over the demonic creature to which we had given birth. We had kindled many fires in the woods before, burning a clear space in the grass, without ever kindling such a fire as this.

As I ran toward the town through the woods, I could see the smoke over the woods behind me marking the spot and the progress of the flames. The first farmer whom I met driving a team, after leaving the woods, inquired the cause of the smoke. I told him. "Well," said he, "it is none of my stuff," and drove along. The next I met was the owner in his field, with whom I returned at once to the woods, running all the way. I had already run two miles. When at length we got into the neighborhood of the flames, we met a carpenter who had been hewing timber, an infirm man who had been driven off by the fire, fleeing with his axe. The farmer returned to hasten more assistance. I, who was spent with running, remained. What could I do alone against a front of flame half a mile wide?

I walked slowly through the wood to Fair Haven Cliff, climbed to the highest rock, and sat down upon it to observe the progress of the flames, which were rapidly approaching me, now about a mile distant from the spot where the fire was kindled. Presently I heard the sound of the distant bell giving the alarm, and I knew that the town was on its way to the scene. Hitherto I had felt like a guilty person,—nothing but shame and regret. But now I settled the matter with myself shortly. I said to myself: "Who are these men who are said to be the owners of these woods, and how am I related to them? I have set fire to the forest, but I have done no wrong therein, and now it is as if the lightning had done it. These flames are but consuming their natural food." (It has never troubled me from that day to this more than if the lightning had done it. The trivial fishing was all that disturbed me and disturbs me still.) So shortly I settled it with myself and stood to watch the approaching flames. It was a glorious spectacle, and I was the only one there to enjoy it. The fire now reached the base of the cliff and then rushed up its sides. The squirrels ran before it in blind haste, and three pigeons dashed into the midst of the smoke. The flames flashed up the pines to their tops, as if they were powder.

When I found I was about to be surrounded by the fire, I retreated and joined the forces now arriving from the town. It took us several hours to surround the flames with our hoes and shovels and by back fires subdue them. In the midst of all I saw the farmer whom I first met, who had turned indifferently away saying it was none of his stuff, striving earnestly to save his corded wood, his stuff, which the fire had already seized and which it after all consumed.

It burned over a hundred acres or more and destroyed much young wood. When I returned home late in the day, with others of my townsmen, I could not help noticing that the crowd who were so ready to condemn the individual who had kindled the fire did not sympathize with the owners of the wood, but were in fact highly elate and as it were thankful for the opportunity which had afforded them so much sport; and it was only half a dozen owners, so called, though not all of them, who looked sour or grieved, and I felt that I had a deeper interest in the woods, knew them better and should feel their loss more, than any or all of them. The farmer whom I had first conducted to the woods was obliged to ask me the shortest way back, through his own lot. Why, then, should the half-dozen owners [and] the individuals who set the fire alone feel sorrow for the loss of the wood, while the rest of the town have their spirits raised? Some of the owners, however, bore their loss like men, but other some declared behind my back that I was a "damned rascal;" and a flibbertigibbet or two, who crowed like the old cock, shouted some reminiscences of "burnt woods" from safe recesses for some years after. I have had nothing to say to any of them. The locomotive engine has since burned over nearly all the same ground and more, and in some measure blotted out the memory of the previous fire. For a long time after I had learned this lesson I marvelled that while matches and tinder were contemporaries the world was not consumed; why the houses that have hearths were not burned before another day; if the flames were not as hungry now as when I waked them. I at once ceased to regard the owners and my own fault,— if fault there was any in the matter,—and attended to the phenomenon before me, determined to make the most of it. To be sure, I felt a little ashamed when I reflected on what a trivial occasion this had happened, that at the time I was no better employed than my townsmen.

That night I watched the fire, where some stumps still flamed at midnight in the midst of the blackened waste, wandering through the woods by myself; and far in the night I threaded my way to the spot where the fire had taken, and discovered the now broiled fish,—which had been dressed,—scattered over the burnt grass.

PERSPECTIVE

DEATH OF A PINE TREE

This afternoon, being on Fair Haven Hill, I heard the sound of a saw, and soon after from the Cliff saw two men sawing down a noble pine beneath, about forty rods off. I resolved to watch it till it fell, the last of a dozen or more which were left when the forest was cut and for fifteen years have waved in solitary majesty over the sprout-land. I saw them like beavers or insects gnawing at the trunk of this noble tree, the diminutive manikins with their cross-cut saw which could scarcely span it. It towered up a hundred feet as I afterward found by measurement, one of the tallest probably in the township and straight as an arrow, but slanting a little toward the hillside, its top seen against the frozen river and the hills of Conantum. I watch closely to see when it begins to move. Now the sawers stop, and with an axe open it a little on the side toward which it leans, that it may break the faster. And now their saw goes again. Now surely it is going; it is inclined one quarter of the quadrant, and, breathless, I expect its crashing fall. But no, I was mistaken; it has not moved an inch; it stands at the same angle as at first. It is fifteen minutes yet to its fall. Still its branches wave in the wind, as if it were destined to stand for a century, and the wind soughs through its needles as of yore; it is still a forest tree, the most majestic tree that waves over Musketaquid. The silvery sheen of the sunlight is reflected from its needles; it still affords an inaccessible crotch for the squirrel's nest; not a lichen has forsaken its mast-like stem, its raking mast,—the hill is the hulk. Now, now's the moment! The manikins at its base are fleeing from their crime. They have dropped the guilty saw and axe. How slowly and majestically it starts! as if it were only swayed by a summer breeze, and would return without a sigh to its location in the air. And now it fans the hillside with its fall, and it lies down to its bed in the valley, from which it is never to rise, as softly as a feather, folding its green mantle about it like a warrior, as if, tired of standing, it embraced the earth with silent joy, returning its elements to the dust again. But hark! there

THE FALL

you only saw, but did not hear. There now comes up a
deafening crash to these rocks, advertising you that even
trees do not die without a groan. It rushes to embrace the
earth, and mingle its elements with the dust. And now all
is still once more and forever, both to eye and ear.

I went down and measured it. It was about four feet in
diameter where it was sawed, about one hundred feet
long. Before I had reached it the axemen had already
half divested it of its branches. Its gracefully spreading
top was a perfect wreck on the hillside as if it had been
made of glass, and the tender cones of one year's growth
upon its summit appealed in vain and too late to the mercy of the chopper. Already he has measured it with his
axe, and marked off the mill-logs it will make. And the
space it occupied in upper air is vacant for the next two
centuries. It is lumber. He has laid waste the air. When
the fish hawk in the spring revisits the banks of the Musketaquid, he will circle in vain to find his accustomed
perch, and the hen-hawk will mourn for the pines lofty
enough to protect her brood. A plant which it has taken
two centuries to perfect, rising by slow stages into the
heavens, has this afternoon ceased to exist. Its sapling top
had expanded to this January thaw as the forerunner of
summers to come. Why does not the village bell sound a
knell? I hear no knell tolled. I see no procession of
mourners in the streets, or the woodland aisles. The squirrel has leaped to another tree; the hawk has circled further off, and has now settled upon a new eyrie, but the
woodman is preparing [to] lay his axe at the root of that
also.

CATCHING A PIG

3:30 P.M.—When I came forth, thinking to empty my
boat and go a-meditating along the river,—for the full
ditches and drenched grass forbade other routes, except
the highway,—and this is one advantage of a boat,—I
learned to my chagrin that Father's pig was gone. He had
leaped out of the pen some time since his breakfast, but
his dinner was untouched. Here was an ugly duty not to

be shirked,—a wild shoat that weighed but ninety to be
tracked, caught, and penned,—an afternoon's work, at
least (if I were lucky enough to accomplish it so soon),
prepared for me, quite different from what I had anticipated. I felt chagrined, it is true, but I could not ignore
the fact nor shirk the duty that lay so near to me. Do the
duty that lies nearest to thee. I proposed to Father to sell
the pig as he was running (somewhere) to a neighbor who
had talked of buying him, making a considerable reduc-
tion. But my suggestion was not acted on, and the respon-
sibilities of the case all devolved on me, for I could run
faster than Father. Father looked to me, and I ceased to
look to the river. Well, let us see if we can track him. Yes,
this is the corner where he got out, making a step of his
trough. Thanks to the rain, his tracks are quite distinct.
Here he went along the edge of the garden over the water and muskmelons, then through the beans and potatoes, and even along the front-yard walk I detect the
print of his divided hoof, his two sharp toes (*ungulæ*). It's
a wonder we did not see him. And here he passed out
under the gate, across the road,—how naked he must
have felt!—into a grassy ditch, and whither next? Is it of
any use to go hunting him up unless you have devised
some mode of catching him when you have found? Of
what avail to know where he has been, even where he is?
He was so shy the little while we had him, of course he
will never come back; he cannot be tempted by a swill-
pail. Who knows how many miles off he is! Perhaps he
has taken the back track and gone to Brighton, or Ohio!
At most, probably we shall only have the satisfaction of
glimpsing the nimble beast at a distance, from time to
time, as he trots swiftly through the green meadows and
corn-fields. But, now I speak, what is that I see pacing
deliberately up the middle of the street forty rods off? It
is *he*. As if to tantalize, to tempt us to waste our afternoon
without further hesitation, he thus offers himself. He
roots a foot or two and then lies down on his belly in the
middle of the street. But think not to catch him a-nap-
ping. He has his eyes about, and his ears too. He has already been chased. He gives that wagon a wide berth,
and now, seeing me, he turns and trots back down the

street. He turns into a front yard. Now if I can only close
that gate upon him ninety-nine hundredths of the work is
done, but ah! he hears me coming afar off, he foresees
the danger, and, with swinish cunning and speed, he
scampers out. My neighbor in the street tries to head him;
he jumps to this side the road, then to that, before him;
but the third time the pig was there first and went by.
"Whose is it?" he shouts. "It's ours." He bolts into that
neighbor's yard and so across his premises. He has been
twice there before, it seems; he knows the road; see what
work he has made in his flower-garden! He must be fond
of bulbs. Our neighbor picks up one tall flower with its
bulb attached, holds it out at arm's length. He is excited
about the pig; it is a subject he is interested in. But where
is [he] gone now? The last glimpse I had of him was as he
went through the cow-yard; here are his tracks again in
this corn-field, but they are lost in the grass. We lose him;
we beat the bushes in vain; he may be far away. But
hark! I heard a grunt. Nevertheless for half an hour I do
not see him that grunted. At last I find fresh tracks along
the river, and again lose them. Each neighbor whose garden I traverse tells me some anecdote of losing pigs, or
the attempt to drive them, by which I am not encouraged. Once more he crosses our first neighbor's garden
and is said to be in the road. But I am not there yet; it is a
good way off. At length my eyes rest on him again, after
three quarters of an hour's separation. There he trots with
the whole road to himself, and now again drops on his
belly in a puddle. Now he starts again, seeing me twenty
rods [off], deliberates, considers which way I want him to
go, and goes the other. There was some chance of driving
him along the sidewalk, or letting him go rather, till he
slipped under our gate again, but of what avail would
that be? How corner and catch him who keeps twenty
rods off? He never lets the open side of the triangle be
less than half a dozen rods wide. There was one place
where a narrower street turned off at right angles with
the main one, just this side our yard, but I could not drive
him past that. Twice he ran up the narrow street, for he
knew I did not wish it, but though the main street was
broad and open and no traveller in sight, when I tried to

drive him past this opening he invariably turned his pig-
gish head toward me, dodged from side to side, and finally ran up the narrow street or down the main one, as if
there were a high barrier erected before him. But really
he is no more obstinate than I. I cannot but respect his
tactics and his independence. He will be he, and I may
be I. He is not unreasonable because he thwarts me, but
only the more reasonable. He has a strong will. He stands
upon his idea. There is a wall across the path not where a
man bars the way, but where he is resolved not to travel.
Is he not superior to man therein? Once more he glides
down the narrow street, deliberates at a corner, chooses
wisely for him, and disappears through an openwork
fence eastward. He has gone to fresh gardens and pastures new. Other neighbors stand in the doorways but
half sympathizing, only observing, "Ugly thing to catch."
"You have a job on your hands." I lose sight of him, but
hear that he is far ahead in a large field. And there we
try to let him alone a while, giving him a wide berth.

At this stage an Irishman was engaged to assist. "I can
catch him," says he, with Buonapartean confidence. He
thinks him a family Irish pig. His wife is with him, bare-
headed, and his little flibbertigibbet of a boy, seven years
old. "Here, Johnny, do you run right off there" (at the
broadest possible angle with his own course). "Oh, but he
can't do anything." "Oh, but I only want him to tell me
where he is,—to keep sight of him." Michael soon discovers that he is not an Irish pig, and his wife and Johnny's
occupation are soon gone. Ten minutes afterward I am
patiently tracking him step by step through a corn-field,
a near-sighted man helping me, and then into garden after garden far eastward, and finally into the highway, at
the grave-yard; but hear and see nothing. One suggests a
dog to track him. Father is meanwhile selling him to the
blacksmith, who also is trying to get sight of him. After
fifteen minutes since he disappeared eastward, I hear
that he has been to the river twice far on [?] the north,
through the first neighbor's premises. I wend that way.
He crosses the street far ahead, Michael behind; he
dodges up an avenue. I stand in the gap there, Michael at
the other end, and now he tries to corner him. But it is a

vain hope to corner him in a yard. I see a carriage-manu-
factory door open. "Let him go in there, Flannery." For
once the pig and I are of one mind; he bolts in, and the
door is closed. Now for a rope. It is a large barn, crowded
with carriages. The rope is at length obtained; the windows are barred with carriages lest he bolt through. He is
resting quietly on his belly in the further corner, thinking
unutterable things.

Now the course recommences within narrower limits.
Bump, bump, bump he goes, against wheels and shafts.
We get no hold yet. He is all ear and eye. Small boys are
sent under the carriages to drive him out. He froths at the
mouth and deters them. At length he is stuck for an instant between the spokes of a wheel, and I am securely
attached to his hind leg. He squeals deafeningly, and is
silent. The rope is attached to a hind leg. The door is
opened, and the *driving* commences. Roll an egg as well.
You may drag him, but you cannot drive him. But he is
in the road, and now another thunder-shower greets us. I
leave Michael with the rope in one hand and a switch in
the other and go home. He seems to be gaining a little
westward. But, after long delay, I look out and find that
he makes but doubtful progress. A boy is made to face
him with a stick, and it is only when the pig springs at
him savagely that progress is made homeward. He will be
killed before he is driven home. I get a wheelbarrow and
go to the rescue. Michael is alarmed. The pig is rabid,
snaps at him. We drag him across the barrow, hold him
down, and so, at last, get him home.

If a wild shoat like this gets loose, first track him if you
can, or otherwise discover where he is. Do not scare him
more than you can help. Think of some yard or building
or other inclosure that will hold him and, by showing
your forces—yet as if uninterested parties—fifteen or
twenty rods off, let him of his own accord enter it. Then
slightly shut the gate. Now corner and tie him and put
him into a cart or barrow.

All progress in driving at last was made by facing and
endeavoring to switch him from home. He rushed upon
you and made a few feet in the desired direction. When I
approached with the barrow he advanced to meet it with
determination.

Nice ending

So I get home at dark, wet through and supperless, covered with mud and wheel-grease, without any rare flowers.

****

Last Friday (the 22d) afternoon (when I was away), Father's pig got out again and took to the riverside. The next day he was heard from, but not found. That night he was seen on an island in the meadow, in the midst of the flood, but thereafter for some time no account of him. J. Farmer advised to go to Ai Hale, just over the Carlisle line. He has got a dog which, if you put him on the track of the pig not more than four hours' old, will pursue and catch him and hold him by the ear without hurting him till you come up. That's the best way. Ten men cannot stop him in the road, but he will go by them. It was generally conceded that the right kind of dog was all that was wanted, like Ai Hale's, one that would hold him by the ear, but not uselessly maim him. One or two said, "If I only had such a one's dog, I'd catch him for so much."

Neighbors sympathized as much as in them lay. It was the town talk; the meetings were held at Wolcott & Holden's. Every man told of his losses and disappointments in this line. One had heard of his pig last up in Westford, but never saw him again; another had only caught his pig by his running against a post so hard as to stun himself for a few moments. It was thought this one must have been born in the woods, for he would run and leap like a wolf. Some advised not to build so very high, but lay the upper board flat over the pen, for then, when he caught by his fore feet, his body would swing under to no purpose. One said you would not catch him to buy a pig out of a drove. Our pig ran as if he *still* had the devil in him. It was generally conceded that a good dog was the desideratum. But thereupon Lawrence, the harness-maker, came forward and told his experience. He once helped hunt a pig in the next town. He weighed two hundred; had been out some time (though not in '75), but they learned where he resorted; but they got a capital dog of the right kind. They had the dog tied lest he should scare the pig too soon. They crawled along very carefully near to the hollow where the pig was till they could hear him. They knew that if he should hear them and he was wide awake, he would dash off with a grunt, and that would be the last of him, but what more could they do? They consulted in a whisper and concluded to let the dog go. They did so, and directly heard an awful yelp; rushed up; the pig was gone, and there lay the dog torn all to pieces! At this there was a universal *haw! haw!* and the reputation of dogs fell, and the chance of catching the pig seemed less.

Two dollars reward was offered to him who would catch and return him without maiming him. At length, the 26th, he was heard from. He was caught and tied in north part of the town. Took to a swamp, as they say they are inclined. He was chased two hours with a spaniel dog, which never faced him, nor touched him, but, as the man said, "tuckered him out," kept him on the go and showed where he was. When at a distance the pig stopped and faced the dog until the pursuers came up. He was brought home the 27th, all his legs tied, and put into his new pen. It was a very deep one. It might have been made deeper, but Father did not wish to build a wall, and the man who caught him and got his two dollars for it thought it ought to hold any decent pig. Father said he didn't wish to keep him in a well.

A PRIVATE MOUNTAIN

There are some things of which I cannot at once tell whether I have dreamed them or they are real; as if they were just, perchance, establishing, or else losing, a real basis in my world. This is especially the case in the early morning hours, when there is a gradual transition from dreams to waking thoughts, from illusions to actualities, as from darkness, or perchance moon and star light, to sunlight. Dreams are real, as is the light of the stars and moon, and theirs is said to be a *dreamy* light. Such early morning thoughts as I speak of occupy a debatable ground between dreams and waking thoughts. They are a sort of permanent dream in my mind. At least, until we have for some time changed our position from prostrate to erect, and commenced or faced some of the duties of the day, we cannot tell what we have dreamed from what we have actually experienced.]

This morning, for instance, for the twentieth time at least, I thought of that mountain in the easterly part of our town (where no high hill actually is) which once or twice I had ascended, and often allowed my thoughts alone to climb. I now contemplate it in my mind as a familiar thought which I have surely had for many years from time to time, but whether anything could have reminded me of it in the middle of yesterday, whether I ever before remembered it in broad daylight, I doubt. I can now eke out the vision I had of it this morning with my old and yesterday forgotten dreams.

My way up used to lie through a dark and unfrequented wood at its base,—I cannot now tell exactly, it was so long ago, under what circumstances I first ascended, only that I shuddered as I went along (I have an indistinct remembrance of having been out overnight alone),—and then I steadily ascended along a rocky ridge half clad with stinted trees, where wild beasts haunted, till I lost myself quite in the upper air and clouds, seeming to pass an imaginary line which separates a hill, mere earth heaped up, from a mountain, into a superterranean grandeur and sublimity. What distinguishes that summit above the earthy line, is that it is unhandselled, awful, grand. It can never become familiar; you are lost the moment you set foot there. You know no path, but wander, thrilled, over the bare and pathless rock, as if it were solidified air and cloud. That rocky, misty summit, secreted in the clouds, was far more thrillingly awful and sublime than the crater of a volcano spouting fire.

This is a business we can partly understand. The perfect mountain height is already thoroughly purified. It is as if you trod with awe the face of a god turned up, unwittingly but helplessly, yielding to the laws of gravity. And are there not such mountains, east or west, from which you may look down on Concord in your thought, and on all the world? In dreams I am shown this height from time to time, and I seem to have asked my fellow once to climb there with me, and yet I am constrained to believe that I never actually ascended it. It chances, now

I think of it, that it rises in my mind where lies the Bury-ing-Hill. You might go through its gate to enter that dark wood, but that hill and its graves are so concealed and obliterated by the awful mountain that I never thought of them as underlying it. Might not the graveyards of the just always be hills, ways by which we ascend and over-look the plain?

But my old way down was different, and, indeed, this was another way up, though I never so ascended. I came out, as I descended, breathing the thicker air. I came out the belt of wood into a familiar pasture, and along down by a wall. Often, as I go along the low side of this pas-ture, I let my thoughts ascend toward the mount, gradu-ally entering the stinted wood (Nature subdued) and the thinner air, and drape themselves with mists. There are ever two ways up: one is through the dark wood, the oth-er through the sunny pasture. That is, I reach and discov-er the mountain only through the dark wood, but I see to my surprise, when I look off between the mists from its summit, how it is ever adjacent to my native fields, nay, imminent over them, and accessible through a sunny pas-ture. Why is it that in the lives of men we hear more of the dark wood than of the sunny pasture?

A hard-featured god reposing, whose breath hangs about his forehead.

ON SEEING

If, about the last of October, you ascend any hill in the outskirts of the town and look over the forest, you will see, amid the brown of other oaks, which are now with-ered, and the green of the pines, the bright-red tops or crescents of the scarlet oaks, very equally and thickly dis-tributed on all sides, even to the horizon. Complete trees standing exposed on the edges of the forest, where you have never suspected them, or their tops only in the re-cesses of the forest surface, or perhaps towering above the surrounding trees, or reflecting a warm rose red from the very edge of the horizon in favorable lights. All this you will see, and much more, if you are prepared to see it,—

if you *look* for it. Otherwise, regular and universal as this phenomenon is, you will think for threescore year and ten that all the wood is at this season sere and brown. Objects are concealed from our view not so much because they are out of the course of our visual ray (continued) as because there is no intention of the mind and eye toward them. We do not realize how far and widely, or how near and narrowly, we are to look. The greater part of the phenomena of nature are for this reason concealed to us all our lives. Here, too, as in political economy, the supply answers to the demand. Nature does not cast pearls before swine. There is just as much beauty visible to us in the landscape as we are prepared to appreciate,—not a grain more. The actual objects which one person will see from a particular hilltop are just as different from those which another will see as the persons are different. The scarlet oak must, in a sense, be in your eye when you go forth. We cannot see anything until we are possessed with the idea of it, and then we can hardly see anything else. In my botanical rambles I find that first the idea, or image, of a plant occupies my thoughts, though it may at first seem very foreign to this locality, and for some weeks or months I go thinking of it and expecting it unconsciously, and at length I surely see it, and it is henceforth an actual neighbor of mine. This is the history of my finding a score or more of rare plants which I could name.

Take one of our selectmen and put him on the highest hill in the township, and tell him to look! What, probably, would he see? What would he *select* to look at? Sharpening his sight to the utmost, and putting on the glasses that suited him best, aye, using a spy-glass if he liked, straining his optic nerve to its utmost, and making a full report. Of course, he would see a Brocken spectre of himself. Now take Julius Cæsar, or Emanuel Swedenborg, or a Fiji-Islander, and set him up there! Let them compare notes afterward. Would it appear that they had enjoyed the same prospect? For aught we know, as strange a man as any of these is always at our elbows. It does not appear that anybody saw Shakespeare when he was about in England looking off, but only some of his raiment.

Why, it takes a sharpshooter to bring down even such
trivial game as snipes and woodcocks; he must take very
particular aim, and know what he is aiming at. He would
stand a very small chance if he fired at random into the
sky, being told that snipes were flying there. And so it is
with him that shoots at beauty. Not till the sky falls will
he catch larks, unless he is a trained sportsman. He will
not bag any if he does not already know its seasons and
haunts and the color of its wing,— if he has not dreamed
of it, so that he can *anticipate* it; then, indeed, he flushes
it at every step, shoots double and on the wing, with both
barrels, even in corn-fields. The sportsman trains himself,
dresses, and watches unweariedly, and loads and primes
for his particular game. He prays for it, and so he gets it.
After due and long preparation, schooling his eye and
hand, dreaming awake and asleep, with gun and paddle
and boat, he goes out after meadow-hens,—which most
of his townsmen never saw nor dreamed of,—paddles for
miles against a head wind, and therefore he gets them.
He had them half-way into his bag when he started, and
has only to shove them down. The fisherman, too, dreams
of fish, till he can almost catch them in his sink-spout.
The hen scratches, and finds her food right under where
she stands; but such is not the way with the hawk.

The true sportsman can shoot you almost any of his
game from his windows. It comes and perches at last on
the barrel of his gun; but the rest of the world never see
it, with the feathers on. He will keep himself supplied by
firing up his chimney. The geese fly exactly under his
zenith, and honk when they get there. Twenty musquash
have the refusal of each one of his traps before it is empty.

ARROWHEADS

It is now high time to look for arrowheads, etc. I spend
many hours every spring gathering the crop which the
melting snow and rain has washed bare. When, at length,
some island in the meadow or some sandy field elsewhere
has been plowed, perhaps for rye, in the fall, I take note

of it, and do not fail to repair thither as soon as the earth begins to be dry in the spring. If the spot chances never to have been cultivated before, I am the first to gather a crop from it. The farmer little thinks that another reaps a harvest which is the fruit of his toil. As much ground is turned up in a day by the plow as Indian implements could not have turned over in a month, and my eyes rest on the evidences of an aboriginal life which passed here a thousand years ago perchance. Especially if the knolls in the meadows are washed by a freshet where they have been plowed the previous fall, the soil will be taken away lower down and the stones left,—the arrowheads, etc., and soapstone pottery amid them,—somewhat as gold is washed in a dish or tom. I landed on two spots this afternoon and picked up a dozen arrowheads. It is one of the regular pursuits of the spring. As much as sportsmen go in pursuit of ducks, and gunners of musquash, and scholars of rare books, and travellers of adventures, and poets of ideas, and all men of money, I go in search of arrowheads when the proper season comes round again. So I help myself to live worthily, and loving my life as I should. It is a good collyrium to look on the bare earth,— to pore over it so much, getting strength to all your senses, like Antæus. If I did not find arrowheads, I might, perchance, begin to pick up crockery and fragments of pipes,—the relics of a more recent man. Indeed, you can hardly name a more innocent or wholesome entertainment. As I am thus engaged, I hear the rumble of the bowling-alley's thunder, which has begun again in the village. It comes before the earliest natural thunder. But what its lightning is, and what atmospheres it purifies, I do not know. Or I might collect the various bones which I come across. They would make a museum that would delight some Owen at last, and what a text they might furnish me for a course of lectures on human life or the like! I might spend my days collecting the fragments of pipes until I found enough, after all my search, to compose one perfect pipe when laid together.

I have not decided whether I had better publish my experience in searching for arrowheads in three volumes, with plates and an index, or try to compress it into one.

These durable implements seem to have been suggested to the Indian mechanic with a view to my entertainment in a succeeding period. After all the labor expended on it, the bolt may have been shot but once perchance, and the shaft which was devoted to it decayed, and there lay the arrowhead, sinking into the ground, awaiting me. They lie all over the hills with like expectation, and in due time the husbandman is sent, and, tempted by the promise of corn or rye, he plows the land and turns them up to my view. Many as I have found, methinks the last one gives me about the same delight that the first did. Some time or other, you would say, it had rained arrowheads, for they lie all over the surface of America. You may have your peculiar tastes. Certain localities in your town may seem from association unattractive and uninhabitable to you. You may wonder that the land bears any money value there, and pity some poor fellow who is said to survive in that neighborhood. But plow up a new field there, and you will find the omnipresent arrow-points strewn over it, and it will appear that the red man, with other tastes and associations, lived there too. No matter how far from the modern road or meeting-house, no matter how near. They lie in the meeting-house cellar, and they lie in the distant cow-pasture. And some collections which were made a century ago by the curious like myself have been dispersed again, and they are still as good as new. You cannot tell the third-hand ones (for they are all second-hand) from the others, such is their persistent out-of-door durability; for they were chiefly made to be lost. They are sown, like a grain that is slow to germinate, broadcast over the earth. Like the dragon's teeth which bore a crop of soldiers, these bear crops of philosophers and poets, and the same seed is just as good to plant again. It is a stone fruit. Each one yields me a thought. I come nearer to the maker of it than if I found his bones. His bones would not prove any wit that wielded them, such as this work of his bones does. It is humanity inscribed on the face of the earth, patent to my eyes as soon as the snow goes off, not hidden away in some crypt or grave or under a pyramid. No disgusting mummy, but a clean stone, the best symbol or letter that could have been transmitted to me.

The Red Man, his mark   ⟶

At every step I see it, and I can easily supply the "Tahatawan" or "Mantatuket" that might have been written if he had had a clerk. It is no single inscription on a particular rock, but a footprint—rather a mind-print—left everywhere, and altogether illegible. No vandals, however vandalic in their disposition, can be so industrious as to destroy them.

Time will soon destroy the works of famous painters and sculptors, but the Indian arrowhead will balk his efforts and Eternity will have to come to his aid. They are not fossil bones, but, as it were, fossil thoughts, forever reminding me of the mind that shaped them. I would fain know that I am treading in the tracks of human game,—that I am on the trail of mind,—and these little reminders never fail to set me right. When I see these signs I know that the subtle spirits that made them are not far off, into whatever form transmuted. What if you do plow and hoe amid them, and swear that not one stone shall be left upon another? They are only the less like to break in that case. When you turn up one layer you bury another so much the more securely. They are at peace with rust. This arrow-headed character promises to outlast all others. The larger pestles and axes may, perchance, grow scarce and be broken, but the arrowhead shall, perhaps, never cease to wing its way through the ages of eternity. It was originally winged for but a short flight, but it still, to my mind's eye, wings its way through the ages, bearing a message from the hand that shot it. Myriads of arrow-points lie sleeping in the skin of the revolving earth, while meteors revolve in space. The footprint, the mind-print of the oldest men. When some Vandal chieftain has razed to the earth the British Museum, and, perchance, the winged bulls from Nineveh shall have lost most if not all of their features, the arrowheads which the museum contains will, perhaps, find themselves at home again in familiar dust, and resume their shining in new springs upon the bared surface of the earth then, to be picked up for the thousandth time by the shepherd or savage that may be wandering there, and once more suggest their story to him. Indifferent they to

British Museums, and, no doubt, Nineveh bulls are old acquaintances of theirs, for they have camped on the plains of Mesopotamia, too, and were buried *with* the winged bulls.

They cannot be said to be lost nor found. Surely their use was not so much to bear its fate to some bird or quadruped, or man, as it was to lie here near the surface of the earth for a perpetual reminder to the generations that come after. As for museums, I think it is better to let Nature take care of our antiquities. These are our antiquities, and they are cleaner to think of than the rubbish of the Tower of London, and they are a more ancient armor than is there. It is a recommendation that they are so inobvious,—that they occur only to the eye and thought that chances to be directed toward them. When you pick up an arrowhead and put it in your pocket, it may say: "Eh, you think you have got me, do you? But I shall wear a hole in your pocket at last, or if you put me in your cabinet, your heir or great-grandson will forget me or throw me out the window directly, or when the house falls I shall drop into the cellar, and there I shall lie quite at home again. Ready to be *found* again, eh? Perhaps some new red man that is to come will fit me to a shaft and make me do his bidding for a bow-shot. What reck I?"

ARROWHEAD'S SPEECH

WALDEN

"I do not propose to write an ode to dejection," Thoreau wrote on the title page of his greatest book, "but to brag as lustily as Chanticleer in the morning, standing on his roost, if only to wake my neighbors up." The influence of his book, however, reached far beyond his neighbors, and has been felt in many countries of the earth. Few writers have brought English prose to the level of beauty and expressiveness that Thoreau here achieves through the discipline of many drafts, as many as seven for some portions of the book. On one level the book records the results of Thoreau's "experiment" in living alone on the shore of Walden Pond, separating the "ends" of life from the "means"; but on its deepest level it becomes an odyssey of the imagination, a hymn to the greatness of the human spirit and its capacities for ennobling itself. Texts of the four key chapters reprinted here are from the definitive Princeton Edition, edited by Lyndon Shanley (1971).

WHERE I LIVED,
AND WHAT I LIVED FOR

AT A CERTAIN SEASON of our life we are accustomed to consider every spot as the possible site of a house. I have thus surveyed the country on every side within a dozen

miles of where I live. In imagination I have bought all
the farms in succession, for all were to be bought, and I
knew their price. I walked over each farmer's premises,
tasted his wild apples, discoursed on husbandry with him,
took his farm at his price, at any price, mortgaging it to
him in my mind; even put a higher price on it,—took
every thing but a deed of it,—took his word for his deed,
for I dearly love to talk,—cultivated it, and him too to
some extent, I trust, and withdrew when I had enjoyed it
long enough, leaving him to carry it on. This experience
entitled me to be regarded as a sort of real-estate broker
by my friends. Wherever I sat, there I might live, and the
landscape radiated from me accordingly. What is a house
but a *sedes*, a seat?—better if a country seat. I discovered
many a site for a house not likely to be soon improved,
which some might have thought too far from the village,
but to my eyes the village was too far from it. Well, there
I might live, I said; and there I did live, for an hour, a
summer and a winter life; saw how I could let the years
run off, buffet the winter through, and see the spring
come in. The future inhabitants of this region, wherever
they may place their houses, may be sure that they have
been anticipated. An afternoon sufficed to lay out the
land into orchard woodlot and pasture, and to decide
what fine oaks or pines should be left to stand before the
door, and whence each blasted tree could be seen to the
best advantage; and then I let it lie, fallow perchance, for
a man is rich in proportion to the number of things which
he can afford to let alone.

My imagination carried me so far that I even had the
refusal of several farms,—the refusal was all I wanted,—
but I never got my fingers burned by actual possession.
The nearest that I came to actual possession was when I
bought the Hollowell Place, and had begun to sort my
seeds, and collected materials with which to make a
wheelbarrow to carry it on or off with; but before the
owner gave me a deed of it, his wife—every man has
such a wife—changed her mind and wished to keep it,
and he offered me ten dollars to release him. Now, to
speak the truth, I had but ten cents in the world, and it
surpassed my arithmetic to tell, if I was that man who

had ten cents, or who had a farm, or ten dollars, or all together. However, I let him keep the ten dollars and the farm too, for I had carried it far enough; or rather, to be generous, I sold him the farm for just what I gave for it, and, as he was not a rich man, made him a present of ten dollars, and still had my ten cents, and seeds, and materials for a wheelbarrow left. I found thus that I had been a rich man without any damage to my poverty. But I retained the landscape, and I have since annually carried off what it yielded without a wheelbarrow. With respect to landscapes,—

> "I am monarch of all I *survey*,
> My right there is none to dispute."

I have frequently seen a poet withdraw, having enjoyed the most valuable part of a farm, while the crusty farmer supposed that he had got a few wild apples only. Why, the owner does not know it for many years when a poet has put his farm in rhyme, the most admirable kind of invisible fence, has fairly impounded it, milked it, skimmed it, and got all the cream, and left the farmer only the skimmed milk.

The real attractions of the Hollowell farm, to me, were; its complete retirement, being about two miles from the village, half a mile from the nearest neighbor, and separated from the highway by a broad field; its bounding on the river, which the owner said protected it by its fogs from frosts in the spring, though that was nothing to me; the gray color and ruinous state of the house and barn, and the dilapidated fences, which put such an interval between me and the last occupant; the hollow and lichen-covered apple trees, gnawed by rabbits, showing what kind of neighbors I should have; but above all, the recollection I had of it from my earliest voyages up the river, when the house was concealed behind a dense grove of red maples, through which I heard the house-dog bark. I was in haste to buy it, before the proprietor finished getting out some rocks, cutting down the hollow apple trees, and grubbing up some young birches which had sprung up in the pasture, or, in short, had made any more of his improvements. To enjoy these advantages I was ready to carry it on; like Atlas, to take the world on my shoulders,—I never heard what compensation he received for that,—and do all those things which had no other motive or excuse but that I might pay for it and be unmolested in my possession of it; for I knew all the while that it would yield the most abundant crop of the kind I wanted if I could only afford to let it alone. But it turned out as I have said.

All that I could say, then, with respect to farming on a large scale, (I have always cultivated a garden,) was, that I had had my seeds ready. Many think that seeds improve with age. I have no doubt that time discriminates between the good and the bad; and when at last I shall plant, I shall be less likely to be disappointed. But I would say to my fellows, once for all, As long as possible live free and uncommitted. It makes but little difference whether you are committed to a farm or the county jail.

Old Cato, whose "De Re Rusticâ" is my "Cultivator," says, and the only translation I have seen makes sheer nonsense of the passage, "When you think of getting a farm, turn it thus in your mind, not to buy greedily; nor spare your pains to look at it, and do not think it enough to go round it once. The oftener you go there the more it will please you, if it is good." I think I shall not buy greedily, but go round and round it as long as I live, and be buried in it first, that it may please me the more at last.

The present was my next experiment of this kind, which I purpose to describe more at length; for convenience, putting the experience of two years into one. As I have said, I do not propose to write an ode to dejection, but to brag as lustily as chanticleer in the morning, standing on his roost, if only to wake my neighbors up.

When first I took up my abode in the woods, that is, began to spend my nights as well as days there, which, by accident, was on Independence Day, or the fourth of July, 1845, my house was not finished for winter, but was merely a defence against the rain, without plastering or chimney, the walls being of rough weather-stained boards, with wide chinks, which made it cool at night.

The upright white hewn studs and freshly planed door and window casings gave it a clean and airy look, especially in the morning, when its timbers were saturated with dew, so that I fancied that by noon some sweet gum would exude from them. To my imagination it retained throughout the day more or less of this auroral character, reminding me of a certain house on a mountain which I had visited the year before. This was an airy and unplastered cabin, fit to entertain a travelling god, and where a goddess might trail her garments. The winds which passed over my dwelling were such as sweep over the ridges of mountains, bearing the broken strains, or celestial parts only, of terrestrial music. The morning wind forever blows, the poem of creation is uninterrupted; but few are the ears that hear it. Olympus is but the outside of the earth every where.

The only house I had been the owner of before, if I except a boat, was a tent, which I used occasionally when making excursions in the summer, and this is still rolled up in my garret; but the boat, after passing from hand to hand, has gone down the stream of time. With this more substantial shelter about me, I had made some progress toward settling in the world. This frame, so slightly clad, was a sort of crystallization around me, and reacted on the builder. It was suggestive somewhat as a picture in outlines. I did not need to go out doors to take the air, for the atmosphere within had lost none of its freshness. It was not so much within doors as behind a door where I sat, even in the rainiest weather. The Harivansa says, "An abode without birds is like a meat without seasoning." Such was not my abode, for I found myself suddenly neighbor to the birds; not by having imprisoned one, but having caged myself near them. I was not only nearer to some of those which commonly frequent the garden and the orchard, but to those wilder and more thrilling songsters of the forest which never, or rarely, serenade a villager,—the wood-thrush, the veery, the scarlet tanager, the field-sparrow, the whippoorwill, and many others.

I was seated by the shore of a small pond, about a mile and a half south of the village of Concord and somewhat higher than it, in the midst of an extensive wood between

that town and Lincoln, and about two miles south of that
our only field known to fame, Concord Battle Ground;
but I was so low in the woods that the opposite shore, half
a mile off, like the rest, covered with wood, was my most
distant horizon. For the first week, whenever I looked out
on the pond it impressed me like a tarn high up on the
side of a mountain, its bottom far above the surface of
other lakes, and, as the sun arose, I saw it throwing off its
nightly clothing of mist, and here and there, by degrees,
its soft ripples or its smooth reflecting surface was revealed, while the mists, like ghosts, were stealthily withdrawing in every direction into the woods, as at the
breaking up of some nocturnal conventicle. The very dew
seemed to hang upon the trees later into the day than
usual, as on the sides of mountains.

This small lake was of most value as a neighbor in the
intervals of a gentle rain storm in August, when, both air
and water being perfectly still, but the sky overcast, mid-
afternoon had all the serenity of evening, and the wood-
thrush sang around, and was heard from shore to shore. A
lake like this is never smoother than at such a time; and
the clear portion of the air above it being shallow and
darkened by clouds, the water, full of light and reflections, becomes a lower heaven itself so much the more
important. From a hill top near by, where the wood had
been recently cut off, there was a pleasing vista southward across the pond, through a wide indentation in the
hills which form the shore there, where their opposite
sides sloping toward each other suggested a stream flowing out in the direction through a wooded valley, but
stream there was none. That way I looked between and
over the near green hills to some distant and higher ones
in the horizon, tinged with blue. Indeed, by standing on
tiptoe I could catch a glimpse of some of the peaks of the
still bluer and more distant mountain ranges in the north-
west, those true-blue coins from heaven's own mint, and
also of some portion of the village. But in other directions, even from this point, I could not see over or beyond
the woods which surrounded me. It is well to have some
water in your neighborhood, to give buoyancy to and
float the earth. One value even of the smallest well is,

that when you look into it you see that earth is not continent but insular. This is as important as that it keeps butter cool. When I looked across the pond from this peak toward the Sudbury meadows, which in time of flood I distinguished elevated perhaps by a mirage in their seething valley, like a coin in a basin, all the earth beyond the pond appeared like a thin crust insulated and floated even by this small sheet of intervening water, and I was reminded that this on which I dwelt was but *dry land*.

Though the view from my door was still more contracted, I did not feel crowded or confined in the least. There was pasture enough for my imagination. The low shrub-oak plateau to which the opposite shore arose, stretched away toward the prairies of the West and the steppes of Tartary, affording ample room for all the roving families of men. "There are none happy in the world but beings who enjoy freely a vast horizon,"—said Damodara, when his herds required new and larger pastures.

Both place and time were changed, and I dwelt nearer to those parts of the universe and to those eras in history which had most attracted me. Where I lived was as far off as many a region viewed nightly by astronomers. We are wont to imagine rare and delectable places in some remote and more celestial corner of the system, behind the constellation of Cassiopeia's Chair, far from noise and disturbance. I discovered that my house actually had its site in such a withdrawn, but forever new and unprofaned, part of the universe. If it were worth the while to settle in those parts near to the Pleiades or the Hyades, to Aldebaran or Altair, then I was really there, or at an equal remoteness from the life which I had left behind, dwindled and twinkling with as fine a ray to my nearest neighbor, and to be seen only in moonless nights by him. Such was that part of creation where I had squatted;—

> "There was a shepherd that did live,
>   And held his thoughts as high
> As were the mounts whereon his flocks
>   Did hourly feed him by."

What should we think of the shepherd's life if his flocks always wandered to higher pastures than his thoughts?

Every morning was a cheerful invitation to make my
life of equal simplicity, and I may say innocence, with
Nature herself. I have been as sincere a worshipper of
Aurora as the Greeks. I got up early and bathed in the
pond; that was a religious exercise, and one of the best
things which I did. They say that characters were engra-
ven on the bathing tub of king Tching-thang to this effect: "Renew thyself completely each day; do it again,
and again, and forever again." I can understand that.
Morning brings back the heroic ages. I was as much affected by the faint hum of a mosquito making its invisible and unimaginable tour through my apartment at earliest dawn, when I was sitting with door and windows
open, as I could be by any trumpet that ever sang of
fame. It was Homer's requiem; itself an Iliad and Odyssey in the air, singing its own wrath and wanderings.
There was something cosmical about it; a standing advertisement, till forbidden, of the everlasting vigor and fertility of the world. The morning, which is the most memorable season of the day, is the awakening hour. Then
there is least somnolence in us; and for an hour, at least,
some part of us awakes which slumbers all the rest of the
day and night. Little is to be expected of that day, if it
can be called a day, to which we are not awakened by
our Genius, but by the mechanical nudgings of some ser-
vitor, are not awakened by our own newly acquired force
and aspirations from within, accompanied by the undula-
tions of celestial music, instead of factory bells, and a fragrance filling the air—to a higher life than we fell asleep
from; and thus the darkness bear its fruit, and prove itself
to be good, no less than the light. That man who does not
believe that each day contains an earlier, more sacred,
and auroral hour than he has yet profaned, has despaired
of life, and is pursuing a descending and darkening way.
After a partial cessation of his sensuous life, the soul of
man, or its organs rather, are reinvigorated each day, and
his Genius tries again what noble life it can make. All
memorable events, I should say, transpire in morning
time and in a morning atmosphere. The Vedas say, "All
intelligences awake with the morning." Poetry and art,
and the fairest and most memorable of the actions of

men, date from such an hour. All poets and heroes, like Memnon, are the children of Aurora, and emit their music at sunrise. To him whose elastic and vigorous thought keeps pace with the sun, the day is a perpetual morning. It matters not what the clocks say or the attitudes and labors of men. Morning is when I am awake and there is a dawn in me. Moral reform is the effort to throw off sleep. Why is it that men give so poor an account of their day if they have not been slumbering? They are not such poor calculators. If they had not been overcome with drowsiness they would have performed something. The millions are awake enough for physical labor; but only one in a million is awake enough for effective intellectual exertion, only one in a hundred millions to a poetic or divine life. To be awake is to be alive. I have never yet met a man who was quite awake. How could I have looked him in the face?

We must learn to reawaken and keep ourselves awake, not by mechanical aids, but by an infinite expectation of the dawn, which does not forsake us in our soundest sleep. I know of no more encouraging fact than the unquestionable ability of man to elevate his life by a conscious endeavor. It is something to be able to paint a particular picture, or to carve a statue, and so to make a few objects beautiful; but it is far more glorious to carve and paint the very atmosphere and medium through which we look, which morally we can do. To affect the quality of the day, that is the highest of arts. Every man is tasked to make his life, even in its details, worthy of the contemplation of his most elevated and critical hour. If we refused, or rather used up, such paltry information as we get, the oracles would distinctly inform us how this might be done.

I went to the woods because I wished to live deliberately, to front only the essential facts of life, and see if I could not learn what it had to teach, and not, when I came to die, discover that I had not lived. I did not wish to live what was not life, living is so dear; nor did I wish to practice resignation, unless it was quite necessary. I wanted to live deep and suck out all the marrow of life, to live so sturdily and Spartan-like as to put to rout all that was not life, to cut a broad swath and shave close, to drive life into a corner, and reduce it to its lowest terms, and, if it proved to be mean, why then to get the whole and genuine meanness of it, and publish its meanness to the world; or if it were sublime, to know it by experience, and be able to give a true account of it in my next excursion. For most men, it appears to me, are in a strange uncertainty about it, whether it is of the devil or of God, and have *somewhat hastily* concluded that it is the chief end of man here to "glorify God and enjoy him forever."

Still we live meanly, like ants; though the fable tells us that we were long ago changed into men; like pygmies we fight with cranes; it is error upon error, and clout upon clout, and our best virtue has for its occasion a superfluous and evitable wretchedness. Our life is frittered away by detail. An honest man has hardly need to count more than his ten fingers, or in extreme cases he may add his ten toes, and lump the rest. Simplicity, simplicity, simplicity! I say, let your affairs be as two or three, and not a hundred or a thousand; instead of a million count half a dozen, and keep your accounts on your thumb nail. In the midst of this chopping sea of civilized life, such are the clouds and storms and quicksands and thousand-and-one items to be allowed for, that a man has to live, if he would not founder and go to the bottom and not make his port at all, by dead reckoning, and he must be a great calculator indeed who succeeds. Simplify, simplify. Instead of three meals a day, if it be necessary eat but one; instead of a hundred dishes, five; and reduce other things in proportion. Our life is like a German Confederacy, made up of petty states, with its boundary forever fluctuating, so that even a German cannot tell you how it is bounded at any moment. The nation itself, with all its so called internal improvements, which, by the way, are all external and superficial, is just such an unwieldy and overgrown establishment, cluttered with furniture and tripped up by its own traps, ruined by luxury and heedless expense, by want of calculation and a worthy aim, as the million households in the land; and the only cure for it as for them is in a rigid economy, a stern and more than Spartan simplicity of life and elevation of purpose.

It lives too fast. Men think that it is essential that the *Nation* have commerce, and export ice, and talk through a telegraph, and ride thirty miles an hour, without a doubt, whether *they* do or not; but whether we should live like baboons or like men, is a little uncertain. If we do not get out sleepers, and forge rails, and devote days and nights to the work, but go to tinkering upon our *lives* to improve *them*, who will build railroads? And if railroads are not built, how shall we get to heaven in season? But if we stay at home and mind our business, who will want railroads? We do not ride on the railroad; it rides upon us. Did you ever think what those sleepers are that underlie the railroad? Each one is a man, an Irish-man, or a Yankee man. The rails are laid on them, and they are covered with sand, and the cars run smoothly over them. They are sound sleepers, I assure you. And every few years a new lot is laid down and run over; so that, if some have the pleasure of riding on a rail, others have the misfortune to be ridden upon. And when they run over a man that is walking in his sleep, a supernumerary sleeper in the wrong position, and wake him up, they suddenly stop the cars, and make a hue and cry about it, as if this were an exception. I am glad to know that it takes a gang of men for every five miles to keep the sleepers down and level in their beds as it is, for this is a sign that they may sometime get up again.

Why should we live with such hurry and waste of life? We are determined to be starved before we are hungry. Men say that a stitch in time saves nine, and so they take a thousand stitches to-day to save nine to-morrow. As for work, we haven't any of any consequence. We have the Saint Vitus' dance, and cannot possibly keep our heads still. If I should only give a few pulls at the parish bell-rope, as for a fire, that is, without setting the bell, there is hardly a man on his farm in the outskirts of Concord, notwithstanding that press of engagements which was his excuse so many times this morning, nor a boy, nor a woman, I might almost say, but would forsake all and follow that sound, not mainly to save property from the flames, but, if we will confess the truth, much more to see it burn, since burn it must, and we, be it known, did not set it on fire,—or to see it put out, and have a hand in it, if that is done as handsomely; yes, even if it were the parish church itself. Hardly a man takes a half hour's nap after dinner, but when he wakes he holds up his head and asks, "What's the news?" as if the rest of mankind had stood his sentinels. Some give directions to be waked every half hour, doubtless for no other purpose; and then, to pay for it, they tell what they have dreamed. After a night's sleep the news is as indispensable as the breakfast. "Pray tell me any thing new that has happened to a man any where on this globe,"—and he reads it over his coffee and rolls, that a man has had his eyes gouged out this morning on the Wachito River; never dreaming the while that he lives in the dark unfathomed mammoth cave of this world, and has but the rudiment of an eye himself.

For my part, I could easily do without the post-office. I think that there are very few important communications made through it. To speak critically, I never received more than one or two letters in my life—I wrote this some years ago—that were worth the postage. The penny post is, commonly, an institution through which you seriously offer a man that penny for his thoughts which is so often safely offered in jest. And I am sure that I never read any memorable news in a newspaper. If we read of one man robbed, or murdered, or killed by accident, or one house burned, or one vessel wrecked, or one steamboat blown up, or one cow run over on the Western Railroad, or one mad dog killed, or one lot of grasshoppers in the winter,—we never need read of another. One is enough. If you are acquainted with the principle, what do you care for a myriad instances and applications? To a philosopher all *news*, as it is called, is gossip, and they who edit and read it are old women over their tea. Yet not a few are greedy after this gossip. There was such a rush, as I hear, the other day at one of the offices to learn the foreign news by the last arrival, that several large squares of plate glass belonging to the establishment were broken by the pressure,—news which I seriously think a ready wit might write a twelvemonth or twelve years beforehand with sufficient accuracy. As for Spain, for instance, if you know how to throw in Don Carlos and the

Infanta, and Don Pedro and Seville and Granada, from time to time in the right proportions,—they may have changed the names a little since I saw the papers, and serve up a bull-fight when other entertainments fail, it will be true to the letter, and give us as good an idea of the exact state or ruin of things in Spain as the most succinct and lucid reports under this head in the newspapers: and as for England, almost the last significant scrap of news from that quarter was the revolution of 1649; and if you have learned the history of her crops for an average year, you never need attend to that thing again, unless your speculations are of a merely pecuniary character. If one may judge who rarely looks into the newspapers, nothing new does ever happen in foreign parts, a French revolution not excepted.

What news! how much more important to know what that is which was never old! "Kieou-pe-yu (great dignitary of the state of Wei) sent a man to Khoung-tseu to know his news. Khoung-tseu caused the messenger to be seated near him, and questioned him in these terms: What is your master doing? The messenger answered with respect: My master desires to diminish the number of his faults, but he cannot accomplish it. The messenger being gone, the philosopher remarked: What a worthy messenger! What a worthy messenger!" The preacher, instead of vexing the ears of drowsy farmers on their day of rest at the end of the week,—for Sunday is the fit conclusion of an ill-spent week, and not the fresh and brave beginning of a new one,—with this one other draggle-tail of a sermon, should shout with thundering voice,— "Pause! Avast! Why so seeming fast, but deadly slow?"

Shams and delusions are esteemed for soundest truths, while reality is fabulous. If men would steadily observe realities only, and not allow themselves to be deluded, life, to compare it with such things as we know, would be like a fairy tale and the Arabian Nights' Entertainments. If we respected only what is inevitable and has a right to be, music and poetry would resound along the streets. When we are unhurried and wise, we perceive that only great and worthy things have any permanent and absolute existence,—that petty fears and petty pleasures are

but the shadow of the reality. This is always exhilarating
and sublime. By closing the eyes and slumbering, and
consenting to be deceived by shows, men establish and
confirm their daily life of routine and habit every where,
which still is built on purely illusory foundations. Children, who play life, discern its true law and relations
more clearly than men, who fail to live it worthily, but
who think that they are wiser by experience, that is, by
failure. I have read in a Hindoo book, that "there was a
king's son, who, being expelled in infancy from his native
city, was brought up by a forester, and, growing up to
maturity in that state, imagined himself to belong to the
barbarous race with which he lived. One of his father's
ministers having discovered him, revealed to him what
he was, and the misconception of his character was re-
moved, and he knew himself to be a prince. So soul,"
continues the Hindoo philosopher, "from the circumstances in which it is placed, mistakes its own character,
until the truth is revealed to it by some holy teacher, and
then it knows itself to be *Brahme*." I perceive that we
inhabitants of New England live this mean life that we
do because our vision does not penetrate the surface of
things. We think that that *is* which *appears* to be. If a
man should walk through this town and see only the reality, where, think you, would the "Mill-dam" go to? If he
should give us an account of the realities he beheld there,
we should not recognize the place in his description.
Look at a meeting-house, or a court-house, or a jail, or a
shop, or a dwelling-house, and say what that thing really
is before a true gaze, and they would all go to pieces in
your account of them. Men esteem truth remote, in the
outskirts of the system, behind the farthest star, before
Adam and after the last man. In eternity there is indeed
something true and sublime. But all these times and
places and occasions are now and here. God himself cul-
minates in the present moment, and will never be more
divine in the lapse of all the ages. And we are enabled to
apprehend at all what is sublime and noble only by the
perpetual instilling and drenching of the reality which
surrounds us. The universe constantly and obediently answers to our conceptions; whether we travel fast or slow,

TRUTH IS
NoT REMOTE
2

the track is laid for us. Let us spend our lives in conceiving then. The poet or the artist never yet had so fair and noble a design but some of his posterity at least could accomplish it.

Let us spend one day as deliberately as Nature, and not be thrown off the track by every nutshell and mosquito's wing that falls on the rails. Let us rise early and fast, or break fast, gently and without perturbation; let company come and let company go, let the bells ring and the children cry,—determined to make a day of it. Why should we knock under and go with the stream? Let us not be upset and overwhelmed in that terrible rapid and whirlpool called a dinner, situated in the meridian shallows. Weather this danger and you are safe, for the rest of the way is down hill. With unrelaxed nerves, with morning vigor, sail by it, looking another way, tied to the mast like Ulysses. If the engine whistles, let it whistle till it is hoarse for its pains. If the bell rings, why should we run? We will consider what kind of music they are like. Let us settle ourselves, and work and wedge our feet downward through the mud and slush of opinion, and prejudice, and tradition, and delusion, and appearance, that alluvion which covers the globe, through Paris and London, through New York and Boston and Concord, through church and state, through poetry and philosophy and religion, till we come to a hard bottom and rocks in place, which we can call *reality*, and say, This is, and no mistake; and then begin, having a *point d'appui*, below freshet and frost and fire, a place where you might found a wall or a state, or set a lamp-post safely, or perhaps a gauge, not a Nilometer, but a Realometer, that future ages might know how deep a freshet of shams and appearances had gathered from time to time. If you stand right fronting and face to face to a fact, you will see the sun glimmer on both its surfaces, as if it were a cimeter, and feel its sweet edge dividing you through the heart and marrow, and so you will happily conclude your mortal career. Be it life or death, we crave only reality. If we are really dying, let us hear the rattle in our throats and feel cold in the extremities; if we are alive, let us go about our business.

Time is but the stream I go a-fishing in. I drink at it; but while I drink I see the sandy bottom and detect how shallow it is. Its thin current slides away, but eternity remains. I would drink deeper; fish in the sky, whose bottom is pebbly with stars. I cannot count one. I know not the first letter of the alphabet. I have always been regretting that I was not as wise as the day I was born. The intellect is a cleaver; it discerns and rifts its way into the secret of things. I do not wish to be any more busy with my hands than is necessary. My head is hands and feet. I feel all my best faculties concentrated in it. My instinct tells me that my head is an organ for burrowing, as some creatures use their snout and fore-paws, and with it I would mine and burrow my way through these hills. I think that the richest vein is somewhere hereabouts; so by the divining rod and thin rising vapors I judge; and here I will begin to mine.

READING

With a little more deliberation in the choice of their pursuits, all men would perhaps become essentially students and observers, for certainly their nature and destiny are interesting to all alike. In accumulating property for ourselves or our posterity, in founding a family or a state, or acquiring fame even, we are mortal; but in dealing with truth we are immortal, and need fear no change nor accident. The oldest Egyptian or Hindoo philosopher raised a corner of the veil from the statue of the divinity; and still the trembling robe remains raised, and I gaze upon as fresh a glory as he did, since it was I in him that was then so bold, and it is he in me that now reviews the vision. No dust has settled on that robe; no time has elapsed since that divinity was revealed. That time which we really improve, or which is improvable, is neither past, present, nor future.

My residence was more favorable, not only to thought, but to serious reading, than a university; and though I was beyond the range of the ordinary circulating library, I had more than ever come within the influence of those books which circulate round the world, whose sentences were first written on bark, and are now merely copied from time to time on to linen paper. Says the poet Mîr Camar Uddîn Mast, "Being seated to run through the region of the spiritual world; I have had this advantage in books. To be intoxicated by a single glass of wine; I have experienced this pleasure when I have drunk the liquor of the esoteric doctrines." I kept Homer's Iliad on my table through the summer, though I looked at his page only now and then. Incessant labor with my hands, at first, for I had my house to finish and my beans to hoe at the same time, made more study impossible. Yet I sustained myself by the prospect of such reading in future. I read one or two shallow books of travel in the intervals of my work, till that employment made me ashamed of myself, and I asked where it was then that *I* lived.

The student may read Homer or Æschylus in the Greek without danger of dissipation or luxuriousness, for it implies that he in some measure emulate their heroes, and consecrate morning hours to their pages. The heroic books, even if printed in the character of our mother tongue, will always be in a language dead to degenerate times; and we must laboriously seek the meaning of each word and line, conjecturing a larger sense than common use permits out of what wisdom and valor and generosity we have. The modern cheap and fertile press, with all its translations, has done little to bring us nearer to the heroic writers of antiquity. They seem as solitary, and the letter in which they are printed as rare and curious, as ever. It is worth the expense of youthful days and costly hours, if you learn only some words of an ancient language, which are raised out of the trivialness of the street, to be perpetual suggestions and provocations. It is not in vain that the farmer remembers and repeats the few Latin words which he has heard. Men sometimes speak as if the study of the classics would at length make way for more modern and practical studies; but the adventurous student will always study classics, in whatever language they may be written and however ancient they may be. For what are the classics but the noblest recorded thoughts of man? They are the only oracles which are not decayed, and there are such answers to the most modern inquiry in them as Delphi and Dodona never gave. We might as well omit to study Nature because she is old. To read well, that is, to read true books in a true spirit, is a noble exercise, and one that will task the reader more than any exercise which the customs of the day esteem. It requires a training such as the athletes underwent, the steady intention almost of the whole life to this object. Books must be read as deliberately and reservedly as they were written. It is not enough even to be able to speak the language of that nation by which they are written, for there is a memorable interval between the spoken and the written language, the language heard and the language read. The one is commonly transitory, a sound, a tongue, a dialect merely, almost brutish, and we learn it unconsciously, like the brutes, of our mothers. The other is the maturity and experience of that; if that is our mother tongue, this is our father tongue, a reserved and select expression, too significant to be heard by the ear, which we must be born again in order to speak. The crowds of men who merely *spoke* the Greek and Latin tongues in the middle ages were not entitled by the accident of birth to *read* the works of genius written in those languages; for these were not written in that Greek or Latin which they knew, but in the select language of literature. They had not learned the nobler dialects of Greece and Rome, but the very materials on which they were written were waste paper to them, and they prized instead a cheap contemporary literature. But when the several nations of Europe had acquired distinct though rude written languages of their own, sufficient for the purposes of their rising literatures, then first learning revived, and scholars were enabled to discern from that remoteness the treasures of antiquity. What the Roman and Grecian multitude could not *hear*, after the lapse of ages a few scholars *read*, and a few scholars only are still reading it.

However much we may admire the orator's occasional bursts of eloquence, the noblest written words are commonly as far behind or above the fleeting spoken language as the firmament with its stars is behind the clouds.

There are the stars, and they who can may read them.
The astronomers forever comment on and observe them.
They are not exhalations like our daily colloquies and va-
porous breath. What is called eloquence in the forum is
commonly found to be rhetoric in the study. The orator
yields to the inspiration of a transient occasion, and
speaks to the mob before him, to those who can *hear* him;
but the writer, whose more equable life is his occasion,
and who would be distracted by the event and the crowd
which inspire the orator, speaks to the intellect and heart
of mankind, to all in any age who can *understand* him.

No wonder that Alexander carried the Iliad with him
on his expeditions in a precious casket. A written word is
the choicest of relics. It is something at once more intimate with us and more universal than any other work of
art. It is the work of art nearest to life itself. It may be
translated into every language, and not only be read but
actually breathed from all human lips;—not be represented on canvas or in marble only, but be carved out of the
breath of life itself. The symbol of an ancient man's
thought becomes a modern man's speech. Two thousand
summers have imparted to the monuments of Grecian literature, as to her marbles, only a maturer golden and
autumnal tint, for they have carried their own serene and
celestial atmosphere into all lands to protect them against
the corrosion of time. Books are the treasured wealth of
the world and the fit inheritance of generations and nations. Books, the oldest and the best, stand naturally and
rightfully on the shelves of every cottage. They have no
cause of their own to plead, but while they enlighten and
sustain the reader his common sense will not refuse them.
Their authors are a natural and irresistible aristocracy in
every society, and more than kings or emperors, exert an
influence on mankind. When the illiterate and perhaps
scornful trader has earned by enterprise and industry his
coveted leisure and independence, and is admitted to the
circles of wealth and fashion, he turns inevitably at last to
those still higher but yet inaccessible circles of intellect
and genius, and is sensible only of the imperfection of his
culture and the vanity and insufficiency of all his riches,
and further proves his good sense by the pains which he

takes to secure for his children that intellectual culture
whose want he so keenly feels; and thus it is that he becomes the founder of a family.

Those who have not learned to read the ancient classics
in the language in which they were written must have a
very imperfect knowledge of the history of the human
race; for it is remarkable that no transcript of them has
ever been made into any modern tongue, unless our civilization itself may be regarded as such a transcript.
Homer has never yet been printed in English, nor Æschylus, nor Virgil even,—works as refined, as solidly
done, and as beautiful almost as the morning itself; for
later writers, say what we will of their genius, have rarely, if ever, equalled the elaborate beauty and finish and
the lifelong and heroic literary labors of the ancients.
They only talk of forgetting them who never knew them.
It will be soon enough to forget them when we have the
learning and the genius which will enable us to attend to
and appreciate them. That age will be rich indeed when
those relics which we call Classics, and the still older and
more than classic but even less known Scriptures of the
nations, shall have still further accumulated, when the
Vaticans shall be filled with Vedas and Zendavestas and
Bibles, with Homers and Dantes and Shakspeares, and all
the centuries to come shall have successively deposited
their trophies in the forum of the world. By such a pile
we may hope to scale heaven at last.

The works of the great poets have never yet been read
by mankind, for only great poets can read them. They
have only been read as the multitude read the stars, at
most astrologically, not astronomically. Most men have
learned to read to serve a paltry convenience, as they
have learned to cipher in order to keep accounts and not
be cheated in trade; but of reading as a noble intellectual
exercise they know little or nothing; yet this only is reading, in a high sense, not that which lulls us as a luxury
and suffers the nobler faculties to sleep the while, but
what we have to stand on tiptoe to read and devote our
most alert and wakeful hours to.

I think that having learned our letters we should read
the best that is in literature, and not be forever repeating

our a b abs, and words of one syllable, in the fourth or
fifth classes, sitting on the lowest and foremost form all
our lives. Most men are satisfied if they read or hear
read, and perchance have been convicted by the wisdom
of one good book, the Bible, and for the rest of their lives
vegetate and dissipate their faculties in what is called
easy reading. There is a work in several volumes in our
Circulating Library entitled Little Reading, which I
thought referred to a town of that name which I had not
been to. There are those who, like cormorants and os-
triches, can digest all sorts of this, even after the fullest
dinner of meats and vegetables, for they suffer nothing to
be wasted. If others are the machines to provide this
provender, they are the machines to read it. They read
the nine thousandth tale about Zebulon and Sephronia,
and how they loved as none had ever loved before, and
neither did the course of their true love run smooth,—at
any rate, how it did run and stumble, and get up again
and go on! how some poor unfortunate got up onto a stee-
ple, who had better never have gone up as far as the
belfry; and then, having needlessly got him up there, the
happy novelist rings the bell for all the world to come
together and hear, O dear! how he did get down again!
For my part, I think that they had better metamorphose
all such aspiring heroes of universal noveldom into man
weathercocks, as they used to put heroes among the con-
stellations, and let them swing round there till they are
rusty, and not come down at all to bother honest men
with their pranks. The next time the novelist rings the
bell I will not stir though the meeting-house burn down.
"The Skip of the Tip-Toe-Hop, a Romance of the Middle
Ages, by the celebrated author of 'Tittle-Tol-Tan,' to appear in monthly parts; a great rush; don't all come together." All this they read with saucer eyes, and erect
and primitive curiosity, and with unwearied gizzard,
whose corrugations even yet need no sharpening, just as
some little four-year-old bencher his two-cent gilt-cov-
ered edition of Cinderella,—without any improvement,
that I can see, in the pronunciation, or accent, or emphasis, or any more skill in extracting or inserting the moral.
The result is dulness of sight, a stagnation of the vital

circulations, and a general deliquium and sloughing off
of all the intellectual faculties. This sort of gingerbread is
baked daily and more sedulously than pure wheat or rye-
and-Indian in almost every oven, and finds a surer market.

The best books are not read even by those who are
called good readers. What does our Concord culture
amount to? There is in this town, with a very few exceptions, no taste for the best or for very good books even in
English literature, whose words all can read and spell.
Even the college-bred and so called liberally educated
men here and elsewhere have really little or no acquaintance with the English classics; and as for the recorded
wisdom of mankind, the ancient classics and Bibles,
which are accessible to all who will know of them, there
are the feeblest efforts any where made to become acquainted with them. I know a woodchopper, of middle
age, who takes a French paper, not for news as he says,
for he is above that, but to "keep himself in practice," he
being a Canadian by birth; and when I ask him what he
considers the best thing he can do in this world, he says,
beside this, to keep up and add to his English. This is
about as much as the college bred generally do or aspire
to do, and they take an English paper for the purpose.
One who has just come from reading perhaps one of the
best English books will find how many with whom he
can converse about it? Or suppose he comes from reading
a Greek or Latin classic in the original, whose praises are
familiar even to the so called illiterate; he will find nobody at all to speak to, but must keep silence about it.
Indeed, there is hardly the professor in our colleges, who,
if he has mastered the difficulties of the language, has
proportionally mastered the difficulties of the wit and poetry of a Greek poet, and has any sympathy to impart to
the alert and heroic reader; and as for the sacred Scriptures, or Bibles of mankind, who in this town can tell me
even their titles? Most men do not know that any nation
but the Hebrews have had a scripture. A man, any man,
will go considerably out of his way to pick up a silver
dollar; but here are golden words, which the wisest men
of antiquity have uttered, and whose worth the wise of

every succeeding age have assured us of;—and yet we
learn to read only as far as Easy Reading, the primers
and classbooks, and when we leave school, the "Little
Reading," and story books, which are for boys and begin-
ners; and our reading, our conversation and thinking, are
all on a very low level, worthy only of pygmies and manikins.

I aspire to be acquainted with wiser men than this our ✳
Concord soil has produced, whose names are hardly
known here. Or shall I hear the name of Plato and never
read his book? As if Plato were my townsman and I never
saw him,—my next neighbor and I never heard him
speak or attended to the wisdom of his words. But how
actually is it? His Dialogues, which contain what was immortal in him, lie on the next shelf, and yet I never read
them. We are underbred and low-lived and illiterate; and
in this respect I confess I do not make any very broad
distinction between the illiterateness of my townsman
who cannot read at all, and the illiterateness of him who
has learned to read only what is for children and feeble
intellects. We should be as good as the worthies of antiquity, but partly by first knowing how good they were.
We are a race of tit-men, and soar but little higher in our
intellectual flights than the columns of the daily paper.

It is not all books that are as dull as their readers. There
are probably words addressed to our condition exactly,
which, if we could really hear and understand, would be
more salutary than the morning or the spring to our lives,
and possibly put a new aspect on the face of things for us.
How many a man has dated a new era in his life from
the reading of a book. The book exists for us perchance
which will explain our miracles and reveal new ones. The
at present unutterable things we may find somewhere uttered. These same questions that disturb and puzzle and
confound us have in their turn occurred to all the wise
men; not one has been omitted; and each has answered
them, according to his ability, by his words and his life.
Moreover, with wisdom we shall learn liberality. The solitary hired man on a farm in the outskirts of Concord,
who has had his second birth and peculiar religious experience, and is driven as he believes into silent gravity and

exclusiveness by his faith, may think it is not true; but Zoroaster, thousands of years ago, travelled the same road and had the same experience; but he, being wise, knew it to be universal, and treated his neighbors accordingly, and is even said to have invented and established worship among men. Let him humbly commune with Zoroaster then, and, through the liberalizing influence of all the worthies, with Jesus Christ himself, and let "our church" go by the board.

We boast that we belong to the nineteenth century and are making the most rapid strides of any nation. But consider how little this village does for its own culture. I do not wish to flatter my townsmen, nor to be flattered by them, for that will not advance either of us. We need to be provoked,—goaded like oxen, as we are, into a trot. We have a comparatively decent system of common schools, schools for infants only; but excepting the half-starved Lyceum in the winter, and latterly the puny beginning of a library suggested by the state, no school for ourselves. We spend more on almost any article of bodily aliment or ailment than on our mental aliment. It is time that we had uncommon schools, that we did not leave off our education when we begin to be men and women. It is time that villages were universities, and their elder inhabitants the fellows of universities, with leisure—if they are indeed so well off—to pursue liberal studies the rest of their lives. Shall the world be confined to one Paris or one Oxford forever? Cannot students be boarded here and get a liberal education under the skies of Concord? Can we not hire some Abelard to lecture to us? Alas! what with foddering the cattle and tending the store, we are kept from school too long, and our education is sadly neglected. In this country, the village should in some respects take the place of the nobleman of Europe. It should be the patron of the fine arts. It is rich enough. It wants only the magnanimity and refinement. It can spend money enough on such things as farmers and traders value, but it is thought Utopian to propose spending money for things which more intelligent men know to be of far more worth. This town has spent seventeen thousand dollars on a town-house, thank fortune or politics, but probably it will not spend so much on living wit, the true meat to put into that shell, in a hundred years. The one hundred and twenty-five dollars annually subscribed for a Lyceum in the winter is better spent than any other equal sum raised in the town. If we live in the nineteenth century, why should we not enjoy the advantages which the nineteenth century offers? Why should our life be in any respect provincial? If we will read newspapers, why not skip the gossip of Boston and take the best newspaper in the world at once?—not be sucking the pap of "neutral family" papers, or browsing "Olive-Branches" here in New England. Let the reports of all the learned societies come to us, and we will see if they know any thing. Why should we leave it to Harper & Brothers and Redding & Co. to select our reading? As the nobleman of cultivated taste surrounds himself with whatever conduces to his culture,—genius—learning—wit—books—paintings—statuary—music—philosophical instruments, and the like; so let the village do,—not stop short at a pedagogue, a parson, a sexton, a parish library, and three selectmen, because our pilgrim forefathers got through a cold winter once on a bleak rock with these. To act collectively is according to the spirit of our institutions; and I am confident that, as our circumstances are more flourishing, our means are greater than the nobleman's. New England can hire all the wise men in the world to come and teach her, and board them round the while, and not be provincial at all. That is the *uncommon* school we want. Instead of noblemen, let us have noble villages of men. If it is necessary, omit one bridge over the river, go round a little there, and throw one arch at least over the darker gulf of ignorance which surrounds us.

HIGHER LAWS

As I came home through the woods with my string of fish, trailing my pole, it being now quite dark, I caught a glimpse of a woodchuck stealing across my path, and felt a strange thrill of savage delight, and was strongly tempted to seize and devour him raw; not that I was hungry

then, except for that wildness which he represented.
Once or twice, however, while I lived at the pond, I
found myself ranging the woods, like a half-starved
hound, with a strange abandonment, seeking some kind
of venison which I might devour, and no morsel could
have been too savage for me. The wildest scenes had become unaccountably familiar. I found in myself, and still
find, an instinct toward a higher, or, as it is named, spiritual life, as do most men, and another toward a primitive
rank and savage one, and I reverence them both. I love
the wild not less than the good. The wildness and adventure that are in fishing still recommended it to me. I like
sometimes to take rank hold on life and spend my day
more as the animals do. Perhaps I have owed to this employment and to hunting, when quite young, my closest
acquaintance with Nature. They early introduce us to
and detain us in scenery with which otherwise, at that
age, we should have little acquaintance. Fishermen, hunters, woodchoppers, and others, spending their lives in the
fields and woods, in a peculiar sense a part of Nature
themselves, are often in a more favorable mood for observing her, in the intervals of their pursuits, than philosophers or poets even, who approach her with expectation.
She is not afraid to exhibit herself to them. The traveller
on the prairie is naturally a hunter, on the head waters of
the Missouri and Columbia a trapper, and at the Falls of
St. Mary a fisherman. He who is only a traveller learns
things at second-hand and by the halves, and is poor authority. We are most interested when science reports
what those men already know practically or instinctively,
for that alone is a true *humanity,* or account of human
experience.

They mistake who assert that the Yankee has few
amusements, because he has not so many public holidays,
and men and boys do not play so many games as they do
in England, for here the more primitive but solitary
amusements of hunting fishing and the like have not yet
given place to the former. Almost every New England
boy among my contemporaries shouldered a fowling
piece between the ages of ten and fourteen; and his hunting and fishing grounds were not limited like the pre-

serves of an English nobleman, but were more boundless even than those of a savage. No wonder, then, that he did not oftener stay to play on the common. But already a change is taking place, owing, not to an increased humanity, but to an increased scarcity of game, for perhaps the hunter is the greatest friend of the animals hunted, not excepting the Humane Society.

Moreover, when at the pond, I wished sometimes to add fish to my fare for variety. I have actually fished from the same kind of necessity that the first fishers did. Whatever humanity I might conjure up against it was all factitious, and concerned my philosophy more than my feelings. I speak of fishing only now, for I had long felt differently about fowling, and sold my gun before I went to the woods. Not that I am less humane than others, but I did not perceive that my feelings were much affected. I did not pity the fishes nor the worms. This was habit. As for fowling, during the last years that I carried a gun my excuse was that I was studying ornithology, and sought only new or rare birds. But I confess that I am now inclined to think that there is a finer way of studying ornithology than this. It requires so much closer attention to the habits of the birds, that, if for that reason only, I have been willing to omit the gun. Yet notwithstanding the objection on the score of humanity, I am compelled to doubt if equally valuable sports are ever substituted for these; and when some of my friends have asked me anxiously about their boys, whether they should let them hunt, I have answered, yes,—remembering that it was one of the best parts of my education,—*make* them hunters, though sportsmen only at first, if possible, mighty hunters at last, so that they shall not find game large enough for them in this or any vegetable wilderness,— hunters as well as fishers of men. Thus far I am of the opinion of Chaucer's nun, who

> "yave not of the text a pulled hen
> That saith that hunters ben not holy men."

There is a period in the history of the individual, as of the race, when the hunters are the "best men," as the Algonquins called them. We cannot but pity the boy who has never fired a gun; he is no more humane, while his education has been sadly neglected. This was my answer with respect to those youths who were bent on this pursuit, trusting that they would soon outgrow it. No humane being, past the thoughtless age of boyhood, will wantonly murder any creature, which holds its life by the same tenure that he does. The hare in its extremity cries like a child. I warn you, mothers, that my sympathies do not always make the usual phil-*anthropic* distinctions.

Such is oftenest the young man's introduction to the forest, and the most original part of himself. He goes thither at first as a hunter and fisher, until at last, if he has the seeds of a better life in him, he distinguishes his proper objects, as a poet or naturalist it may be, and leaves the gun and fish-pole behind. The mass of men are still and always young in this respect. In some countries a hunting parson is no uncommon sight. Such a one might make a good shepherd's dog, but is far from being the Good Shepherd. I have been surprised to consider that the only obvious employment, except wood-chopping, ice-cutting, or the like business, which ever to my knowledge detained at Walden Pond for a whole half day any of my fellow-citizens, whether fathers or children of the town, with just one exception, was fishing. Commonly they did not think that they were lucky, or well paid for their time, unless they got a long string of fish, though they had the opportunity of seeing the pond all the while. They might go there a thousand times before the sediment of fishing would sink to the bottom and leave their purpose pure; but no doubt such a clarifying process would be going on all the while. The governor and his council faintly remember the pond, for they went a-fishing there when they were boys; but now they are too old and dignified to go a-fishing, and so they know it no more forever. Yet even they expect to go to heaven at last. If the legislature regards it, it is chiefly to regulate the number of hooks to be used there; but they know nothing about the hook of hooks with which to angle for the pond itself, impaling the legislature for a bait. Thus, even in civilized communities, the embryo man passes through the hunter stage of development.

I have found repeatedly, of late years, that I cannot fish without falling a little in self-respect. I have tried it again and again. I have skill at it, and, like many of my fellows, a certain instinct for it, which revives from time to time, but always when I have done I feel that it would have been better if I had not fished. I think that I do not mistake. It is a faint intimation, yet so are the first streaks of morning. There is unquestionably this instinct in me which belongs to the lower orders of creation; yet with every year I am less a fisherman, though without more humanity or even wisdom; at present I am no fisherman at all. But I see that if I were to live in a wilderness I should again be tempted to become a fisher and hunter in earnest. Beside, there is something essentially unclean about this diet and all flesh, and I began to see where housework commences, and whence the endeavor, which costs so much, to wear a tidy and respectable appearance each day, to keep the house sweet and free from all ill odors and sights. Having been my own butcher and scullion and cook, as well as the gentleman for whom the dishes were served up, I can speak from an unusually complete experience. The practical objection to animal food in my case was its uncleanness; and, besides, when I had caught and cleaned and cooked and eaten my fish, they seemed not to have fed me essentially. It was insignificant and unnecessary, and cost more than it came to. A little bread or a few potatoes would have done as well, with less trouble and filth. Like many of my contemporaries, I had rarely for many years used animal food, or tea, or coffee, &c.; not so much because of any ill effects which I had traced to them, as because they were not agreeable to my imagination. The repugnance to animal food is not the effect of experience, but is an instinct. It appeared more beautiful to lie low and fare hard in many respects; and though I never did so, I went far enough to please my imagination. I believe that every man who has ever been earnest to preserve his higher or poetic faculties in the best condition has been particularly inclined to abstain from animal food, and from much food of any kind. It is a significant fact, stated by entomologists, I find it in Kirby and Spence, that "some in-

sects in their perfect state, though furnished with organs
of feeding, make no use of them;" and they lay it down
as "a general rule, that almost all insects in this state eat
much less than in that of larvæ. The voracious caterpillar
when transformed into a butterfly,". . . "and the glutton-
ous maggot when become a fly," content themselves with
a drop or two of honey or some other sweet liquid. The
abdomen under the wings of the butterfly still represents
the larva. This is the tid-bit which tempts his insectivo-
rous fate. The gross feeder is a man in the larva state; and
there are whole nations in that condition, nations without
fancy or imagination, whose vast abdomens betray them.

It is hard to provide and cook so simple and clean a
diet as will not offend the imagination; but this, I think, is
to be fed when we feed the body; they should both sit
down at the same table. Yet perhaps this may be done.
The fruits eaten temperately need not make us ashamed
of our appetites, nor interrupt the worthiest pursuits. But
put an extra condiment into your fish, and it will poison
you. It is not worth the while to live by rich cookery.
Most men would feel shame if caught preparing with
their own hands precisely such a dinner, whether of animal or vegetable food, as is every day prepared for them
by others. Yet till this is otherwise we are not civilized,
and, if gentlemen and ladies, are not true men and wom-
en. This certainly suggests what change is to be made. It
may be vain to ask why the imagination will not be rec-
onciled to flesh and fat. I am satisfied that it is not. Is it
not a reproach that man is a carnivorous animal? True,
he can and does live, in a great measure, by preying on
other animals; but this is a miserable way,—as any one
who will go to snaring rabbits, or slaughtering lambs,
may learn,—and he will be regarded as a benefactor of
his race who shall teach man to confine himself to a more
innocent and wholesome diet. Whatever my own practice
may be, I have no doubt that it is a part of the destiny of
the human race, in its gradual improvement, to leave off
eating animals, as surely as the savage tribes have left off
eating each other when they came in contact with the
more civilized.

If one listens to the faintest but constant suggestions of

his genius, which are certainly true, he sees not to what extremes, or even insanity, it may lead him; and yet that way, as he grows more resolute and faithful, his road lies. The faintest assured objection which one healthy man feels will at length prevail over the arguments and customs of mankind. No man ever followed his genius till it misled him. Though the result were bodily weakness, yet perhaps no one can say that the consequences were to be regretted, for these were a life in conformity to higher principles. If the day and the night are such that you greet them with joy, and life emits a fragrance like flowers and sweet-scented herbs, is more elastic, more starry, more immortal,—that is your success. All nature is your congratulation, and you have cause momentarily to bless yourself. The greatest gains and values are farthest from being appreciated. We easily come to doubt if they exist. We soon forget them. They are the highest reality. Perhaps the facts most astounding and most real are never communicated by man to man. The true harvest of my daily life is somewhat as intangible and indescribable as the tints of morning or evening. It is a little star-dust caught, a segment of the rainbow which I have clutched.

Yet, for my part, I was never unusually squeamish; I could sometimes eat a fried rat with a good relish, if it were necessary. I am glad to have drunk water so long, for the same reason that I prefer the natural sky to an opium-eater's heaven. I would fain keep sober always; and there are infinite degrees of drunkenness. I believe that water is the only drink for a wise man; wine is not so noble a liquor; and think of dashing the hopes of a morning with a cup of warm coffee, or of an evening with a dish of tea! Ah, how low I fall when I am tempted by them! Even music may be intoxicating. Such apparently slight causes destroyed Greece and Rome, and will destroy England and America. Of all ebriosity, who does not prefer to be intoxicated by the air he breathes? I have found it to be the most serious objection to coarse labors long continued, that they compelled me to eat and drink coarsely also. But to tell the truth, I find myself at present somewhat less particular in these respects. I carry less religion to the table, ask no blessing; not because I am wiser than I was, but, I am obliged to confess, because, however much it is to be regretted, with years I have grown more coarse and indifferent. Perhaps these questions are entertained only in youth, as most believe of poetry. My practice is "nowhere," my opinion is here. Nevertheless I am far from regarding myself as one of those privileged ones to whom the Ved refers when it says, that "he who has true faith in the Omnipresent Supreme Being may eat all that exists," that is, is not bound to inquire what is his food, or who prepares it; and even in their case it is to be observed, as a Hindoo commentator has remarked, that the Vedant limits this privilege to "the time of distress."

Who has not sometimes derived an inexpressible satisfaction from his food in which appetite had no share? I have been thrilled to think that I owed a mental perception to the commonly gross sense of taste, that I have been inspired through the palate, that some berries which I had eaten on a hill-side had fed my genius. "The soul not being mistress of herself," says Thseng-tseu, "one looks, and one does not see; one listens, and one does not hear; one eats, and one does not know the savor of food." He who distinguishes the true savor of his food can never be a glutton; he who does not cannot be otherwise. A puritan may go to his brown-bread crust with as gross an appetite as ever an alderman to his turtle. Not that food which entereth into the mouth defileth a man, but the appetite with which it is eaten. It is neither the quality nor the quantity, but the devotion to sensual savors; when that which is eaten is not a viand to sustain our animal, or inspire our spiritual life, but food for the worms that possess us. If the hunter has a taste for mud-turtles, muskrats, and other such savage tid-bits, the fine lady indulges a taste for jelly made of a calf's foot, or for sardines from over the sea, and they are even. He goes to the mill-pond, she to her preserve-pot. The wonder is how they, how you and I, can live this slimy beastly life, eating and drinking.

Our whole life is startlingly moral. There is never an instant's truce between virtue and vice. Goodness is the only investment that never fails. In the music of the harp which trembles round the world it is the insisting on this which thrills us. The harp is the travelling patterer for the Universe's Insurance Company, recommending its laws, and our little goodness is all the assessment that we pay. Though the youth at last grows indifferent, the laws of the universe are not indifferent, but are forever on the side of the most sensitive. Listen to every zephyr for some reproof, for it is surely there, and he is unfortunate who does not hear it. We cannot touch a string or move a stop but the charming moral transfixes us. Many an irksome noise, go a long way off, is heard as music, a proud sweet satire on the meanness of our lives.

We are conscious of an animal in us, which awakens in proportion as our higher nature slumbers. It is reptile and sensual, and perhaps cannot be wholly expelled; like the worms which, even in life and health, occupy our bodies. Possibly we may withdraw from it, but never change its nature. I fear that it may enjoy a certain health of its own; that we may be well, yet not pure. The other day I picked up the lower jaw of a hog, with white and sound teeth and tusks, which suggested that there was an animal health and vigor distinct from the spiritual. This creature succeeded by other means than temperance and purity. "That in which men differ from brute beasts," says Mencius, "is a thing very inconsiderable; the common herd lose it very soon; superior men preserve it carefully." Who knows what sort of life would result if we had attained to purity? If I knew so wise a man as could teach me purity I would go to seek him forthwith. "A command over our passions, and over the external senses of the body, and good acts, are declared by the Ved to be indispensable in the mind's approximation to God." Yet the spirit can for the time pervade and control every member and function of the body, and transmute what in form is the grossest sensuality into purity and devotion. The generative energy, which, when we are loose, dissipates and makes us unclean, when we are continent invigorates and inspires us. Chastity is the flowering of man; and what are called Genius, Heroism, Holiness, and the like, are but various fruits which succeed it. Man flows at once to God when the channel of purity is open.

By turns our purity inspires and our impurity casts us
down. He is blessed who is assured that the animal is dying out in him day by day, and the divine being established. Perhaps there is none but has cause for shame on
account of the inferior and brutish nature to which he is
allied. I fear that we are such gods or demigods only as
fauns and satyrs, the divine allied to beasts, the creatures
of appetite, and that, to some extent, our very life is our
disgrace.—

> "How happy's he who hath due place assigned
> To his beasts and disaforested his mind!
>
> *   *   *
>
> Can use his horse, goat, wolf, and ev'ry beast,
> And is not ass himself to the rest!
> Else man not only is the herd of swine,
> But he's those devils too which did incline
> Them to a headlong rage, and made them worse."

All sensuality is one, though it takes many forms; all
purity is one. It is the same whether a man eat, or drink,
or cohabit, or sleep sensually. They are but one appetite,
and we only need to see a person do any one of these
things to know how great a sensualist he is. The impure
can neither stand nor sit with purity. When the reptile is
attacked at one mouth of his burrow, he shows himself at
another. If you would be chaste, you must be temperate.
What is chastity? How shall a man know if he is chaste?
He shall not know it. We have heard of this virtue, but
we know not what it is. We speak conformably to the
rumor which we have heard. From exertion come wisdom and purity; from sloth ignorance and sensuality. In
the student sensuality is a sluggish habit of mind. An unclean person is universally a slothful one, one who sits by
a stove, whom the sun shines on prostrate, who reposes
without being fatigued. If you would avoid uncleanness,
and all the sins, work earnestly, though it be at cleaning a
stable. Nature is hard to be overcome, but she must be
overcome. What avails it that you are Christian, if you
are not purer than the heathen, if you deny yourself no
more, if you are not more religious? I know of many sys-

tems of religion esteemed heathenish whose precepts fill the reader with shame, and provoke him to new endeavors, though it be to the performance of rites merely.

I hesitate to say these things, but it is not because of the subject,—I care not how obscene my *words* are,—but because I cannot speak of them without betraying my impurity. We discourse freely without shame of one form of sensuality, and are silent about another. We are so degraded that we cannot speak simply of the necessary functions of human nature. In earlier ages, in some countries, every function was reverently spoken of and regulated by law. Nothing was too trivial for the Hindoo lawgiver, however offensive it may be to modern taste. He teaches how to eat, drink, cohabit, void excrement and urine, and the like, elevating what is mean, and does not falsely excuse himself by calling these things trifles.

Every man is the builder of a temple, called his body, to the god he worships, after a style purely his own, nor can he get off by hammering marble instead. We are all sculptors and painters, and our material is our own flesh and blood and bones. Any nobleness begins at once to refine a man's features, any meanness or sensuality to imbrute them.

John Farmer sat at his door one September evening, after a hard day's work, his mind still running on his labor more or less. Having bathed he sat down to recreate his intellectual man. It was a rather cool evening, and some of his neighbors were apprehending a frost. He had not attended to the train of his thoughts long when he heard some one playing on a flute, and that sound harmonized with his mood. Still he thought of his work; but the burden of his thought was, that though this kept running in his head, and he found himself planning and contriving it against his will, yet it concerned him very little. It was no more than the scurf of his skin, which was constantly shuffled off. But the notes of the flute came home to his ears out of a different sphere from that he worked in, and suggested work for certain faculties which slumbered in him. They gently did away with the street, and the village, and the state in which he lived. A voice said to him,—Why do you stay here and live this mean moil-

ing life, when a glorious existence is possible for you?
Those same stars twinkle over other fields than these.—
But how to come out of this condition and actually migrate thither? All that he could think of was to practise
some new austerity, to let his mind descend into his body
and redeem it, and treat himself with ever increasing
respect.

CONCLUSION

To the sick the doctors wisely recommend a change of
air and scenery. Thank Heaven, here is not all the world.
The buck-eye does not grow in New England, and the
mocking-bird is rarely heard here. The wild-goose is
more of a cosmopolite than we; he breaks his fast in Canada, takes a luncheon in the Ohio, and plumes himself for
the night in a southern bayou. Even the bison, to some
extent, keeps pace with the seasons, cropping the pastures
of the Colorado only till a greener and sweeter grass
awaits him by the Yellowstone. Yet we think that if rail-
fences are pulled down, and stone-walls piled up on our
farms, bounds are henceforth set to our lives and our
fates decided. If you are chosen town-clerk, forsooth, you
cannot go to Tierra del Fuego this summer: but you may
go to the land of infernal fire nevertheless. The universe
is wider than our views of it.

Yet we should oftener look over the tafferel of our
craft, like curious passengers, and not make the voyage
like stupid sailors picking oakum. The other side of the
globe is but the home of our correspondent. Our voyag-
ing is only great-circle sailing, and the doctors prescribe
for diseases of the skin merely. One hastens to Southern
Africa to chase the giraffe; but surely that is not the game
he would be after. How long, pray, would a man hunt
giraffes if he could? Snipes and woodcocks also may afford rare sport; but I trust it would be nobler game to
shoot one's self.—

> "Direct your eye sight inward, and you'll find
> A thousand regions in your mind
> Yet undiscovered. Travel them, and be
> Expert in home-cosmography."

What does Africa,—what does the West stand for? Is not
our own interior white on the chart? black though it may
prove, like the coast, when discovered. Is it the source of
the Nile, or the Niger, or the Mississippi, or a North-West
Passage around this continent, that we would find? Are
these the problems which most concern mankind? Is
Franklin the only man who is lost, that his wife should be
so earnest to find him? Does Mr. Grinnell know where he
himself is? Be rather the Mungo Park, the Lewis and
Clarke and Frobisher, of your own streams and oceans;
explore your own higher latitudes,—with shiploads of
preserved meats to support you, if they be necessary; and
pile the empty cans sky-high for a sign. Were preserved
meats invented to preserve meat merely? Nay, be a Columbus to whole new continents and worlds within you,
opening new channels, not of trade, but of thought. Every man is the lord of a realm beside which the earthly
empire of the Czar is but a petty state, a hummock left
by the ice. Yet some can be patriotic who have no *self-*
respect, and sacrifice the greater to the less. They love
the soil which makes their graves, but have no sympathy
with the spirit which may still animate their clay. Patriotism is a maggot in their heads. What was the meaning of
that South-Sea Exploring Expedition, with all its parade
and expense, but an indirect recognition of the fact, that
there are continents and seas in the moral world, to
which every man is an isthmus or an inlet, yet unexplored by him, but that it is easier to sail many thousand
miles through cold and storm and cannibals, in a government ship, with five hundred men and boys to assist one,
than it is to explore the private sea, the Atlantic and Pacific Ocean of one's being alone.—

> "*Erret, et extremos alter scrutetur Iberos.*
> *Plus habet hic vitæ, plus habet ille viæ.*"

> Let them wander and scrutinize the outlandish
> Australians.
> I have more of God, they more of the road.

It is not worth the while to go round the world to count
the cats in Zanzibar. Yet do this even till you can do better, and you may perhaps find some "Symmes' Hole" by
which to get at the inside at last. England and France,

Spain and Portugal, Gold Coast and Slave Coast, all front
on this private sea; but no bark from them has ventured
out of sight of land, though it is without doubt the direct
way to India. If you would learn to speak all tongues and
conform to the customs of all nations, if you would travel
farther than all travellers, be naturalized in all climes,
and cause the Sphinx to dash her head against a stone,
even obey the precept of the old philosopher, and Explore thyself. Herein are demanded the eye and the
nerve. Only the defeated and deserters go to the wars,
cowards that run away and enlist. Start now on that farthest western way, which does not pause at the Mississippi or the Pacific, nor conduct toward a worn-out China
or Japan, but leads on direct a tangent to this sphere,
summer and winter, day and night, sun down, moon
down, and at last earth down too.

It is said that Mirabeau took to highway robbery "to
ascertain what degree of resolution was necessary in order to place one's self in formal opposition to the most
sacred laws of society." He declared that "a soldier who
fights in the ranks does not require half so much courage
as a foot-pad,"—"that honor and religion have never
stood in the way of a well-considered and a firm resolve."
This was manly, as the world goes; and yet it was idle, if
not desperate. A saner man would have found himself
often enough "in formal opposition" to what are deemed
"the most sacred laws of society," through obedience to
yet more sacred laws, and so have tested his resolution
without going out of his way. It is not for a man to put
himself in such an attitude to society, but to maintain
himself in whatever attitude he find himself through obedience to the laws of his being, which will never be one
of opposition to a just government, if he should chance to
meet with such.

I left the woods for as good a reason as I went there.
Perhaps it seemed to me that I had several more lives to
live, and could not spare any more time for that one. It is
remarkable how easily and insensibly we fall into a particular route, and make a beaten track for ourselves. I
had not lived there a week before my feet wore a path
from my door to the pond-side; and though it is five or

six years since I trod it, it is still quite distinct. It is true, I fear that others may have fallen into it, and so helped to keep it open. The surface of the earth is soft and impressible by the feet of men; and so with the paths which the mind travels. How worn and dusty, then, must be the highways of the world, how deep the ruts of tradition and conformity! I did not wish to take a cabin passage, but rather to go before the mast and on the deck of the world, for there I could best see the moonlight amid the mountains. I do not wish to go below now.

I learned this, at least, by my experiment; that if one advances confidently in the direction of his dreams, and endeavors to live the life which he has imagined, he will meet with a success unexpected in common hours. He will put some things behind, will pass an invisible boundary; new, universal, and more liberal laws will begin to establish themselves around and within him; or the old laws be expanded, and interpreted in his favor in a more liberal sense, and he will live with the license of a higher order of beings. In proportion as he simplifies his life, the laws of the universe will appear less complex, and solitude will not be solitude, nor poverty poverty, nor weakness weakness. If you have built castles in the air, your work need not be lost; that is where they should be. Now put the foundations under them.

It is a ridiculous demand which England and America make, that you shall speak so that they can understand you. Neither men nor toad-stools grow so. As if that were important, and there were not enough to understand you without them. As if Nature could support but one order of understandings, could not sustain birds as well as quadrupeds, flying as well as creeping things, and *hush* and *who*, which Bright can understand, were the best English. As if there were safety in stupidity alone. I fear chiefly lest my expression may not be *extra- vagant* enough, may not wander far enough beyond the narrow limits of my daily experience, so as to be adequate to the truth of which I have been convinced. *Extra vagance!* it depends on how you are yarded. The migrating buffalo, which seeks new pastures in another latitude, is not extravagant like the cow which kicks over the pail, leaps the cow-yard fence, and runs after her calf, in milking time. I desire to speak somewhere *without* bounds; like a man in a waking moment, to men in their waking moments; for I am convinced that I cannot exaggerate enough even to lay the foundation of a true expression. Who that has heard a strain of music feared then lest he should speak extravagantly any more forever? In view of the future or possible, we should live quite laxly and undefined in front, our outlines dim and misty on that side; as our shadows reveal an insensible perspiration toward the sun. The volatile truth of our words should continually betray the inadequacy of the residual statement. Their truth is instantly *translated*; its literal monument alone remains. The words which express our faith and piety are not definite; yet they are significant and fragrant like frankincense to superior natures.

Why level downward to our dullest perception always, and praise that as common sense? The commonest sense is the sense of men asleep, which they express by snoring. Sometimes we are inclined to class those who are once-and-a-half witted with the half-witted, because we appreciate only a third part of their wit. Some would find fault with the morning-red, if they ever got up early enough. "They pretend," as I hear, "that the verses of Kabir have four different senses; illusion, spirit, intellect, and the exoteric doctrine of the Vedas;" but in this part of the world it is considered a ground for complaint if a man's writings admit of more than one interpretation. While England endeavors to cure the potato-rot, will not any endeavor to cure the brain-rot, which prevails so much more widely and fatally?

I do not suppose that I have attained to obscurity, but I should be proud if no more fatal fault were found with my pages on this score than was found with the Walden ice. Southern customers objected to its blue color, which is the evidence of its purity, as if it were muddy, and preferred the Cambridge ice, which is white, but tastes of weeds. The purity men love is like the mists which envelop the earth, and not like the azure ether beyond.

Some are dinning in our ears that we Americans, and moderns generally, are intellectual dwarfs compared with

the ancients, or even the Elizabethan men. But what is
that to the purpose? A living dog is better than a dead
lion. Shall a man go and hang himself because he belongs
to the race of pygmies, and not be the biggest pygmy
that he can? Let every one mind his own business, and
endeavor to be what he was made.

Why should we be in such desperate haste to succeed,
and in such desperate enterprises? If a man does not keep
pace with his companions, perhaps it is because he hears
a different drummer. Let him step to the music which he
hears, however measured or far away. It is not important
that he should mature as soon as an apple-tree or an oak.
Shall he turn his spring into summer? If the condition of
things which we were made for is not yet, what were any
reality which we can substitute? We will not be shipwrecked on a vain reality. Shall we with pains erect a
heaven of blue glass over ourselves, though when it is
done we shall be sure to gaze still at the true ethereal
heaven far above, as if the former were not?

There was an artist in the city of Kouroo who was disposed to strive after perfection. One day it came into his
mind to make a staff. Having considered that in an imperfect work time is an ingredient, but into a perfect
work time does not enter, he said to himself, It shall be
perfect in all respects, though I should do nothing else in
my life. He proceeded instantly to the forest for wood,
being resolved that it should not be made of unsuitable
material; and as he searched for and rejected stick after
stick, his friends gradually deserted him, for they grew
old in their works and died, but he grew not older by a
moment. His singleness of purpose and resolution, and his
elevated piety, endowed him, without his knowledge,
with perennial youth. As he made no compromise with
Time, Time kept out of his way, and only sighed at a
distance because he could not overcome him. Before he
had found a stock in all respects suitable the city of
Kouroo was a hoary ruin, and he sat on one of its mounds
to peel the stick. Before he had given it the proper shape
the dynasty of the Candahars was at an end, and with the
point of the stick he wrote the name of the last of that
race in the sand, and then resumed his work. By the time

he had smoothed and polished the staff Kalpa was no
longer the pole-star; and ere he had put on the ferule and
the head adorned with precious stones, Brahma had
awoke and slumbered many times. But why do I stay to
mention these things? When the finishing stroke was put
to his work, it suddenly expanded before the eyes of the
astonished artist into the fairest of all the creations of
Brahma. He had made a new system in making a staff, a
world with full and fair proportions; in which, though the
old cities and dynasties had passed away, fairer and more
glorious ones had taken their places. And now he saw by
the heap of shavings still fresh at his feet, that, for him
and his work, the former lapse of time had been an illusion, and that no more time had elapsed than is required
for a single scintillation from the brain of Brahma to fall
on and inflame the tinder of a mortal brain. The material
was pure, and his art was pure; how could the result be
other than wonderful?

No face which we can give to a matter will stead us so
well at last as the truth. This alone wears well. For the
most part, we are not where we are, but in a false position. Through an infirmity of our natures, we suppose a
case, and put ourselves into it, and hence are in two cases
at the same time, and it is doubly difficult to get out. In
sane moments we regard only the facts, the case that is.
Say what you have to say, not what you ought. Any truth
is better than make-believe. Tom Hyde, the tinker, standing on the gallows, was asked if he had any thing to say.
"Tell the tailors," said he, "to remember to make a knot
in their thread before they take the first stitch." His companion's prayer is forgotten.

However mean your life is, meet it and live it; do not
shun it and call it hard names. It is not so bad as you are.
It looks poorest when you are richest. The fault-finder
will find faults even in paradise. Love your life, poor as it
is. You may perhaps have some pleasant, thrilling, glorious hours, even in a poor-house. The setting sun is reflected from the windows of the alms-house as brightly as
from the rich man's abode; the snow melts before its door
as early in the spring. I do not see but a quiet mind may
live as contentedly there, and have as cheering thoughts,

as in a palace. The town's poor seem to me often to live
the most independent lives of any. May be they are simply great enough to receive without misgiving. Most
think that they are above being supported by the town;
but it oftener happens that they are not above supporting
themselves by dishonest means, which should be more
disreputable. Cultivate poverty like a garden herb, like
sage. Do not trouble yourself much to get new things,
whether clothes or friends. Turn the old; return to them.
Things do not change; we change. Sell your clothes and
keep your thoughts. God will see that you do not want
society. If I were confined to a corner of a garret all my
days, like a spider, the world would be just as large to me
while I had my thoughts about me. The philosopher said:
"From an army of three divisions one can take away its
general, and put it in disorder; from the man the most
abject and vulgar one cannot take away his thought." Do
not seek so anxiously to be developed, to subject yourself
to many influences to be played on; it is all dissipation.
Humility like darkness reveals the heavenly lights. The
shadows of poverty and meanness gather around us, "and
lo! creation widens to our view." We are often reminded
that if there were bestowed on us the wealth of Crœsus,
our aims must still be the same, and our means essentially
the same. Moreover, if you are restricted in your range
by poverty, if you cannot buy books and newspapers, for
instance, you are but confined to the most significant and
vital experiences; you are compelled to deal with the material which yields the most sugar and the most starch. It
is life near the bone where it is sweetest. You are de-
fended from being a trifler. No man loses ever on a lower
level by magnanimity on a higher. Superfluous wealth
can buy superfluities only. Money is not required to buy
one necessary of the soul.

I live in the angle of a leaden wall, into whose compo-
sition was poured a little alloy of bell metal. Often, in the
repose of my mid-day, there reaches my ears a confused
tintinnabulum from without. It is the noise of my contemporaries. My neighbors tell me of their adventures
with famous gentlemen and ladies, what notabilities they
met at the dinner-table; but I am no more interested in

such things than in the contents of the Daily Times. The interest and the conversation are about costume and manners chiefly; but a goose is a goose still, dress it as you will. They tell me of California and Texas, of England and the Indies, of the Hon. Mr. _____ of Georgia or of Massachusetts, all transient and fleeting phenomena, till I am ready to leap from their court-yard like the Mameluke bey. I delight to come to my bearings,—not walk in procession with pomp and parade, in a conspicuous place, but to walk even with the Builder of the universe, if I may,—not to live in this restless, nervous, bustling, trivial Nineteenth Century, but stand or sit thoughtfully while it goes by. What are men celebrating? They are all on a committee of arrangements, and hourly expect a speech from somebody. God is only the president of the day, and Webster is his orator. I love to weigh, to settle, to gravitate toward that which most strongly and rightfully attracts me;—not hang by the beam of the scale and try to weigh less,—not suppose a case, but take the case that is; to travel the only path I can, and that on which no power can resist me. It affords me no satisfaction to commence to spring an arch before I have got a solid foundation. Let us not play at kittly-benders. There is a solid bottom every where. We read that the traveller asked the boy if the swamp before him had a hard bottom. The boy replied that it had. But presently the traveller's horse sank in up to the girths, and he observed to the boy, "I thought you said that this bog had a hard bottom." "So it has," answered the latter, "but you have not got half way to it yet." So it is with the bogs and quicksands of society; but he is an old boy that knows it. Only what is thought said or done at a certain rare coincidence is good. I would not be one of those who will foolishly drive a nail into mere lath and plastering; such a deed would keep me awake nights. Give me a hammer, and let me feel for the furring. Do not depend on the putty. Drive a nail home and clinch it so faithfully that you can wake up in the night and think of your work with satisfaction,—a work at which you would not be ashamed to invoke the Muse. So will help you God, and so only. Every nail driven should be as another rivet in the machine of the universe, you carrying on the work.

Rather than love, than money, than fame, give me truth.

I sat at a table where were rich food and wine in abundance, and obsequious attendance, but sincerity and truth were not; and I went away hungry from the inhospitable board. The hospitality was as cold as the ices. I thought that there was no need of ice to freeze them. They talked to me of the age of the wine and the fame of the vintage; but I thought of an older, a newer, and purer wine, of a more glorious vintage, which they had not got, and could not buy. The style, the house and grounds and "entertainment" pass for nothing with me. I called on the king, but he made me wait in his hall, and conducted like a man incapacitated for hospitality. There was a man in my neighborhood who lived in a hollow tree. His manners were truly regal. I should have done better had I called on him.

How long shall we sit in our porticoes practising idle and musty virtues, which any work would make impertinent? As if one were to begin the day with long-suffering, and hire a man to hoe his potatoes; and in the afternoon go forth to practise Christian meekness and charity with goodness aforethought! Consider the China pride and stagnant self-complacency of mankind. This generation reclines a little to congratulate itself on being the last of an illustrious line; and in Boston and London and Paris and Rome, thinking of its long descent, it speaks of its progress in art and science and literature with satisfaction. There are the Records of the Philosophical Societies, and the public Eulogies of *Great Men!* It is the good Adam contemplating his own virtue. "Yes, we have done great deeds, and sung divine songs, which shall never die,"—that is, as long as *we* can remember them. The learned societies and great men of Assyria,—where are they? What youthful philosophers and experimentalists we are! There is not one of my readers who has yet lived a whole human life. These may be but the spring months in the life of the race. If we have had the seven-years' itch, we have not seen the seventeen-year locust yet in Concord. We are acquainted with a mere pellicle of the globe on which we live. Most have not delved six feet beneath the surface, nor leaped as many above it. We know not where we are. Beside, we are sound asleep nearly half our time. Yet we esteem ourselves wise, and have an established order on the surface.

Truly, we are deep thinkers, we are ambitious spirits! As I
stand over the insect crawling amid the pine needles on
the forest floor, and endeavoring to conceal itself from
my sight, and ask myself why it will cherish those humble thoughts, and hide its head from me who might perhaps be its benefactor, and impart to its race some cheering information, I am reminded of the greater Benefactor
and Intelligence, that stands over me the human insect.

There is an incessant influx of novelty into the world,
and yet we tolerate incredible dulness. I need only suggest what kind of sermons are still listened to in the most
enlightened countries. There are such words as joy and
sorrow, but they are only the burden of a psalm, sung
with a nasal twang, while we believe in the ordinary and
mean. We think that we can change our clothes only. It is
said that the British Empire is very large and respectable,
and that the United States are a first-rate power. We do
not believe that a tide rises and falls behind every man
which can float the British Empire like a chip, if he
should ever harbor it in his mind. Who knows what sort
of seventeen-year locust will next come out of the
ground? The government of the world I live in was not
framed, like that of Britain, in after-dinner conversations
over the wine.

The life in us is like the water in the river. It may rise
this year higher than man has ever known it, and flood
the parched uplands; even this may be the eventful year,
which will drown out all our muskrats. It was not always
dry land where we dwell. I see far inland the banks
which the stream anciently washed, before science began
to record its freshets. Every one has heard the story
which has gone the rounds of New England, of a strong
and beautiful bug which came out of the dry leaf of an
old table of apple-tree wood, which had stood in a farmer's kitchen for sixty years, first in Connecticut, and afterward in Massachusetts,—from an egg deposited in the
living tree many years earlier still, as appeared by counting the annual layers beyond it; which was heard gnawing out for several weeks, hatched perchance by the heat
of an urn. Who does not feel his faith in a resurrection
and immortality strengthened by hearing of this? Who

knows what beautiful and winged life, whose egg has been buried for ages under many concentric layers of woodenness in the dead dry life of society, deposited at first in the alburnum of the green and living tree, which has been gradually converted into the semblance of its well-seasoned tomb,—heard perchance gnawing out now for years by the astonished family of man, as they sat round the festive board,—may unexpectedly come forth from amidst society's most trivial and handselled furniture, to enjoy its perfect summer life at last!

I do not say that John or Jonathan will realize all this; but such is the character of that morrow which mere lapse of time can never make to dawn. The light which puts out our eyes is darkness to us. Only that day dawns to which we are awake. There is more day to dawn. The sun is but a morning star.

SLAVERY IN
MASSACHUSETTS

"Slavery in Massachusetts" is Thoreau's vehement response to the apprehension in Boston in 1854 of the fugitive slave, Anthony Burns, and his forced return by state authorities to his owner in Virginia. Thoreau's wrath overflowed initially into his journal, from which he later quarried the material for a speech before a gathering of anti-slavery protesters at Framingham. William Lloyd Garrison printed the speech in The Liberator *for July 21, 1854, with additional material that Thoreau had not read at the protest meeting; and it was reprinted immediately by Horace Greeley in the New York* Tribune *and elsewhere. This essay may be interpreted as Thoreau's application of the principle enunciated in "Resistance to Civil Government" that governments exceed their rightful authority when they apply force to the resolution of moral issues. The text is from* Reform Papers *in the Princeton Edition (1973) edited by Wendell Glick.*

I LATELY ATTENDED A MEETING of the citizens of Concord, expecting, as one among many, to speak on the subject of slavery in Massachusetts; but I was surprised and disappointed to find that what had called my townsmen together was the destiny of Nebraska, and not of Massachusetts, and that what I had to say would be entirely out of order. I had thought that the house was on fire, and not the prairie; but though several of the citizens of Massachusetts are now in prison for attempting to rescue a slave from her own clutches, not one of the speakers at that meeting expressed regret for it, not one even referred to it. It was only the disposition of some wild lands a thousand miles off, which appeared to concern them. The inhabitants of Concord are not prepared to stand by one of their own bridges, but talk only of taking up a position on the highlands beyond the Yellowstone river. Our Buttricks, and Davises, and Hosmers are retreating thither, and I fear that they will have no Lexington Common between them and the enemy. There is not one slave in Nebraska; there are perhaps a million slaves in Massachusetts.

They who have been bred in the school of politics fail now and always to face the facts. Their measures are half measures and make-shifts, merely. They put off the day of settlement indefinitely, and meanwhile the debt accumulates. Though the Fugitive Slave Law had not been the subject of discussion on that occasion, it was at length faintly resolved by my townsmen, at an adjourned meeting, as I learn, that the compromise compact of 1820 having been repudiated by one of the parties, 'Therefore, . . . the Fugitive Slave Law must be repealed.' But this is not the reason why an iniquitous law should be repealed. The fact which the politician faces is merely, that there is less honor among thieves than was supposed, and not the fact that they are thieves.

As I had no opportunity to express my thoughts at that meeting, will you allow me to do so here?

Again it happens that the Boston Court House is full of armed men, holding prisoner and trying a MAN, to find out if he is not really a SLAVE. Does any one think that Justice or God awaits Mr. Loring's decision? For him to sit there deciding still, when this question is already decided from eternity to eternity, and the unlettered slave himself, and the multitude around, have long since heard and assented to the decision, is simply to make himself ridiculous. We may be tempted to ask from whom he received his commission, and who he is that received it; what novel statutes he obeys, and what precedents are to him of authority. Such an arbiter's very existence is an impertinence. We do not ask him to make up his mind, but to make up his pack.

I listen to hear the voice of a Governor, Commander-in-Chief of the forces of Massachusetts. I hear only the creaking of crickets and the hum of insects which now fill the summer air. The Governor's exploit is to review the troops on muster days. I have seen him on horse-back, with his hat off, listening to a chaplain's prayer. It chances that is all I have ever seen of a Governor. I think that I could manage to get along without one. If *he* is not of the least use to prevent my being kidnapped, pray of what important use is he likely to be to me? When freedom is most endangered, he dwells in the deepest obscurity. A distinguished clergyman told me that he chose the profession of a clergyman, because it afforded the most leisure for literary pursuits. I would recommend to him the profession of a Governor.

Three years ago, also, when the Simm's tragedy was acted, I said to myself, there is such an officer, if not such a man, as the Governor of Massachusetts,—what has he been about the last fortnight? Has he had as much as he could do to keep on the fence during this moral earth-quake? It seemed to me that no keener satire could have been aimed at, no more cutting insult have been offered to that man, than just what happened—the absence of all inquiry after him in that crisis. The worst and the most I chance to know of him is, that he did not improve that opportunity to make himself known, and worthily known. He could at least have *resigned* himself into fame. It appeared to be forgotten that there was such a man, or such an office. Yet no doubt he was endeavoring to fill the gubernatorial chair all the while. He was no Governor of mine. He did not govern me.

But at last, in the present case, the Governor was heard from. After he and the United States Government had perfectly succeeded in robbing a poor innocent black man of his liberty for life, and, as far as they could, of his

Creator's likeness in his breast, he made a speech to his accomplices, at a congratulatory supper!

I have read a recent law of this State, making it penal for 'any officer of the Commonwealth' to 'detain, or aid in the . . . detention,' any where within its limits, 'of any person, for the reason that he is claimed as a fugitive slave.' Also, it was a matter of notoriety that a writ of replevin to take the fugitive out of the custody of the United States Marshal could not be served, for want of sufficient force to aid the officer.

I had thought that the Governor was in some sense the executive officer of the State; that it was his business, as a Governor, to see that the laws of the State were executed; while, as a man, he took care that he did not, by so doing, break the laws of humanity; but when there is any special important use for him, he is useless, or worse than useless, and permits the laws of the State to go unexecuted. Perhaps I do not know what are the duties of a Governor; but if to be a Governor requires to subject one's self to so much ignominy without remedy, if it is to put a restraint upon my manhood, I shall take care never to be Governor of Massachusetts. I have not read far in the statutes of this Commonwealth. It is not profitable reading. They do not always say what is true; and they do not always mean what they say. What I am concerned to know is, that that man's influence and authority were on the side of the slaveholder, and not of the slave—of the guilty, and not of the innocent—of injustice, and not of justice. I never saw him of whom I speak; indeed, I did not know that he was Governor until this event occurred. I heard of him and Anthony Burns at the same time, and thus, undoubtedly, most will hear of him. So far am I from being governed by him. I do not mean that it was any thing to his discredit that I had not heard of him, only that I heard what I did. The worst I shall say of him is, that he proved no better than the majority of his constituents would be likely to prove. In my opinion, he was not equal to the occasion.

The whole military force of the State is at the service of a Mr. Suttle, a slaveholder from Virginia, to enable him to catch a man whom he calls his property; but not a soldier is offered to save a citizen of Massachusetts from being kidnapped! Is this what all these soldiers, all this *training* has been for these seventy-nine years past? Have they been trained merely to rob Mexico, and carry back fugitive slaves to their masters?

These very nights, I heard the sound of a drum in our streets. There were men *training* still; and for what? I could with an effort pardon the cockerels of Concord for crowing still, for they, perchance, had not been beaten that morning; but I could not excuse this rub-a-dub of the 'trainers'. The slave was carried back by exactly such as these, i.e., by the soldier, of whom the best you can say in this connection is, that he is a fool made conspicuous by a painted coat.

Three years ago, also, just a week after the authorities of Boston assembled to carry back a perfectly innocent man, and one whom they knew to be innocent, into slavery, the inhabitants of Concord caused the bells to be rung and the cannons to be fired, to celebrate their liberty—and the courage and love of liberty of their ancestors who fought at the bridge. As if *those* three millions had fought for the right to be free themselves, but to hold in slavery three million others. Now-a-days, men wear a fool's cap, and call it a liberty cap. I do not know but there are some, who, if they were tied to a whipping-post, and could but get one hand free, would use it to ring the bells and fire the cannons, to celebrate *their* liberty. So some of my townsmen took the liberty to ring and fire; that was the extent of their freedom; and when the sound of the bells died away, their liberty died away also; when the powder was all expended, their liberty went off with the smoke.

The joke could be no broader, if the inmates of the prisons were to subscribe for all the powder to be used in such salutes, and hire the jailers to do the firing and ringing for them, while they enjoyed it through the grating.

This is what I thought about my neighbors.

Every humane and intelligent inhabitant of Concord, when he or she heard those bells and those cannons, thought not with pride of the events of the 19th of April, 1775, but with shame of the events of the 12th of April,

1851. But now we have half buried that old shame under a new one.

Massachusetts sat waiting Mr. Loring's decision, as if it could in any way affect her own criminality. Her crime, the most conspicuous and fatal crime of all, was permitting him to be the umpire in such a case. It was really the trial of Massachusetts. Every moment that she hesitated to set this man free—every moment that she now hesitates to atone for her crime, she is convicted. The Commissioner on her case is God; not Edward G. God, but simple God.

I wish my countrymen to consider, that whatever the human law may be, neither an individual nor a nation can ever commit the least act of injustice against the obscurest individual, without having to pay the penalty for it. A government which deliberately enacts injustice, and persists in it, will at length ever become the laughing-stock of the world.

Much has been said about American slavery, but I think that we do not even yet realize what slavery is. If I were seriously to propose to Congress to make mankind into sausages, I have no doubt that most of the members would smile at my proposition, and if any believed me to be in earnest, they would think that I proposed something much worse than Congress had ever done. But if any of them will tell me that to make a man into a sausage would be much worse,—would be any worse, than to make him into a slave,—than it was to enact the Fugitive Slave Law, I will accuse him of foolishness, of intellectual incapacity, of making a distinction without a difference. The one is just as sensible a proposition as the other.

I heard a good deal said about trampling this law under foot. Why, one need not go out of his way to do that. This law rises not to the level of the head or the reason; its natural habitat is in the dirt. It was born and bred, and has its life only in the dust and mire, on a level with the feet, and he who walks with freedom, and does not with Hindoo mercy avoid treading on every venomous reptile, will inevitably tread on it, and so trample it under foot,— and Webster, its maker, with it, like the dirt-bug and its ball.

Recent events will be valuable as a criticism on the administration of justice in our minds, or, rather, as showing what are the true resources of justice in any community. It has come to this, that the friends of liberty, the friends of the slave, have shuddered when they have understood that his fate was left to the legal tribunals of the country to be decided. Free men have no faith that justice will be awarded in such a case; the judge may decide this way or that; it is a kind of accident, at best. It is evident that he is not a competent authority in so important a case. It is no time, then, to be judging according to his precedents, but to establish a precedent for the future. I would much rather trust to the sentiment of the people. In their vote, you would get something of some value, at least, however small; but, in the other case, only the trammelled judgment of an individual, of no significance, be it which way it might.

It is to some extent fatal to the courts, when the people are compelled to go behind them. I do not wish to believe that the courts were made for fair weather, and for very civil cases merely,—but think of leaving it to any court in the land to decide whether more than three millions of people, in this case, a sixth part of a nation, have a right to be freemen or not! But it has been left to the courts of *justice*, so-called—to the Supreme Court of the land— and, as you all know, recognizing no authority but the Constitution, it has decided that the three millions are, and shall continue to be, slaves. Such judges as these are merely the inspectors of a pick-lock and murderer's tools, to tell him whether they are in working order or not, and there they think that their responsibility ends. There was a prior case on the docket, which they, as judges appointed by God, had no right to skip; which having been justly settled, they would have been saved from this humiliation. It was the case of the murderer himself.

The law will never make men free; it is men who have got to make the law free. They are the lovers of law and order, who observe the law when the government breaks it.

Among human beings, the judge whose words seal the fate of a man furthest into eternity, is not he who merely pronounces the verdict of the law, but he, whoever he may be, who, from a love of truth, and unprejudiced by any custom or enactment of men, utters a true opinion or *sentence* concerning him. He it is that *sentences* him. Whoever has discerned truth, has received his commission from a higher source than the chiefest justice in the world, who can discern only law. He finds himself constituted judge of the judge.—Strange that it should be necessary to state such simple truths.

I am more and more convinced that, with reference to any public question, it is more important to know what the country thinks of it, than what the city thinks. The city does not *think* much. On any moral question, I would rather have the opinion of Boxboro than of Boston and New York put together. When the former speaks, I feel as if somebody *had* spoken, as if *humanity* was yet, and a reasonable being had asserted its rights,—as if some unprejudiced men among the country's hills had at length turned their attention to the subject, and by a few sensible words redeemed the reputation of the race. When, in some obscure country town, the farmers come together to a special town meeting, to express their opinion on some subject which is vexing the land, that, I think, is the true Congress, and the most respectable one that is ever assembled in the United States.

It is evident that there are, in this Commonwealth, at least, two parties, becoming more and more distinct—the party of the city, and the party of the country. I know that the country is mean enough, but I am glad to believe that there is a slight difference in her favor. But as yet, she has few, if any organs, through which to express herself. The editorials which she reads, like the news, come from the sea-board. Let us, the inhabitants of the country, cultivate self-respect. Let us not send to the city for aught more essential than our broadcloths and groceries, or, if we read the opinions of the city, let us entertain opinions of our own.

Among measures to be adopted, I would suggest to make as earnest and vigorous an assault on the Press as has already been made, and with effect, on the Church. The Church has much improved within a few years; but

the Press is almost, without exception, corrupt. I believe
that, in this country, the press exerts a greater and a more
pernicious influence than the Church did in its worst period. We are not a religious people, but we are a nation
of politicians. We do not care for the Bible, but we do
care for the newspaper. At any meeting of politicians,—
like that at Concord the other evening, for instance,—
how impertinent it would be to quote from the Bible!
how pertinent to quote from a newspaper or from the
Constitution! The newspaper is a Bible which we read
every morning and every afternoon, standing and sitting,
riding and walking. It is a Bible which every man carries
in his pocket, which lies on every table and counter, and
which the mail, and thousands of missionaries, are continually dispensing. It is, in short, the only book which
America has printed, and which America reads. So wide
is its influence. The editor is a preacher whom you voluntarily support. Your tax is commonly one cent daily, and
it costs nothing for pew hire. But how many of these
preachers preach the truth? I repeat the testimony of
many an intelligent foreigner, as well as my own convictions, when I say, that probably no country was ever
ruled by so mean a class of tyrants as, with a few noble
exceptions, are the editors of the periodical press in *this*
country. And as they live and rule only by their servility,
and appealing to the worst, and not the better nature of
man, the people who read them are in the condition of
the dog that returns to his vomit.

The *Liberator* and the *Commonwealth* were the only
papers in Boston, as far as I know, which made themselves heard in condemnation of the cowardice and
meanness of the authorities of that city, as exhibited in
'51. The other journals, almost without exception, by
their manner of referring to and speaking of the Fugitive
Slave Law, and the carrying back of the slave Simms,
insulted the common sense of the country, at least. And,
for the most part, they did this, one would say, because
they thought so to secure the approbation of their patrons, not being aware that a sounder sentiment prevailed
to any extent in the heart of the Commonwealth. I am
told that some of them have improved of late; but they

are still eminently time-serving. Such is the character they have won.

But, thank fortune, this preacher can be even more easily reached by the weapons of the reformer than could the recreant priest. The free men of New England have only to refrain from purchasing and reading these sheets, have only to withhold their cents, to kill a score of them at once. One whom I respect told me that he purchased Mitchell's *Citizen* in the cars, and then threw it out the window. But would not his contempt have been more fatally expressed, if he had not bought it?

Are they Americans? are they New Englanders? are they inhabitants of Lexington, and Concord, and Framingham, who read and support the Boston *Post, Mail, Journal, Advertiser, Courier,* and *Times?* Are these the Flags of our Union? I am not a newspaper reader, and may omit to name the worst.

Could slavery suggest a more complete servility than some of these journals exhibit? Is there any dust which their conduct does not lick, and make fouler still with its slime? I do not know whether the Boston *Herald* is still in existence, but I remember to have seen it about the streets when Simms was carried off. Did it not act its part well—serve its master faithfully? How could it have gone lower on its belly? How can a man stoop lower than he is low? do more than put his extremities in the place of the head he has? than make his head his lower extremity? When I have taken up this paper with my cuffs turned up, I have heard the gurgling of the sewer through every column. I have felt that I was handling a paper picked out of the public gutters, a leaf from the gospel of the gambling-house, the groggery and the brothel, harmonizing with the gospel of the Merchants' Exchange.

The majority of the men of the North, and of the South, and East, and West, are not men of principle. If they vote, they do not send men to Congress on errands of humanity, but while their brothers and sisters are being scourged and hung for loving liberty, while—I might here insert all that slavery implies and is,—it is the mismanagement of wood and iron and stone and gold which concerns them. Do what you will, O Government! with

my wife and children, my mother and brother, my father
and sister, I will obey your commands to the letter. It will
indeed grieve me if you hurt them, if you deliver them to
overseers to be hunted by hounds or to be whipped to
death; but nevertheless, I will peaceably pursue my chosen calling on this fair earth, until perchance, one day,
when I have put on mourning for them dead, I shall have
persuaded you to relent. Such is the attitude, such are the
words of Massachusetts.

Rather than do thus, I need not say what match I
would touch, what system endeavor to blow up,—but as I
love my life, I would side with the light, and let the dark
earth roll from under me, calling my mother and my
brother to follow.

I would remind my countrymen, that they are to be
men first, and Americans only at a late and convenient
hour. No matter how valuable law may be to protect
your property, even to keep soul and body together, if it
do not keep you and humanity together.

I am sorry to say, that I doubt if there is a judge in
Massachusetts who is prepared to resign his office, and
get his living innocently, whenever it is required of him
to pass sentence under a law which is merely contrary to
the law of God. I am compelled to see that they put
themselves, or rather, are by character, in this respect,
exactly on a level with the marine who discharges his
musket in any direction he is ordered to. They are just as
much tools and as little men. Certainly, they are not the
more to be respected, because their master enslaves their
understandings and consciences, instead of their bodies.

The judges and lawyers,—simply as such, I mean,—
and all men of expediency, try this case by a very low
and incompetent standard. They consider not whether
the Fugitive Slave Law is right, but whether it is what
they call *constitutional*. Is virtue constitutional, or vice?
Is equity constitutional, or iniquity? In important moral
and vital questions like this, it is just as impertinent to ask
whether it is profitable or not. They persist in being the
servants of the worst of men, and not the servants of humanity. The question is not whether you or your grandfather, seventy years ago, did not enter into an agreement

to serve the devil, and that service is not accordingly now due; but whether you will not now, for once and at last, serve God,—in spite of your own past recreancy, or that of your ancestor,—by obeying that eternal and only just CONSTITUTION, which He, and not any Jefferson or Adams, has written in your being.

The amount of it is, if the majority vote the devil to be God, the minority will live and behave accordingly, and obey the successful candidate, trusting that some time or other, by some Speaker's casting vote, perhaps, they may reinstate God. This is the highest principle I can get out of or invent for my neighbors. These men act as if they believed that they could safely slide down hill a little way—or a good way—and would surely come to a place, by and by, where they could begin to slide up again. This is expediency, or choosing that course which offers the slightest obstacles to the feet, that is, a down-hill one. But there is no such thing as accomplishing a righteous reform by the use of 'expediency.' There is no such thing as sliding up hill. In morals, the only sliders are backsliders.

Thus we steadily worship Mammon, both School, and State, and Church, and the Seventh Day curse God with a tintamar from one end of the Union to the other.

Will mankind never learn that policy is not morality—that it never secures any moral right, but considers merely what is expedient? chooses the available candidate, who is invariably the devil,—and what right have his constituents to be surprised, because the devil does not behave like an angel of light? What is wanted is men, not of policy, but of probity—who recognize a higher law than the Constitution, or the decision of the majority. The fate of the country does not depend on how you vote at the polls—the worst man is as strong as the best at that game; it does not depend on what kind of paper you drop into the ballot-box once a year, but on what kind of man you drop from your chamber into the street every morning.

What should concern Massachusetts is not the Nebraska Bill, nor the Fugitive Slave Bill, but her own slaveholding and servility. Let the State dissolve her union with the slaveholder. She may wriggle and hesitate, and ask leave

to read the Constitution once more; but she can find no
respectable law or precedent which sanctions the continu-
ance of such a Union for an instant.

Let each inhabitant of the State dissolve his union with
her, as long as she delays to do her duty.

The events of the past month teach me to distrust
Fame. I see that she does not finely discriminate, but
coarsely hurrahs. She considers not the simple heroism of
an action, but only as it is connected with its apparent
consequences. She praises till she is hoarse the easy exploit of the Boston tea party, but will be comparatively
silent about the braver and more disinterestedly heroic
attack on the Boston Court-House, simply because it was
unsuccessful!

Covered with disgrace, the State has sat down coolly to
try for their lives and liberties the men who attempted to
do its duty for it. And this is called *justice!* They who
have shown that they can behave particularly well may
perchance be put under bonds for *their good behavior.*
They whom truth requires at present to plead guilty, are
of all the inhabitants of the State, pre-eminently innocent. While the Governor, and the Mayor, and countless
officers of the Commonwealth, are at large, the champions of liberty are imprisoned.

Only they are guiltless, who commit the crime of contempt of such a court. It behoves every man to see that
his influence is on the side of justice, and let the courts
make their own characters. My sympathies in this case
are wholly with the accused, and wholly against the ac-
cusers and their judges. Justice is sweet and musical; but
injustice is harsh and discordant. The judge still sits
grinding at his organ, but it yields no music, and we hear
only the sound of the handle. He believes that all the
music resides in the handle, and the crowd toss him their
coppers the same as before.

Do you suppose that that Massachusetts which is now
doing these things,—which hesitates to crown these men,
some of whose lawyers, and even judges, perchance, may
be driven to take refuge in some poor quibble, that they
may not wholly outrage their instinctive sense of justice,—do you suppose that she is any thing but base and

servile? that she is the champion of liberty?

Show me a free State, and a court truly of justice, and I will fight for them, if need be; but show me Massachusetts, and I refuse her my allegiance, and express contempt for her courts.

The effect of a good government is to make life more valuable,—of a bad one, to make it less valuable. We can afford that railroad, and all merely material stock, should lose some of its value for that only compels us to live more simply and economically; but suppose that the value of life itself should be diminished! How can we make a less demand on man and nature, how live more economically in respect to virtue and all noble qualities, than we do? I have lived for the last month,—and I think that every man in Massachusetts capable of the sentiment of patriotism must have had a similar experience,—with the sense of having suffered a vast and indefinite loss. I did not know at first what ailed me. At last it occurred to me that what I had lost was a country. I had never respected the Government near to which I had lived, but I had foolishly thought that I might manage to live here, minding my private affairs, and forget it. For my part, my old and worthiest pursuits have lost I cannot say how much of their attraction, and I feel that my investment in life here is worth many per cent. less since Massachusetts last deliberately sent back an innocent man, Anthony Burns, to slavery. I dwelt before, perhaps, in the illusion that my life passed somewhere only *between* heaven and hell, but now I cannot persuade myself that I do not dwell *wholly within* hell. The site of that political organization called Massachusetts is to me morally covered with volcanic scoriæ and cinders, such as Milton describes in the infernal regions. If there is any hell more unprincipled than our rulers, and we, the ruled, I feel curious to see it. Life itself being worth less, all things with it, which minister to it, are worth less. Suppose you have a small library, with pictures to adorn the walls—a garden laid out around—and contemplate scientific and literary pursuits, &c., and discover all at once that your villa, with all its contents, is located in hell, and that the justice of the peace has a cloven foot and a forked tail—do not these things suddenly lose their value in your eyes?

I feel that, to some extent, the State has fatally interfered with my lawful business. It has not only interrupted me in my passage through Court street on errands of trade, but it has interrupted me and every man on his onward and upward path, on which he had trusted soon to leave Court street far behind. What right had it to remind me of Court street? I have found that hollow which even I had relied on for solid.

I am surprised to see men going about their business as if nothing had happened. I say to myself—Unfortunates! they have not heard the news. I am surprised that the man whom I just met on horseback should be so earnest to overtake his newly-bought cows running away—since all property is insecure—and if they do not run away again, they may be taken away from him when he gets them. Fool! does he not know that his seed-corn is worth less this year—that all beneficent harvests fail as you approach the empire of hell? No prudent man will build a stone house under these circumstances, or engage in any peaceful enterprise which it requires a long time to accomplish. Art is as long as ever, but life is more interrupted and less available for a man's proper pursuits. It is not an era of repose. We have used up all our inherited freedom. If we would save our lives, we must fight for them.

I walk toward one of our ponds, but what signifies the beauty of nature when men are base? We walk to lakes to see our serenity reflected in them; when we are not serene, we go not to them. Who can be serene in a country where both the rulers and the ruled are without principle? The remembrance of my country spoils my walk. My thoughts are murder to the State, and involuntarily go plotting against her.

But it chanced the other day that I scented a white water-lily, and a season I had waited for had arrived. It is the emblem of purity. It bursts up so pure and fair to the eye, and so sweet to the scent, as if to show us what purity and sweetness reside in, and can be extracted from, the slime and muck of earth. I think I have plucked the first one that has opened for a mile. What confirmation of our hopes is in the fragrance of this flower! I shall not so soon despair of the world for it, notwithstanding slavery, and the cowardice and want of principle of Northern men. It suggests what kind of laws have prevailed longest and widest, and still prevail, and that the time may come when man's deeds will smell as sweet. Such is the odor which the plant emits. If Nature can compound this fragrance still annually, I shall believe her still young and full of vigor, her integrity and genius unimpaired, and that there is virtue even in man, too, who is fitted to perceive and love it. It reminds me that Nature has been partner to no Missouri Compromise. I scent no compromise in the fragrance of the water-lily. It is not a *Nymphœa Douglassii*. In it, the sweet, and pure, and innocent, are wholly sundered from the obscene and baleful. I do not scent in this the time-serving irresolution of a Massachusetts Governor, nor of a Boston Mayor. So behave that the odor of your actions may enhance the general sweetness of the atmosphere, that when we behold or scent a flower, we may not be reminded how inconsistent your deeds are with it; for all odor is but one form of advertisement of a moral quality, and if fair actions had not been performed, the lily would not smell sweet. The foul slime stands for the sloth and vice of man, the decay of humanity; the fragrant flower that springs from it, for the purity and courage which are immortal.

Slavery and servility have produced no sweet-scented flower annually, to charm the senses of men, for they have no real life: they are merely a decaying and a death, offensive to all healthy nostrils. We do not complain that they *live*, but that they do not *get buried*. Let the living bury them; even they are good for manure.

THE SHIPWRECK

An indefatigable walker, Thoreau on four separate occasions took walking trips on Cape Cod, twice in the company of his friend, Ellery Channing, who edited with Thoreau's sister Sophia the volume Cape Cod *three years after Thoreau's death. Thoreau's sharp eye misses none of the essential details of the seashore; but what he sees quickly becomes a microcosm of a larger vision of the world, of human life, and time. This text reproduces that portion of the first printing in* Putnam's Monthly Magazine *for June 1855, that describes Thoreau's initial visit.*

WISHING TO GET A BETTER VIEW than I had yet had of the ocean, which, we are told, covers more than two-thirds of the globe, but of which a man who lives a few miles inland may never see any trace, more than of another world, I made a visit to Cape Cod in October, '49, and another the succeeding June, the first time with a single companion, the last time alone. I have spent, in all, ten days on the Cape, but, having come so fresh to the sea, have got but little salted. My readers must expect only so much saltness as the land-breeze acquires from blowing over an arm of the sea, or is tasted on the windows and on the bark of trees twenty miles inland after September gales.

Cape Cod is the bared and bended arm of Massachusetts; the shoulder is at Buzzard's Bay, the elbow, or crazy-bone, at Cape Mallebarre, the wrist at Truro, and the sandy fist at Provincetown—behind which the State stands on her guard, with her back to the Green Mountains, and her feet planted on the floor of the ocean, like an athlete protecting her bay—boxing with northeast storms, and, ever and anon, heaving up her Atlantic adversary from the lap of earth; ready to thrust forward her other fist, which keeps guard the while upon her breast at Cape Ann.

On studying the map, I saw that there must be an uninterrupted beach on the east or outside of the fore-arm of the Cape, more than thirty miles from the general line of the coast, which would afford a good sea view; but that, on account of an opening in the beach, forming the entrance to Nanset Harbor, in Orleans, I must strike it in Eastham, if I approached it by land, and probably I could walk thence straight to Race Point, about twenty-eight miles, and not meet with any obstruction.

We left Concord, Massachusetts, on Tuesday, October 9th, 1849. On reaching Boston, we found that the Provincetown steamer, which should have got in the day before, had not yet arrived, on account of a violent storm; and, as we noticed in the streets a large handbill, on which were the words, "Death! 145 lives lost at Cohasset!" we decided to go by way of Cohasset. There were many Irish in the cars, going to identify bodies and to sympathize with the survivors, and also to attend the funeral which was to take place in the afternoon. When we arrived at Cohasset, it appeared that nearly all the passengers were bound for the beach, which was about a mile distant, and many other persons were flocking in from the neighboring country. There were several hundreds of them streaming off over Cohasset common in that direction—some on foot and some in wagons—and, among them, I noticed some sportsmen in their hunting jackets, with their guns and game-bags and dogs. As we passed the grave-yard we saw a large hole, like a cellar, freshly dug there, and, just before reaching the shore, by a pleasantly winding and rocky road, we met several hay-

riggings and farm wagons coming away toward the meeting-house, each loaded with three large, rough deal boxes. We needed not to ask what was in them. The owners
of the wagons were made the undertakers. Many horses
in carriages were fastened to the fences near the shore,
and, for a mile or more, up and down, the beach was
covered with people looking out for bodies and examining the fragments of the wreck. This is the rockiest shore
in Massachusetts, from Nantasket to Scituate—hard sieni-
tic rocks, which the waves have laid bare, but have not
been able to crumble. It has been the scene of many a
shipwreck.

The brig St. John, from Galway, Ireland, laden with
emigrants, was wrecked on Sunday morning; it was now
Tuesday morning, and the sea was still breaking violently
on the rocks. There were eighteen or twenty of the same
large boxes that I have mentioned, lying on a green hill-
side, a few rods from the water, and surrounded by a
crowd. The bodies which had been recovered, twenty-
seven or eight in all, had been collected there. Some were
rapidly nailing down the lids, others were carting the
boxes away, and others were lifting the lids, which were
yet loose, and peeping under the cloths—for each body,
with such rags as still adhered to it, was covered loosely
with a white sheet. I witnessed no signs of grief, but there
was a sober dispatch of business which was affecting. One
man was seeking to identify a particular body, and one
undertaker or carpenter was calling to another to know in
what box a certain child was put. I saw many marble feet
and matted heads as the cloths were raised, and one livid,
swollen and mangled body of a drowned girl—who probably had intended to go out to service in some American
family—to which some rags still adhered, with a string,
half concealed by the flesh, about its swollen neck; the
coiled-up wreck of a human hulk, gashed by the rocks or
fishes, so that the bones and muscle were exposed, but
quite bloodless—merely red and white—with wide-open
and staring eyes, yet lusterless, dead-lights; or, like the
cabin windows of a stranded vessel, filled with sand.
Sometimes there were two or more children, or a parent
and child in the same box, and on the lid would perhaps

be written with red chalk, "Bridget such-a-one, and sister's child." The surrounding sward was covered with bits of sails and clothing. I have since heard, from one who lives by this beach, that a woman who had come over before, but had left her infant behind for her sister to bring, came and looked into these boxes, and saw in one,—probably the same whose superscription I have quoted—her child in her sister's arms, as if the sister had meant to be found thus; and, within three days after, the mother died from the effect of that sight.

We turned from this and walked along the rocky shore. In the first cave were strewn, what seemed the fragments of a vessel, in small pieces mixed with sand and sea-weed, and great quantities of feathers; but it looked so old and rusty, that I, at first, took it to be some old wreck which had lain there many years; I even thought of Capt. Kidd, and that the feathers were those which sea-fowl had cast there; and, perhaps, there might be some tradition about it in the neighborhood. I asked a sailor if that was the St. John. He said it was. I asked him where she struck. He pointed to a rock in front of us, a mile from the shore, called the Grampus Rock, and added:—

"You can see a part of her now sticking up; it looks like a small boat."

I saw it. It was thought to be held by the chain-cables and the anchors. I asked if the bodies which I saw were all that were drowned.

"Not a quarter of them," said he.

"Where are the rest?"

"Most of them right underneath that piece you see."

It appeared to us that there was enough rubbish to make the wreck of a large vessel in this cove alone, and that it would take many days to cart it off. It was several feet deep, and here and there was a bonnet or a jacket on it. In the very midst of the crowd about this wreck, there were men with carts busily collecting the sea-weed which the storm had cast up, and conveying it beyond the reach of the tide, though they were often obliged to separate fragments of clothing from it, and they might, at any moment, have found a human body under it. Drown who might, they did not forget that this weed was a valuable manure. This shipwreck had not produced a visible vibration in the fabric of society.

About a mile south we could see, rising above the rocks, the masts of the British brig which the St. John had endeavored to follow, which had slipped her cables, and, by good luck, run into the mouth of Cohasset Harbor. A little further along the shore we saw a man's clothes on a rock; further, a woman's scarf, a gown, a straw bonnet, the brig's caboose, and one of her masts high and dry, broken into several pieces. In another rocky cove, several rods from the water, and behind rocks twenty feet high, lay a part of one side of the vessel still hanging together. It was, perhaps, forty feet long, by fourteen wide. I was even more astonished at the power of the waves, exhibited on this shattered fragment, than I had been at the sight of the smaller fragments before. The largest timbers and iron braces were broken superfluously, and I saw that no material could withstand the power of the waves; that iron must go to pieces in such a case, and an iron vessel would be cracked up like an egg-shell on the rocks. Some of these timbers, however, were so rotten that I could almost thrust my umbrella through them. They told us that some were saved on this piece, and also showed where the sea had heaved it into this cove, which was now dry. When I saw where it had come in, and in what condition, I wondered that any had been saved on it. A little further on, a crowd of men was collected around the mate of the St. John, who was telling his story. He was a slim-looking youth, who spoke of the captain as the master, and seemed a little excited. He was saying that when they jumped into the boat, she filled, and the vessel lurching, the weight of the water in the boat caused the painter to break, and so they were separated. Whereat one man came away, saying:—

"Well, I don't see but he tells a straight story enough. You see, the weight of the water in the boat broke the painter. A boat full of water is very heavy—" and so on, in a loud and impertinently earnest tone, as if he had a bet depending on it, but had no humane interest in the matter. Another, a large man, stood near by upon a rock, gazing into the sea, and chewing large quids of tobacco, as if that habit were forever confirmed with him.

"Come," says another to his companion, "let's be off. We've seen the whole of it. It's no use to stay to the funeral."

Further, we saw one standing upon a rock, who, we were told, was one that was saved. He was a sober-looking man, dressed in a jacket and gray pantaloons, with his hands in the pockets. I asked him a few questions, which he answered; but he seemed unwilling to talk about it, and soon walked away. By his side stood one of the lifeboat men, in an oil-cloth jacket, who told us how they went to the relief of the British brig, thinking that the boat of the St. John, which they passed on the way, held all her crew,—for the waves prevented their seeing those who were on the vessel, though they might have saved some had they known there were any there. A little further was the flag of the St. John spread on a rock to dry, and held down by stones at the corners. This frail but essential and significant portion of the vessel, which had so long been the sport of the winds, was sure to reach the shore. There were one or two houses visible from these rocks, in which were some of the survivors, recovering from the shock which their bodies and minds had sustained. One was not expected to live.

We kept on down the shore as far as a promontory called White-head, that we might see more of the Cohasset Rocks. In a little cove, within half a mile, there were an old man and his son collecting, with their team, the sea-weed which that fatal storm had cast up, as serenely employed as if there had never been a wreck in the world, though they were within sight of the Grampus Rock on which the St. John had struck. The old man had heard that there was a wreck, and knew most of the particulars, but he said that he had not been up there since it happened. It was the wrecked weed that concerned him most, rock-weed, kelp, and sea-weed as he named them, which he carted to his barn-yard; and those bodies were to him but other weeds which the tide cast up, but which were of no use to him. We afterwards came to the lifeboat in its harbor, waiting for another emergency,—and in the afternoon we saw the funeral procession at a distance, at the head of which walked the captain with the other survivors.

On the whole, it was not so impressive a scene as I might have expected. If I had found one body cast upon the beach in some lonely place, it would have affected me more. I sympathized rather with the winds and waves, as if to toss and mangle these poor human bodies was the order of the day. If this was the law of Nature, why waste any time in awe or pity? If the last day were come, we should not think so much about the separation of friends or the blighted prospects of individuals. I saw that corpses might be multiplied, as on the field of battle, till they no longer affected us in any degree, as exceptions to the common lot of humanity. Take all the grave-yards together, they are always the majority. It is the individual and private that demands our sympathy. A man can attend but one funeral in the course of his life, can behold but one corpse. Yet I saw that the inhabitants of the shore would be not a little affected by this event. They would watch there many days and nights for the sea to give up its dead, and their imaginations and sympathies would supply the place of mourners far away, who, as yet, knew not of the wreck. Many days after this, something white was seen floating on the water by one who was sauntering on the beach. It was approached in a boat, and found to be the body of a woman, which had risen in an upright position, whose white cap was blown back with the wind. I saw that the beauty of the shore itself was wrecked for many a lonely walker there, until he could perceive, at last, how its beauty was enhanced by wrecks like this, and it acquired thus a rarer and sublimer beauty still.

Why care for these dead bodies? They really have no friends but the worms or fishes. Their owners were coming to the New World, as Columbus and the Pilgrims did, they were within a mile of its shores; but, before they could reach it, they emigrated to a newer world than ever Columbus dreamed of, yet one of whose existence we believe that there is far more universal and convincing evidence—though it has not yet been discovered by science—than Columbus had of this; not merely mariners' tales and some paltry driftwood and sea-weed, but a continual drift and instinct to all our shores and continents. I saw their empty hulks that came to land; but they themselves, meanwhile, were cast upon some shore yet further west, toward which we are all tending, and which we shall reach at last, it may be through storm and darkness, as they did. No doubt, we have reason to thank God, that they have not been "shipwrecked into life again." The mariner who makes the safest port in Heaven, perchance, seems to his friends on earth to be shipwrecked, for they deem Boston harbor the better place; though, perhaps, invisible to them, a skillful pilot comes to meet him, and the fairest and balmiest gales blow off that coast, his good ship makes the land in halcyon days, and he kisses the shore in rapture there, while his old hulk tosses in the surf here. It is hard to part with one's body, but no doubt, it is easy enough to do without it when once it is gone. All their plans and hopes burst like a bubble! Infants by the score dashed on the rocks by the enraged Atlantic Ocean! No, no! If the St. John did not make her port here, she has been telegraphed there. The strongest wind cannot stagger a Spirit; it is a Spirit's breath. A just man's purpose cannot be split on any Grampus or material rock, but itself will split rocks till it succeeds.

A PLEA FOR CAPTAIN JOHN BROWN*

Like "Slavery in Massachusetts," "A Plea for Captain John Brown" originated as a polemic address, in this instance delivered by Thoreau before a tense assemblage made up of his Concord townspeople in 1859. That John Brown's action at Harper's Ferry was reprehensible to the majority of the community carried no weight with Thoreau, at this point in his life deeply disturbed over the slavery issue. After repeating the speech in Boston and Worcester, Thoreau contributed his text to James Redpath for a gathering of anti-slavery pieces from many other contributors, including Emerson, under the title Echoes of Harper's Ferry. *Published in the spring of 1860, the book was intended by both Thoreau and Redpath to generate revenue for the benefit of John Brown's widow and children. The text printed here is from* Reform Papers (1973) *in the Princeton Edition, edited by Wendell Glick.*

I TRUST THAT YOU WILL PARDON me for being here. I do not wish to force my thoughts upon you, but I feel forced myself. Little as I know of Captain Brown, I would fain

---

* Read to the citizens of Concord, Mass., Sunday Evening, October 30, 1859. Also as the fifth lecture of the Fraternity Course in Boston, November 1; and at Worcester, November 3.

do my part to correct the tone and the statements of the newspapers, and of my countrymen generally, respecting his character and actions. It costs us nothing to be just. We can at least express our sympathy with, and admiration of, him and his companions, and that is what I now propose to do.

First, as to his history.

I will endeavor to omit, as much as possible, what you have already read. I need not describe his person to you, for probably most of you have seen and will not soon forget him. I am told that his grandfather, John Brown, was an officer in the Revolution; that he himself was born in Connecticut about the beginning of this century, but early went with his father to Ohio. I heard him say that his father was a contractor who furnished beef to the army there, in the war of 1812; that he accompanied him to the camp, and assisted him in that employment, seeing a good deal of military life, more, perhaps, than if he had been a soldier, for he was often present at the councils of the officers. Especially, he learned by experience how armies are supplied and maintained in the field—a work which, he observed, requires at least as much experience and skill as to lead them in battle. He said that few persons had any conception of the cost, even the pecuniary cost, of firing a single bullet in war. He saw enough, at any rate, to disgust him with a military life, indeed to excite in him a great abhorrence of it; so much so, that though he was tempted by the offer of some petty office in the army, when he was about eighteen, he not only declined that, but he also refused to train when warned, and was fined for it. He then resolved that he would never have anything to do with any war, unless it were a war for liberty.

When the troubles in Kansas began, he sent several of his sons thither to strengthen the party of the Free State men, fitting them out with such weapons as he had; telling them that if the troubles should increase, and there should be need of him, he would follow to assist them with his hand and counsel. This, as you all know, he soon after did; and it was through his agency, far more than any other's, that Kansas was made free.

For a part of his life he was a surveyor, and at one time
he was engaged in wool-growing, and he went to Europe
as an agent about that business. There, as every where, he
had his eyes about him, and made many original observations. He said, for instance, that he saw why the soil of
England was so rich, and that of Germany (I think it was)
so poor, and he thought of writing to some of the
crowned heads about it. It was because in England the
peasantry live on the soil which they cultivate, but in
Germany they are gathered into villages, at night. It is a
pity that he did not make a book of his observations.

I should say that he was an old-fashioned man in his
respect for the Constitution, and his faith in the perma-
nence of this Union. Slavery he deemed to be wholly opposed to these, and he was its determined foe.

He was by descent and birth a New England farmer, a
man of great common sense, deliberate and practical as
that class is, and tenfold more so. He was like the best of
those, who stood at Concord Bridge once, on Lexington
Common, and on Bunker Hill, only he was firmer and
higher principled than any that I have chanced to hear of
as there. It was no abolition lecturer that converted him.
Ethan Allen and Stark, with whom he may in some respects be compared, were rangers in a lower and less important field. They could bravely face their country's
foes, but he had the courage to face his country herself,
when she was in the wrong. A Western writer says, to
account for his escape from so many perils, that he was
concealed under a "rural exterior;" as if, in that prairie
land, a hero should, by good rights, wear a citizen's dress
only.

He did not go to the college called Harvard, good old
Alma Mater as she is. He was not fed on the pap that is
there furnished. As he phrased it, "I know no more of
grammar than one of your calves." But he went to the
great university of the West, where he sedulously pur-
sued the study of Liberty, for which he had early betrayed a fondness, and having taken many degrees, he
finally commenced the public practice of Humanity in
Kansas, as you all know. Such were *his humanities*, and

not any study of grammar. He would have left a Greek accent slanting the wrong way, and righted up a falling man.

He was one of that class of whom we hear a great deal, but, for the most part, see nothing at all—the Puritans. It would be in vain to kill him. He died lately in the time of Cromwell, but he reappeared here. Why should he not? Some of the Puritan stock are said to have come over and settled in New England. They were a class that did something else than celebrate their forefathers' day, and eat parched corn in remembrance of that time. They were neither Democrats nor Republicans, but men of simple habits, straightforward, prayerful; not thinking much of rulers who did not fear God, not making many compromises, nor seeking after available candidates.

"In his camp," as one has recently written, and as I have myself heard him state, "he permitted no profanity; no man of loose morals was suffered to remain there, unless, indeed, as a prisoner of war. 'I would rather,' said he, 'have the small-pox, yellow fever, and cholera, all together in my camp, than a man without principle. . . . It is a mistake, sir, that our people make, when they think that bullies are the best fighters, or that they are the fit men to oppose these Southerners. Give me men of good principles,—God-fearing men,—men who respect themselves, and with a dozen of them I will oppose any hundred such men as these Buford ruffians.'" He said that if one offered himself to be a soldier under him, who was forward to tell what he could or would do, if he could only get sight of the enemy, he had but little confidence in him.

He was never able to find more than a score or so of recruits whom he would accept, and only about a dozen, among them his sons, in whom he had perfect faith. When he was here, some years ago, he showed to a few a little manuscript book,—his "orderly book" I think he called it,—containing the names of his company in Kansas, and the rules by which they bound themselves; and he stated that several of them had already sealed the contract with their blood. When some one remarked that, with the addition of a chaplain, it would have been a perfect Cromwellian troop, he observed that he would have been glad to add a chaplain to the list, if he could have found one who could fill that office worthily. It is easy enough to find one for the United States army. I believe that he had prayers in his camp morning and evening, nevertheless.

He was a man of Spartan habits, and at sixty was scrupulous about his diet at your table, excusing himself by saying that he must eat sparingly and fare hard, as became a soldier or one who was fitting himself for difficult enterprises, a life of exposure.

A man of rare common sense and directness of speech, as of action; a transcendentalist above all, a man of ideas and principles,—that was what distinguished him. Not yielding to a whim or transient impulse, but carrying out the purpose of a life. I noticed that he did not overstate any thing, but spoke within bounds. I remember, particularly, how, in his speech here, he referred to what his family had suffered in Kansas, without ever giving the least vent to his pent-up fire. It was a volcano with an ordinary chimney-flue. Also referring to the deeds of certain Border Ruffians, he said, rapidly paring away his speech, like an experienced soldier, keeping a reserve of force and meaning, "They had a perfect right to be hung." He was not in the least a rhetorician, was not talking to Buncombe or his constituents any where, had no need to invent any thing, but to tell the simple truth, and communicate his own resolution; therefore he appeared incomparably strong, and eloquence in Congress and elsewhere seemed to me at a discount. It was like the speeches of Cromwell compared with those of an ordinary king.

As for his tact and prudence, I will merely say, that at a time when scarcely a man from the Free States was able to reach Kansas by any direct route, at least without having his arms taken from him, he, carrying what imperfect guns and other weapons he could collect, openly and slowly drove an ox-cart through Missouri, apparently in the capacity of a surveyor, with his surveying compass exposed in it, and so passed unsuspected, and had ample opportunity to learn the designs of the enemy. For some time after his arrival he still followed the same profession. When, for instance, he saw a knot of the ruffians on the prairie, discussing, of course, the single topic which then occupied their minds, he would, perhaps, take his compass and one of his sons, and proceed to run an imaginary line right through the very spot on which that conclave had assembled, and when he came up to them, he would naturally pause and have some talk with them, learning their news, and, at last, all their plans perfectly; and having thus completed his real survey, he would resume his imaginary one, and run on his line till he was out of sight.

When I expressed surprise that he could live in Kansas at all, with a price set upon his head, and so large a number, including the authorities, exasperated against him, he accounted for it by saying, "It is perfectly well understood that I will not be taken." Much of the time for some years he has had to skulk in swamps, suffering from poverty and from sickness, which was the consequence of exposure, befriended only by Indians and a few whites. But though it might be known that he was lurking in a particular swamp, his foes commonly did not care to go in after him. He could even come out into a town where there were more Border Ruffians than Free State men, and transact some business, without delaying long, and yet not be molested; for said he, "No little handful of men were willing to undertake it, and a large body could not be got together in season."

As for his recent failure, we do not know the facts about it. It was evidently far from being a wild and desperate attempt. His enemy, Mr. Vallandigham, is compelled to say, that "it was among the best planned and executed conspiracies that ever failed."

Not to mention his other successes, was it a failure, or did it show a want of good management, to deliver from bondage a dozen human beings, and walk off with them by broad daylight, for weeks if not months, at a leisurely pace, through one State after another, for half the length of the North, conspicuous to all parties, with a price set upon his head, going into a court room on his way and telling what he had done, thus convincing Missouri that it

was not profitable to try to hold slaves in his neighborhood?—and this, not because the government menials
were lenient, but because they were afraid of him.

Yet he did not attribute his success, foolishly, to "his
star," or to any magic. He said, truly, that the reason why
such greatly superior numbers quailed before him, was,
as one of his prisoners confessed, because they *lacked a
cause*—a kind of armor which he and his party never
lacked. When the time came, few men were found willing to lay down their lives in defence of what they knew
to be wrong; they did not like that this should be their
last act in this world.

But to make haste to *his* last act, and its effects.

The newspapers seem to ignore, or perhaps are really
ignorant of the fact, that there are at least as many as two
or three individuals to a town throughout the North, who
think much as the present speaker does about him and his
enterprise. I do not hesitate to say that they are an important and growing party. We aspire to be something more
than stupid and timid chattels, pretending to read history
and our bibles, but desecrating every house and every
day we breathe in. Perhaps anxious politicians may prove
that only seventeen white man and five negroes were
concerned in the late enterprise, but their very anxiety to
prove this might suggest to themselves that all is not told.
Why do they still dodge the truth? They are so anxious
because of a dim consciousness of the fact, which they do
not distinctly face, that at least a million of the free inhabitants of the United States would have rejoiced if it
had succeeded. They at most only criticise the tactics.
Though we wear no crape, the thought of that man's position and probable fate is spoiling many a man's day
here at the North for other thinking. If any one who has
seen him here can pursue successfully any other train of
thought, I do not know what he is made of. If there is any
such who gets his usual allowance of sleep, I will warrant
him to fatten easily under any circumstances which do
not touch his body or purse. I put a piece of paper and a
pencil under my pillow, and when I could not sleep, I
wrote in the dark.

On the whole, my respect for my fellow-men, except as

one may outweigh a million, is not being increased these days. I have noticed the cold-blooded way in which newspaper writers and men generally speak of this event, as if an ordinary malefactor, though one of unusual "pluck,"—as the Governor of Virginia is reported to have said, using the language of the cock-pit, "the gamest man he ever saw,"—had been caught, and were about to be hung. He was not dreaming of his foes when the governor thought he looked so brave. It turns what sweetness I have to gall, to hear, or hear of, the remarks of some of my neighbors. When we heard at first that he was dead, one of my townsmen observed that "he died as the fool dieth;" which pardon me, for an instant suggested a likeness in him dying to my neighbor living. Others, craven-hearted, said disparagingly, that "he threw his life away," because he resisted the government. Which way have they thrown *their* lives, pray?—Such as would praise a man for attacking singly an ordinary band of thieves or murderers. I hear another ask, Yankee-like, "What will he gain by it?" as if he expected to fill his pockets by this enterprise. Such a one has no idea of gain but in this worldly sense. If it does not lead to a "surprise" party, if he does not get a new pair of boots, or a vote of thanks, it must be a failure. "But he won't gain any thing by it." Well, no, I don't suppose he could get four-and-sixpence a day for being hung, take the year round; but then he stands a chance to save a considerable part of his soul—and *such* a soul!—when *you* do not. No doubt you can get more in your market for a quart of milk than for a quart of blood, but that is not the market that heroes carry their blood to.

Such do not know that like the seed is the fruit, and that, in the moral world, when good seed is planted, good fruit is inevitable, and does not depend on our watering and cultivating; that when you plant, or bury, a hero in his field, a crop of heroes is sure to spring up. This is a seed of such force and vitality, that it does not ask our leave to germinate.

The momentary charge at Balaclava, in obedience to a blundering command, proving what a perfect machine the soldier is, has, properly enough, been celebrated by a poet laureate; but the steady, and for the most part successful charge of this man, for some years, against the legions of Slavery, in obedience to an infinitely higher command, is as much more memorable than that, as an intelligent and conscientious man is superior to a machine. Do you think that that will go unsung?

"Served him right"—"A dangerous man"—"He is undoubtedly insane." So they proceed to live their sane, and wise, and altogether admirable lives, reading their Plutarch a little, but chiefly pausing at that feat of Putnam, who was let down into a wolf's den; and in this wise they nourish themselves for brave and patriotic deeds some time or other. The Tract Society could afford to print that story of Putnam. You might open the district schools with the reading of it, for there is nothing about Slavery or the Church in it; unless it occurs to the reader that some pastors are *wolves* in sheep's clothing. "The American Board of Commissioners for Foreign Missions" even, might dare to protest against *that* wolf. I have heard of boards, and of American boards, but it chances that I never heard of this particular lumber till lately. And yet I hear of Northern men, women, and children, by families, buying a "life membership" in such societies as these;—a life-membership in the grave! You can get buried cheaper than that.

Our foes are in our midst and all about us. There is hardly a house but is divided against itself, for our foe is the all but universal woodenness of both head and heart, the want of vitality in man, which is the effect of our vice; and hence are begotten fear, superstition, bigotry, persecution, and slavery of all kinds. We are mere figureheads upon a hulk, with livers in the place of hearts. The curse is the worship of idols, which at length changes the worshipper into a stone image himself; and the New Englander is just as much an idolater as the Hindoo. This man was an exception, for he did not set up even a political graven image between him and his God.

A church that can never have done with excommunicating Christ while it exists! Away with your broad and flat churches, and your narrow and tall churches! Take a step forward, and invent a new style of out-houses. Invent a salt that will save you, and defend our nostrils.

The modern Christian is a man who has consented to say all the prayers in the liturgy, provided you will let him go straight to bed and sleep quietly afterward. All his prayers begin with "Now I lay me down to sleep," and he is forever looking forward to the time when he shall go to his "*long* rest." He has consented to perform certain old established charities, too, after a fashion, but he does not wish to hear of any new-fangled ones; he doesn't wish to have any supplementary articles added to the contract, to fit it to the present time. He shows the whites of his eyes on the Sabbath, and the blacks all the rest of the week. The evil is not merely a stagnation of blood, but a stagnation of spirit. Many, no doubt, are well disposed, but sluggish by constitution and by habit, and they cannot conceive of a man who is actuated by higher motives than they are. Accordingly they pronounce this man insane, for they know that *they* could never act as he does, as long as they are themselves.

We dream of foreign countries, of other times and races of men, placing them at a distance in history or space; but let some significant event like the present occur in our midst, and we discover, often, this distance and this strangeness between us and our nearest neighbors. *They* are our Austrias, and Chinas, and South Sea Islands. Our crowded society becomes well spaced all at once, clean and handsome to the eye, a city of magnificent distances. We discover why it was that we never got beyond compliments and surfaces with them before; we become aware of as many versts between us and them as there are between a wandering Tartar and a Chinese town. The thoughtful man becomes a hermit in the thoroughfares of the market-place. Impassable seas suddenly find their level between us, or dumb steppes stretch themselves out there. It is the difference of constitution, of intelligence, and faith, and not streams and mountains, that make the true and impassable boundaries between individuals and between states. None but the like-minded can come plenipotentiary to our court.

I read all the newspapers I could get within a week after this event, and I do not remember in them a single

expression of sympathy for these men. I have since seen
one noble statement, in a Boston paper, not editorial.
Some voluminous sheets decided not to print the full report of Brown's words to the exclusion of other matter. It
was as if a publisher should reject the manuscript of the
New Testament, and print Wilson's last speech. The same
journal which contained this pregnant news, was chiefly
filled, in parallel columns, with the reports of the political
conventions that were being held. But the descent to
them was too steep. They should have been spared this
contrast, been printed in an extra at least. To turn from
the voices and deeds of earnest men to the *cackling* of
political conventions! Office seekers and speech-makers,
who do not so much as lay an honest egg, but wear their
breasts bare upon an egg of chalk! Their great game is
the game of straws, or rather that universal aboriginal
game of the platter, at which the Indians cried *hub, bub!*
Exclude the reports of religious and political conventions,
and publish the words of a living man.

But I object not so much to what they have omitted as
to what they have inserted. Even the *Liberator* called it
"a misguided, wild, and apparently insane . . . effort." As
for the herd of newspapers and magazines, I do not
chance to know an editor in the country who will deliberately print anything which he knows will ultimately and
permanently reduce the number of his subscribers. They
do not believe that it would be expedient. How then can
they print truth? If we do not say pleasant things, they
argue, nobody will attend to us. And so they do like some
travelling auctioneers, who sing an obscene song in order
to draw a crowd around them. Republican editors,
obliged to get their sentences ready for the morning edition, and accustomed to look at every thing by the twilight of politics, express no admiration, nor true sorrow
even, but call these men "deluded fanatics"—"mistaken
men"—"insane," or "crazed." It suggests what a *sane* set
of editors we are blessed with, *not* "mistaken men"; who
know very well on which side their bread is buttered, at
least.

A man does a brave and humane deed, and at once, on
all sides, we hear people and parties declaring, "I didn't

do it, nor countenance *him* to do it, in any conceivable way. It can't be fairly inferred from my past career." I, for one, am not interested to hear you define your position. I don't know that I ever was, or ever shall be. I think it is mere egotism, or impertinent at this time. Ye needn't take so much pains to wash your skirts of him. No intelligent man will ever be convinced that he was any creature of yours. He went and came, as he himself informs us, "under the auspices of John Brown and nobody else." The Republican party does not perceive how many his *failure* will make to vote more correctly than they would have them. They have counted the votes of Pennsylvania & Co., but they have not correctly counted Captain Brown's vote. He has taken the wind out of their sails, the little wind they had, and they may as well lie to and repair.

What though he did not belong to your clique! Though you may not approve of his method or his principles, recognize his magnanimity. Would you not like to claim kindredship with him in that, though in no other thing he is like, or likely, to you? Do you think that you would lose your reputation so? What you lost at the spile, you would gain at the bung.

If they do not mean all this, then they do not speak the truth, and say what they mean. They are simply at their old tricks still.

"It was always conceded to him," *says one who calls him crazy,* "that he was a conscientious man, very modest in his demeanor, apparently inoffensive, until the subject of Slavery was introduced, when he would exhibit a feeling of indignation unparalleled."

The slave-ship is on her way, crowded with its dying victims; new cargoes are being added in mid ocean; a small crew of slaveholders, countenanced by a large body of passengers, is smothering four millions under the hatches, and yet the politician asserts that the only proper way by which deliverance is to be obtained, is by "the quiet diffusion of the sentiments of humanity," without any "outbreak." As if the sentiments of humanity were ever found unaccompanied by its deeds, and you could disperse them, all finished to order, the pure article, as easily as water with a watering-pot, and so lay the dust. What is that that I hear cast overboard? The bodies of the dead that have found deliverance. That is the way we are "diffusing" humanity, and its sentiments with it.

Prominent and influential editors, accustomed to deal with politicians, men of an infinitely lower grade, say, in their ignorance, that he acted "on the principle of revenge." They do not know the man. They must enlarge themselves to conceive of him. I have no doubt that the time will come when they will begin to see him as he was. They have got to conceive of a man of faith and of religious principle, and not a politician or an Indian; of a man who did not wait till he was personally interfered with, or thwarted in some harmless business, before he gave his life to the cause of the oppressed.

If Walker may be considered the representative of the South, I wish I could say that Brown was the representative of the North. He was a superior man. He did not value his bodily life in comparison with ideal things. He did not recognize unjust human laws, but resisted them as he was bid. For once we are lifted out of the trivialness and dust of politics into the region of truth and manhood. No man in America has ever stood up so persistently and effectively for the dignity of human nature, knowing himself for a man, and the equal of any and all governments. In that sense he was the most American of us all. He needed no babbling lawyer, making false issues, to defend him. He was more than a match for all the judges that American voters, or office-holders of whatever grade, can create. He could not have been tried by a jury of his peers, because his peers did not exist. When a man stands up serenely against the condemnation and vengeance of mankind, rising above them literally *by a whole body*,—even though he were of late the vilest murderer, who has settled that matter with himself,—the spectacle is a sublime one,—didn't ye know it, ye Liberators, ye Tribunes, ye Republicans?—and we become criminal in comparison. Do yourselves the honor to recognize him. He needs none of your respect.

As for the Democratic journals, they are not human enough to affect me at all. I do not feel indignation at any thing they may say.

I am aware that I anticipate a little, that he was still, at the last accounts, alive in the hands of his foes; but that being the case, I have all along found myself thinking and speaking of him as physically dead.

I do not believe in erecting statues to those who still live in our hearts, whose bones have not yet crumbled in the earth around us, but I would rather see the statue of Captain Brown in the Massachusetts State-House yard, than that of any other man whom I know. I rejoice that I live in this age—that I am his contemporary.

What a contrast, when we turn to that political party which is so anxiously shuffling him and his plot out of its way, and looking around for some available slaveholder, perhaps, to be its candidate, at least for one who will execute the Fugitive Slave Law, and all those other unjust laws which he took up arms to annul!

Insane! A father and six sons, and one son-in-law, and several more men besides;—as many at least as twelve disciples,—all struck with insanity at once; while the sane tyrant holds with a firmer gripe than ever his four millions of slaves, and a thousand sane editors, his abettors, are saving their country and their bacon! Just as insane were his efforts in Kansas. Ask the tyrant who is his most dangerous foe, the sane man or the insane. Do the thousands who know him best, who have rejoiced at his deeds in Kansas, and have afforded him material aid there, think him insane? Such a use of this word is a mere trope with most who persist in using it, and I have no doubt that many of the rest have already in silence retracted their words.

Read his admirable answers to Mason and others. How they are dwarfed and defeated by the contrast! On the one side, half brutish, half timid questioning; on the other, truth, clear as lightning, crashing into their obscene temples. They are made to stand with Pilate, and Gessler, and the Inquisition. How ineffectual their speech and action! and what a void their silence! They are but helpless tools in this great work. It was no human power that gathered them about this preacher.

What have Massachusetts and the North sent a few *sane* representatives to Congress for, of late years?—to declare with effect what kind of sentiments? All their speeches put together and boiled down,—and probably they themselves will confess it,—do not match for manly directness and force, and for simple truth, the few casual remarks of crazy John Brown, on the floor of the Harper's Ferry engine house;—that man whom you are about to hang, to send to the other world, though not to represent *you* there. No, he was not our representative in any sense. He was too fair a specimen of a man to represent the like of us. Who, then, *were* his constituents? If you read his words understandingly you will find out. In his case there is no idle eloquence, no made, nor maiden speech, no compliments to the oppressor. Truth is his inspirer, and earnestness the polisher of his sentences. He could afford to lose his Sharps' rifles, while he retained his faculty of speech, a Sharps' rifle of infinitely surer and longer range.

And the *New York Herald* reports the conversation *"verbatim"!* It does not know of what undying words it is made the vehicle.

I have no respect for the penetration of any man who can read the report of that conversation, and still call the principal in it insane. It has the ring of a saner sanity than an ordinary discipline and habits of life, than an ordinary organization, secure. Take any sentence of it—"Any questions that I can honorably answer, I will; not otherwise. So far as I am myself concerned, I have told every thing truthfully. I value my word, sir." The few who talk about his vindictive spirit, while they really admire his heroism, have no test by which to detect a noble man, no amalgam to combine with his pure gold. They mix their own dross with it.

It is a relief to turn from these slanders to the testimony of his more truthful, but frightened, jailers and hangmen. Governor Wise speaks far more justly and appreciatingly of him than any Northern editor, or politician, or public personage, that I chance to have heard from. I know that you can afford to hear him again on this subject. He says: "They are themselves mistaken who take him to be a madman. . . . He is cool, collected, and indomitable, and it is but just to him to say, that he was humane to his prisoners. . . . And he inspired me with great trust in his integrity as a man of truth. He is a fanatic, vain and garrulous," (I leave that part to Mr. Wise) "but firm, truthful, and intelligent. His men, too, who survive, are like him. . . . Colonel Washington says that he was the coolest and firmest man he ever saw in defying danger and death. With one son dead by his side, and another shot through, he felt the pulse of his dying son with one hand, and held his rifle with the other, and commanded his men with the utmost composure, encouraging them to be firm, and to sell their lives as dear as they could. Of the three white prisoners, Brown, Stevens, and Coppoc, it was hard to say which was most firm. . . ."

Almost the first Northern men whom the slaveholder has learned to respect!

The testimony of Mr. Vallandigham, though less valuable, is of the same purport, that "it is vain to underrate either the man or his conspiracy . . . He is the farthest possible remove from the ordinary ruffian, fanatic, or madman."

"All is quiet at Harper's Ferry," says the journals. What is the character of that calm which follows when the law and the slaveholder prevail? I regard this event as a touchstone designed to bring out, with glaring distinctness, the character of this government. We needed to be thus assisted to see it by the light of history. It needed to see itself. When a government puts forth its strength on the side of injustice, as ours to maintain Slavery and kill the liberators of the slave, it reveals itself a merely brute force, or worse, a demoniacal force. It is the head of the Plug Uglies. It is more manifest than ever that tyranny rules. I see this government to be effectually allied with France and Austria in oppressing mankind. There sits a tyrant holding fettered four millions of slaves; here comes their heroic liberator. This most hypocritical and diabolical government looks up from its seat on the gasping four millions, and inquires with an assumption of innocence, "What do you assault me for? Am I not an honest man? Cease agitation on this subject, or I will make a slave of you, too, or else hang you."

We talk about a *representative* government; but what a monster of a government is that where the noblest fac-

ulties of the mind, and the *whole* heart, are not *represented*. A semi-human tiger or ox, stalking over the earth,
with its heart taken out and the top of its brain shot
away. Heroes have fought well on their stumps when
their legs were shot off, but I never heard of any good
done by such a government as that.

The only government that I recognize,—and it matters
not how few are at the head of it, or how small its
army,—is that power that establishes justice in the land,
never that which establishes injustice. What shall we
think of a government to which all the truly brave and
just men in the land are enemies, standing between it and
those whom it oppresses? A government that pretends to
be Christian and crucifies a million Christs every day!

Treason! Where does such treason take its rise? I cannot help thinking of you as you deserve, ye governments.
Can you dry up the fountains of thought? High treason,
when it is resistance to tyranny here below, has its origin
in, and is first committed by the power that makes and
forever recreates man. When you have caught and hung
all these human rebels, you have accomplished nothing
but your own guilt, for you have not struck at the fountain head. You presume to contend with a foe against
whom West Point cadets and rifled cannon *point* not.
Can all the art of the cannon-founder tempt matter to
turn against its maker? Is the form in which the founder
thinks he casts it more essential than the constitution of it
and of himself?

The United States have a coffle of four millions of
slaves. They are determined to keep them in this condition; and Massachusetts is one of the confederated overseers to prevent their escape. Such are not all the inhabitants of Massachusetts, but such are they who rule and are
obeyed here. It was Massachusetts, as well as Virginia,
that put down this insurrection at Harper's Ferry. She
sent the marines there, and she will have to pay the penalty of her sin.

Suppose that there is a society in this State that out of
its own purse and magnanimity saves all the fugitive
slaves that run to us, and protects our colored fellow-citizens, and leaves the other work to the Government, so-

called. Is not that government fast losing its occupation, and becoming contemptible to mankind? If private men are obliged to perform the offices of government, to protect the weak and dispense justice, then the government becomes only a hired man, or clerk, to perform menial or indifferent services. Of course, that is but the shadow of a government whose existence necessitates a Vigilant Committee. What should we think of the oriental Cadi even, behind whom worked in secret a Vigilant Committee? But such is the character of our Northern States generally; each has its Vigilant Committee. And, to a certain extent, these crazy governments recognize and accept this relation. They say, virtually, "We'll be glad to work for you on these terms, only don't make a noise about it." And thus the government, its salary being insured, withdraws into the back shop, taking the constitution with it, and bestows most of its labor on repairing that. When I hear it at work sometimes, as I go by, it reminds me, at best, of those farmers who in winter contrive to turn a penny by following the coopering business. And what kind of spirit is their barrel made to hold? They speculate in stocks, and bore holes in mountains, but they are not competent to lay out even a decent highway. The only *free* road, the Underground Railroad, is owned and managed by the Vigilant Committee. *They* have tunnelled under the whole breadth of the land. Such a government is losing its power and respectability as surely as water runs out of a leaky vessel, and is held by one that can contain it.

I hear many condemn these men because they were so few. When were the good and the brave ever in a majority? Would you have had him wait till that time came?— till you and I came over to him? The very fact that he had no rabble or troop of hirelings about him would alone distinguish him from ordinary heroes. His company was small indeed, because few could be found worthy to pass muster. Each one who there laid down his life for the poor and oppressed, was a picked man, called out of many thousands, if not millions; apparently a man of principle, of rare courage and devoted humanity, ready to sacrifice his life at any moment for the benefit of his fellow man. It may be doubted if there were as many more their equals in these respects in all the country—I speak of his followers only—for their leader, no doubt, scoured the land far and wide, seeking to swell his troop. These alone were ready to step between the oppressor and the oppressed. Surely, they were the very best men you could select to be hung. That was the greatest compliment which this country could pay them. They were ripe for her gallows. She has tried a long time, she has hung a good many, but never found the right one before.

When I think of him, and his six sons, and his son in law,—not to enumerate the others,—enlisted for this fight; proceeding coolly, reverently, humanely to work, for months if not years, sleeping and waking upon it, summering and wintering the thought, without expecting any reward but a good conscience, while almost all America stood ranked on the other side, I say again that it affects me as a sublime spectacle. If he had had any journal advocating *"his cause,"* any organ as the phrase is, monotonously and wearisomely playing the same old tune, and then passing round the hat, it would have been fatal to his efficiency. If he had acted in any way so as to be let alone by the government, he might have been suspected. It was the fact that the tyrant must give place to him, or he to the tyrant, that distinguished him from all the reformers of the day that I know.

It was his peculiar doctrine that a man has a perfect right to interfere by force with the slaveholder, in order to rescue the slave. I agree with him. They who are continually shocked by slavery have some right to be shocked by the violent death of the slaveholder, but no others. Such will be more shocked by his life than by his death. I shall not be forward to think him mistaken in his method who quickest succeeds to liberate the slave. I speak for the slave when I say, that I prefer the philanthropy of Captain Brown to that philanthropy which neither shoots me nor liberates me. At any rate, I do not think it is quite sane for one to spend his whole life in talking or writing about this matter, unless he is continuously inspired, and I have not done so. A man may have other affairs to attend to. I do not wish to kill nor to be killed, but I can foresee circumstances in which both these things would be by me unavoidable. We preserve the so-called "peace" of our community by deeds of petty violence every day. Look at the policeman's billy and hand cuffs! Look at the jail! Look at the gallows! Look at the chaplain of the regiment! We are hoping only to live safely on the outskirts of *this* provisional army. So we defend ourselves and our hen roosts, and maintain slavery. I know that the mass of my countrymen think that the only righteous use that can be made of Sharps' rifles and revolvers is to fight duels with them, when we are insulted by other nations, or to hunt Indians, or shoot fugitive slaves with them, or the like. I think that for once the Sharps' rifles and the revolvers were employed in a righteous cause. The tools were in the hands of one who could use them.

The same indignation that is said to have cleared the temple once will clear it again. The question is not about the weapon, but the spirit in which you use it. No man has appeared in America as yet who loved his fellow man so well, and treated him so tenderly. He lived for him. He took up his life and he laid it down for him. What sort of violence is that which is encouraged, not by soldiers but by peaceable citizens, not so much by lay-men as by ministers of the gospel, not so much by the fighting sects as by the Quakers, and not so much by Quaker men as by Quaker women?

This event advertises me that there is such a fact as death—the possibility of a man's dying. It seems as if no man had ever died in America before, for in order to die you must first have lived. I dont believe in the hearses and palls and funerals that they have had. There was no death in the case, because there had been no life; they merely rotted or sloughed off, pretty much as they had rotted or sloughed along. No temple's vail was rent, only a hole dug somewhere. Let the dead bury their dead. The best of them fairly ran down like a clock. Franklin—Washington—they were let off without dying; they were merely missing one day. I hear a good many pretend that they are going to die;—or that they have died for aught that I know. Nonsense! I'll defy them to do it. They haven't got life enough in them. They'll deliquesce like fungi, and keep a hundred eulogists mopping the spot where they left off. Only half a dozen or so have died since the world began. Do you think that you are going to die, sir? No! there's no hope of you. You haven't got your lesson yet. You've got to stay after school. We make a needless ado about capital punishment—taking lives, when there is no life to take. *Memento mori!* We don't understand that sublime sentence which some worthy got sculptured on his gravestone once. We've interpreted it in a grovelling and snivelling sense; we've wholly forgotten how to die.

But be sure you do die, nevertheless. Do your work, and finish it. If you know how to begin, you will know when to end.

These men, in teaching us how to die, have at the same time taught us how to live. If this man's acts and words do not create a revival, it will be the severest possible satire on the acts and words that do. It is the best news that America has ever heard. It has already quickened the feeble pulse of the North, and infused more and more generous blood into her veins and heart, than any number of years of what is called commercial and political prosperity could. How many a man who was lately contemplating suicide has now something to live for!

One writer says that Brown's peculiar monomania made him to be "dreaded by the Missourians as a supernatural being." Sure enough, a hero in the midst of us cowards is always so dreaded. He is just that thing. He shows himself superior to nature. He has a spark of divinity in him.

> "Unless about himself he can
> Erect himself, how poor a thing is man!"

Newspaper editors argue also that it is proof of his *insanity* that he thought he was appointed to do this work which he did—that he did not suspect himself for a moment! They talk as if it were impossible that a man could be "divinely appointed" in these days to do any work whatever; as if vows and religion were out of date as connected with any man's daily work,—as if the agent to abolish Slavery could only be somebody appointed by the

President, or by some political party. They talk as if a man's death were a failure, and his continued life, be it of whatever character, were a success.

When I reflect to what a cause this man devoted himself, and how religiously, and then reflect to what cause his judges and all who condemn him so angrily and fluently devote themselves, I see that they are as far apart as the heavens and earth are asunder.

The amount of it is, our *"leading men"* are a harmless kind of folk, and they know *well enough* that *they* were not divinely appointed, but elected by the votes of their party.

Who is it whose safety requires that Captain Brown be hung? Is it indispensable to any Northern man? Is there no resource but to cast these men also to the Minotaur? If you do not wish it say so distinctly. While these things are being done, beauty stands veiled and music is a screeching lie. Think of him—of his rare qualities! such a man as it takes ages to make, and ages to understand; no mock hero, nor the representative of any party. A man such as the sun may not rise upon again in this benighted land. To whose making went the costliest material, the finest adamant; sent to be the redeemer of those in captivity. And the only use to which you can put him is to hang him at the end of a rope! You who pretend to care for Christ crucified, consider what you are about to do to him who offered himself to be the savior of four millions of men.

Any man knows when he is justified, and all the wits in the world cannot enlighten him on that point. The murderer always knows that he is justly punished; but when a government takes the life of a man without the consent of his conscience, it is an audacious government, and is taking a step towards its own dissolution. Is it not possible that an individual may be right and a government wrong? Are laws to be enforced simply because they were made? or declared by any number of men to be good, if they are *not* good? Is there any necessity for a man's being a tool to perform a deed of which his better nature disapproves? Is it the intention of law-makers that *good* men shall be hung ever? Are judges to interpret the law according to the letter, and not the spirit? What right have *you* to enter into a compact with yourself that you *will* do thus or so, against the light within you? Is it for *you* to *make up* your mind—to form any resolution whatever—and not accept the convictions that are forced upon you, and which ever pass your understanding? I do not believe in lawyers, in that mode of attacking or defending a man, because you descend to meet the judge on his own ground, and, in cases of the highest importance, it is of no consequence whether a man breaks a human law or not. Let lawyers decide trivial cases. Business men may arrange that among themselves. If they were the interpreters of the everlasting laws which rightfully bind man, that would be another thing. A counterfeiting law-factory, standing half in a slave land and half in a free! What kind of laws for free men can you expect from that?

I am here to plead his cause with you. I plead not for his life, but for his character—his immortal life; and so it becomes your cause wholly, and is not his in the least. Some eighteen hundred years ago Christ was crucified; this morning, perchance, Captain Brown was hung. These are the two ends of a chain which is not without its links. He is not Old Brown any longer; he is an Angel of Light.

I see now that it was necessary that the bravest and humanest man in all the country should be hung. Perhaps he saw it himself. I *almost fear* that I may yet hear of his deliverance, doubting if a prolonged life, if *any* life, can do as much good as his death.

"Misguided"! "Garrulous"! "Insane"! "Vindictive"! So ye write in your easy chairs, and thus he wounded responds from the floor of the Armory, clear as a cloudless sky, true as the voice of nature is: "No man sent me here; it was my own prompting and that of my Maker. I acknowledge no master in human form."

And in what a sweet and noble strain he proceeds, addressing his captors, who stand over him: "I think, my friends, you are guilty of a great wrong against God and humanity, and it would be perfectly right for any one to interfere with you so far as to free those you wilfully and wickedly hold in bondage."

And referring to his movement: "It is, in my opinion, the greatest service a man can render to God."

"I pity the poor in bondage that have none to help them; that is why I am here; not to gratify any personal animosity, revenge, or vindictive spirit. It is my sympathy with the oppressed and the wronged, that are as good as you, and as precious in the sight of God."

You don't know your testament when you see it.

"I want you to understand that I respect the rights of the poorest and weakest of colored people, oppressed by the slave power, just as much as I do those of the most wealthy and powerful."

"I wish to say, furthermore, that you had better, all you people at the South, prepare yourselves for a settlement of that question, that must come up for settlement sooner than you are prepared for it. The sooner you are prepared the better. You may dispose of me very easily. I am nearly disposed of now; but this question is still to be settled—this negro question, I mean; the end of that is not yet."

I foresee the time when the painter will paint that scene, no longer going to Rome for a subject; the poet will sing it; the historian record it; and, with the Landing of the Pilgrims and the Declaration of Independence, it will be the ornament of some future national gallery, when at least the present form of Slavery shall be no more here. We shall then be at liberty to weep for Captain Brown. Then, and not till then, we will take our revenge.

WALKING

First published by James T. Fields in The Atlantic
Monthly *a month after Thoreau's death in May of 1862,
"Walking" was a fusion of two lectures entitled "Walking" and "The Wild" that Thoreau delivered repeatedly
in the decade of the 1850s. The integration of the two
parts is accomplished with consummate skill. Thoreau's
walks become metaphorical crusades to the "Holy
Land," into the mythical West, through the "wild,"
since "in wildness is the preservation of the world." A
prophetic environmental statement, the essay abounds
as well in memorable, evocative phrases. "I believe in
the forest," Thoreau assures his readers, "and in the
meadow, and in the night in which the corn grows."
The text reproduced here is from* The Atlantic Monthly
for June 1862.

I WISH TO SPEAK A WORD for Nature, for absolute freedom and wildness, as contrasted with a freedom and culture merely civil,—to regard man as an inhabitant, or a
part and parcel of Nature, rather than a member of society. I wish to make an extreme statement, if so I may
make an emphatic one, for there are enough champions
of civilization: the minister, and the school-committee,
and every one of you will take care of that.

I have met with but one or two persons in the course of

my life who understood the art of Walking, that is, of
taking walks,—who had a genius, so to speak, for *sauntering:* which word is beautifully derived "from idle people
who roved about the country, in the Middle Ages, and
asked charity, under pretence of going *à la Sainte Terre,*"
to the Holy Land, till the children exclaimed, "There
goes a *Sainte-Terrer,*" a Saunterer,—a Holy-Lander.
They who never go to the Holy Land in their walks, as
they pretend, are indeed mere idlers and vagabonds; but
they who do go there are saunterers in the good sense,
such as I mean. Some, however, would derive the word
from *sans terre,* without land or a home, which, therefore, in the good sense, will mean, having no particular
home, but equally at home everywhere. For this is the
secret of successful sauntering. He who sits still in a
house all the time may be the greatest vagrant of all; but
the saunterer, in the good sense, is no more vagrant than
the meandering river, which is all the while sedulously
seeking the shortest course to the sea. But I prefer the
first, which, indeed, is the most probable derivation. For
every walk is a sort of crusade, preached by some Peter
the Hermit in us, to go forth and reconquer this Holy
Land from the hands of the Infidels.

It is true, we are but faint-hearted crusaders, even the
walkers, nowadays, who undertake no persevering, never-
ending enterprises. Our expeditions are but tours, and
come round again at evening to the old hearth-side from
which we set out. Half the walk is but retracing our steps.
We should go forth on the shortest walk, perchance, in
the spirit of undying adventure, never to return,—prepared to send back our embalmed hearts only as relics to
our desolate kingdoms. If you are ready to leave father
and mother, and brother and sister, and wife and child
and friends, and never see them again,—if you have paid
your debts, and made your will, and settled all your affairs, and are a free man, then you are ready for a walk.

To come down to my own experience, my companion
and I, for I sometimes have a companion, take pleasure in
fancying ourselves knights of a new, or rather an old, order,—not Equestrians or Chevaliers, not Ritters or Riders,
but Walkers, a still more ancient and honorable class, I

trust. The chivalric and heroic spirit which once belonged
to the Rider seems now to reside in, or perchance to have
subsided into, the Walker,—not the Knight, but Walker
Errant. He is a sort of fourth estate, outside of Church
and State and People.

We have felt that we almost alone hereabouts practised
this noble art; though, to tell the truth, at least, if their
own assertions are to be received, most of my townsmen
would fain walk sometimes, as I do, but they cannot. No
wealth can buy the requisite leisure, freedom, and independence, which are the capital in this profession. It
comes only by the grace of God. It requires a direct dis-
pensation from Heaven to become a walker. You must be
born into the family of the Walkers. *Ambulator nascitur,
non fit.* Some of my townsmen, it is true, can remember
and have described to me some walks which they took
ten years ago, in which they were so blessed as to lose
themselves for half an hour in the woods; but I know very
well that they have confined themselves to the highway
ever since, whatever pretensions they may make to belong to this select class. No doubt they were elevated for
a moment as by the reminiscence of a previous state of
existence, when even they were foresters and outlaws.

> "When he came to grene wode,
>   In a mery mornynge,
> There he herde the notes small
>   Of byrdes mery syngynge.
>
> "It is ferre gone, sayd Robyn,
>   That I was last here;
> Me lyste a lytell for to shote
>   At the donne dere."

I think that I cannot preserve my health and spirits,
unless I spend four hours a day at least—and it is commonly more than that—sauntering through the woods
and over the hills and fields, absolutely free from all
worldly engagements. You may safely say, A penny for
your thoughts, or a thousand pounds. When sometimes I
am reminded that the mechanics and shopkeepers stay in
their shops not only all the forenoon, but all the afternoon
too, sitting with crossed legs, so many of them,—as if the
legs were made to sit upon, and not to stand or walk

upon,—I think that they deserve some credit for not having all committed suicide long ago.

I, who cannot stay in my chamber for a single day without acquiring some rust, and when sometimes I have stolen forth for a walk at the eleventh hour of four o'clock in the afternoon, too late to redeem the day, when the shades of night were already beginning to be mingled with the daylight, have felt as if I had committed some sin to be atoned for,—I confess that I am astonished at the power of endurance, to say nothing of the moral insensibility, of my neighbors who confine themselves to shops and offices the whole day for weeks and months, ay, and years almost together. I know not what manner of stuff they are of,—sitting there now at three o'clock in the afternoon, as if it were three o'clock in the morning. Bonaparte may talk of the three-o'clock-in-the-morning courage, but it is nothing to the courage which can sit down cheerfully at this hour in the afternoon over against one's self whom you have known all the morning, to starve out a garrison to whom you are bound by such strong ties of sympathy. I wonder that about this time, or say between four and five o'clock in the afternoon, too late for the morning papers and too early for the evening ones, there is not a general explosion heard up and down the street, scattering a legion of antiquated and housebred notions and whims to the four winds for an airing,—and so the evil cure itself.

How womankind, who are confined to the house still more than men, stand it I do not know; but I have ground to suspect that most of them do not *stand* it at all. When, early in a summer afternoon, we have been shaking the dust of the village from the skirts of our garments, making haste past those houses with purely Doric or Gothic fronts, which have such an air of repose about them, my companion whispers that probably about these times their occupants are all gone to bed. Then it is that I appreciate the beauty and the glory of architecture, which itself never turns in, but forever stands out and erect, keeping watch over the slumberers.

No doubt temperament, and, above all, age, have a good deal to do with it. As a man grows older, his ability to sit still and follow in-door occupations increases. He grows vespertinal in his habits as the evening of life approaches, till at last he comes forth only just before sundown, and gets all the walk that he requires in half an hour.

But the walking of which I speak has nothing in it akin to taking exercise, as it is called, as the sick take medicine at stated hours,—as the swinging of dumbbells or chairs; but is itself the enterprise and adventure of the day. If you would get exercise, go in search of the springs of life. Think of a man's swinging dumbbells for his health, when those springs are bubbling up in far-off pastures unsought by him!

Moreover, you must walk like a camel, which is said to be the only beast which ruminates when walking. When a traveller asked Wordsworth's servant to show him her master's study, she answered, "Here is his library, but his study is out of doors."

Living much out of doors, in the sun and wind, will no doubt produce a certain roughness of character,—will cause a thicker cuticle to grow over some of the finer qualities of our nature, as on the face and hands, or as severe manual labor robs the hands of some of their delicacy of touch. So staying in the house, on the other hand, may produce a softness and smoothness, not to say thinness of skin, accompanied by an increased sensibility to certain impressions. Perhaps we should be more susceptible to some influences important to our intellectual and moral growth, if the sun had shone and the wind blown on us a little less; and no doubt it is a nice matter to proportion rightly the thick and thin skin. But methinks that is a scurf that will fall off fast enough,—that the natural remedy is to be found in the proportion which the night bears to the day, the winter to the summer, thought to experience. There will be so much the more air and sunshine in our thoughts. The callous palms of the laborer are conversant with finer tissues of self-respect and heroism, whose touch thrills the heart, than the languid fingers of idleness. That is mere sentimentality that lies abed by day and thinks itself white, far from the tan and callus of experience.

unconscious
prophetic
usage

When we walk, we naturally go to the fields and woods: what would become of us, if we walked only in a garden or a mall? Even some sects of philosophers have felt the necessity of importing the woods to themselves, since they did not go to the woods. "They planted groves and walks of Platanes," where they took *subdiales ambulationes* in porticos open to the air. Of course it is of no use to direct our steps to the woods, if they do not carry us thither. I am alarmed when it happens that I have walked a mile into the woods bodily, without getting there in spirit. In my afternoon walk I would fain forget all my morning occupations and my obligations to society. But it sometimes happens that I cannot easily shake off the village. The thought of some work will run in my head, and I am not where my body is,—I am out of my senses. In my walks I would fain return to my senses. What business have I in the woods, if I am thinking of something out of the woods? I suspect myself, and cannot help a shudder, when I find myself so implicated even in what are called good works,—for this may sometimes happen.

My vicinity affords many good walks; and though for so many years I have walked almost every day, and sometimes for several days together, I have not yet exhausted them. An absolutely new prospect is a great happiness, and I can still get this any afternoon. Two or three hours' walking will carry me to as strange a country as I expect ever to see. A single farm-house which I had not seen before is sometimes as good as the dominions of the King of Dahomey. There is in fact a sort of harmony discoverable between the capabilities of the landscape within a circle of ten miles' radius, or the limits of an afternoon walk, and the threescore years and ten of human life. It will never become quite familiar to you.

Nowadays almost all man's improvements, so called, as the building of houses, and the cutting down of the forest and of all large trees, simply deform the landscape, and make it more and more tame and cheap. A people who would begin by burning the fences and let the forest stand! I saw the fences half consumed, their ends lost in the middle of the prairie, and some worldly miser with a

surveyor looking after his bounds, while heaven had tak-
en place around him, and he did not see the angels going
to and fro, but was looking for an old post-hole in the
midst of paradise. I looked again, and saw him standing in
the middle of a boggy, stygian fen, surrounded by devils,
and he had found his bounds without a doubt, three little
stones, where a stake had been driven, and looking nearer,
I saw that the Prince of Darkness was his surveyor.

I can easily walk ten, fifteen, twenty, any number of
miles, commencing at my own door, without going by
any house, without crossing a road except where the fox
and the mink do: first along by the river, and then the
brook, and then the meadow and the wood-side. There
are square miles in my vicinity which have no inhabitant.
From many a hill I can see civilization and the abodes of
man afar. The farmers and their works are scarcely more
obvious than woodchucks and their burrows. Man and his
affairs, church and state and school, trade and commerce,
and manufactures and agriculture, even politics, the most
alarming of them all,—I am pleased to see how little
space they occupy in the landscape. Politics is but a narrow field, and that still narrower highway yonder leads to
it. I sometimes direct the traveller thither. If you would
go to the political world, follow the great road,—follow
that market-man, keep his dust in your eyes, and it will
lead you straight to it; for it, too, has its place merely,
and does not occupy all space. I pass from it as from a
beanfield into the forest, and it is forgotten. In one half-
hour I can walk off to some portion of the earth's surface
where a man does not stand from one year's end to another, and there, consequently, politics are not, for they
are but as the cigar-smoke of a man.

The village is the place to which the roads tend, a sort
of expansion of the highway, as a lake of a river. It is the
body of which roads are the arms and legs,—a trivial or
quadrivial place, the thoroughfare and ordinary of travellers. The word is from the Latin villa, which, together
with via, a way, or more anciently ved and vella, Varro
derives from veho, to carry, because the villa is the place
to and from which things are carried. They who got their
living by teaming were said vellaturam facere. Hence,

too, apparently, the Latin word *vilis* and our *vile*, also *villain*. This suggests what kind of degeneracy villagers are liable to. They are wayworn by the travel that goes by and over them, without travelling themselves.

Some do not walk at all; others walk in the highways; a few walk across lots. Roads are made for horses and men of business. I do not travel in them much, comparatively, because I am not in a hurry to get to any tavern or grocery or livery-stable or depot to which they lead. I am a good horse to travel, but not from choice a roadster. The landscape-painter uses the figures of men to mark a road. He would not make that use of my figure. I walk out into a Nature such as the old prophets and poets, Menu, Moses, Homer, Chaucer, walked in. You may name it America, but it is not America: neither Americus Vespucius, nor Columbus, nor the rest were the discoverers of it. There is a truer account of it in mythology than in any history of America, so called, that I have seen.

However, there are a few old roads that may be trodden with profit, as if they led somewhere now that they are nearly discontinued. There is the Old Marlborough Road, which does not go to Marlborough now, methinks, unless that is Marlborough where it carries me. I am the bolder to speak of it here, because I presume that there are one or two such roads in every town.

THE OLD MARLBOROUGH ROAD.

Where they once dug for money,
But never found any;
Where sometimes Martial Miles
Singly files,
And Elijah Wood,
I fear for no good:
No other man,
Save Elisha Dugan,—
O man of wild habits,
Partridges and rabbits,
Who hast no cares
Only to set snares,
Who liv'st all alone,
Close to the bone,
And where life is sweetest

Constantly eatest.
When the spring stirs my blood
  With the instinct to travel,
  I can get enough gravel
On the Old Marlborough Road.
  Nobody repairs it,
  For nobody wears it;
  It is a living way,
  As the Christians say.
Not many there be
  Who enter therein,
Only the guests of the
  Irishman Quin.
What is it, what is it,
  But a direction out there,
And the bare possibility
  Of going somewhere?
  Great guide-boards of stone,
  But travellers none;
  Cenotaphs of the towns
  Named on their crowns.
  It is worth going to see
  Where you *might* be.
  What king
  Did the thing,
  I am still wondering;
  Set up how or when,
  By what selectmen,
  Gourgas or Lee,
  Clark or Darby?
  They're a great endeavor
  To be something forever;
  Blank tablets of stone,
  Where a traveller might groan,
  And in one sentence
  Grave all that is known;
  Which another might read,
  In his extreme need.
  I know one or two
  Lines that would do,
  Literature that might stand
  All over the land,
  Which a man could remember
  Till next December,
  And read again in the spring,

After the thawing.
If with fancy unfurled
You leave your abode,
You may go round the world
By the Old Marlborough Road.

At present, in this vicinity, the best part of the land is not private property; the landscape is not owned, and the walker enjoys comparative freedom. But possibly the day will come when it will be partitioned off into so-called pleasure-grounds, in which a few will take a narrow and exclusive pleasure only,—when fences shall be multiplied, and man-traps and other engines invented to confine men to the *public* road, and walking over the surface of God's earth shall be construed to mean trespassing on some gentleman's grounds. To enjoy a thing exclusively is commonly to exclude yourself from the true enjoyment of it. Let us improve our opportunities, then, before the evil days come.

What is it that makes it so hard sometimes to determine whither we will walk? I believe that there is a subtle magnetism in Nature, which, if we unconsciously yield to it, will direct us aright. It is not indifferent to us which way we walk. There is a right way; but we are very liable from heedlessness and stupidity to take the wrong one. We would fain take that walk, never yet taken by us through this actual world, which is perfectly symbolical of the path which we love to travel in the interior and ideal world; and sometimes, no doubt, we find it difficult to choose our direction, because it does not yet exist distinctly in our idea.

When I go out of the house for a walk, uncertain as yet whither I will bend my steps, and submit myself to my instinct to decide for me, I find, strange and whimsical as it may seem, that I finally and inevitably settle southwest, toward some particular wood or meadow or deserted pasture or hill in that direction. My needle is slow to settle,— varies a few degrees, and does not always point due southwest, it is true, and it has good authority for this variation, but it always settles between west and south-southwest. The future lies that way to me, and the earth

seems more unexhausted and richer on that side. The outline which would bound my walks would be, not a circle,
but a parabola, or rather like one of those cometary orbits
which have been thought to be non-returning curves, in
this case opening westward, in which my house occupies
the place of the sun. I turn round and round irresolute
sometimes for a quarter of an hour, until I decide, for the
thousandth time, that I will walk into the southwest or
west. Eastward I go only by force; but westward I go
free. Thither no business leads me. It is hard for me to
believe that I shall find fair landscapes or sufficient wildness and freedom behind the eastern horizon. I am not
excited by the prospect of a walk thither; but I believe
that the forest which I see in the western horizon stretches
uninterruptedly towards the setting sun, and that there
are no towns nor cities in it of enough consequence to
disturb me. Let me live where I will, on this side is the
city, on that the wilderness, and ever I am leaving the
city more and more, and withdrawing into the wilderness. I should not lay so much stress on this fact, if I did
not believe that something like this is the prevailing tendency of my countrymen. I must walk toward Oregon,
and not toward Europe. And that way the nation is moving, and I may say that mankind progress from east to
west. Within a few years we have witnessed the phenomenon of a southeastward migration, in the settlement of
Australia; but this affects us as a retrograde movement,
and, judging from the moral and physical character of
the first generation of Australians, has not yet proved a
successful experiment. The eastern Tartars think that
there is nothing west beyond Thibet. "The world ends
there," say they; "beyond there is nothing but a shoreless
sea." It is unmitigated East where they live.

We go eastward to realize history and study the works
of art and literature, retracing the steps of the race; we go
westward as into the future, with a spirit of enterprise
and adventure. The Atlantic is a Lethean stream, in our
passage over which we have had an opportunity to forget
the Old World and its institutions. If we do not succeed
this time, there is perhaps one more chance for the race
left before it arrives on the banks of the Styx; and that is
in the Lethe of the Pacific, which is three times as wide.

I know not how significant it is, or how far it is an evidence of singularity, that an individual should thus consent in his pettiest walk with the general movement of the race; but I know that something akin to the migratory instinct in birds and quadrupeds,—which, in some instances, is known to have affected the squirrel tribe, impelling them to a general and mysterious movement, in which they were seen, say some, crossing the broadest rivers, each on its particular chip, with its tail raised for a sail, and bridging narrower streams with their dead,— that something like the *furor* which affects the domestic cattle in the spring, and which is referred to a worm in their tails,—affects both nations and individuals, either perennially or from time to time. Not a flock of wild geese cackles over our town, but it to some extent unsettles the value of real estate here, and, if I were a broker, I should probably take that disturbance into account.

> "Than longen folk to gon on pilgrimages,
> And palmeres for to seken strange strondes."

Every sunset which I witness inspires me with the desire to go to a West as distant and as fair as that into which the sun goes down. He appears to migrate westward daily, and tempt us to follow him. He is the Great Western Pioneer whom the nations follow. We dream all night of those mountain-ridges in the horizon, though they may be of vapor only, which were last gilded by his rays. The island of Atlantis, and the islands and gardens of the Hesperides, a sort of terrestrial paradise, appear to have been the Great West of the ancients, enveloped in mystery and poetry. Who has not seen in imagination, when looking into the sunset sky, the gardens of the Hesperides, and the foundation of all those fables?

Columbus felt the westward tendency more strongly than any before. He obeyed it, and found a New World for Castile and Leon. The herd of men in those days scented fresh pastures, from afar.

> "And now the sun had stretched out all the hills,
> And now was dropped into the western bay;
> At last *he* rose, and twitched his mantle blue;
> To-morrow to fresh woods and pastures new."

Where on the globe can there be found an area of equal extent with that occupied by the bulk of our States, so fertile and so rich and varied in its productions, and at the same time so habitable by the European, as this is? Michaux, who knew but part of them, says that "the species of large trees are much more numerous in North America than in Europe; in the United States there are more than one hundred and forty species that exceed thirty feet in height; in France there are but thirty that attain this size." Later botanists more than confirm his observations. Humboldt came to America to realize his youthful dreams of a tropical vegetation, and he beheld it in its greatest perfection in the primitive forests of the Amazon, the most gigantic wilderness on the earth, which he has so eloquently described. The geographer Guyot, himself a European, goes farther,—farther than I am ready to follow him; yet not when he says,—"As the plant is made for the animal, as the vegetable world is made for the animal world, America is made for the man of the Old World. . . . The man of the Old World sets out upon his way. Leaving the highlands of Asia, he descends from station to station towards Europe. Each of his steps is marked by a new civilization superior to the preceding, by a greater power of development. Arrived at the Atlantic, he pauses on the shore of this unknown ocean, the bounds of which he knows not, and turns upon his footprints for an instant." When he has exhausted the rich soil of Europe, and reinvigorated himself, "then recommences his adventurous career westward as in the earliest ages." So far Guyot.

From this western impulse coming in contact with the barrier of the Atlantic sprang the commerce and enterprise of modern times. The younger Michaux, in his "Travels West of the Alleghanies in 1802," says that the common inquiry in the newly settled West was, " 'From what part of the world have you come?' As if these vast and fertile regions would naturally be the place of meeting and common country of all the inhabitants of the globe."

To use an obsolete Latin word, I might say, *Ex Oriente lux; ex Occidente* FRUX. From the East light; from the West fruit.

Sir Francis Head, an English traveller and a Governor-General of Canada, tells us that "in both the northern and southern hemispheres of the New World, Nature has not only outlined her works on a larger scale, but has painted the whole picture with brighter and more costly colors than she used in delineating and in beautifying the Old World. . . . The heavens of America appear infinitely higher, the sky is bluer, the air is fresher, the cold is intenser, the moon looks larger, the stars are brighter, the thunder is louder, the lightning is vivider, the wind is stronger, the rain is heavier, the mountains are higher, the rivers longer, the forests bigger, the plains broader." This statement will do at least to set against Buffon's account of this part of the world and its productions.

Linnæus said long ago, "Nescio quæ facies *læta, glabra* plantis Americanis: I know not what there is of joyous and smooth in the aspect of American plants"; and I think that in this country there are no, or at most very few, *Africanæ bestiæ,* African beasts, as the Romans called them, and that in this respect also it is peculiarly fitted for the habitation of man. We are told that within three miles of the centre of the East-Indian city of Singapore, some of the inhabitants are annually carried off by tigers; but the traveller can lie down in the woods at night almost anywhere in North America without fear of wild beasts.

These are encouraging testimonies. If the moon looks larger here than in Europe, probably the sun looks larger also. If the heavens of America appear infinitely higher, and the stars brighter, I trust that these facts are symbolical of the height to which the philosophy and poetry and religion of her inhabitants may one day soar. At length, perchance, the immaterial heaven will appear as much higher to the American mind, and the intimations that star it as much brighter. For I believe that climate does thus react on man,—as there is something in the mountain-air that feeds the spirit and inspires. Will not man grow to greater perfection intellectually as well as physically under these influences? Or is it unimportant how many foggy days there are in his life? I trust that we shall be more imaginative, that our thoughts will be clearer, fresher, and more ethereal, as our sky,—our understand-

ing more comprehensive and broader, like our plains,—
our intellect generally on a grander scale, like our thunder and lightning, our rivers and mountains and forests,—and our hearts shall even correspond in breadth
and depth and grandeur to our inland seas. Perchance
there will appear to the traveller something, he knows not
what, of *lœta* and *glabra*, of joyous and serene, in our
very faces. Else to what end does the world go on, and
why was America discovered?

To Americans I hardly need to say,—

> "Westward the star of empire takes its way."

As a true patriot, I should be ashamed to think that Adam
in paradise was more favorably situated on the whole
than the backwoodsman in this country.

Our sympathies in Massachusetts are not confined to
New England; though we may be estranged from the
South, we sympathize with the West. There is the home
of the younger sons, as among the Scandinavians they
took to the sea for their inheritance. It is too late to be
studying Hebrew; it is more important to understand
even the slang of to-day.

Some months ago I went to see a panorama of the
Rhine. It was like a dream of the Middle Ages. I floated
down its historic stream in something more than imagination, under bridges built by the Romans, and repaired by
later heroes, past cities and castles whose very names
were music to my ears, and each of which was the subject
of a legend. There were Ehrenbreitstein and Rolandseck
and Coblentz, which I knew only in history. They were
ruins that interested me chiefly. There seemed to come
up from its waters and its vine-clad hills and valleys a
hushed music as of Crusaders departing for the Holy
Land. I floated along under the spell of enchantment, as
if I had been transported to an heroic age, and breathed
an atmosphere of chivalry.

Soon after, I went to see a panorama of the Mississippi,
and as I worked my way up the river in the light of to-
day, and saw the steamboats wooding up, counted the
rising cities, gazed on the fresh ruins of Nauvoo, beheld
the Indians moving west across the stream, and, as before
I had looked up the Moselle, now looked up the Ohio and

the Missouri, and heard the legends of Dubuque and of
Wenona's Cliff,—still thinking more of the future than of
the past or present,—I saw that this was a Rhine stream
of a different kind; that the foundations of castles were
yet to be laid, and the famous bridges were yet to be
thrown over the river; and I felt that *this was the heroic
age itself*, though we know it not, for the hero is commonly the simplest and obscurest of men.

The West of which I speak is but another name for the
Wild; and what I have been preparing to say is, that in
Wildness is the preservation of the world. Every tree
sends its fibres forth in search of the Wild. The cities
import it at any price. Men plough and sail for it. From
the forest and wilderness come the tonics and barks
which brace mankind. Our ancestors were savages. The
story of Romulus and Remus being suckled by a wolf is
not a meaningless fable. The founders of every State
which has risen to eminence have drawn their nourishment and vigor from a similar wild source. It was because
the children of the Empire were not suckled by the wolf
that they were conquered and displaced by the children
of the Northern forests who were.

I believe in the forest, and in the meadow, and in the
night in which the corn grows. We require an infusion of
hemlock-spruce or arbor-vitæ in our tea. There is a difference between eating and drinking for strength and
from mere gluttony. The Hottentots eagerly devour the
marrow of the koodoo and other antelopes raw, as a matter of course. Some of our Northern Indians eat raw the
marrow of the Arctic reindeer, as well as various other
parts, including the summits of the antlers, as long as
they are soft. And herein, perchance, they have stolen a
march on the cooks of Paris. They get what usually goes
to feed the fire. This is probably better than stall-fed beef
and slaughter-house pork to make a man of. Give me a
wildness whose glance no civilization can endure,—as if
we lived on the marrow of koodoos devoured raw.

There are some intervals which border the strain of the
wood-thrush, to which I would migrate,—wild lands
where no settler has squatted; to which, methinks, I am
already acclimated.

The African hunter Cummings tells us that the skin of
the eland, as well as that of most other antelopes just
killed, emits the most delicious perfume of trees and
grass. I would have every man so much like a wild ante-
lope, so much a part and parcel of Nature, that his very
person should thus sweetly advertise our senses of his
presence, and remind us of those parts of Nature which
he most haunts. I feel no disposition to be satirical, when
the trapper's coat emits the odor of musquash even; it is a
sweeter scent to me than that which commonly exhales
from the merchant's or the scholar's garments. When I go
into their wardrobes and handle their vestments, I am
reminded of no grassy plains and flowery meads which
they have frequented, but of dusty merchants' exchanges
and libraries rather.

A tanned skin is something more than respectable, and
perhaps olive is a fitter color than white for a man,—a
denizen of the woods. "The pale white man!" I do not
wonder that the African pitied him. Darwin the naturalist says, "A white man bathing by the side of a Tahitian
was like a plant bleached by the gardener's art, compared
with a fine, dark green one, growing vigorously in the
open fields."

Ben Jonson exclaims,—

> "How near to good is what is fair!"

So I would say,—

> "How near to good is what is *wild!*"

Life consists with wildness. The most alive is the wildest.
Not yet subdued to man, its presence refreshes him. One
who pressed forward incessantly and never rested from
his labors, who grew fast and made infinite demands on
life, would always find himself in a new country or wilderness, and surrounded by the raw material of life. He
would be climbing over the prostrate stems of primitive
forest-trees.

Hope and the future for me are not in lawns and cultivated fields, not in towns and cities, but in the impervious
and quaking swamps. When, formerly, I have analyzed
my partiality for some farm which I had contemplated

purchasing, I have frequently found that I was attracted
solely by a few square rods of impermeable and unfath-
omable bog,—a natural sink in one corner of it. That was
the jewel which dazzled me. I derive more of my subsistence from the swamps which surround my native town
than from the cultivated gardens in the village. There are
no richer parterres to my eyes than the dense beds of
dwarf andromeda (*Cassandra calyculata*) which cover
these tender places on the earth's surface. Botany cannot
go farther than tell me the names of the shrubs which
grow there,—the high-blueberry, panicled andromeda,
lamb-kill, azalea, and rhodora,—all standing in the quaking sphagnum. I often think that I should like to have my
house front on this mass of dull red bushes, omitting other flower plots and borders, transplanted spruce and trim
box, even gravelled walks,—to have this fertile spot under my windows, not a few imported barrow-fulls of soil
only to cover the sand which was thrown out in digging
the cellar. Why not put my house, my parlor, behind this
plot, instead of behind that meagre assemblage of curiosities, that poor apology for a Nature and Art, which I call
my front-yard? It is an effort to clear up and make a
decent appearance when the carpenter and mason have
departed, though done as much for the passer-by as the
dweller within. The most tasteful front-yard fence was
never an agreeable object of study to me; the most elaborate ornaments, acorn-tops, or what not, soon wearied
and disgusted me. Bring your sills up to the very edge of
the swamp, then, (though it may not be the best place for
a dry cellar,) so that there be no access on that side to
citizens. Front-yards are not made to walk in, but, at
most, through, and you could go in the back way.

Yes, though you may think me perverse, if it were proposed to me to dwell in the neighborhood of the most
beautiful garden that ever human art contrived, or else of
a dismal swamp, I should certainly decide for the swamp.
How vain, then, have been all your labors, citizens, for
me!

My spirits infallibly rise in proportion to the outward
drearinesss. Give me the ocean, the desert, or the wilderness! In the desert, pure air and solitude compensate for

want of moisture and fertility. The traveller Burton says
of it,—"Your *morale* improves; you become frank and
cordial, hospitable and single-minded. . . . In the desert,
spirituous liquors excite only disgust. There is a keen enjoyment in a mere animal existence." They who have
been travelling long on the steppes of Tartary say,—"On
reëntering cultivated lands, the agitation, perplexity, and
turmoil of civilization oppressed and suffocated us; the
air seemed to fail us, and we felt every moment as if
about to die of asphyxia." When I would recreate myself,
I seek the darkest wood, the thickest and most intermina-
ble, and, to the citizen, most dismal swamp. I enter a
swamp as a sacred place,—a *sanctum sanctorum*. There
is the strength, the marrow of Nature. The wild-wood
covers the virgin mould,—and the same soil is good for
men and for trees. A man's health requires as many acres
of meadow to his prospect as his farm does loads of
muck. There are the strong meats on which he feeds. A
town is saved, not more by the righteous men in it than
by the woods and swamps that surround it. A township
where one primitive forest waves above, while another
primitive forest rots below,—such a town is fitted to raise
not only corn and potatoes, but poets and philosophers for
the coming ages. In such a soil grew Homer and Confucius and the rest, and out of such a wilderness comes the
Reformer eating locusts and wild honey.

To preserve wild animals implies generally the creation
of a forest for them to dwell in or resort to. So is it with
man. A hundred years ago they sold bark in our streets
peeled from our own woods. In the very aspect of those
primitive and rugged trees, there was, methinks, a tanning principle which hardened and consolidated the fibres of men's thoughts. Ah! already I shudder for these
comparatively degenerate days of my native village,
when you cannot collect a load of bark of good thickness,—and we no longer produce tar and turpentine.

The civilized nations—Greece, Rome, England—have
been sustained by the primitive forests which anciently
rotted where they stand. They survive as long as the soil
is not exhausted. Alas for human culture! little is to be
expected of a nation, when the vegetable mould is ex-

hausted, and it is compelled to make manure of the bones
of its fathers. There the poet sustains himself merely by
his own superfluous fat, and the philosopher comes down
on his marrow-bones.

It is said to be the task of the American "to work the
virgin soil," and that "agriculture here already assumes
proportions unknown everywhere else." I think that the
farmer displaces the Indian even because he redeems the
meadow, and so makes himself stronger and in some respects more natural. I was surveying for a man the other
day a single straight line one hundred and thirty-two rods
long, through a swamp, at whose entrance might have
been written the words which Dante read over the entrance to the infernal regions,—"Leave all hope, ye that
enter,"—that is, of ever getting out again; where at one
time I saw my employer actually up to his neck and
swimming for his life in his property, though it was still
winter. He had another similar swamp which I could not
survey at all, because it was completely under water, and
nevertheless, with regard to a third swamp, which I did
survey from a distance, he remarked to me, true to his
instincts, that he would not part with it for any consideration, on account of the mud which it contained. And
that man intends to put a girdling ditch round the whole
in the course of forty months, and so redeem it by the
magic of his spade. I refer to him only as the type of a
class.

The weapons with which we have gained our most important victories, which should be handed down as heir-
looms from father to son, are not the sword and the lance,
but the bush-whack, the turf-cutter, the spade, and the
bog-hoe, rusted with the blood of many a meadow, and
begrimed with the dust of many a hard-fought field. The
very winds blew the Indian's cornfield into the meadow,
and pointed out the way which he had not the skill to
follow. He had no better implement with which to in-
trench himself in the land than a clamshell. But the farmer is armed with plough and spade.

In Literature it is only the wild that attracts us. Dulness
is but another name for tameness. It is the uncivilized free
and wild thinking in "Hamlet" and the "Iliad," in all the

Scriptures and Mythologies, not learned in the schools, that delights us. As the wild duck is more swift and beautiful than the tame, so is the wild—the mallard—thought, which 'mid falling dews wings its way above the fens. A truly good book is something as natural, and as unexpectedly and unaccountably fair and perfect, as a wild flower discovered on the prairies of the West or in the jungles of the East. Genius is a light which makes the darkness visible, like the lightning's flash, which perchance shatters the temple of knowledge itself,—and not a taper lighted at the hearth-stone of the race, which pales before the light of common day.

English literature, from the days of the minstrels to the Lake Poets,—Chaucer and Spenser and Milton, and even Shakespeare, included,—breathes no quite fresh and in this sense wild strain. It is an essentially tame and civilized literature, reflecting Greece and Rome. Her wilderness is a green-wood,—her wild man a Robin Hood. There is plenty of genial love of Nature, but not so much of Nature herself. Her chronicles inform us when her wild animals, but not when the wild man in her, became extinct.

The science of Humboldt is one thing, poetry is another thing. The poet to-day, notwithstanding all the discoveries of science, and the accumulated learning of mankind, enjoys no advantage over Homer.

Where is the literature which gives expression to Nature? He would be a poet who could impress the winds and streams into his service, to speak for him; who nailed words to their primitive senses, as farmers drive down stakes in the spring, which the frost has heaved; who derived his words as often as he used them,—transplanted them to his page with earth adhering to their roots; whose words were so true and fresh and natural that they would appear to expand like the buds at the approach of spring, though they lay half-smothered between two musty leaves in a library,—ay, to bloom and bear fruit there, after their kind, annually, for the faithful reader, in sympathy with surrounding Nature.

I do not know of any poetry to quote which adequately expresses this yearning for the Wild. Approached from

this side, the best poetry is tame. I do not know where to
find in any literature, ancient or modern, any account
which contents me of that Nature with which even I am
acquainted. You will perceive that I demand something
which no Augustan nor Elizabethan age, which no *culture*, in short, can give. Mythology comes nearer to it
than anything. How much more fertile a Nature, at least,
has Grecian mythology its root in than English literature!
Mythology is the crop which the Old World bore before
its soil was exhausted, before the fancy and imagination
were affected with blight; and which it still bears, wherever its pristine vigor is unabated. All other literatures
endure only as the elms which overshadow our houses;
but this is like the great dragon-tree of the Western Isles,
as old as mankind, and, whether that does or not, will
endure as long; for the decay of other literatures makes
the soil in which it thrives.

The West is preparing to add its fables to those of the
East. The valleys of the Ganges, the Nile, and the Rhine,
having yielded their crop, it remains to be seen what the
valleys of the Amazon, the Plate, the Orinoco, the St.
Lawrence, and the Mississippi will produce. Perchance,
when, in the course of ages, American liberty has become
a fiction of the past,—as it is to some extent a fiction of
the present,—the poets of the world will be inspired by
American mythology.

The wildest dreams of wild men, even, are not the less
true, though they may not recommend themselves to the
sense which is most common among Englishmen and
Americans to-day. It is not every truth that recommends
itself to the common sense. Nature has a place for the
wild clematis as well as for the cabbage. Some expressions
of truth are reminiscent,—others merely *sensible*, as the
phrase is,—others prophetic. Some forms of disease, even,
may prophesy forms of health. The geologist has discovered that the figures of serpents, griffins, flying dragons,
and other fanciful embellishments of heraldry, have their
prototypes in the forms of fossil species which were extinct before man was created, and hence "indicate a faint
and shadowy knowledge of a previous state of organic
existence." The Hindoos dreamed that the earth rested on

an elephant, and the elephant on a tortoise, and the tortoise on a serpent; and though it may be an unimportant coincidence, it will not be out of place here to state, that a fossil tortoise has lately been discovered in Asia large enough to support an elephant. I confess that I am partial to these wild fancies, which transcend the order of time and development. They are the sublimest recreation of the intellect. The partridge loves peas, but not those that go with her into the pot.

In short, all good things are wild and free. There is something in a strain of music, whether produced by an instrument or by the human voice,—take the sound of a bugle in a summer night, for instance,—which by its wildness, to speak without satire, reminds me of the cries emitted by wild beasts in their native forests. It is so much of their wildness as I can understand. Give me for my friends and neighbors wild men, not tame ones. The wildness of the savage is but a faint symbol of the awful ferity with which good men and lovers meet.

I love even to see the domestic animals reassert their native rights,—any evidence that they have not wholly lost their original wild habits and vigor; as when my neighbor's cow breaks out of her pasture early in the spring and boldly swims the river, a cold, gray tide, twenty-five or thirty rods wide, swollen by the melted snow. It is the buffalo crossing the Mississippi. This exploit confers some dignity on the herd in my eyes,—already dignified. The seeds of instinct are preserved under the thick hides of cattle and horses, like seeds in the bowels of the earth, an indefinite period.

Any sportiveness in cattle is unexpected. I saw one day a herd of a dozen bullocks and cows running about and frisking in unwieldly sport, like huge rats, even like kittens. They shook their heads, raised their tails, and rushed up and down a hill, and I perceived by their horns, as well as by their activity, their relation to the deer tribe. But, alas! a sudden loud *Whoa!* would have damped their ardor at once, reduced them from venison to beef, and stiffened their sides and sinews like the locomotive. Who but the Evil One has cried," "Whoa!" to mankind? Indeed, the life of cattle, like that of many men, is but a

sort of locomotiveness; they move a side at a time, and
man, by his machinery, is meeting the horse and ox half-
way. Whatever part the whip has touched is thenceforth
palsied. Who would ever think of a *side* of any of the
supple cat tribe, as we speak of a *side* of beef?

I rejoice that horses and steers have to be broken before
they can be made the slaves of men, and that men themselves have some wild oats still left to sow before they
become submissive members of society. Undoubtedly, all
men are not equally fit subjects for civilization; and because the majority, like dogs and sheep, are tame by inherited disposition, this is no reason why the others
should have their natures broken that they may be reduced to the same level. Men are in the main alike, but
they were made several in order that they might be various. If a low use is to be served, one man will do nearly
or quite as well as another; if a high one, individual excellence is to be regarded. Any man can stop a hole to
keep the wind away, but no other man could serve so
rare a use as the author of this illustration did. Confucius
says,—"The skins of the tiger and the leopard, when they
are tanned, are as the skins of the dog and the sheep
tanned." But it is not the part of a true culture to tame
tigers, any more than it is to make sheep ferocious; and
tanning their skins for shoes is not the best use to which
they can be put.

When looking over a list of men's names in a foreign
language, as of military officers, or of authors who have
written on a particular subject, I am reminded once more
that there is nothing in a name. The name Menschikoff,
for instance, has nothing in it to my ears more human
than a whisker, and it may belong to a rat. As the names
of the Poles and Russians are to us, so are ours to them. It
is as if they had been named by the child's rigmarole,—*I
cry wiery ichery van, tittle-tol-tan.* I see in my mind a
herd of wild creatures swarming over the earth, and to
each the herdsman has affixed some barbarous sound in
his own dialect. The names of men are of course as cheap
and meaningless as *Bose* and *Tray*, the names of dogs.

Methinks it would be some advantage to philosophy, if

men were named merely in the gross, as they are known. It
would be necessary only to know the genus, and perhaps
the race or variety, to know the individual. We are not
prepared to believe that every private soldier in a Roman
army had a name of his own,—because we have not supposed that he had a character of his own. At present our
only true names are nicknames. I knew a boy who, from
his peculiar energy, was called "Buster" by his playmates,
and this rightly supplanted his Christian name. Some travellers tell us that an Indian had no name given him at first,
but earned it, and his name was his fame; and among some
tribes he acquired a new name with every new exploit. It is
pitiful when a man bears a name for convenience merely,
who has earned neither name nor fame.

I will not allow mere names to make distinctions for
me, but still see men in herds for all them. A familiar
name cannot make a man less strange to me. It may be
given to a savage who retains in secret his own wild title
earned in the woods. We have a wild savage in us, and a
savage name is perchance somewhere recorded as ours. I
see that my neighbor, who bears the familiar epithet William, or Edwin, takes it off with his jacket. It does not
adhere to him when asleep or in anger, or aroused by any
passion or inspiration. I seem to hear pronounced by
some of his kin at such a time his original wild name in
some jaw-breaking or else melodious tongue.

Here is this vast, savage, howling mother of ours, Nature, lying all around, with such beauty, and such affection for her children, as the leopard; and yet we are so
early weaned from her breast to society, to that culture
which is exclusively an interaction of man on man,—a
sort of breeding in and in, which produces at most a
merely English nobility, a civilization destined to have a
speedy limit.

In society, in the best institutions of men, it is easy to
detect a certain precocity. When we should still be growing children, we are already little men. Give me a culture
which imports much muck from the meadows, and deep-
ens the soil,—not that which trusts to heating manures,
and improved implements and modes of culture only!

Many a poor sore-eyed student that I have heard of would grow faster, both intellectually and physically, if, instead of sitting up so very late, he honestly slumbered a fool's allowance.

There may be an excess even of informing light. Niépce, a Frenchman, discovered "actinism," that power in the sun's rays which produces a chemical effect,—that granite rocks, and stone structures, and statues of metal, "are all alike destructively acted upon during the hours of sunshine, and, but for provisions of Nature no less wonderful, would soon perish under the delicate touch of the most subtile of the agencies of the universe." But he observed that "those bodies which underwent this change during the daylight possessed the power of restoring themselves to their original conditions during the hours of night, when this excitement was no longer influencing them." Hence it has been inferred that "the hours of darkness are as necessary to the inorganic creation as we know night and sleep are to the organic kingdom." Not even does the moon shine every night, but gives place to darkness.

I would not have every man nor every part of a man cultivated, any more than I would have every acre of earth cultivated: part will be tillage, but the greater part will be meadow and forest, not only serving an immediate use, but preparing a mould against a distant future, by the annual decay of the vegetation which it supports.

There are other letters for the child to learn than those which Cadmus invented. The Spaniards have a good term to express this wild and dusky knowledge,—*Gramâtica parda*, tawny grammar,—a kind of mother-wit derived from that same leopard to which I have referred.

We have heard of a Society for the Diffusion of Useful Knowledge. It is said that knowledge is power; and the like. Methinks there is equal need of a Society for the Diffusion of Useful Ignorance, what we will call Beautiful Knowledge, a knowledge useful in a higher sense: for what is most of our boasted so-called knowledge but a conceit that we know something, which robs us of the advantage of our actual ignorance? What we call knowledge is often our positive ignorance; ignorance our nega-

tive knowledge. By long years of patient industry and
reading of the newspapers—for what are the libraries of
science but files of newspapers?—a man accumulates a
myriad facts, lays them up in his memory, and then
when in some spring of his life he saunters abroad into
the Great Fields of thought, he, as it were, goes to grass
like a horse, and leaves all his harness behind in the stable. I would say to the Society for the Diffusion of Useful
Knowledge, sometimes,—Go to grass. You have eaten hay
long enough. The spring has come with its green crop.
The very cows are driven to their country pastures before
the end of May; though I have heard of one unnatural
farmer who kept his cow in the barn and fed her on hay
all the year round. So, frequently, the Society for the Diffusion of Useful Knowledge treats its cattle.

A man's ignorance sometimes is not only useful, but
beautiful,—while his knowledge, so called, is oftentimes
worse than useless, besides being ugly. Which is the best
man to deal with,—he who knows nothing about a subject, and, what is extremely rare, knows that he knows
nothing, or he who really knows something about it, but
thinks that he knows all?

My desire for knowledge is intermittent; but my desire
to bathe my head in atmospheres unknown to my feet is
perennial and constant. The highest that we can attain to
is not Knowledge, but Sympathy with Intelligence. I do
not know that this higher knowledge amounts to anything
more definite than a novel and grand surprise on a sudden revelation of the insufficiency of all that we called
Knowledge before,—a discovery that there are more
things in heaven and earth than are dreamed of in our
philosophy. It is the lighting up of the mist by the sun.
Man cannot *know* in any higher sense than this, any more
than he can look serenely and with impunity in the face
of the sun: 'Ωϛ τὶ νοῶν, οὐ κεῖνον νοήσειϛ,—"You will not
perceive that, as perceiving a particular thing," say the
Chaldean Oracles.

There is something servile in the habit of seeking after
a law which we may obey. We may study the laws of
matter at and for our convenience, but a successful life
knows no law. It is an unfortunate discovery certainly,

that of a law which binds us where we did not know
before that we were bound. Live free, child of the
mist,—and with respect to knowledge we are all children
of the mist. The man who takes the liberty to live is superior to all the laws, by virtue of his relation to the law-
maker. "That is active duty," says the Vishnu Purana,
"which is not for our bondage; that is knowledge which is
for our liberation: all other duty is good only unto weariness; all other knowledge is only the cleverness of an artist."

It is remarkable how few events or crises there are in
our histories; how little exercised we have been in our
minds; how few experiences we have had. I would fain
be assured that I am growing apace and rankly, though
my very growth disturb this dull equanimity,—though it
be with struggle through long, dark, muggy nights or seasons of gloom. It would be well, if all our lives were a
divine tragedy even, instead of this trivial comedy or
farce. Dante, Bunyan, and others, appear to have been
exercised in their minds more than we: they were subjected to a kind of culture such as our district schools and
colleges do not contemplate. Even Mahomet, though
many may scream at his name, had a good deal more to
live for, ay, and to die for, than they have commonly.

When, at rare intervals, some thought visits one, as perchance he is walking on a railroad, then indeed the cars
go by without his hearing them. But soon, by some inexo-
rable law, our life goes by and the cars return.

> "Gentle breeze, that wanderest unseen,
> And bendest the thistles round Loira of storms,
> Traveller of the windy glens,
> Why hast thou left my ear so soon?"

While almost all men feel an attraction drawing them
to society, few are attracted strongly to Nature. In their
relation to Nature men appear to me for the most part,
notwithstanding their arts, lower than the animals. It is
not often a beautiful relation, as in the case of the animals. How little appreciation of the beauty of the landscape there is among us! We have to be told that the

Greeks called the world Κόσμος, Beauty, or Order, but we do not see clearly why they did so, and we esteem it at best only a curious philological fact.

For my part, I feel that with regard to Nature I live a sort of border life, on the confines of a world into which I make occasional and transient forays only, and my patriotism and allegiance to the State into whose territories I seem to retreat are those of a moss-trooper. Unto a life which I call natural I would gladly follow even a will-o'-the-wisp through bogs and sloughs unimaginable, but no moon nor fire-fly has shown me the causeway to it. Nature is a personality so vast and universal that we have never seen one of her features. The walker in the familiar fields which stretch around my native town sometimes finds himself in another land than is described in their owners' deeds, as it were in some faraway field on the confines of the actual Concord, where her jurisdiction ceases, and the idea which the word Concord suggests ceases to be suggested. These farms which I have myself surveyed, those bounds which I have set up appear dimly still as through a mist; but they have no chemistry to fix them; they fade from the surface of the glass; and the picture which the painter painted stands out dimly from beneath. The world with which we are commonly acquainted leaves no trace, and it will have no anniversary.

I took a walk on Spaulding's Farm the other afternoon. I saw the setting sun lighting up the opposite side of a stately pine wood. Its golden rays straggled into the aisles of the wood as into some noble hall. I was impressed as if some ancient and altogether admirable and shining family had settled there in that part of the land called Concord, unknown to me,—to whom the sun was servant,—who had not gone into society in the village,—who had not been called on. I saw their park, their pleasure-ground, beyond through the wood, in Spaulding's cranberry-meadow. The pines furnished them with gables as they grew. Their house was not obvious to vision; the trees grew through it. I do not know whether I heard the sounds of a suppressed hilarity or not. They seemed to recline on the sunbeams. They have sons and daughters. They are quite well. The farmer's cart-path, which leads directly through their hall, does not in the least put them out,—as the muddy bottom of a pool is sometimes seen through the reflected skies. They never heard of Spaulding, and do not know that he is their neighbor,—notwithstanding I heard him whistle as he drove his team through the house. Nothing can equal the serenity of their lives. Their coat of arms is simply a lichen. I saw it painted on the pines and oaks. Their attics were in the tops of the trees. They are of no politics. There was no noise of labor. I did not perceive that they were weaving or spinning. Yet I did detect, when the wind lulled and hearing was done away, the finest imaginable sweet musical hum,—as of a distant hive in May, which perchance was the sound of their thinking. They had no idle thoughts, and no one without could see their work, for their industry was not as in knots and excrescences embayed.

But I find it difficult to remember them. They fade irrevocably out of my mind even now while I speak and endeavor to recall them, and recollect myself. It is only after a long and serious effort to recollect my best thoughts that I become again aware of their cohabitancy. If it were not for such families as this, I think I should move out of Concord.

We are accustomed to say in New England that few and fewer pigeons visit us every year. Our forests furnish no mast for them. So, it would seem, few and fewer thoughts visit each growing man from year to year, for the grove in our minds is laid waste,—sold to feed unnecessary fires of ambition, or sent to mill, and there is scarcely a twig left for them to perch on. They no longer build nor breed with us. In some more genial season, perchance, a faint shadow flits across the landscape of the mind, cast by the *wings* of some thought in its vernal or autumnal migration, but, looking up, we are unable to detect the substance of the thought itself. Our winged thoughts are turned to poultry. They no longer soar, and they attain only to a Shanghai and Cochin-China grandeur. Those *gra-a-ate thoughts*, those *gra-a-ate men* you hear of!

We hug the earth,—how rarely we mount! Methinks we might elevate ourselves a little more. We might climb a tree, at least. I found my account in climbing a tree once. It was a tall white pine, on the top of a hill; and though I got well pitched, I was well paid for it, for I discovered new mountains in the horizon which I had never seen before,—so much more of the earth and the heavens. I might have walked about the foot of the tree for threescore years and ten, and yet I certainly should never have seen them. But, above all, I discovered around me,—it was near the end of June,—on the ends of the topmost branches only, a few minute and delicate red cone-like blossoms, the fertile flower of the white pine looking heavenward. I carried straightway to the village the topmost spire, and showed it to stranger jurymen who walked the streets,—for it was court-week,—and to farmers and lumber-dealers and wood-choppers and hunters, and not one had ever seen the like before, but they wondered as at a star dropped down. Tell of ancient architects finishing their works on the tops of columns as perfectly as on the lower and more visible parts! Nature has from the first expanded the minute blossoms of the forest only toward the heavens, above men's heads and unobserved by them. We see only the flowers that are under our feet in the meadows. The pines have developed their delicate blossoms on the highest twigs of the wood every summer for ages, as well over the heads of Nature's red children as of her white ones; yet scarcely a farmer or hunter in the land has ever seen them.

Above all, we cannot afford not to live in the present. He is blessed over all mortals who loses no moment of the passing life in remembering the past. Unless our philosophy hears the cock crow in every barn-yard within our horizon, it is belated. That sound commonly reminds us that we are growing rusty and antique in our employments and habits of thought. His philosophy comes down to a more recent time than ours. There is something suggested by it that is a newer treatment,—the gospel according to this moment. He has not fallen astern; he has got up early, and kept up early, and to be where he is is to be in season, in the foremost rank of time. It is an expression of the health and soundness of Nature, a brag for all the world,—healthiness as of a spring burst forth, a new fountain of the Muses, to celebrate this last instant of time. Where he lives no fugitive slave laws are passed. Who has not betrayed his master many times since last he heard that note?

The merit of this bird's strain is in its freedom from all plaintiveness. The singer can easily move us to tears or to laughter, but where is he who can excite in us a pure morning joy? When, in doleful dumps, breaking the awful stillness of our wooden sidewalk on a Sunday, or, perchance, a watcher in the house of mourning, I hear a cockerel crow far or near, I think to myself, "There is one of us well, at any rate,"—and with a sudden gush return to my senses.

We had a remarkable sunset one day last November. I was walking in a meadow, the source of a small brook, when the sun at last, just before setting, after a cold gray day, reached a clear stratum in the horizon, and the softest, brightest morning sunlight fell on the dry grass and on the stems of the trees in the opposite horizon, and on the leaves of the shrub-oaks on the hill-side, while our shadows stretched long over the meadow eastward, as if we were the only motes in its beams. It was such a light as we could not have imagined a moment before, and the air also was so warm and serene that nothing was wanting to make a paradise of that meadow. When we reflected that this was not a solitary phenomenon, never to happen again, but that it would happen forever and ever an infinite number of evenings, and cheer and reassure the latest child that walked there, it was more glorious still.

The sun sets on some retired meadow, where no house is visible, with all the glory and splendor that it lavishes on cities, and, perchance, as it has never set before,—where there is but a solitary marsh-hawk to have his wings gilded by it, or only a musquash looks out from his cabin, and there is some little black-veined brook in the midst of the marsh, just beginning to meander, winding

slowly round a decaying stump. We walked in so pure
and bright a light, gilding the withered grass and leaves,
so softly and serenely bright, I thought I had never
bathed in such a golden flood, without a ripple or a mur-
mur to it. The west side of every wood and rising ground
gleamed like the boundary of Elysium, and the sun on
our backs seemed like a gentle herdsman driving us home
at evening.

So we saunter toward the Holy Land, till one day the
sun shall shine more brightly than ever he has done, shall
perchance shine into our minds and hearts, and light up
our whole lives with a great awakening light, as warm
and serene and golden as on a bank-side in autumn.

AUTUMNAL TINTS

"Autumnal Tints" is not only a memorial to the acuteness of Thoreau's vision; it recalls also one of Thoreau's favorite themes that the beauty that surrounds us is unseen if the eye of the beholder is closed to it. Auditors of Thoreau who heard his lecture on autumnal tints— among them Bronson Alcott—testified that their perceptiveness to fall colors was sharpened by Thoreau's remarks. Thoreau prepared this essay for publication in The Atlantic Monthly *along with "Walking" and "Life without Principle" in the final months of his life; and it appeared posthumously in the* Atlantic *for October 1862. The text reproduced here is from that printing.*

EUROPEANS COMING TO AMERICA are surprised by the brilliancy of our autumnal foliage. There is no account of such a phenomenon in English poetry, because the trees acquire but few bright colors there. The most that Thomson says on this subject in his "Autumn" is contained in the lines,

> "But see the fading many-colored woods,
> Shade deepening over shade, the country
>   round
> Imbrown; a crowded umbrage, dusk and
>   dun,
> Of every hue, from wan declining green to
>   sooty dark":—

and in the line in which he speaks of

> "Autumn beaming o'er the yellow woods."

The autumnal change of our woods has not made a deep impression on our own literature yet. October has hardly tinged our poetry.

A great many, who have spent their lives in cities, and have never chanced to come into the country at this season, have never seen this, the flower, or rather the ripe fruit, of the year. I remember riding with one such citizen, who, though a fortnight too late for the most brilliant tints, was taken by surprise, and would not believe that there had been any brighter. He had never heard of this phenomenon before. Not only many in our towns have never witnessed it, but it is scarcely remembered by the majority from year to year.

Most appear to confound changed leaves with withered ones, as if they were to confound ripe apples with rotten ones. I think that the change to some higher color in a leaf is an evidence that it has arrived at a late and perfect maturity, answering to the maturity of fruits. It is generally the lowest and oldest leaves which change first. But as the perfect winged and usually bright-colored insect is short-lived, so the leaves ripen but to fall.

Generally, every fruit, on ripening, and just before it falls, when it commences a more independent and individual existence, requiring less nourishment from any source, and that not so much from the earth through its stem as from the sun and air, acquires a bright tint. So do leaves. The physiologist says it is "due to an increased absorption of oxygen." That is the scientific account of the matter,—only a reassertion of the fact. But I am more interested in the rosy cheek than I am to know what particular diet the maiden fed on. The very forest and herbage, the pellicle of the earth, must acquire a bright color, an evidence of its ripeness,—as if the globe itself were a fruit on its stem, with ever a cheek toward the sun.

Flowers are but colored leaves, fruits but ripe ones. The edible part of most fruits is, as the physiologist says, "the parenchyma or fleshly tissue of the leaf" of which they are formed.

Our appetites have commonly confined our views of ripeness and its phenomena, color, mellowness, and perfectness, to the fruits which we eat, and we are wont to forget that an immense harvest which we do not eat, hardly use at all, is annually ripened by Nature. At our annual Cattle Shows and Horticultural Exhibitions, we make, as we think, a great show of fair fruits, destined, however, to a rather ignoble end, fruits not valued for their beauty chiefly. But round about and within our towns there is annually another show of fruits, on an infinitely grander scale, fruits which address our taste for beauty alone.

October is the month of painted leaves. Their rich glow now flashes round the world. As fruits and leaves and the day itself acquire a bright tint just before they fall, so the year near its setting. October is its sunset sky; November the later twilight.

I formerly thought that it would be worth the while to get a specimen leaf from each changing tree, shrub, and herbaceous plant, when it had acquired its brightest characteristic color, in its transition from the green to the brown state, outline it, and copy its color exactly, with paint, in a book, which should be entitled, *"October, or Autumnal Tints"*;—beginning with the earliest reddening,—Woodbine and the lake of radical leaves, and coming down through the Maples, Hickories, and Sumachs, and many beautifully freckled leaves less generally known, to the latest Oaks and Aspens. What a memento such a book would be! You would need only to turn over its leaves to take a ramble through the autumn woods whenever you pleased. Or if I could preserve the leaves themselves, unfaded, it would be better still. I have made but little progress toward such a book, but I have endeavored, instead, to describe all these bright tints in the order in which they present themselves. The following are some extracts from my notes.

The Purple Grasses.

By the twentieth of August, everywhere in woods and swamps, we are reminded of the fall, both by the richly spotted Sarsaparilla-leaves and Brakes, and the withering and blackened Skunk-Cabbage and Hellebore, and, by the river-side, the already blackening Pontederia.

The Purple Grass (*Eragrostis pectinacea*) is now in the height of its beauty. I remember still when I first noticed this grass particularly. Standing on a hillside near our river, I saw, thirty or forty rods off, a stripe of purple half a dozen rods long, under the edge of a wood, where the ground sloped toward a meadow. It was as high-colored and interesting, though not quite so bright, as the patches of Rhexia, being a darker purple, like a berry's stain laid on close and thick. On going to and examining it, I found it to be a kind of grass in bloom, hardly a foot high, with but few green blades, and a fine spreading panicle of purple flowers, a shallow, purplish mist trembling around me. Close at hand it appeared but a dull purple, and made little impression on the eye; it was even difficult to detect; and if you plucked a single plant, you were surprised to find how thin it was, and how little color it had. But viewed at a distance in a favorable light, it was of a fine lively purple, flower-like, enriching the earth. Such puny causes combine to produce these decided effects. I was the more surprised and charmed because grass is commonly of a sober and humble color.

With its beautiful purple blush it reminds me, and supplies the place, of the Rhexia, which is now leaving off, and it is one of the most interesting phenomena of August. The finest patches of it grow on waste strips or selvages of land at the base of dry hills, just above the edge of the meadows, where the greedy mower does not deign to swing his scythe; for this is a thin and poor grass, beneath his notice. Or, it may be, because it is so beautiful he does not know that it exists; for the same eye does not see this and Timothy. He carefully gets the meadow hay and the more nutritious grasses which grow next to that, but he leaves this fine purple mist for the walker's harvest,—fodder for his fancy stock. Higher up the hill, perchance, grow also Blackberries, John's-Wort, and neglected, withered, and wiry June-Grass. How fortunate that it grows in such places, and not in the midst of the rank grasses which are annually cut! Nature thus keeps use and

beauty distinct. I know many such localities, where it
does not fail to present itself annually, and paint the
earth with its blush. It grows on the gentle slopes, either
in a continuous patch or in scattered and rounded tufts a
foot in diameter, and it lasts till it is killed by the first
smart frosts.

In most plants the corolla or calyx is the part which
attains the highest color, and is the most attractive; in
many it is the seed-vessel or fruit; in others, as the Red
Maple, the leaves; and in others still it is the very culm
itself which is the principal flower or blooming part.

The last is especially the case with the Poke or Garget
(*Phytolacca decandra*). Some which stand under our
cliffs quite dazzle me with their purple stems now and
early in September. They are as interesting to me as most
flowers, and one of the most important fruits of our autumn. Every part is flower, (or fruit,) such is its superfluity of color,—stem, branch, peduncle, pedicel, petiole,
and even the at length yellowish purple-veined leaves. Its
cylindrical racemes of berries of various hues, from green
to dark purple, six or seven inches long, are gracefully
drooping on all sides, offering repasts to the birds; and
even the sepals from which the birds have picked the
berries are a brilliant lake-red, with crimson flame-like
reflections, equal to anything of the kind,—all on fire
with ripeness. Hence the *lacca*, from *lac*, lake. There are
at the same time flower-buds, flowers, green berries, dark
purple or ripe ones, and these flower-like sepals, all on
the same plant.

We love to see any redness in the vegetation of the
temperate zone. It is the color of colors. This plant speaks
to our blood. It asks a bright sun on it to make it show to
best advantage, and it must be seen at this season of the
year. On warm hill-sides its stems are ripe by the twenty-
third of August. At that date I walked through a beautiful
grove of them, six or seven feet high, on the side of one
of our cliffs, where they ripen early. Quite to the ground
they were a deep brilliant purple with a bloom, contrast-
ing with the still clear green leaves. It appears a rare triumph of Nature to have produced and perfected such a
plant, as if this were enough for a summer. What a per-

fect maturity it arrives at! It is the emblem of a successful
life concluded by a death not premature, which is an ornament to Nature. What if we were to mature as perfectly, root and branch, glowing in the midst of our decay,
like the Poke! I confess that it excites me to behold them.
I cut one for a cane, for I would fain handle and lean on
it. I love to press the berries between my fingers, and see
their juice staining my hand. To walk amid these upright,
branching casks of purple wine, which retain and diffuse
a sunset glow, tasting each one with your eye, instead of
counting the pipes on a London dock, what a privilege!
For Nature's vintage is not confined to the vine. Our poets
have sung of wine, the product of a foreign plant which
commonly they never saw, as if our own plants had no
juice in them more than the singers. Indeed, this has been
called by some the American Grape and, though a native
of America, its juices are used in some foreign countries
to improve the color of the wine; so that the poetaster
may be celebrating the virtues of the Poke without knowing it. Here are berries enough to paint afresh the western sky, and play the bacchanal with, if you will. And
what flutes its ensanguined stems would make, to be used
in such a dance! It is truly a royal plant. I could spend the
evening of the year musing amid the Poke-stems. And
perchance amid these groves might arise at last a new
school of philosophy or poetry. It lasts all through September.

At the same time with this, or near the end of August,
a to me very interesting genus of grasses, Andropogons,
or Beard-Grasses, is in its prime. *Andropogon furcatus,*
Forked Beard-Grass, or call it Purple-Fingered Grass; *Andropogon scoparius,* Purple Wood-Grass; and *Andropogon* (now called *Sorghum*) *nutans,* Indian-Grass. The
first is a very tall and slender-culmed grass, three to seven
feet high, with four or five purple finger-like spokes
raying upward from the top. The second is also quite
slender, growing in tufts two feet high by one wide, with
culms often somewhat curving, which, as the spikes go
out of bloom, have a whitish fuzzy look. These two are
prevailing grasses at this season on dry and sandy fields
and hill-sides. The culms of both, not to mention their

pretty flowers, reflect a purple tinge, and help to declare
the ripeness of the year. Perhaps I have the more sympathy with them because they are despised by the farmer,
and occupy sterile and neglected soil. They are high-colored, like ripe grapes, and express a maturity which the
spring did not suggest. Only the August sun could have
thus burnished these culms and leaves. The farmer has
long since done his upland haying, and he will not conde-
scend to bring his scythe to where these slender wild
grasses have at length flowered thinly; you often see
spaces of bare sand amid them. But I walk encouraged
between the tufts of Purple Wood-Grass, over the sandy
fields, and along the edge of the Shrub-Oaks, glad to recognize these simple contemporaries. With thoughts cutting a broad swathe I "get" them, with horse-raking
thoughts I gather them into windrows. The fine-eared
poet may hear the whetting of my scythe. These two
were almost the first grasses that I learned to distinguish,
for I had not known by how many friends I was surrounded,—I had seen them simply as grasses standing.
The purple of their culms also excites me like that of the
Poke-Weed stems.

Think what refuge there is for one, before August is
over, from college commencements and society that iso-
lates! I can skulk amid the tufts of Purple Wood-Grass on
the borders of the "Great Fields." Wherever I walk these
afternoons, the Purple-Fingered Grass also stands like a
guide-board, and points my thoughts to more poetic
paths than they have lately travelled.

A man shall perhaps rush by and trample down plants
as high as his head, and cannot be said to know that they
exist, though he may have cut many tons of them, lit-
tered his stables with them, and fed them to his cattle for
years. Yet, if he ever favorably attends to them, he may
be overcome by their beauty. Each humblest plant, or
weed, as we call it, stands there to express some thought
or mood of ours; and yet how long it stands in vain! I had
walked over those Great Fields so many Augusts, and
never yet distinctly recognized these purple companions
that I had there. I had brushed against them and trodden
on them, forsooth; and now, at last, they, as it were, rose

up and blessed me. Beauty and true wealth are always
thus cheap and despised. Heaven might be defined as the
place which men avoid. Who can doubt that these grasses, which the farmer says are of no account to him, find
some compensation in your appreciation of them? I may
say that I never saw them before,—though, when I came
to look them face to face, there did come down to me a
purple gleam from previous years; and now, wherever I
go, I see hardly anything else. It is the reign and presidency of the Andropogons.

Almost the very sands confess the ripening influence of
the August sun, and methinks, together with the slender
grasses waving over them, reflect a purple tinge. The im-
purpled sands! Such is the consequence of all this sunshine absorbed into the pores of plants and of the earth.
All sap or blood is now wine-colored. At last we have not
only the purple sea, but the purple land.

The Chestnut Beard-Grass, Indian-Grass, or Wood-
Grass, growing here and there in waste places, but more
rare than the former, (from two to four or five feet high,)
is still handsomer and of more vivid colors than its conge-
ners, and might well have caught the Indian's eye. It has
a long, narrow, one-sided, and slightly nodding panicle of
bright purple and yellow flowers, like a banner raised
above its reedy leaves. These bright standards are now
advanced on the distant hill-sides, not in large armies, but
in scattered troops or single file, like the red men. They
stand thus fair and bright, representative of the race
which they are named after, but for the most part unobserved as they. The expression of this grass haunted me
for a week, after I first passed and noticed it, like the
glance of an eye. It stands like an Indian chief taking a
last look at his favorite hunting-grounds.

The Red Maple.

By the twenty-fifth of September, the Red Maples generally are beginning to be ripe. Some large ones have
been conspicuously changing for a week, and some single
trees are now very brilliant. I notice a small one, half a
mile off across a meadow, against the green wood-side

there, a far brighter red than the blossoms of any tree in
summer, and more conspicuous. I have observed this tree
for several autumns invariably changing earlier than its
fellows, just as one tree ripens its fruit earlier than another. It might serve to mark the season, perhaps. I should be
sorry, if it were cut down. I know of two or three such
trees in different parts of our town, which might, perhaps, be propagated from, as early ripeners or September
trees, and their seed be advertised in the market, as well
as that of radishes, if we cared as much about them.

At present, these burning bushes stand chiefly along
the edge of the meadows, or I distinguish them afar on
the hillsides here and there. Sometimes you will see many
small ones in a swamp turned quite crimson when all other trees around are still perfectly green, and the former
appear so much the brighter for it. They take you by
surprise, as you are going by on one side, across the fields,
thus early in the season, as if it were some gay encamp-
ment of the red men, or other foresters, of whose arrival
you had not heard.

Some single trees, wholly bright scarlet, seen against
others of their kind still freshly green, or against evergreens, are more memorable than whole groves will be
by-and-by. How beautiful, when a whole tree is like one
great scarlet fruit full of ripe juices, every leaf, from lowest limb to topmost spire, all aglow, especially if you look
toward the sun! What more remarkable object can there
be in the landscape? Visible for miles, too fair to be believed. If such a phenomenon occurred but once, it would
be handed down by tradition to posterity, and get into
the mythology at last.

The whole tree thus ripening in advance of its fellows
attains a singular preëminence, and sometimes maintains
it for a week or two. I am thrilled at the sight of it, bearing aloft its scarlet standard for the regiment of green-
clad foresters around, and I go half a mile out of my way
to examine it. A single tree becomes thus the crowning
beauty of some meadowy vale, and the expression of the
whole surrounding forest is at once more spirited for it.

A small Red Maple has grown, perchance, far away at
the head of some retired valley, a mile from any road,

unobserved. It has faithfully discharged the duties of a
Maple there, all winter and summer, neglected none of
its economies, but added to its stature in the virtue which
belongs to a Maple, by a steady growth for so many
months, never having gone gadding abroad, and is nearer
heaven than it was in the spring. It has faithfully hus-
banded its sap, and afforded a shelter to the wandering
bird, has long since ripened its seeds and committed them
to the winds, and has the satisfaction of knowing, perhaps, that a thousand little well-behaved Maples are already settled in life somewhere. It deserves well of Ma-
pledom. Its leaves have been asking it from time to time,
in a whisper, "When shall we redden?" And now, in this
month of September, this month of travelling, when men
race hastening to the sea-side, or the mountains, or the
lakes, this modest Maple, still without budging an inch,
travels in its reputation,—runs up its scarlet flag on that
hill-side, which shows that it has finished its summer's
work before all other trees, and withdraws from the contest. At the eleventh hour of the year, the tree which no
scrutiny could have detected here when it was most industrious is thus, by the tint of its maturity, by its very
blushes, revealed at last to the careless and distant traveller, and leads his thoughts away from the dusty road into
those brave solitudes which it inhabits. It flashes out conspicuous with all the virtue and beauty of a Maple,—
Acer rubrum. We may now read its title, or *rubric*, clear.
Its *virtues, not its sins, are as scarlet*.

Notwithstanding the Red Maple is the most intense
scarlet of any of our trees, the Sugar-Maple has been the
most celebrated, and Michaux in his "Sylva" does not
speak of the autumnal color of the former. About the second of October, these trees, both large and small, are
most brilliant, though many are still green. In "sprout-
lands" they seem to vie with one another, and ever some
particular one in the midst of the crowd will be of a peculiarly pure scarlet, and by its more intense color attract
our eye even at a distance, and carry off the palm. A
large Red-Maple swamp, when at the height of its
change, is the most obviously brilliant of all tangible
things, where I dwell, so abundant is this tree with us. It

varies much both in form and color. A great many are
merely yellow, more scarlet, others scarlet deepening into
crimson, more red than common. Look at yonder swamp
of Maples mixed with Pines, at the base of a Pine-clad
hill, a quarter of a mile off, so that you get the full effect
of the bright colors, without detecting the imperfections
of the leaves, and see their yellow, scarlet, and crimson
fires, of all tints, mingled and contrasted with the green.
Some Maples are yet green, only yellow or crimson-
tipped on the edges of their flakes, like the edges of a
Hazel-Nut burr; some are wholly brilliant scarlet, raying
out regularly and finely every way, bilaterally, like the
vines of a leaf; others, of more irregular form, when I
turn my head slightly, emptying out some of its earthiness and concealing the trunk of the tree, seem to rest
heavily flake on flake, like yellow and scarlet clouds,
wreath upon wreath, or like snow-drifts driving through
the air, stratified by the wind. It adds greatly to the beauty of such a swamp at this season, that, even though there
may be no other trees interspersed, it is not seen as a
simple mass of color, but, different trees being of different colors and hues, the outline of each crescent tree-top
is distinct, and where one laps on to another. Yet a painter would hardly venture to make them thus distinct a
quarter of a mile off.

As I go across a meadow directly toward a low rising
ground this bright afternoon, I see, some fifty rods off
toward the sun, the top of a Maple swamp just appearing
over the sheeny russet edge of the hill, a stripe apparently
twenty rods long by ten feet deep, of the most intensely
brilliant scarlet, orange, and yellow, equal to any flowers
or fruits, or any tints ever painted. As I advance, lowering
the edge of the hill which makes the firm foreground or
lower frame of the picture, the depth of the brilliant
grove revealed steadily increases, suggesting that the
whole of the inclosed valley is filled with such color. One
wonders that the tithing-men and fathers of the town are
not out to see what the trees mean by their high colors
and exuberance of spirits, fearing that some mischief is
brewing. I do not see what the Puritans did at this season,
when the Maples blaze out in scarlet. They certainly

could not have worshipped in groves then. Perhaps that is
what they built meeting-houses and fenced them round
with horse-sheds for.

The Elm.

Now, too, the first of October, or later, the Elms are at
the height of their autumnal beauty, great brownish-
yellow masses, warm from their September oven, hanging over the highway. Their leaves are perfectly ripe. I
wonder if there is any answering ripeness in the lives of
the men who live beneath them. As I look down our
street, which is lined with them, they remind me both by
their form and color of yellowing sheaves of grain, as if
the harvest had indeed come to the village itself, and we
might expect to find some maturity and *flavor* in the
thoughts of the villagers at last. Under those bright rustling yellow piles just ready to fall on the heads of the
walkers, how can any crudity or greenness of thought or
act prevail? When I stand where half a dozen large Elms
droop over a house, it is as if I stood within a ripe pump-
kin-rind, and I feel as mellow as if I were the pulp,
though I may be somewhat stringy and seedy withal.
What is the late greenness of the English Elm, like a cu-
cumber out of season, which does not know when to have
done, compared with the early and golden maturity of
the American tree? The street is the scene of a great har-
vest-home. It would be worth the while to set out these
trees, if only for their autumnal value. Think of these
great yellow canopies or parasols held over our heads and
houses by the mile together, making the village all one
and compact,—an *ulmarium*, which is at the same time a
nursery of men! And then how gently and unobserved
they drop their burden and let in the sun when it is wanted, their leaves not heard when they fall on our roofs and
in our streets; and thus the village parasol is shut up and
put away! I see the market-man driving into the village,
and disappearing under its canopy of Elm-tops, with *his*
crop, as into a great granary or barnyard. I am tempted
to go thither as to a husking of thoughts, now dry and
ripe, and ready to be separated from their integuments;

but, alas! I foresee that it will be chiefly husks and little
thought, blasted pig-corn, fit only for cob-meal,—for, as
you sow, so shall you reap.

Fallen Leaves.

By the sixth of October the leaves generally begin to
fall, in successive showers, after frost or rain; but the
principal leaf-harvest, the acme of the *Fall*, is commonly
about the sixteenth. Some morning at that date there is
perhaps a harder frost than we have seen, and ice formed
under the pump, and now, when the morning wind rises,
the leaves come down in denser showers than ever. They
suddenly form thick beds or carpets on the ground, in
this gentle air, or even without wind, just the size and
form of the tree above. Some trees, as small Hickories,
appear to have dropped their leaves instantaneously, as a
soldier grounds arms at a signal; and those of the Hickory, being bright yellow still, though withered, reflect a
blaze of light from the ground where they lie. Down they
have come on all sides, at the first earnest touch of autumn's wand, making a sound like rain.

Or else it is after moist and rainy weather that we notice how great a fall of leaves there has been in the night,
though it may not yet be the touch that loosens the Rock-
Maple leaf. The streets are thickly strewn with the trophies, and fallen Elm-leaves make a dark brown pavement under our feet. After some remarkably warm
Indian-summer day or days, I perceive that it is the unusual heat which, more than anything, causes the leaves
to fall, there having been, perhaps, no frost nor rain for
some time. The intense heat suddenly ripens and wilts
them, just as it softens and ripens peaches and other
fruits, and causes them to drop.

The leaves of late Red Maples, still bright, strew the
earth, often crimson-spotted on a yellow ground, like
some wild apples,—though they preserve these bright
colors on the ground but a day or two, especially if it
rains. On causeways I go by trees here and there all bare
and smoke-like, having lost their brilliant clothing; but
there it lies, nearly as bright as ever, on the ground on

one side, and making nearly as regular a figure as lately
on the tree. I would rather say that I first observe the
trees thus flat on the ground like a permanent colored
shadow, and they suggest to look for the boughs that bore
them. A queen might be proud to walk where these gal-
lant trees have spread their bright cloaks in the mud. I
see wagons roll over them as a shadow or a reflection,
and the drivers heed them just as little as they did their
shadows before.

Birds'-nests, in the Huckleberry and other shrubs, and
in trees, are already being filled with the withered leaves.
So many have fallen in the woods, that a squirrel cannot
run after a falling nut without being heard. Boys are raking them in the streets, if only for the pleasure of dealing
with such clean crisp substances. Some sweep the paths
scrupulously neat, and then stand to see the next breath
strew them with new trophies. The swamp-floor is thickly
covered, and the *Lycopodium lucidulum* looks suddenly
greener amid them. In dense woods they half-cover pools
that are three or four rods long. The other day I could
hardly find a well-known spring, and even suspected that
it had dried up, for it was completely concealed by freshly fallen leaves; and when I swept them aside and revealed it, it was like striking the earth, with Aaron's rod,
for a new spring. Wet grounds about the edges of
swamps look dry with them. At one swamp, where I was
surveying, thinking to step on a leafy shore from a rail, I
got into the water more than a foot deep.

When I go to the river the day after the principal fall
of leaves, the sixteenth, I find my boat all covered, bottom and seats, with the leaves of the Golden Willow under which it is moored, and I set sail with a cargo of them
rustling under my feet. If I empty it, it will be full again
to-morrow. I do not regard them as litter, to be swept
out, but accept them as suitable straw or matting for the
bottom of my carriage. When I turn up into the mouth of
the Assabet, which is wooded, large fleets of leaves are
floating on its surface, as it were getting out to sea, with
room to tack; but next the shore, a little farther up, they
are thicker than foam, quite concealing the water for a
rod in width, under and amid the Alders, Button-Bushes,

and Maples, still perfectly light and dry, with fibre unrelaxed; and at a rocky bend where they are met and stopped by the morning wind, they sometimes form a broad and dense crescent quite across the river. When I turn my prow that way, and the wave which it makes strikes them, list what a pleasant rustling from these dry substances grating on one another! Often it is their undulation only which reveals the water beneath them. Also every motion of the wood-turtle on the shore is betrayed by their rustling there. Or even in mid-channel, when the wind rises, I hear them blown with a rustling sound. Higher up they are slowly moving round and round in some great eddy which the river makes, as that at the "Leaning Hemlocks," where the water is deep, and the current is wearing into the bank.

Perchance, in the afternoon of such a day, when the water is perfectly calm and full of reflections, I paddle gently down the main stream, and, turning up the Assabet, reach a quiet cove, where I unexpectedly find myself surrounded by myriads of leaves, like fellow-voyagers, which seem to have the same purpose, or want of purpose, with myself. See this great fleet of scattered leaf-boats which we paddle amid, in this smooth river-bay, each one curled up on every side by the sun's skill, each nerve a stiff spruce-knee,—like boats of hide, and of all patterns, Charon's boat probably among the rest, and some with lofty prows and poops, like the stately vessels of the ancients, scarcely moving in the sluggish current,—like the great fleets, the dense Chinese cities of boats, with which you mingle on entering some great mart, some New York or Canton, which we are all steadily approaching together. How gently each has been deposited on the water! No violence has been used towards them yet, though, perchance, palpitating hearts were present at the launching. And painted ducks, too, the splendid wood-duck among the rest, often come to sail and float amid the painted leaves,—barks of a nobler model still!

What wholesome herb-drinks are to be had in the swamps now! What strong medicinal, but rich, scents from the decaying leaves! The rain falling on the freshly

dried herbs and leaves, and filling the pools and ditches
into which they have dropped thus clean and rigid, will
soon convert them into tea,—green, black, brown, and
yellow teas, of all degrees of strength, enough to set all
Nature a-gossiping. Whether we drink them or not, as
yet, before their strength is drawn, these leaves, dried on
great Nature's coppers, are of such various pure and delicate tints as might make the fame of Oriental teas.

How they are mixed up, of all species, Oak and Maple
and Chestnut and Birch! But Nature is not cluttered with
them; she is a perfect husbandman; she stores them all.
Consider what a vast crop is thus annually shed on the
earth! This, more than any mere grain or seed, is the
great harvest of the year. The trees are now repaying the
earth with interest what they have taken from it. They
are discounting. They are about to add a leaf's thickness
to the depth of the soil. This is the beautiful way in
which Nature gets her muck, while I chaffer with this
man and that, who talks to me about sulphur and the cost
of carting. We are all the richer for their decay. I am
more interested in this crop than in the English grass
alone or in the corn. It prepares the virgin mould for
future cornfields and forests, on which the earth fattens.
It keeps our homestead in good heart.

For beautiful variety no crop can be compared with
this. Here is not merely the plain yellow of the grains,
but nearly all the colors that we know, the brightest blue
not excepted: the early blushing Maple, the Poison-Su-
mach blazing its sins as scarlet, the mulberry Ash, the
rich chrome-yellow of the Poplars, the brilliant red
Huckleberry, with which the hills' backs are painted, like
those of sheep. The frost touches them, and, with the
slightest breath of returning day or jarring of earth's axle,
see in what showers they come floating down! The
ground is all party-colored with them. But they still live
in the soil, whose fertility and bulk they increase, and in
the forests that spring from it. They stoop to rise, to
mount higher in coming years, by subtle chemistry,
climbing by the sap in the trees, and the sapling's first
fruits thus shed, transmuted at last, may adorn its crown,
when, in after-years, it has become the monarch of the
forest.

It is pleasant to walk over the beds of these fresh, crisp, and rustling leaves. How beautifully they go to their graves! how gently lay themselves down and turn to mould!—painted of a thousand hues, and fit to make the beds of us living. So they troop to their last resting-place, light and frisky. They put on no weeds, but merrily they go scampering over the earth, selecting the spot, choosing a lot, ordering no iron fence, whispering all through the woods about it,—some choosing the spot where the bodies of men are mouldering beneath, and meeting them half-way. How many flutterings before they rest quietly in their graves! They that soared so loftily, how contentedly they return to dust again, and are laid low, resigned to lie and decay at the foot of the tree, and afford nourishment to new generations of their kind, as well as to flutter on high! They teach us how to die. One wonders if the time will ever come when men, with their boasted faith in immortality, will lie down as gracefully and as ripe,—with such an Indian-summer serenity will shed their bodies, as they do their hair and nails.

When the leaves fall, the whole earth is a cemetery pleasant to walk in. I love to wander and muse over them in their graves. Here are no lying nor vain epitaphs. What though you own no lot at Mount Auburn? Your lot is surely cast somewhere in this vast cemetery, which has been consecrated from of old. You need attend no auction to secure a place. There is room enough here. The Loose-strife shall bloom and the Huckleberry-bird sing over your bones. The woodman and hunter shall be your sextons, and the children shall tread upon the borders as much as they will. Let us walk in the cemetery of the leaves,—this is your true Greenwood Cemetery.

The Sugar-Maple.

But think not that the splendor of the year is over; for as one leaf does not make a summer, neither does one fallen leaf make an autumn. The smallest Sugar-Maples in our streets make a great show as early as the fifth of October, more than any other trees there. As I look up the Main Street, they appear like painted screens standing before the houses; yet many are green. But now, or

generally by the seventeenth of October, when almost all
Red Maples, and some White Maples, are bare, the large
Sugar-Maples also are in their glory, glowing with yellow
and red, and show unexpectedly bright and delicate tints.
They are remarkable for the contrast they often afford of
deep blushing red on one half and green on the other.
They become at length dense masses of rich yellow with
a deep scarlet blush, or more than blush, on the exposed
surfaces. They are the brightest trees now in the street.

The large ones on our Common are particularly beautiful. A delicate, but warmer than golden yellow is now the
prevailing color, with scarlet cheeks. Yet, standing on the
east side of the Common just before sundown, when the
western light is transmitted through them, I see that their
yellow even, compared with the pale lemon yellow of an
Elm close by, amounts to a scarlet, without noticing the
bright scarlet portions. Generally, they are great regular
oval masses of yellow and scarlet. All the sunny warmth
of the season, the Indian summer, seems to be absorbed
in their leaves. The lowest and inmost leaves next the
bole are, as usual, of the most delicate yellow and green,
like the complexion of young men brought up in the
house. There is an auction on the Common today, but its
red flag is hard to be discerned amid this blaze of color.

Little did the fathers of the town anticipate this brilliant success, when they caused to be imported from farther in the country some straight poles with their tops cut
off, which they called Sugar-Maples; and, as I remember,
after they were set out, a neighboring merchant's clerk,
by way of jest, planted beans about them. Those which
were then jestingly called bean-poles are to-day far the
most beautiful objects noticeable in our streets. They are
worth all and more than they have cost,—though one of
the selectmen, while setting them out, took the cold
which occasioned his death,—if only because they have
filled the open eyes of children with their rich color un-
stintedly so many Octobers. We will not ask them to yield
us sugar in the spring, while they afford us so fair a prospect in the autumn. Wealth in-doors may be the inheritance of few, but it is equally distributed on the Common. All children alike can revel in this golden harvest.

Surely trees should be set in our streets with a view to their October splendor; though I doubt whether this is ever considered by the "Tree Society." Do you not think it will make some odds to these children that they were brought up under the Maples? Hundreds of eyes are steadily drinking in this color, and by these teachers even the truants are caught and educated the moment they step abroad. Indeed, neither the truant nor the studious is at present taught color in the schools. These are instead of the bright colors in apothecaries' shops and city windows. It is a pity that we have no more *Red* Maples, and some Hickories, in our streets as well. Our paint-box is very imperfectly filled. Instead of, or beside, supplying such paint-boxes as we do, we might supply these natural colors to the young. Where else will they study color under greater advantages? What School of Design can vie with this? Think how much the eyes of painters of all kinds, and of manufacturers of cloth and paper, and paper-stainers, and countless others, are to be educated by these autumnal colors. The stationer's envelopes may be of various tints, yet not so various as those of the leaves of a single tree. If you want a different shade or tint of a particular color, you have only to look farther within or without the tree or the wood. These leaves are not many dipped in one dye, as at the dye-house, but they are dyed in light of infinitely various degrees of strength, and left to set and dry there.

Shall the names of so many of our colors continue to be derived from those of obscure foreign localities, as Naples yellow, Prussian blue, raw Sienna, burnt Umber, Gamboge?—(surely the Tyrian purple must have faded by this time)—or from comparatively trivial articles of commerce,—chocolate, lemon, coffee, cinnamon, claret?—(shall we compare our Hickory to a lemon, or a lemon to a Hickory?)—or from ores and oxides which few ever see? Shall we so often, when describing to our neighbors the color of something we have seen, refer them, not to some natural object in our neighborhood, but perchance to a bit of earth fetched from the other side of the planet, which possibly they may find at the apothecary's, but which probably neither they nor we ever saw? Have we not an *earth* under our feet,—ay, and a sky over our heads? Or is the last *all* ultramarine? What do we know of sapphire, amethyst, emerald, ruby, amber, and the like,—most of us who take these names in vain? Leave these precious words to cabinet-keepers, virtuosos, and maids-of-honor,—to the Nabobs, Begums, and Chobdars of Hindostan, or wherever else. I do not see why, since America and her autumn woods have been discovered, our leaves should not compete with the precious stones in giving names to colors; and, indeed, I believe that in course of time the names of some of our trees and shrubs, as well as flowers, will get into our popular chromatic nomenclature.

But of much more importance than a knowledge of the names and distinctions of color is the joy and exhilaration which these colored leaves excite. Already these brilliant trees throughout the street, without any more variety, are at least equal to an annual festival and holiday, or a week of such. These are cheap and innocent gala-days, celebrated by one and all without the aid of committees or marshals, such a show as may safely be licensed, not attracting gamblers or rum-sellers, nor requiring any special police to keep the peace. And poor indeed must be that New-England village's October which has not the Maple in its streets. This October festival costs no powder, nor ringing of bells, but every tree is a living liberty-pole on which a thousand bright flags are waving.

No wonder that we must have our annual Cattle-Show, and Fall Training, and perhaps Cornwallis, our September Courts, and the like. Nature herself holds her annual fair in October, not only in the streets, but in every hollow and on every hill-side. When lately we looked into that Red-Maple swamp all a-blaze, where the trees were clothed in their vestures of most dazzling tints, did it not suggest a thousand gypsies beneath,—a race capable of wild delight,—or even the fabled fawns, satyrs, and wood-nymphs come back to earth? Or was it only a congregation of wearied wood-choppers, or of proprietors come to inspect their lots, that we thought of? Or, earlier still, when we paddled on the river through that fine-grained September air, did there not appear to be something new going on under the sparkling surface of the stream, a shaking of props, at least, so that we made haste in order to be up in time? Did not the rows of yellowing Willows and Button-Bushes on each side seem like rows of booths, under which, perhaps, some fluviatile egg-pop equally yellow was effervescing? Did not all these suggest that man's spirits should rise as high as Nature's,—should hang out their flag, and the routine of his life be interrupted by an analogous expression of joy and hilarity?

No annual training or muster of soldiery, no celebration with its scarfs and banners, could import into the town a hundredth part of the annual splendor of our October. We have only to set the trees, or let them stand, and Nature will find the colored drapery,—flags of all her nations, some of whose private signals hardly the botanist can read,—while we walk under the triumphal arches of the Elms. Leave it to Nature to appoint the days, whether the same as in neighboring States or not, and let the clergy read her proclamations, if they can understand them. Behold what a brilliant drapery is her Woodbine flag! What public-spirited merchant, think you, has contributed this part of the show? There is no handsomer shingling and paint than this vine, at present covering a whole side of some houses. I do not believe that the Ivy *never sear* is comparable to it. No wonder it has been extensively introduced into London. Let us have a good many Maples and Hickories and Scarlet Oaks, then, I say. Blaze away! Shall that dirty roll of bunting in the gun-house be all the colors a village can display? A village is not complete, unless it have these trees to mark the season in it. They are important, like the town-clock. A village that has them not will not be found to work well. It has a screw loose, an essential part is wanting. Let us have Willows for spring, Elms for summer, Maples and Walnuts and Tupeloes for autumn, Evergreens for winter, and Oaks for all seasons. What is a gallery in a house to a gallery in the streets, which every market-man rides through, whether he will or not? Of course, there is not a picture-gallery in the country which would be worth so much to us as is the western view at sunset under the Elms of our main street. They are the frame to a picture

which is daily painted behind them. An avenue of Elms
as large as our largest and three miles long would seem to
lead to some admirable place, though only C_____were
at the end of it.

A village needs these innocent stimulants of bright and
cheering prospects to keep off melancholy and superstition. Show me two villages, one embowered in trees and
blazing with all the glories of October, the other a merely
trivial and treeless waste, or with only a single tree or two
for suicides, and I shall be sure that in the latter will be
found the most starved and bigoted religionists and the
most desperate drinkers. Every wash-tub and milk-can
and gravestone will be exposed. The inhabitants will dis-
appear abruptly behind their barns and houses, like desert Arabs amid their rocks, and I shall look to see spears
in their hands. They will be ready to accept the most
barren and forlorn doctrine,—as that the world is speedily coming to an end, or has already got to it, or that they
themselves are turned wrong side outward. They will
perchance crack their dry joints at one another and call it
a spiritual communication.

But to confine ourselves to the Maples. What if we
were to take half as much pains in protecting them as we
do in setting them out,—not stupidly tie our horses to our
dahlia-stems?

What meant the fathers by establishing this *perfectly
living* institution before the church,—this institution
which needs no repairing nor repainting, which is continually enlarged and repaired by its growth? Surely they

> "Wrought in a sad sincerity;
> Themselves from God they could not free;
> They *planted* better than they knew;—
> The conscious *trees* to beauty grew."

Verily these Maples are cheap preachers, permanently
settled, which preach their half-century, and century, ay,
and century-and-a-half sermons, with constantly increasing unction and influence, ministering to many generations of men; and the least we can do is to supply them
with suitable colleagues as they grow infirm.

The Scarlet Oak.

Belonging to a genus which is remarkable for the beautiful form of its leaves, I suspect that some Scarlet-Oak leaves surpass those of all other Oaks in the rich and wild beauty of their outlines. I judge from an acquaintance with twelve species, and from drawings which I have seen of many others.

Stand under this tree and see how finely its leaves are cut against the sky,—as it were, only a few sharp points extending from a midrib. They look like double, treble, or quadruple crosses. They are far more ethereal than the less deeply scolloped Oak-leaves. They have so little leafy *terra firma* that they appear melting away in the light, and scarcely obstruct our view. The·leaves of very young plants are, like those of full-grown Oaks of other species, more entire, simple, and lumpish in their outlines; but these, raised high on old trees, have solved the leafy problem. Lifted higher and higher, and sublimated more and more, putting off some earthiness and cultivating more intimacy with the light each year, they have at length the least possible amount of earthy matter, and the greatest spread and grasp of skyey influences. There they dance, arm in arm with the light,—tripping it on fantastic points, fit partners in those aërial halls. So intimately mingled are they with it, that, what with their slenderness and their glossy surfaces you can hardly tell at last what in the dance is leaf and what is light. And when no zephyr stirs, they are at most but a rich tracery to the forest-windows.

I am again struck with their beauty, when, a month later, they thickly strew the ground in the woods, piled one upon another under my feet. They are then brown above, but purple beneath. With their narrow lobes and their bold deep scollops reaching almost to the middle, they suggest that the material must be cheap, or else there has been a lavish expense in their creation, as if so much had been cut out. Or else they seem to us the remnants of the stuff out of which leaves have been cut with a die. Indeed, when they lie thus one upon another, they remind me of a pile of scrap-tin.

Or bring one home, and study it closely at your leisure, by the fireside. It is a type, not from any Oxford font, not in the Basque nor the arrow-headed character, not found on the Rosetta Stone, but destined to be copied in sculpture one day, if they ever get to whittling stone here. What a wild and pleasing outline, a combination of graceful curves and angles! The eye rests with equal delight on what is not leaf and on what is leaf,—on the broad, free, open sinuses, and on the long, sharp, bristle-pointed lobes. A simple oval outline would include it all, if you connected the points of the leaf; but how much richer is it than that, with its half-dozen deep scollops, in which the eye and thought of the beholder are embayed! If I were a drawing-master, I would set my pupils to copying these leaves, that they might learn to draw firmly and gracefully.

Regarded as water, it is like a pond with half a dozen broad rounded promontories extending nearly to its middle, half from each side, while its watery bays extend far inland, like sharp friths, at each of whose heads several fine streams empty in,—almost a leafy archipelago.

But it oftener suggests land, and, as Dionysius and Pliny compared the form of the Morea to that of the leaf of the Oriental Plane-tree, so this leaf reminds me of some fair wild island in the ocean, whose extensive coast, alternate rounded bays with smooth strands, and sharp-pointed rocky capes, mark it as fitted for the habitation of man, and destined to become a centre of civilization at last. To the sailor's eye, it is a much-indented shore. Is it not, in fact, a shore to the aërial ocean, on which the windy surf beats? At sight of this leaf we are all mariners,—if not vikings, buccaneers, and filibusters. Both our love of repose and our spirit of adventure are addressed. In our most casual glance, perchance, we think, that, if we succeed in doubling those sharp capes, we shall find deep, smooth, and secure havens in the ample bays. How different from the White-Oak leaf, with its rounded headlands, on which no light-house need be placed! That is an England, with its long civil history, that may be

read. This is some still unsettled New-found Island or
Celebes. Shall we go and be rajahs there?

By the twenty-sixth of October the large Scarlet Oaks
are in their prime, when other Oaks are usually withered.
They have been kindling their fires for a week past, and
now generally burst into a blaze. This alone of *our* indig-
enous deciduous trees (excepting the Dogwood, of which
I do not know half a dozen, and they are but large
bushes) is now in its glory. The two Aspens and the Sugar-Maple come nearest to it in date, but they have lost
the greater part of their leaves. Of evergreens, only the
Pitch-Pine is still commonly bright.

But it requires a particular alertness, if not devotion to
these phenomena, to appreciate the wide-spread, but late
and unexpected glory of the Scarlet Oaks. I do not speak
here of the small trees and shrubs, which are commonly
observed, and which are now withered, but of the large
trees. Most go in and shut their doors, thinking that bleak
and colorless November has already come, when some of
the most brilliant and memorable colors are not yet lit.

This very perfect and vigorous one, about forty feet
high, standing in an open pasture, which was quite glossy
green on the twelfth, is now, the twenty-sixth, completely
changed to bright dark scarlet,—every leaf, between you
and the sun, as if it had been dipped into a scarlet dye.
The whole tree is much like a heart in form, as well as
color. Was not this worth waiting for? Little did you
think, ten days ago, that that cold green tree would assume such color as this. Its leaves are still firmly attached,
while those of other trees are falling around it. It seems to
say,—"I am the last to blush, but I blush deeper than any
of ye. I bring up the rear in my red coat. We Scarlet
ones, alone of Oaks, have not given up the fight."

The sap is now, and even far into November, frequently flowing fast in these trees, as in Maples in the spring;
and apparently their bright tints, now that most other
Oaks are withered, are connected with this phenomenon.
They are full of life. It has a pleasantly astringent, acorn-
like taste, this strong Oak-wine, as I find on tapping them
with my knife.

Looking across this woodland valley, a quarter of a

mile wide, how rich those Scarlet Oaks, embosomed in
Pines, their bright red branches intimately intermingled
with them! They have their full effect there. The Pine-
boughs are the green calyx to their red petals. Or, as we
go along a road in the woods, the sun striking endwise
through it, and lighting up the red tents of the Oaks,
which on each side are mingled with the liquid green of
the Pines, makes a very gorgeous scene. Indeed, without
the evergreens for contrast, the autumnal tints would lose
much of their effect.

The Scarlet Oak asks a clear sky and the brightness of
late October days. These bring out its colors. If the sun
goes into a cloud, they become comparatively indistinct.
As I sit on a cliff in the southwest part of our town, the
sun is now getting low, and the woods in Lincoln, south
and east of me, are lit up by its more level rays; and in
the Scarlet Oaks, scattered so equally over the forest,
there is brought out a more brilliant redness than I had
believed was in them. Every tree of this species which is
visible in those directions, even to the horizon, now stands
out distinctly red. Some great ones lift their red backs
high above the woods, in the next town, like huge roses
with a myriad of fine petals; and some more slender ones,
in a small grove of White Pines on Pine Hill in the east,
on the very verge of the horizon, alternating with the
Pines on the edge of the grove, and shouldering them
with their red coats, look like soldiers in red amid hunters
in green. This time it is Lincoln green, too. Till the sun
got low, I did not believe that there were so many red-
coats in the forest army. Theirs is an intense burning red,
which would lose some of its strength, methinks, with every step you might take toward them; for the shade that
lurks amid their foliage does not report itself at this distance, and they are unanimously red. The focus of their
reflected color is in the atmosphere far on this side. Every
such tree becomes a nucleus of red, as it were, where,
with the declining sun, that color grows and glows. It is
partly borrowed fire, gathering strength from the sun on
its way to your eye. It has only some comparatively dull
red leaves for a rallying-point, or kindling-stuff, to start
it, and it becomes an intense scarlet or red mist, or fire,
which finds fuel for itself in the very atmosphere. So vi-

vacious is redness. The very rails reflect a rosy light at this hour and season. You see a redder tree than exists.

If you wish to count the Scarlet Oaks, do it now. In a clear day stand thus on a hill-top in the woods, when the sun is an hour high, and every one within range of your vision, excepting in the west, will be revealed. You might live to the age of Methuselah and never find a tithe of them, otherwise. Yet sometimes even in a dark day I have thought them as bright as I ever saw them. Looking westward, their colors are lost in a blaze of light; but in other directions the whole forest is a flower-garden, in which these late roses burn, alternating with green, while the so-called "gardeners," walking here and there, perchance, beneath, with spade and water-pot, see only a few little asters amid withered leaves.

These are *my* China-asters, *my* late garden-flowers. It costs me nothing for a gardener. The falling leaves, all over the forest, are protecting the roots of my plants. Only look at what is to be seen, and you will have garden enough, without deepening the soil in your yard. We have only to elevate our view a little, to see the whole forest as a garden. The blossoming of the Scarlet Oak,— the forest-flower, surpassing all in splendor (at least since the Maple)! I do not know but they interest me more than the Maples, they are so widely and equally dispersed throughout the forest; they are so hardy, a nobler tree on the whole;—our chief November flower, abiding the approach of winter with us, imparting warmth to early November prospects. It is remarkable that the latest bright color that is general should be this deep, dark scarlet and red, the intensest of colors. The ripest fruit of the year; like the cheek of a hard, glossy, red apple from the cold Isle of Orleans, which will not be mellow for eating till next spring! When I rise to a hill-top, a thousand of these great Oak roses, distributed on every side, as far as the horizon! I admire them four or five miles off! This my unfailing prospect for a fortnight past! This late forest-flower surpasses all that spring or summer could do. Their colors were but rare and dainty specks comparatively (created for the near-sighted, who walk amid the humblest herbs and underwoods), and made no impression on a distant eye. Now it is an extended forest or a mountain-side, through or along which we journey from day to day, that bursts into bloom. Comparatively, our gardening is on a petty scale,—the gardener still nursing a few asters amid dead weeds, ignorant of the gigantic asters and roses, which, as it were, overshadow him, and ask for none of his care. It is like a little red paint ground on a saucer, and held up against the sunset sky. Why not take more elevated and broader views, walk in the great garden, not skulk in a little "debauched" nook of it? consider the beauty of the forest, and not merely of a few impounded herbs?

Let your walks now be a little more adventurous; ascend the hills. If, about the last of October, you ascend any hill in the outskirts of our town, and probably of yours, and look over the forest, you may see—well, what I have endeavored to describe. All this you surely will see, and much more, if you are prepared to see it,—if you look for it. Otherwise, regular and universal as this phenomenon is, whether you stand on the hill-top or in the hollow, you will think for threescore years and ten that all the wood is, at this season, sear and brown. Objects are concealed from our view, not so much because they are out of the course of our visual ray as because we do not bring our minds and eyes to bear on them; for there is no power to see in the eye itself, any more than in any other jelly. We do not realize how far and widely, or how near and narrowly, we are to look. The greater part of the phenomena of Nature are for this reason concealed from us all our lives. The gardener sees only the gardener's garden. Here, too, as in political economy, the supply answers to the demand. Nature does not cast pearls before swine. There is just as much beauty visible to us in the landscape as we are prepared to appreciate,— not a grain more. The actual objects which one man will see from a particular hill-top are just as different from those which another will see as the beholders are different. The Scarlet Oak must, in a sense, be in your eye when you go forth. We cannot see anything until we are possessed with the idea of it, take it into our heads,—and then we can hardly see anything else. In my botanical rambles, I find, that, first, the idea, or image, of a plant

occupies my thoughts, though it may seem very foreign
to this locality,—no nearer than Hudson's Bay,—and for
some weeks or months I go thinking of it, and expecting
it, unconsciously, and at length I surely see it. This is the
history of my finding a score or more of rare plants,
which I could name. A man sees only what concerns him.
A botanist absorbed in the study of grasses does not distinguish the grandest Pasture Oaks. He, as it were, tram-
ples down Oaks unwittingly in his walk, or at most sees
only their shadows. I have found that it required a different intention of the eye, in the same locality, to see different plants, even when they were closely allied, as *Jun-
caceœ* and *Gramineœ*: when I was looking for the
former, I did not see the latter in the midst of them. How
much more then, it requires different intentions of the
eye and of the mind to attend to different departments of
knowledge! How differently the poet and the naturalist
look at objects!

Take a New-England selectman, and set him on the
highest of our hills, and tell him to look,—sharpening his
sight to the utmost, and putting on the glasses that suit
him best, (ay, using a spy-glass, if he likes,)—and make a
full report. What, probably, will he *spy*?—what will he
select to look at? Of course, he will see a Brocken spectre
of himself. He will see several meeting-houses, at least,
and, perhaps, that somebody ought to be assessed higher
than he is, since he has so handsome a wood-lot. Now
take Julius Cæsar, or Immanuel Swedenborg, or a Fegee-
Islander, and set him up there. Or suppose all together,
and let them compare notes afterward. Will it appear
that they have enjoyed the same prospect? What they
will see will be as different as Rome was from Heaven or
Hell, or the last from the Fegee Islands. For aught we
know, as strange a man as any of these is always at our
elbow.

Why, it takes a sharp-shooter to bring down even such
trivial games as snipes and woodcocks; he must take very
particular aim, and know what he is aiming at. He would
stand a very small chance, if he fired at random into the
sky, being told that snipes were flying there. And so is it
with him that shoots at beauty; though he wait till the sky

falls, he will not bag any, if he does not already know its
seasons and haunts, and the color of its wing,—if he has
not dreamed of it, so that he can *anticipate* it; then, indeed, he flushes it at every step, shoots double and on the
wing, with both barrels, even in cornfields. The sportsman trains himself, dresses and watches unweariedly, and
loads and primes for his particular game. He prays for it,
and offers sacrifices, and so he gets it. After due and long
preparation, schooling his eye and hand, dreaming awake
and asleep, with gun and paddle and boat he goes out
after meadow-hens, which most of his townsmen never
saw nor dreamed of, and paddles for miles against a
head-wind, and wades in water up to his knees, being out
all day without his dinner, and *therefore* he gets them.
He had them half-way into his bag when he started, and
has only to shove them down. The true sportsman can
shoot you almost any of his game from his windows: what
else has he windows or eyes for? It comes and perches at
last on the barrel of his gun; but the rest of the world
never see it *with the feathers on*. The geese fly exactly
under his zenith, and honk when they get there, and he
will keep himself supplied by firing up his chimney;
twenty musquash have the refusal of each one of his traps
before it is empty. If he lives, and his game-spirit increases, heaven and earth shall fail him sooner than
game; and when he dies, he will go to more extensive,
and, perchance, happier hunting-grounds. The fisherman, too, dreams of fish, sees a bobbing cork in his
dreams, till he can almost catch them in his sink-spout. I
knew a girl who, being sent to pick huckleberries, picked
wild gooseberries by the quart, where no one else knew
that there were any, because she was accustomed to pick
them up country where she came from. The astronomer
knows where to go star-gathering, and sees one clearly in
his mind before any have seen it with a glass. The hen
scratches and finds her food right under where she
stands; but such is not the way with the hawk.

These bright leaves which I have mentioned are not
the exception, but the rule; for I believe that all leaves,
even grasses and mosses, acquire brighter colors just be-

fore their fall. When you come to observe faithfully the changes of each humblest plant, you find that each has, sooner or later, its peculiar autumnal tint; and if you undertake to make a complete list of the bright tints, it will be nearly as long as a catalogue of the plants in your vicinity.

LIFE WITHOUT PRINCIPLE

*One of Thoreau's most (hortatory) pieces, "Life without
Principle" brims with denunciations of the way Thoreau
perceived that his neighbors were spending their lives.
Like* Walden, *"Life without Principle" is a plea for personal purity, which Thoreau believed it impossible to
achieve and to preserve if one acquiesced to the prevalent values of getting and spending, gossiping, and
reading trash. "If we have thus desecrated ourselves,—
as who has not?—the remedy [Thoreau prescribed] will
be by wariness and devotion to reconsecrate ourselves,
and make once more a fane of the mind." Under many
titles, on many occasions, Thoreau delivered these ad-
monitions in lectures, readying them for posthumous
publication in* The Atlantic Monthly *for October 1863, as
he declined into death. The sharp imperatives of the essay do not sound like the words of a dying man. The
text reproduced here is from* Reform Papers (1973) *in
the definitive Princeton Edition of Thoreau's Writings,
edited by Wendell Glick.*

AT A LYCEUM, not long since, I felt that the lecturer had
chosen a theme too foreign to himself, and so failed to
interest me as much as he might have done. He described
things not in or near to his heart, but toward his extrem-

ities and superficies. There was, in this sense, no truly central or centralizing thought in the lecture. I would have had him deal with his privatest experience, as the poet does. The greatest compliment that was ever paid me was when one asked me what *I thought*, and attended to my answer. I am surprised, as well as delighted, when this happens, it is such a rare use he would make of me, as if he were acquainted with the tool. Commonly, if men want anything of me, it is only to know how many acres I make of their land,—since I am a surveyor,—or, at most, what trivial news I have burdened myself with. They never will go to law for my meat; they prefer the shell. A man once came a considerable distance to ask me to lecture on Slavery; but on conversing with him, I found that he and his clique expected seven-eighths of the lecture to be theirs, and only one-eighth mine; so I declined. I take it for granted, when I am invited to lecture anywhere,—for I have had a little experience in that business,—that there is a desire to hear what *I think* on some subject, though I may be the greatest fool in the country,—and not that I should say pleasant things merely, or such as the audience will assent to; and I resolve, accordingly, that I will give them a strong dose of myself. They have sent for me, and engaged to pay for me, and I am determined that they shall have me, though I bore them beyond all precedent.

So now I would say something similar to you, my readers. Since *you* are my readers, and I have not been much of a traveller, I will not talk about people a thousand miles off, but come as near home as I can. As the time is short, I will leave out all the flattery, and retain all the criticism.

Let us consider the way in which we spend our lives.

This world is a place of business. What an infinite bustle! I am awaked almost every night by the panting of the locomotive. It interrupts my dreams. There is no sabbath. It would be glorious to see mankind at leisure for once. It is nothing but work, work, work. I cannot easily buy a blank-book to write thoughts in; they are commonly ruled for dollars and cents. An Irishman, seeing me making a minute in the fields, took it for granted that I was calculating my wages. If a man was tossed out of a window when an infant, and so made a cripple for life, or scared out of his wits by the Indians, it is regretted chiefly because he was thus incapacitated for—business! I think that there is nothing, not even crime, more opposed to poetry, to philosophy, ay, to life itself, than this incessant business.

There is a coarse and boisterous money-making fellow in the outskirts of our town, who is going to build a bank-wall under the hill along the edge of his meadow. The powers have put this into his head to keep him out of mischief, and he wishes me to spend three weeks digging there with him. The result will be that he will perhaps get some more money to hoard, and leave for his heirs to spend foolishly. If I do this, most will commend me as an industrious and hard-working man; but if I choose to devote myself to certain labors which yield more real profit, though but little money, they may be inclined to look on me as an idler. Nevertheless, as I do not need the police of meaningless labor to regulate me, and do not see anything absolutely praiseworthy in this fellow's undertaking, any more than in many an enterprise of our own or foreign governments, however amusing it may be to him or them, I prefer to finish my education at a different school.

If a man walk in the woods for love of them half of each day, he is in danger of being regarded as a loafer; but if he spends his whole day as a speculator, shearing off those woods and making earth bald before her time, he is esteemed an industrious and enterprising citizen. As if a town had no interest in its forests but to cut them down!

Most men would feel insulted, if it were proposed to employ them in throwing stones over a wall, and then in throwing them back, merely that they might earn their wages. But many are no more worthily employed now. For instance: just after sunrise, one summer morning, I noticed one of my neighbors walking beside his team, which was slowly drawing a heavy hewn stone swung under the axle, surrounded by an atmosphere of industry,— his day's work begun,—his brow commenced to sweat,—

a reproach to all sluggards and idlers,—pausing abreast
the shoulders of his oxen, and half turning round with a
flourish of his merciful whip, while they gained their
length on him. And I thought, Such is the labor which the
American Congress exists to protect,—honest, manly
toil,—honest as the day is long,—that makes his bread
taste sweet, and keeps society sweet,—which all men respect and have consecrated: one of the sacred band, doing the needful, but irksome drudgery. Indeed, I felt a
slight reproach, because I observed this from the window,
and was not abroad and stirring about a similar business.
The day went by, and at evening I passed the yard of
another neighbor, who keeps many servants, and spends
much money foolishly, while he adds nothing to the common stock, and there I saw the stone of the morning lying
beside a whimsical structure intended to adorn this Lord
Timothy Dexter's premises, and the dignity forthwith departed from the teamster's labor, in my eyes. In my opinion, the sun was made to light worthier toil than this. I
may add, that his employer has since run off, in debt to a
good part of the town, and, after passing through Chancery, has settled somewhere else, there to become once
more a patron of the arts.

The ways by which you may get money almost without
exception lead downward. To have done anything by
which you earned money *merely* is to have been truly
idle or worse. If the laborer gets no more than the wages
which his employer pays him, he is cheated, he cheats
himself. If you would get money as a writer or lecturer,
you must be popular, which is to go down perpendicular-
ly. Those services which the community will most readily
pay for it is most disagreeable to render. You are paid for
being something less than a man. The State does not commonly reward a genius any more wisely. Even the poet-
laureate would rather not have to celebrate the accidents
of royalty. He must be bribed with a pipe of wine; and
perhaps another poet is called away from his muse to
gauge that very pipe. As for my own business, even that
kind of surveying which I could do with most satisfaction
my employers do not want. They would prefer that I
should do my work coarsely and not too well, ay, not well

enough. When I observe that there are different ways of
surveying, my employer commonly asks which will give
him the most land, not which is most correct. I once invented a rule for measuring cord-wood, and tried to introduce it in Boston; but the measurer there told me that
the sellers did not wish to have their wood measured correctly,—that he was already too accurate for them, and
therefore they commonly got their wood measured in
Charlestown before crossing the bridge.

The aim of the laborer should be, not to get his living,
to get "a good job," but to perform well a certain work;
and, even in a pecuniary sense, it would be economy for
a town to pay its laborers so well that they would not feel
that they were working for low ends, as for a livelihood
merely, but for scientific, or even moral ends. Do not hire
a man who does your work for money, but him who does
it for love of it.

It is remarkable that there are few men so well employed, so much to their minds, but that a little money or
fame would commonly buy them off from their present
pursuit. I see advertisements for *active* young men, as if
activity were the whole of a young man's capital. Yet I
have been surprised when one has with confidence proposed to me, a grown man, to embark in some enterprise
of his, as if I had absolutely nothing to do, my life having
been a complete failure hitherto. What a doubtful compliment this is to pay me! As if he had met me half-way
across the ocean beating up against the wind, but bound
nowhere, and proposed to me to go along with him! If I
did, what do you think the underwriters would say? No,
no! I am not without employment at this stage of the
voyage. To tell the truth, I saw an advertisement for able-
bodied seamen, when I was a boy, sauntering in my native port, and as soon as I came of age I embarked.

The community has no bribe that will tempt a wise
man. You may raise money enough to tunnel a mountain,
but you cannot raise money enough to hire a man who is
minding *his own* business. An efficient and valuable man
does what he can, whether the community pay him for it
or not. The inefficient offer their inefficiency to the
highest bidder, and are forever expecting to be put into

office. One would suppose that they were rarely disappointed.

Perhaps I am more than usually jealous with respect to my freedom. I feel that my connection with and obligation to society are still very slight and transient. Those slight labors which afford me a livelihood, and by which it is allowed that I am to some extent serviceable to my contemporaries, are as yet commonly a pleasure to me, and I am not often reminded that they are a necessity. So far I am successful. But I foresee, that, if my wants should be much increased, the labor required to supply them would become a drudgery. If I should sell both my forenoons and afternoons to society, as most appear to do, I am sure, that, for me, there would be nothing left worth living for. I trust that I shall never thus sell my birthright for a mess of pottage. I wish to suggest that a man may be very industrious, and yet not spend his time well. There is no more fatal blunderer than he who consumes the greater part of his life getting his living. All great enterprises are self-supporting. The poet, for instance, must sustain his body by his poetry, as a steam planing-mill feeds its boilers with the shavings it makes. You must get your living by loving. But as it is said of the merchants that ninety-seven in a hundred fail, so the life of men generally, tried by this standard, is a failure, and bankruptcy may be surely prophesied.

Merely to come into the world the heir of a fortune is not to be born, but to be still-born, rather. To be supported by the charity of friends, or a government-pension,—provided you continue to breathe,—by whatever fine synonymes you describe these relations, is to go into the almshouse. On Sundays the poor debtor goes to church to take an account of stock, and finds, of course, that his outgoes have been greater than his income. In the Catholic Church, especially, they go into Chancery, make a clean confession, give up all, and think to start again. Thus men will lie on their backs, talking about the fall of man, and never make an effort to get up.

As for the comparative demand which men make on life, it is an important difference between two, that the one is satisfied with a level success, that his marks can all

be hit by point-blank shots, but the other, however low
and unsuccessful his life may be, constantly elevates his
aim, though at a very slight angle to the horizon. I should
much rather be the last man,—though, as the Orientals
say, "Greatness doth not approach him who is forever
looking down; and all those who are looking high are
growing poor."

It is remarkable that there is <u>little or nothing</u> to be remembered <u>written on the subject of getting a living</u>: how
to make getting a living not merely honest and honorable, but altogether inviting and glorious; for if *getting* a
living is not so, then living is not. One would think, from
looking at literature, that this question had never disturbed a solitary individual's musings. Is it that men are
too much disgusted with their experience to speak of it?
The lesson of value which money teaches, which the Author of the Universe has taken so much pains to teach us,
we are inclined to skip altogether. As for the means of
living, it is wonderful how indifferent men of all classes
are about it, even reformers, so-called,—whether they in-
herit, or earn, or steal it. I think that society has done
nothing for us in this respect, or at least has undone what
she has done. Cold and hunger seem more friendly to my
nature than those methods which men have adopted and
advise to ward them off.

The title *wise* is, for the most part, falsely applied.
How can one be a wise man, if he does not know any
better how to live than other men?—if he is only more
cunning and intellectually subtle? Does Wisdom work in
a tread-mill? or does she teach how to succeed *by her
example?* Is there any such thing as wisdom not applied
to life? Is she merely the miller who grinds the finest
logic? It is pertinent to ask if Plato got his *living* in a
better way or more successfully than his contemporaries,—or did he succumb to the difficulties of life like
other men? Did he seem to prevail over some of them
merely by indifference, or by assuming grand airs? or
find it easier to live, because his aunt remembered him in
her will? The ways in which most men get their living,
that is, live, are mere make-shifts, and a shirking of the
real business of life,—chiefly because they do not know,

but partly because they do not mean, any better.

The rush to California, for instance, and the attitude, not merely of merchants, but of philosophers and prophets, so called, in relation to it, reflect the greatest disgrace on mankind. That so many are ready to live by luck, and so get the means of commanding the labor of others less lucky, without contributing any value to society! And that is called enterprise! I know of no more startling development of the immorality of trade, and all the common modes of getting a living. The philosophy and poetry and religion of such a mankind are not worth the dust of a puff-ball. The hog that gets his living by rooting, stirring up the soil so, would be ashamed of such company. If I could command the wealth of all the worlds by lifting my finger, I would not pay *such* a price for it. Even Mahomet knew that God did not make this world in jest. It makes God to be a moneyed gentleman who scatters a handful of pennies in order to see mankind scramble for them. The world's raffle! A subsistence in the domains of Nature a thing to be raffled for! What a comment, what a satire on our institutions! The conclusion will be, that mankind will hang itself upon a tree. And have all the precepts in all the Bibles taught men only this? and is the last and most admirable invention of the human race only an improved muck-rake? Is this the ground on which Orientals and Occidentals meet? Did God direct us so to get our living, digging where we never planted,— and He would, perchance, reward us with lumps of gold?

God gave the righteous man a certificate entitling him to food and raiment, but the unrighteous man found a *facsimile* of the same in God's coffers, and appropriated it, and obtained food and raiment like the former. It is one of the most extensive systems of counterfeiting that the world has seen. I did not know that mankind were suffering for want of gold. I have seen a little of it. I know that it is very malleable, but not so malleable as wit. A grain of gold will gild a great surface, but not so much as a grain of wisdom.

The gold-digger in the ravines of the mountains is as much a gambler as his fellow in the saloons of San Francisco. What difference does it make, whether you shake

dirt or shake dice? If you win, society is the loser. The
gold-digger is the enemy of the honest laborer, whatever
checks and compensations there may be. It is not enough
to tell me that you worked hard to get your gold. So does
the Devil work hard. The way of transgressors may be
hard in many respects. The humblest observer who goes
to the mines sees and says that gold-digging is of the
character of a lottery; the gold thus obtained is not the
same thing with the wages of honest toil. But, practically,
he forgets what he has seen, for he has seen only the fact,
not the principle, and goes into trade there, that is, buys a
ticket in what commonly proves another lottery, where
the fact is not so obvious.

After reading Howitt's account of the Australian gold-
diggings one evening, I had in my mind's eye, all night,
the numerous valleys, with their streams, all cut up with
foul pits, from ten to one hundred feet deep, and half a
dozen feet across, as close as they can be dug, and partly
filled with water,—the locality to which men furiously
rush to probe for their fortunes,—uncertain where they
shall break ground,—not knowing but the gold is under
their camp itself,—sometimes digging one hundred and
sixty feet before they strike the vein, or then missing it by
a foot,—turned into demons, and regardless of each other's rights, in their thirst for riches,—whole valleys, for
thirty miles, suddenly honey-combed by the pits of the
miners, so that even hundreds are drowned in them,—
standing in water, and covered with mud and clay, they
work night and day, dying of exposure and disease. Having read this, and partly forgotten it, I was thinking, acci-
dentally, of my own unsatisfactory life, doing as others
do; and with that vision of the diggings still before me, I
asked myself, why I might not be washing some gold daily, though it were only the finest particles,—why I might
not sink a shaft down to the gold within me, and work
that mine. *There* is a Ballarat, a Bendigo for you,—what
though it were a Sulky Gully? At any rate, I might pursue some path, however solitary and narrow and crooked,
in which I could walk with love and reverence. Wherever
a man separates from the multitude, and goes his own
way in this mood, there indeed is a fork in the road,

though ordinary travellers may see only a gap in the paling. His solitary path across-lots will turn out the *higher way* of the two.

Men rush to California and Australia as if the true gold were to be found in that direction; but that is to go to the very opposite extreme to where it lies. They go prospecting farther and farther away from the true lead, and are most unfortunate when they think themselves most successful. Is not our *native* soil auriferous? Does not a stream from the golden mountains flow through our native valley? and has not this for more than geologic ages been bringing down the shining particles and forming the nuggets for us? Yet, strange to tell, if a digger steal away, prospecting for this true gold, into the unexplored solitudes around us, there is no danger that any will dog his steps, and endeavor to supplant him. He may claim and undermine the whole valley even, both the cultivated and the uncultivated portions, his whole life long in peace, for no one will ever dispute his claim. They will not mind his cradles or his toms. He is not confined to a claim twelve feet square, as at Ballarat, but may mine anywhere, and wash the whole wide world in his tom.

Howitt says of the man who found the great nugget which weighed twenty-eight pounds, at the Bendigo diggings in Australia:—"He soon began to drink; got a horse and rode all about, generally at full gallop, and when he met people, called out to inquire if they knew who he was, and then kindly informed them that he was 'the bloody wretch that had found the nugget.' At last he rode full speed against a tree, and nearly knocked his brains out." I think, however, there was no danger of that, for he had already knocked his brains out against the nugget. Howitt adds, "He is a hopelessly ruined man." But he is a type of the class. They are all fast men. Hear some of the names of the places where they dig:—"Jackass Flat,"— "Sheep's-Head Gully,"—"Murderer's Bar," etc. Is there no satire in these names? Let them carry their ill-gotten wealth where they will, I am thinking it will still be "Jackass Flat," if not "Murderer's Bar," where they live.

The last resource of our energy has been the robbing of graveyards on the Isthmus of Darien, an enterprise which

appears to be but in its infancy; for, according to late
accounts, an act has passed its second reading in the legislature of New Granada, regulating this kind of mining;
and a correspondent of the *Tribune* writes:—"In the dry
season, when the weather will permit of the country being properly prospected, no doubt other rich *'guacas'*
[that is, graveyards] will be found." To emigrants he
says:—"Do not come before December; take the Isthmus
route in preference to the Boca del Toro one; bring no
useless baggage, and do not cumber yourself with a tent;
but a good pair of blankets will be necessary; a pick,
shovel, and axe of good material will be almost all that is
required": advice which might have been taken from the
"Burker's Guide." And he concludes with this line in Ital-
ics and small capitals: "*If you are doing well at home,*
STAY THERE," which may fairly be interpreted to mean,
"If you are getting a good living by robbing graveyards
at home, stay there."

But why go to California for a text? She is the child of
New England, bred at her own school and church.

It is remarkable that among all the preachers there are
so few moral teachers. The prophets are employed in excusing the ways of men. Most reverend seniors, the *illu-
minati* of the age, tell me, with a gracious, reminiscent
smile, betwixt an aspiration and a shudder, not to be too
tender about these things,—to lump all that, that is, make
a lump of gold of it. The highest advice I have heard on
these subjects was grovelling. The burden of it was,—It is
not worth your while to undertake to reform the world in
this particular. Do not ask how your bread is buttered; it
will make you sick, if you do,—and the like. A man had
better starve at once than lose his innocence in the process of getting his bread. If within the sophisticated man
there is not an unsophisticated one, then he is but one of
the Devil's angels. As we grow old, we live more coarsely,
we relax a little in our disciplines, and, to some extent,
cease to obey our finest instincts. But we should be fastid-
ious to the extreme of sanity, disregarding the gibes of
those who are more unfortunate than ourselves.

In our science and philosophy, even, there is commonly
no true and absolute account of things. The spirit of sect

and bigotry has planted its hoof amid the stars. You have only to discuss the problem, whether the stars are inhabited or not, in order to discover it. Why must we daub the heavens as well as the earth? It was an unfortunate discovery that Dr. Kane was a Mason, and that Sir John Franklin was another. But it was a more cruel suggestion that possibly that was the reason why the former went in search of the latter. There is not a popular magazine in this country that would dare to print a child's thought on important subjects without comment. It must be submitted to the D.D.s. I would it were the chickadee-dees.

You come from attending the funeral of mankind to attend to a natural phenomenon. A little thought is sexton to all the world.

I hardly know an *intellectual* man, even, who is so broad and truly liberal that you can think aloud in his society. Most with whom you endeavor to talk soon come to a stand against some institution in which they appear to hold stock,—that is, some particular, not universal, way of viewing things. They will continually thrust their own low roof, with its narrow skylight, between you and the sky, when it is the unobstructed heavens you would view. Get out of the way with your cobwebs, wash your windows, I say! In some lyceums they tell me that they have voted to exclude the subject of religion. But how do I know what their religion is, and when I am near to or far from it? I have walked into such an arena and done my best to make a clean breast of what religion I have experienced, and the audience never suspected what I was about. The lecture was as harmless as moonshine to them. Whereas, if I had read to them the biography of the greatest scamps in history, they might have thought that I had written the lives of the deacons of their church. Ordinarily, the inquiry is, Where did you come from? or, Where are you going? That was a more pertinent question which I overheard one of my auditors put to another once,—"What does he lecture for?" It made me quake in my shoes.

To speak impartially, the best men that I know are not serene, a world in themselves. For the most part, they dwell in forms, and flatter and study effect only more

finely than the rest. We select granite for the underpinning of our houses and barns; we build fences of stone;
but we do not ourselves rest on an underpinning of gra-
nitic truth, the lowest primitive rock. Our sills are rotten.
What stuff is the man made of who is not coexistent in
our thought with the purest and subtilest truth? I often
accuse my finest acquaintances of an immense frivolity;
for, while there are manners and compliments we do not
meet, we do not teach one another the lessons of honesty
and sincerity that the brutes do, or of steadiness and solidity that the rocks do. The fault is commonly mutual,
however; for we do not habitually demand any more of
each other.

That excitement about Kossuth, consider how characteristic, but superficial, it was!—only another kind of
politics or dancing. Men were making speeches to him all
over the country, but each expressed only the thought, or
the want of thought, of the multitude. No man stood on
truth. They were merely banded together, as usual, one
leaning on another, and all together on nothing; as the
Hindoos made the world rest on an elephant, the elephant on a tortoise, and the tortoise on a serpent, and had
nothing to put under the serpent. For all fruit of that stir
we have the Kossuth hat.

Just so hollow and ineffectual, for the most part, is our
ordinary conversation. Surface meets surface. When our
life ceases to be inward and private, conversation degen-
erates into mere gossip. We rarely meet a man who can
tell us any news which he has not read in a newspaper, or
been told by his neighbor; and, for the most part, the
only difference between us and our fellow is, that he has
seen the newspaper, or been out to tea, and we have not.
In proportion as our inward life fails, we go more constantly and desperately to the post-office. You may depend on it, that the poor fellow who walks away with the
greatest number of letters, proud of his extensive correspondence, has not heard from himself this long while.

I do not know but it is too much to read one newspaper
a week. I have tried it recently, and for so long it seems
to me that I have not dwelt in my native region. The sun,
the clouds, the snow, the trees say not so much to me.

You cannot serve two masters. It requires more than a day's devotion to know and to possess the wealth of a day.

We may well be ashamed to tell what things we have read or heard in our day. I do not know why my news should be so trivial,—considering what one's dreams and expectations are, why the developments should be so paltry. The news we hear, for the most part, is not news to our genius. It is the stalest repetition. You are often tempted to ask, why such stress is laid on a particular experience which you have had,—that, after twenty-five years, you should meet Hobbins, Registrar of Deeds, again on the sidewalk. Have you not budged an inch, then? Such is the daily news. Its facts appear to float in the atmosphere, insignificant as the sporules of fungi, and impinge on some neglected *thallus*, or surface of our minds, which affords a basis for them, and hence a parasitic growth. We should wash ourselves clean of such news. Of what consequence, though our planet explode, if there is no character involved in the explosion? In health we have not the least curiosity about such events. We do not live for idle amusement. I would not run round a corner to see the world blow up.

All summer, and far into the autumn, perchance, you unconsciously went by the newspapers and the news, and now you find it was because the morning and the evening were full of news to you. Your walks were full of incidents. You attended, not to the affairs of Europe, but to your own affairs in Massachusetts fields. If you chance to live and move and have your being in that thin stratum in which the events that make the news transpire,— thinner than the paper on which it is printed,—then these things will fill the world for you; but if you soar above or dive below that plane, you cannot remember nor be reminded of them. Really to see the sun rise or go down every day, so to relate ourselves to a universal fact, would preserve us sane forever. Nations! What are nations? Tartars, and Huns, and Chinamen! Like insects, they swarm. The historian strives in vain to make them memorable. It is for want of a man that there are so many men. It is individuals that populate the world. Any man thinking may say with the Spirit of Lodin,—

> "I look down from my height on nations,
> And they become ashes before me;—
> Calm is my dwelling in the clouds;
> Pleasant are the great fields of my rest."

Pray, let us live without being drawn by dogs, Esquimaux-fashion, tearing over hill and dale, and biting each other's ears.

Not without a slight shudder at the danger, I often perceive how near I had come to admitting into my mind the details of some trivial affair,—the news of the street; and I am astonished to observe how willing men are to lumber their minds with such rubbish,—to permit idle rumors and incidents of the most insignificant kind to intrude on ground which should be sacred to thought. Shall the mind be a public arena, where the affairs of the street and the gossip of the tea-table chiefly are discussed? Or shall it be a quarter of heaven itself,—an hypæthral temple, consecrated to the service of the gods? I find it so difficult to dispose of the few facts which to me are significant, that I hesitate to burden my attention with those which are insignificant, which only a divine mind could illustrate. Such is, for the most part, the news in newspapers and conversation. It is important to preserve the mind's chastity in this respect. Think of admitting the details of a single case of the criminal court into our thoughts, to stalk profanely through their very *sanctum sanctorum* for an hour, ay, for many hours! to make a very bar-room of the mind's inmost apartment, as if for so long the dust of the street had occupied us,—the very street itself, with all its travel, its bustle, and filth had passed through our thoughts' shrine! Would it not be an intellectual and moral suicide? When I have been compelled to sit spectator and auditor in a court-room for some hours, and have seen my neighbors, who were not compelled, stealing in from time to time, and tiptoeing about with washed hands and faces, it has appeared to my mind's eye, that, when they took off their hats, their ears suddenly expanded into vast hoppers for sound, between which even their narrow heads were crowded.

Like the vanes of windmills, they caught the broad, but shallow stream of sound, which, after a few titillating gyrations in their coggy brains, passed out the other side. I wondered if, when they got home, they were as careful to wash their ears as before their hands and faces. It has seemed to me, at such a time, that the auditors, and the witnesses, the jury and the counsel, the judge and the criminal at the bar,—if I may presume him guilty before he is convicted,—were all equally criminal, and a thunderbolt might be expected to descend and consume them all together.

By all kinds of traps and sign-boards, threatening the extreme penalty of the divine law, exclude such trespassers from the only ground which can be sacred to you. It is so hard to forget what it is worse than useless to remember! If I am to be a thoroughfare, I prefer that it be of the mountain-brooks, the Parnassian streams, and not the town-sewers. There is inspiration, that gossip which comes to the ear of the attentive mind from the courts of heaven. There is the profane and stale revelation of the bar-room and the police court. The same ear is fitted to receive both communications. Only the character of the hearer determines to which it shall be open, and to which closed. I believe that the mind can be permanently profaned by the habit of attending to trivial things, so that all our thoughts shall be tinged with triviality. Our very intellect shall be macadamized, as it were,—its foundation broken into fragments for the wheels of travel to roll over; and if you would know what will make the most durable pavement, surpassing rolled stones, spruce blocks, and asphaltum, you have only to look into some of our minds which have been subjected to this treatment so long.

If we have thus desecrated ourselves,—as who has not?—the remedy will be by wariness and devotion to reconsecrate ourselves, and make once more a fane of the mind. We should treat our minds, that is, ourselves, as innocent and ingenuous children, whose guardians we are, and be careful what objects and what subjects we thrust on their attention. Read not the Times. Read the Eternities. Conventionalities are at length as bad as im-

purities. Even the facts of science may dust the mind by
their dryness, unless they are in a sense effaced each
morning, or rather rendered fertile by the dews of fresh
and living truth. Knowledge does not come to us by details, but in flashes of light from heaven. Yes, every
thought that passes through the mind helps to wear and
tear it, and to deepen the ruts, which, as in the streets of
Pompeii, evince how much it has been used. How many
things there are concerning which we might well deliberate, whether we had better know them,—had better let
their peddling-carts be driven, even at the slowest trot or
walk, over that bridge of glorious span by which we trust
to pass at last from the farthest brink of time to the nearest shore of eternity! Have we no culture, no refinement,—but skill only to live coarsely and serve the Devil?—to acquire a little worldly wealth, or fame, or liberty,
and make a false show with it, as if we were all husk and
shell, with no tender and living kernel to us? Shall our
institutions be like those chestnut-burs which contain
abortive nuts, perfect only to prick the fingers?

America is said to be the arena on which the battle of
freedom is to be fought; but surely it cannot be freedom
in a merely political sense that is meant. Even if we grant
that the American has freed himself from a political tyrant, he is still the slave of an economical and moral tyrant.
Now that the republic—the *res-publica*—has been settled, it is time to look after the *res-privata*,—the private
state,—to see, as the Roman senate charged its consuls,
"*ne quid res*-PRIVATA *detrimenti caperet*," that the *private* state receive no detriment.

Do we call this the land of the free? What is it to be
free from King George and continue the slaves of King
Prejudice? What is it to be born free and not to live free?
What is the value of any political freedom, but as a
means to moral freedom? Is it a freedom to be slaves, or a
freedom to be free, of which we boast? We are a nation
of politicians, concerned about the outmost defences only
of freedom. It is our children's children who may perchance be really free. We tax ourselves unjustly. There is
a part of us which is not represented. It is taxation without representation. We quarter troops, we quarter fools

and cattle of all sorts upon ourselves. We quarter our gross bodies on our poor souls, till the former eat up all the latter's substance.

With respect to a true culture and manhood, we are essentially provincial still, not metropolitan,—mere Jonathans. We are provincial, because we do not find at home our standards,—because we do not worship truth, but the reflection of truth,—because we are warped and narrowed by an exclusive devotion to trade and commerce and manufactures and agriculture and the like, which are but means, and not the end.

So is the English Parliament provincial. Mere country-bumpkins, they betray themselves, when any more important question arises for them to settle, the Irish question, for instance,—the English question why did I not say? Their natures are subdued to what they work in. Their "good breeding" respects only secondary objects. The finest manners in the world are awkwardness and fatuity, when contrasted with a finer intelligence. They appear but as the fashions of past days,—mere courtliness, knee-buckles and small-clothes, out of date. It is the vice, but not the excellence of manners, that they are continually being deserted by the character; they are cast-off clothes or shells, claiming the respect which belonged to the living creature. You are presented with the shells instead of the meat, and it is no excuse generally, that, in the case of some fishes, the shells are of more worth than the meat. The man who thrusts his manners upon me does as if he were to insist on introducing me to his cabinet of curiosities, when I wished to see himself. It was not in this sense that the poet Decker called Christ "the first true gentleman that ever breathed." I repeat that in this sense the most splendid court in Christendom is provincial, having authority to consult about Transalpine interests only, and not the affairs of Rome. A praetor or proconsul would suffice to settle the questions which absorb the attention of the English Parliament and the American Congress.

Government and legislation! these I thought were respectable professions. We have heard of heaven-born Numas, Lycurguses, and Solons, in the history of the world,

whose *names* at least may stand for ideal legislators; but
think of legislating to *regulate* the breeding of slaves, or
the exportation of tobacco! What have divine legislators
to do with the exportation or the importation of tobacco?
what humane ones with the breeding of slaves? Suppose
you were to submit the question to any son of God,—and
has He no children in the nineteenth century? is it a family which is extinct?—in what condition would you get it
again? What shall a State like Virginia say for itself at the
last day, in which these have been the principal, the staple productions? What ground is there for patriotism in
such a State? I derive my facts from statistical tables
which the States themselves have published.

A commerce that whitens every sea in quest of nuts
and raisins, and makes slaves of its sailors for this purpose! I saw, the other day, a vessel which had been
wrecked, and many lives lost, and her cargo of rags, juniper-berries, and bitter almonds were strewn along the
shore. It seemed hardly worth the while to tempt the
dangers of the sea between Leghorn and New York for
the sake of a cargo of juniper-berries and bitter almonds.
America sending to the Old World for her bitters! Is not
the sea-brine, is not shipwreck, bitter enough to make the
cup of life go down here? Yet such, to a great extent, is
our boasted commerce; and there are those who style
themselves statesmen and philosophers who are so blind
as to think that progress and civilization depend on precisely this kind of interchange and activity,—the activity
of flies about a molasses-hogshead. Very well, observes
one, if men were oysters. And very well, answer I, if men
were mosquitoes.

Lieutenant Herndon, whom our Government sent to
explore the Amazon, and, it is said, to extend the area of
Slavery, observed that there was wanting there "an industrious and active population, who know what the com-
forts of life are, and who have artificial wants to draw out
the great resources of the country." But what are the "artificial wants" to be encouraged? Not the love of luxuries,
like the tobacco and slaves of, I believe, his native Virginia, nor the ice and granite and other material wealth of
our native New England; nor are "the great resources of

a country" that fertility or barrenness of soil which produces these. The chief want, in every State that I have
been into, was a high and earnest purpose in its inhabitants. This alone draws out "the great resources" of Nature, and at last taxes her beyond her resources; for man
naturally dies out of her. When we want culture more
than potatoes, and illumination more than sugar-plums,
then the great resources of world are taxed and drawn
out, and the result, or staple production, is, not slaves, nor
operatives, but men,—those rare fruits called heroes,
saints, poets, philosophers, and redeemers.

In short, as a snow-drift is formed where there is a lull
in the wind, so, one would say, where there is a lull of
truth, an institution springs up. But the truth blows right
on over it, nevertheless, and at length blows it down.

What is called politics is comparatively something so
superficial and inhuman, that, practically, I have never
fairly recognized that it concerns me at all. The newspapers, I perceive, devote some of their columns specially to
politics or government without charge; and this, one
would say, is all that saves it; but, as I love literature, and,
to some extent, the truth also, I never read those columns
at any rate. I do not wish to blunt my sense of right so
much. I have not got to answer for having read a single
President's Message. A strange age of the world this,
when empires, kingdoms, and republics come a-begging
to a private man's door, and utter their complaints at his
elbow! I cannot take up a newspaper but I find that some
wretched government or other, hard pushed, and on its
last legs, is interceding with me, the reader, to vote for
it,—more importunate than an Italian beggar; and if I
have a mind to look at its certificate, made, perchance,
by some benevolent merchant's clerk, or the skipper that
brought it over, for it cannot speak a word of English
itself, I shall probably read of the eruption of some Vesu-
vius, or the overflowing of some Po, true or forged, which
brought it into this condition. I do not hesitate, in such a
case, to suggest work, or the almshouse; or why not keep
its castle in silence, as I do commonly? The poor President, what with preserving his popularity and doing his
duty, is completely bewildered. The newspapers are the

ruling power. Any other government is reduced to a few
marines at Fort Independence. If a man neglects to read
the Daily Times, Government will go down on its knees
to him, for this is the only treason in these days.

Those things which now most engage the attention of
men, as politics and the daily routine, are, it is true, vital
functions of human society, but should be unconsciously
performed, like the corresponding functions of the physical body. They are *infra*-human, a kind of vegetation. I
sometimes awake to a half-consciousness of them going
on about me, as a man may become conscious of some of
the process of digestion in a morbid state, and so have the
dyspepsia, as it is called. It is as if a thinker submitted
himself to be rasped by the great gizzard of creation.
Politics is, as it were, the gizzard of society, full of grit
and gravel, and the two political parties are its two opposite halves,—sometimes split into quarters, it may be,
which grind on each other. Not only individuals, but
States, have thus a confirmed dyspepsia, which expresses
itself, you can imagine by what sort of eloquence. Thus
our life is not altogether a forgetting, but also, alas! to a
great extent, a remembering of that which we should
never have been conscious of, certainly not in our waking
hours. Why should we not meet, not always as dyspeptics,
to tell our bad dreams, but sometimes as *eu*peptics, to
congratulate each other on the ever glorious morning? I
do not make an exorbitant demand, surely.

A THOREAU CHRONOLOGY

[* Included wholly or in part in this volume]

1817 Born at Concord, Mass., grandson of a French-Huguenot immigrant from the Isle of Jersey, the third of four children.

1833 Enrolled at Harvard University, after study at Concord Academy.

1835 Taught school at Canton, Mass.; met Orestes Brownson.

1837 Graduated from Harvard. Taught briefly in the Concord schools. Began *Journal.**

1838 Opened (with brother, John) a private school in Concord. Gave the first of many lectures before the Concord Lyceum. Made first of three visits to Maine.

1839 Took the boat trip with John later to be recorded in *A Week on the Concord and Merrimack Rivers.**

1840 Proposal of marriage to Ellen Sewall rejected. Wrote *The Service*, rejected by Margaret Fuller for *The Dial*.

1841 Moved to the Emerson home as caretaker in Emerson's absence. "Friendship"* published in *The Dial*, later in *A Week*.

1842 Brother John died suddenly of lockjaw. "Natural

History of Massachusetts" published in *The Dial*. Met Hawthorne, who had taken up residence in Concord.

1843   A productive year. "The Landlord" and "Paradise (to be) Regained" published in *The Democratic Review;* "A Winter Walk"* in *The Dial;* "Walk to Wachusett" in *Boston Miscellany*. Served as tutor to family of William Emerson on Staten Island. Met Horace Greeley. Aided Emerson in editing *The Dial*.

1844   "Herald of Freedom" and Oriental pieces published in *The Dial*. Inadvertently set fire to the Concord woods.

1845   Built his house on Emerson's land at Walden Pond, beginning his "experiment" in living there on July 4. "Wendell Phillips Before Concord Lyceum" published in *The Liberator*.

1846   Visited the Maine woods. Spent night in jail for refusal to pay poll tax to support the Mexican War, an experience later described in "Resistance to Civil Government."*

1847   "Thomas Carlyle and his Works" published in *Graham's Magazine*. Left Walden Pond (Sept. 6) to live at Emerson's home.

1848   "Ktaadn and the Maine Woods,"* based on the 1846 journey, published in *The Union Magazine*.

1849   *A Week on the Concord and Merrimack Rivers** published at Thoreau's expense. "Resistance to Civil Government"* published in Elizabeth Peabody's *Aesthetic Papers*. Made first visit to Cape Cod. Sister Helen died of tuberculosis.

1850   Made second visit to Cape Cod to search for body of Margaret Fuller, drowned in sinking of the *Elizabeth*. Spent a week in Canada with Ellery Channing.

1853   Portions of *A Yankee in Canada* published in *Putnam's Magazine*. Revisited the Maine woods.

1854 *Walden** published by Ticknor and Fields in edition of 2,000 copies. "Slavery in Massachusetts"* delivered at Framingham anti-slavery convention and published in expanded version in *The Liberator*.

1855 Portions of *Cape Cod** published in *Putnam's Magazine*. Enervated and in poor health in early part of the year.

1856 Met Walt Whitman. Described his impressions of Whitman and of 1856 *Leaves of Grass* in letter of Dec. 7, 1856, to H. G. O. Blake.*

1857 Revisited Cape Cod and the Maine woods. Met John Brown.

1858 "Chesuncook," based on second visit to the Maine woods in 1853, published in *Atlantic Monthly*. Upbraided editor James Russell Lowell for editorial license. Camped on Mt. Monadnock with H. G. O. Blake.

1859 "A Plea for Captain John Brown"* delivered in Concord as an address on October 30, later published in James Redpath's *Echoes of Harper's Ferry* (1860). Father dies.

1860 "The Last Days of John Brown" published in *The Liberator;* "The Succession of Forest Trees" in *Transactions of the Middlesex Agricultural Society for the Year 1860*.

1861 Traveled to Minnesota with Horace Mann in search of health. At work editing his manuscripts. Ravaged by tuberculosis.

1862 Died, May 6. "Wild Apples," "Autumnal Tints,"* and "Walking"* published posthumously in *Atlantic Monthly*.

1863 "Life without Principle"* and "Night and Moonlight" published in *Atlantic Monthly*. *Excursions* published.

1864 "The Wellfleet Oysterman" and "The Highland Light" published in *Atlantic Monthly*. *The Maine*

*Woods** published, edited by Sophia Thoreau and Ellery Channing.

1865 *Cape Cod** published, edited by Sophia Thoreau and Ellery Channing. *Letters to Various Persons** published, edited by Emerson.

1866 *A Yankee in Canada, with Anti-Slavery and Reform Papers** published, probably edited principally by Ellery Channing.

1881 *Early Spring in Massachusetts* published, edited from Thoreau's *Journal* by H. G. O. Blake, followed in 1884 by *Summer*, 1887 by *Winter*, and 1892 by *Autumn*.

1902 *The Service* published.

1905 *Sir Walter Raleigh* published.

1906 *Walden (Manuscript) Edition* (including the *Journal*) published by Houghton Mifflin in 20 volumes.

A THOREAU BIBLIOGRAPHY

The Writings of Henry D. Thoreau, currently being edited at Princeton University and published by the Princeton University Press, will supplant all other editions as definitive when completed. Six volumes are now in print, bearing the seal of the Center for Editions of American Authors of the Modern Language Association of America: *Walden* (1971), *The Maine Woods* (1972), *Reform Papers* (1973), *Early Essays and Miscellanies* (1975), *A Week on the Concord and Merrimack Rivers* (1980), and Volume I of the *Journal* (1981). For works of Thoreau that have not yet been authoritatively edited by the Princeton scholars, the *Walden Edition* of 1906 (Houghton Mifflin) is standard.

Thoreau scholarship in periodicals and books is now massive. Excellent introductions are *The New Thoreau Handbook,* ed. Walter Harding and Michael Meyer (New York, 1980), and the annual summaries in Chapter I of *American Literary Scholarship* (Duke University Press, 1963–1981). *Studies in the American Renaissance,* ed. Joel Myerson (Twayne), annually publishes articles dealing with Thoreau, as do the periodicals *ESQ* (University of Washington), *The Thoreau Society Bulletin* (SUNY at Geneseo), *The Concord Saunterer* (Concord, Mass.), and *The Thoreau Quarterly* (University of Minnesota). The most comprehensive collections of Thoreau criticism are Wendell Glick, *The Recognition of Henry David Thoreau* (Ann Arbor, 1969); Walter Harding, *Thoreau: A Century of Criticism* (Dallas, 1954); John Hicks, *Thoreau in our Season* (Amherst, 1966); and Sherman Paul, *Thoreau: A Collection of Critical Essays* in the Prentice-Hall series (Englewood Cliffs, N.J., 1962). Until the definitive editions are issued from Princeton, Thoreau's poetry is available in the *Collected Poems of Henry Thoreau*, ed. Carl F. Bode (Baltimore, 1964), and his correspondence in *The Correspondence of Henry David Thoreau*, ed. Walter Harding and Carl F. Bode (New York, 1958).

Of the many biographies of Thoreau, Walter Harding's *The Days of Henry Thoreau* (New York, 1966) supersedes all others in its comprehensiveness. It may be supplemented by Henry S. Canby's *Thoreau* (Boston, 1939), and the perceptive early study by the English critic, H. S. Salt, *The Life of Henry David Thoreau* (London, 1890). The most original and influential studies of Thoreau in the last two decades, however, have tended toward analyses of his aesthetics and his philosophy; and he is rapidly emerging as a profound and original thinker and an astute theorist of art and language. Students of Thoreau should study with care, therefore, such volumes as Francis O. Matthiessen's *American Renaissance* (New York, 1941), Sherman Paul's *The Shores of America* (Urbana, 1958), Charles Anderson's *The Magic Circle of Walden* (New York, 1968), Stanley Cavell's *The Senses of Walden* (New York, 1972 and San Francisco, 1981), and Frederick Garber's *Thoreau's Redemptive Imagination* (New York, 1977). Nor should they neglect general studies of the Transcendental Movement, one of the most recent and helpful being Lawrence Buell, *Literary Transcendentalism: Style and Vision in the American Renaissance* (Ithaca, 1973).